The Devil and The River

R.J. ELLORY

An Orion paperback

First published in Great Britain in 2013
by Orion Books
This paperback edition published in 2014
by Orion Books,
an imprint of The Orion Publishing Group Ltd,
Orion House, 5 Upper St Martin's Lane,
London WC2H 9EA

An Hachette UK company

1 3 5 7 9 10 8 6 4 2

A CIP catalogue record for this book
is available from the British Library.

ISBN 978-1-4091-2133-6

Typeset at The Spartan Press Ltd,
Lymington, Hants

Printed and bound in Great Britain by Clays Ltd, St Ives plc

The Orion Publishing Group's policy is to use papers that
are natural, renewable and recyclable products and
made from wood grown in sustainable forests. The logging
and manufacturing processes are expected to conform to
the environmental regulations of the country of origin.

www.orionbooks.co.uk

'An awesome achievement . . . a thriller of such power, scope and accomplishment that fanfares should herald its arrival'

Guardian

'Voodoo and murders and gothically imposing southern dynasties – what's not to like? There are moments of genuine chills, fearsomely speedy page-turning and real humour . . . an enjoyable summer read' *Observer*

'A great read' *Irish Examiner*

'R. J. Ellory sets out his stall with terrific vim and a gripping premise in his latest thriller . . . an energetic and winning exercise in pulp fiction with a Southern Gothic flavour' *Metro*

'Ellory's complex procedurals feel influenced by *The Wire* and the hard-boiled cop thrillers of the 1970s. The accumulation of detail is accompanied by a powerful sense of location and well-paced action sequences. In this siren-filled world there are no easy answers. The result is vivid storytelling with a dark heart and an angry conscience' *Financial Times*

'Classic noir, a journey to the dark corners of man's foolishness, where nothing is ever what it seems and no one can ever be trusted. Ellory is beginning to sound like the master [James Ellroy]. I can think of no higher praise' *Daily Mail*

'A pedal to the metal thriller' *Irish Independent*

'Ellory's the real deal, giving us another horrific chunk of small-town American violence, neglect and psychopathy. ****'

Daily Mirror

By R.J. Ellory

R.J. Ellory is the author of eleven novels including the bestselling *A Quiet Belief in Angels*, which was a Richard & Judy Book Club selection and won the Nouvel Observateur Crime Fiction Prize in 2008, and *A Simple Act of Violence*, which was the 2010 winner of the Old Peculier Crime Novel of the Year. *A Quiet Belief in Angels* has also been optioned for film, and Ellory has written the screenplay for its Oscar-winning French director, Olivier Dahan.

R.J. Ellory's other novels have been translated into twenty-five languages, and he has won the USA Excellence Award for Best Mystery, the *Strand* Magazine Best Thriller 2009, the Quebec Laureat, the Livre de Poche Award, and the Readers' Prize for the Festivals of St. Maur and Avignon. He has been shortlisted for a further twelve awards in numerous countries and four Daggers from the UK Crime Writers' Association.

Despite the American settings of his novels, Ellory is British and currently lives in England with his wife and son. To find out more visit www.rjellory.com

'What's past is prologue'

William Shakespeare, *The Tempest*

1

Wednesday, July 24, 1974

When the rains came, they found the girl's face. Just her face. At least that was how it appeared. And then came her hand—small and white and fine like porcelain. It surfaced from the black mud and showed itself. Just her face and her hand, the rest of her still submerged. To look down toward the riverbank and see just her hand and her face was surreal and disturbing. And John Gaines—who had lately, and by providence or default, come to the position of sheriff of Whytesburg, Breed County, Mississippi, and before that had come alive from the nine circles of hell that was the war in Vietnam, who was himself born in Lafayette, a Louisianan from the start—crouched on his haunches and surveyed the scene with a quiet mind and a steady eye.

The discovery had been called in by a passerby, and Gaines's deputy, Richard Hagen, had driven down there and radioed the Sheriff's Office dispatcher, Barbara Jacobs, and she had called Gaines and told him all that was known.

A girl's face has surfaced from the riverbank.

When Gaines arrived, Hagen was still gasping awkwardly, swallowing two or three mouthfuls of air at a time. He bore the distressed and pallid hue of a dying man, though he was not dying, merely in shock. Hagen had not been to war; he was not inured to such things as this, and thus such things were alien and anathema to his sensibilities. The town of Whytesburg—seated awkwardly in the triangle between the Hattiesburg-intent I-59, and the I-18, itself all fired up to reach Mobile—was a modest town with modest ways, the sort of place they rolled up the sidewalk at sunset, where such things as these did not occur too frequently, which was a good thing for all concerned.

But Gaines had been to war. He had seen the nine circles.

And sometimes, listening to the small complaints of smaller

1

minds—the vandalized mailbox, the illegally parked car, the spilled trash can—Gaines would imagine himself walking the complainant through a burned-out ville. *Here*, he would say, *is a dead child in the arms of her dead mother, the pair of them fused together for eternity by heat and napalm. And here is a young man with half a face and no eyes at all. Can you imagine the last thing he might have seen?* And the complainant would be silent and would then look at Gaines with eyes wide, with lips parted, with sweat-varnished skin, both breathless and without words. *Now*, Gaines would say to them, *now let us speak of these small and inconsequential things*.

There were parts of humanity that were left behind in war, and they would never be recovered.

But this? This was enough to reach even Gaines. A dead girl. Perhaps drowned, perhaps murdered and buried beneath the mud. It would be a raw task to excavate her, and the task had best begin before the rains returned. It was no later than ten, but already the temperature was rising. Gaines predicted storms, perhaps worse.

He called to Hagen, told him to radio Dispatch and get people out here.

"What people?" Hagen asked.

"Call your brother. Tell him to come with his camera. Get Jim Hughes and both his boys. That should do us. Tell 'em to bring shovels, rope, buckets, a couple of blankets, some tarps, as well."

"Should I tell 'em why, Sheriff?"

"No. You just tell 'em they're needed for an hour or more. And get Barbara checking for any outstanding missing persons reports for teenage white girls. I don't know of any, but have her check."

Hagen went to the black-and-white. Gaines walked down to the riverbank and stood twelve or fifteen feet from the girl. If he could have washed off her face, maybe he would have recognized her.

Ninety-three percent of abduction victims were dead within three hours. Dead before anyone even knew they were missing. Couldn't file a missing persons report for forty-eight hours. Do the math. It didn't work out well in most cases.

Gaines's heart then began an awkward rhythm, a flurry of irregular beats, not dissimilar to the rush of medic-administered Dexedrine he'd been given in-country. *This will keep you awake*, he was told back then, and he had taken it and then stayed awake for hours, awake until his nerves screamed for some small respite.

Now—once again—his throat was tight, as if a hand had closed

2

around it. He felt sick. His mouth was dry. He was unable to blink, the dry surfaces of his eyes adhered to his inner lids.

Oh God, what was this girl doing here?

And seeing this girl brought back memories of another child . . .

The child that never was . . .

He could hear Hagen on the radio. People would come—Jim Hughes and his eldest sons, Hagen's brother—and photographs would be taken. Gaines would survey the area for anything indicative of foul play, and then they would reach into the blackness and bring the girl out. Then, and only then, would they know what fate had befallen her, a fate that had buried her in the riverbank before her life had even really begun.

The rain did come, an hour later. The rain was black. Gaines would remember it that way. It fell as straight as gravity, and it was hard and cold and bitter on his lips. He had seen the pictures taken, and then he and Hagen and Hagen's brother, Jim Hughes and his two sons, had started working their hands into the mud around the girl in an effort to release her. They knelt there, all six of them, and they tried to work ropes down under her, beneath her neck, her arms, her waist, her thighs. And then they had to lie down, for the mud was black and depthless, and it sucked relentlessly. And the smell was damp and rank and fetid. It was a smell that filled Gaines's nostrils, a smell that he would always remember. The smell of blood and mud and stagnant water, all blended together into some unholy brew. And there was fear. Only later would he understand this. That he had smelled his own fear. That he had smelled the fear of the others. Fear of what had happened to this girl, that something terrible would be revealed, that her body would surface in pieces perhaps. Fear for themselves, that the mud was too deep, too strong, that they—in their efforts to help, unable to leave her, unable to do anything but persevere—would be drawn into the blackness as well.

Back there, back in the war, perhaps in the hours following his return from some long-range recon patrol, Gaines would walk down to the medical tent and watch the sawbones at work. Hands, arms, legs, feet. A bucket of devastated limbs beneath each makeshift operating table. Perhaps he'd believed that if he could grow immune to such things in reality, he could grow immune to the images in his mind. It had not worked. The mind was stronger than anything reality could present.

3

He saw those things now. He saw them in the face of the girl they were bringing up from the mud.

And when they brought her out, when they saw the deep crevasse that had been cut into her torso, the way it had been bound together again like laces in a shoe, they were bereft of all words.

Finally, it was Jim Hughes who opened his mouth, and he simply said, "Oh my God . . . Oh my God almighty . . ." His voice was all but a whisper, and those words drifted out into the mist and humidity, and they were swallowed without echo.

No one asked who she was, and it was as if no one wanted to know. Not yet.

They paused for a little while, almost unable to look at her, and then they worked on silently, nothing but the heaves and grunts of effort as they brought her onto the tarp and lifted her free from the darkness of her grave.

And the rain fell, and the rain was black, and it did not stop.

The one thing that combat gave you was a willingness to expect everything and nothing at the same time. It took hold of your need for prediction, and it kicked it right out of you. Run for three days; stand still for four. Move at a moment's notice; go back the way you came. And all of it without explanation as to why. *How come this is so utterly, utterly fucked?* someone asked. *Because this is the way God made it* was the answer given. *How else d'you think he gets his rocks off?* After a few weeks, a couple of months perhaps, you realized that there was no one who gave a single, solitary crap about where you were.

One time, Gaines had taken a forty-five-minute chopper ride with six dead guys. Just Gaines, the pilot, and half a dozen dead guys. Some were in body bags, some just wrapped in their ponchos. Ten minutes in and Gaines unzipped them, uncovered their faces, and they all had their eyes open. He had talked for thirty minutes straight. He'd told them everything he felt, everything he feared. They did not judge him. They were just there. Gaines knew they understood. He also knew that Plato was right, that only the dead had seen the end of war. He believed that had he not done that, he would not have been able to go back. He unloaded those good ol' boys and then returned in the same chopper. He could still smell their dead-stink for five clicks.

That same smell overwhelmed Gaines as they carried the girl away. The rain had washed her clean. She was fifteen or sixteen years old; she was naked; and a crudely sewn wound divided her body from neck to navel. It had been sewn with heavy twine, and the mud had worked its way inside her. Even as her pale frame was carried to a tarp above the bank, the mud appeared and disappeared again like small black tongues from the stitched mouths of the wound. Gaines watched the men as they transported her—a line of sad faces, like early-morning soldiers on the base-bound liberty bus. Fun is done. Girls and liquor are all left behind. Like the faces of those transporting the dead to a chopper, the weight of the body in the poncho, their faces grim and resolute, eyes squinting through half-closed lids, almost as if they believed that to see half of this was to be somehow safe from the rest. The precise and torturous gravity of conscience, the burden of guilt, the weight of the dead.

And then Gaines noticed the trees, these arched and disheveled figures, and he believed that had they not already skewed and stretched their roots into rank and fetid earth, they would have come forward, shuffling and awkward, stinking their way out of the filth and shit of the swamps, and they would have suffocated them all within a tangled, knotted argument of arthritic branches and spiders' webs of Spanish moss. There would always be some grotesque and gothic manner of death, but this would perhaps be the worst.

The sorry gang carried her as quickly as they could, the mud dragging at their feet, the rain hammering down, drowning all words, drowning the sound of six men as they stumbled up the bank.

The memory of the dead is the greatest burden of all. That's what Lieutenant Ron Wilson had once opined in a field beyond 25th Division Headquarters at Cu Chi in February of 1968. He uttered those words to Gaines, the very last words ever to leave his lips, and he uttered it in the handful of seconds between changing his damp socks and the arrival of the bullet that killed him. There were no sounds—neither from the bullet itself, haphazardly fired without aim, merely a vague hope that somewhere it would find a target, nor from Lieutenant Wilson's lips. The bullet entered his throat at the base and severed his spinal cord somewhere among the cervical vertebrae. For a brief while, his eyes were still alive, his lips playing with something akin to a reflective smile, as if *The memory of the dead is the greatest burden of all* had been the precursor, the intro-duction to something else. Lieutenant Wilson was a philosopher. He quoted Arnold Bennett aphorisms about time and human industry. He was a good lieutenant, more a leader than a follower, a characteristic founded more in his vague distrust of others rather than any real sense of trust in himself. Gaines did not know what Wilson had done before the war. Later, after Wilson had been choppered away, he had asked the other guys in the platoon. *Who was Wilson? Before the war, I mean. Who was he?* They did not know either, or they did not say. Where he had come from was of no great concern. His life before was irrelevant. The life after was all that concerned them, and for Lieutenant Wilson there would be none.

Gaines remembered Wilson's face—the moment alive, the moment of death—as they reached Jim Hughes's flatbed with their grim burden. They laid the girl out on the rough, waterlogged boards, and Gaines set one half of the tarp beneath her, the other half over her, and he instructed Hughes to drive, his two sons up front, and he would follow them in his squad car back to town. He told Hagen to radio in and request both Dr. Thurston and the coroner be at the Coroner's Office upon their return.

It was now two o'clock in the afternoon. It had taken the better part of four hours to release the girl's body from the mud.

In a little while, once her body had been handed over to the coroner, Gaines would begin the onerous task of identifying whose child this was. And once identified, the task would be to find her parents and deliver the truth. There would be no triangled stars and stripes. There would be no telegram. There would be John Gaines, sheriff of Whytesburg, lately of the nine circles of hell that was Vietnam, standing on a mother's porch with his eyes cast down and his hat in his hands.

2

I remember it like my own name.

That day.

That Thursday.

I remember waking with a sense of urgency, of excitement, anticipation.

I remember the light through the window beside my bed, the way it glowed through the curtain. I remember the texture of the fabric, the motes of dust illuminated like microscopic fireflies.

It was as if I had slept for a thousand years, but sleep had let me go without any effort at all. I felt as if I could just burst with energy.

I rose and washed and dressed. I tied my laces and hurried downstairs.

"Maryanne!" my mother called when she heard my footsteps in the hall. "You come on here and get some breakfast before you go out playing!"

I was not hungry, but I ate. I ate quickly, like a child with endless siblings, hurrying through the food before one of them could snatch it away.

"Now, I need you back before dark," my mother said. "I said you could go today, but I don't want a repeat of last time. I'm not coming out looking for you at ten o'clock at night, young lady. You hear me?"

"Yes, Mom."

"And that Wade boy . . . You remember that they're different from us, Maryanne. Don't you go falling in love with a Wade, now."

"Mom—"

She smiled. She was teasing me.

"And Nancy will be with you, right?"

"Yes, Mom."

"And Michael Webster?"

"Yes, Mom."

"Okay, well, I don't want to hear that you've been giving him any trouble, either. He's the oldest one among you, and if you cause trouble, he'll be the one to get a harsh word from Sheriff Bicklow."

"Mom, we're not going to cause any trouble. I promise. And Michael is not going to have to speak to Sheriff Bicklow. And I don't love Matthias, and I don't love Eugene—"

"Well, that's good to hear, young lady. Even if you fell head over heels for either one of those Wade boys—" She hesitated mid-sentence. A curious expression appeared and was gone just as quickly.

"Okay," she said. "Enjoy yourself. But back before dark, and if I have to come looking for you . . ."

"I'll be back before dark, Mom."

"And I suppose Matthias Wade will be providing food for everyone, as usual . . ."

"He'll bring a basket, I'm sure. He always does."

"Well, as long as you understand that this sort of special treatment won't go on forever. He's a young man, Maryanne. He's all of twenty years old, and I am not so sure that I approve of this friendship . . ."

"We're just friends, Mom. Me and Nancy and the others. We're just friends, okay?"

"And there's the other Wade girl . . . the youngest one. What's her name?"

"Della."

"Well, make sure that you don't leave her out of your plans. Nothing worse for a child than to feel that they're the odd one out."

"I won't, Mom. I promise. Now, can I go, pleeease . . . ?"

My mother smiled then, and there was such warmth and love and care in her smile that I could do nothing but smile back.

I reached the door, and she snapped me back with a single "Maryanne," as if I was tied by elastic.

"Your room?"

"Tonight, Mom. I promise. I promise I'll clean it tonight. Really, I will."

"Be gone," she said, and flicked the dish towel toward me as if shooing a fly.

I was gone like a rocket, like a thunderbolt, haring out of the house and down the path, turning left at the end of the road and running until I felt my legs would fall right off.

I knew my mother was right. However much I might think about Matthias Wade, or think I loved him, or even wish that Eugene Wade would get his head out of his books every once in a while and kiss me, the fact still remained that the Wade family was the Wade family, and—to me—they seemed to be the richest and most powerful family in the world. And their daddy, Earl Wade, well, he scared me ever such a little. I mean, I knew he must be lonely and maybe even a bit crazy perhaps, but still he scared me. The way he stood at the top of the stairs and looked down at us. The way it seemed to take some Herculean effort to crack his face with a smile. The way he referred to us as "incorrigible" and "wearisome" and "vexatious." Seemed to me that a man like that, a man who seemed to have no friends, would appreciate some noise and laughter in the house, but no, apparently not.

I mean, with everything that happened with his wife, I could sort of understand what he might have gone through. Well, no, perhaps not. I am looking at this in hindsight, as an adult, and I can appreciate what might have happened to him, but then—all of fourteen years old—what could I have known? He was a scary man. That was all he was to me. He was Earl Wade—businessman, landowner, involved in politics, always engaged in serious discussions with serious men that could not be disturbed. You tiptoed in the Wade house—that's if you ever got inside. The few occasions I did go in, creeping around like a church mouse with Della and Eugene and Catherine and Matthias, I could sense that even they were wary of upsetting his humor. He had a temper. I knew that much. I heard him hollering at Matthias one time.

"You think you can just waltz in and out of this house as if you own it? Is that what you think? You might be my eldest son, Matthias, but that does not mean you can freeload off of me for the rest of your life. You may have done well in your studies, and you may have earned yourself a place at one of the best colleges in the country, but that does not mean that you can spend the entirety of your summers lazing around like some sort of superficial Hollywood playboy. You are not Jay Gatsby, young man . . ."

I did not know who Jay Gatsby was, but it sounded like he wasn't the sort of person Earl Wade wished his son to be.

And so it was, in some narrow place between the wealth and power of the Wades and the simple reality of my friendship with Nancy Denton, that we found a handful of years that would influence all of our lives for the rest of our lives. It could have been different—so very, very different—but the cruel reality of life is that the things we hope for and the things we have are rarely, if ever, the same.

There are small truths and big truths, just as there are small lies and big lies, and alongside those truths and lies run the questions that were never asked and those that were never answered.

The worst of all is the latter. What happened? What really

9

happened? Why did something so good become something so awfully, terribly bad?

Was it us? Did we make it happen? Did those seven human beings—myself, Nancy Denton, the four Wade children, and Michael Webster—just by circumstance and coincidence, just because we were all in the same place at the same time, conjure up some dreadful enchantment that captured our hearts and souls and directed them toward tragedy?

Is that what happened?

It was a long, long time before I understood that there might never be an answer to that question.

It was the not knowing that killed us all, if not physically, then in our hearts and minds.

A little something in all of us died that day, and perhaps we will never know why.

3

Whytesburg coroner, Victor Powell, was present in the doorway as the pickup and two squad cars drew to a halt ahead of the squat building. He merely nodded as Gaines exited the vehicle, waited in silence as the men lifted the girl's body from the bed of the truck and carried it around toward him.

It was a funeral procession, plain and simple, their expressions grave, their hands and faces smeared with mud, their hair plastered to their heads as if painted with a crude brush.

Gaines excused them when the girl had been delivered, thanked them for their help, their time.

He shook hands with each of them in turn, stood there beside Deputy Hagen as the pickup pulled away and headed back into town.

Gaines turned then, nodded at Hagen, and they went inside to join Powell.

Powell was silent and motionless, looking down at the naked teenager on the slab. Her skin was alabaster white, almost faintly blue beneath the lights. The mud from the riverbank filled the spaces between her fingers and toes; it had welled in the sunken sockets of her eyes; it filled her ears and her nose. Her hair was a dense mass of ragged tails—all of this as if a monochrome photograph had been taken of some weathered statue. It was a surreal and disturbing image, an image that would join so many others that crowded Gaines's mind. But it was here in Whytesburg, and such images—at least for him—should have belonged solely to a war on the other side of the world.

"Any ideas?" Powell asked.

Hagen shook his head. "Doesn't look familiar to me."

"She could be from anywhere," Gaines said. "She doesn't have to be one of ours."

"Well, I'd say she's somewhere between fifteen and eighteen," Powell said. He took a tape measure from a trolley against the wall and measured her. "Five foot four. At a guess, maybe ninety-five pounds. I can give you specifics when I've cleaned her up."

Gaines reached out his hand. His fingers hovered over the crude stitching that dissected her torso. Of this no one had yet spoken. He did not touch her, almost could not bring himself to, and he withdrew his hand slowly.

"Get back to the office," he told Hagen. "Put a wire out, all surrounding counties, and get every missing persons report on female teenagers for the last month." He looked across at Powell. "How long has she been dead, d'you think?"

"Decomp is minimal . . . At a guess, I'd say a week, two at most, but I need to do the autopsy. I can give you a better indication in a couple of hours. I need to take liver temp, find out how cold it was where she was buried and factor that in . . ."

"So beautiful," Hagen said, hesitating at the door. "This is just horrific."

"Go, Richard," Gaines said. "I want to find out who she is as soon as possible."

Hagen departed, glancing back toward the girl twice more before he disappeared from the end of the corridor.

"What can you say?" Powell asked, a rhetorical question. "Such things happen. Infrequently, thank God, but they do happen."

"This incision," Gaines said. "What the hell is that?"

"Who knows, John? Who knows? People do what people do, and sometimes there's no explaining it."

Gaines heard Hagen's car pull away, and almost without pause, the sound of another car slowing to a halt on the gravel in front of the building. That would be Bob Thurston, Whytesburg's doctor. Thurston was a good man, a good friend, and Gaines was relieved that he would be present. He did not want Victor Powell to have to endure such a difficult task alone.

"So do the autopsy," Gaines said. "Let me know as soon as you have anything. I'll get back to the office and start working through whatever missing persons reports have been filed. My fear is that she's from a long way off and we won't find out who she is."

"I'll get pictures done once I've cleaned her up," Powell said. "You can get those out on the wire . . ."

"For sure," Gaines said. "But I have to be honest, Victor . . . There's always the chance that we'll never know."

"I know it's hard to be positive at a time like this," Powell said, "but jumping to conclusions about what might or might not have happened here is going to do us no good. This is rare. A killing in Whytesburg. A murder here? It doesn't happen, John, not from one year to the next. I can't have seen more than half a dozen murders in Whytesburg—in the county, for that matter—in all my career. However, it has happened now. She's someone's daughter, and that someone needs to know."

Gaines turned as Thurston started down the corridor. "Bob's here," he said.

"What's this about a dead girl in the riverbank?" Thurston asked before he entered the room.

Gaines extended his hand, and they shook.

Thurston was trying to smile, trying to be businesslike, but when he saw the girl laid out on the slab, he visibly paled.

"Oh my Lord . . . ," he said.

"We figure she's somewhere between fifteen and eighteen," Powell said. "This incision along the length of her torso might be the cause of death. I'm ready to start the autopsy. I could use your help, if you're willing."

Thurston had not moved. His eyes wide, his face seemed like some ever-shifting confusion of frowns and unspoken questions.

"I've sent Hagen to check on any outstanding reports," Gaines said. "I can't think of any from here for months, but she could have come from anywhere. All we do know is that we have to identify her and find out how she died . . ."

Thurston set his bag down on the floor. He stepped forward and placed his hand on the edge of the table. For a moment it seemed as though he were trying to steady himself.

"No . . . ," he whispered.

Gaines looked at Powell. Powell frowned and shook his head.

"Bob? You okay?" Powell asked.

Both Gaines and Powell watched as Bob Thurston reached out his right hand and touched the girl's face. The gesture was gentle, strangely paternal even, and Gaines was both bemused and unsettled by Thurston's reaction.

"Christ, Bob, anyone'd think you knew her," he said.

Thurston turned and looked at Gaines. Was there a tear in his eye?

"I do," Thurston said.

"What?"

"I know who this is," he said, and his voice cracked.

Gaines stepped forward. "You what?" he repeated, scarcely believing what he was hearing.

"I've delivered every child in this town for thirty years," Thurston said, "and even those who were born before I got here have come to me with influenza and broken bones and poison ivy. I know this girl, John. I *knew* her. I am looking at her now, and it doesn't make sense . . ."

"That she's dead . . . Of course that doesn't make sense," Powell said. "A dead child can never make sense."

"I don't mean that, Victor," Thurston said. "Look at her. Look at her face. Who does she remind you of?"

Powell frowned. He stepped closer, looked down at the girl's face. It was half a minute, perhaps more, and then some sort of slow-dawning realization seemed to register in his eyes.

"She looks like Judith," Powell said. "Oh my God . . . no . . ."

"What is going on here?" Gaines said, agitation evident in his voice. "What the hell is going on here?"

"This can't be," Powell said. "This can't be . . . No, no, this isn't right . . . This isn't right at all . . ."

"She was found buried, you say?" Thurston asked.

"Yes," Gaines replied. "We just dug her out of the riverbank. She was buried—"

"In the mud," Powell said.

"I've heard of it before," Thurston said. "It has happened before . . ."

"Jesus Christ, you guys, what the hell are you talking about? If someone doesn't start explaining what the hell is going on here, I'm arresting the pair of you for withholding evidence."

"You know Judith Denton," Powell said.

"Sure I know Judith," Gaines replied.

"This is her daughter, John. This is Nancy Denton, Judith's daughter."

Gaines shook his head. "Judith doesn't have a daughter—"

"Doesn't now," Thurston interjected, "but she did."

"I'm confused," Gaines said. "Doesn't now, but did have a daughter . . . a daughter when? What daughter? You're not making any sense."

"*This* doesn't make any sense," Thurston said. "The fact that she is here and still a teenager is the thing that doesn't make any sense."

"Why? Why doesn't it make sense?"

"Because she's been missing for a long time, John," Powell said. He looked at Thurston. "How long, Bob? How long since she went missing?"

14

"It was in fifty-four," Thurston replied. "She went missing toward the end of 1954."

Powell exhaled audibly and closed his eyes for a moment. "Well, we found her, didn't we? Twenty years it took, but we found her . . . and she was here all along . . ."

"Twenty years?" Gaines asked. "1954? You can't be serious. There must be a mistake. This can't be her. How can she have gone missing twenty years ago and still look the same?"

"I guess she was dead within hours or days of her disappearance," Powell said, "and whoever did this to her, well, they buried her in the mud, and the mud kept her just as she was."

"This is unbelievable," Gaines said.

"Believe it," Thurston said. "This is Nancy Denton. No doubt, no question, no hesitation. I knew it the moment I saw her."

"And we have to tell her mother," Powell said.

"You want me to come with you, John?" Thurston asked.

Gaines shook his head. "No, I need you here with Victor. I need the autopsy done. I need to find out how she died. I need . . ." He stepped away from the table and started toward the door, turning back as he reached it and looking at both Thurston and Powell in turn. Then he looked at the body on the table once again. "You have to be right. You have to be sure. You have to tell me that there is no chance it could be someone else."

"It's her, John," Thurston said. "I treated her a dozen times for colds and coughs, measles one time, I think . . . I would know this girl anywhere."

"Good God almighty," Gaines said. "I need . . . I need . . ."

"You need to go tell Judith Denton that her daughter's come home . . ."

Gaines stood stock-still for just a second, and then he turned and walked down the corridor.

Thurston looked at Powell. Powell looked down at Nancy.

"So let's find out what happened to you, my dear," he said softly, and began to roll up his sleeves.

4

Judith Denton was damaged below the waterline. She seemed to have been born under a black star that had followed her for life. She was raised in the jumble of shacks at the edge of the county line, amid dark cedar swamps, the trees dressed in Spanish moss and Virginia creeper as if some huge spider had spent eons building defenses. The land was poisoned with Australian pine, with mela-leuca trees and Brazilian pepper, and what little irrigation could be mustered from the bayous did not make the farming any easier. Judith's father—Marcus—was an itinerant journeyman, a guitar player, a field hand, and always ready for *the next big thing*. His left nostril was gapped with an upside-down *V*, a gash too severe to heal and close, and the scar from the upward arc of a shrub knife had dissected his cheek, his eyelid, and his forehead with a pale line that disappeared somewhere within his hair. Years before, there was fighting down here, boxers who would grease their ears and shoulders so they could never be held. Marcus Denton was in there taking bets, making a handful of dollars from sweaty men aiming to thump one another senseless. He was a small and furtive character, always on the edge of things, his skin the color of sour cream. His wife, Evangelina, her shoes perforated with rot, her skirt nothing more than a ragtag collection of mismatched shirt pockets stitched to a slip, followed on behind him like he might one day know something of worth. Such a day never came. Judith—the only child of this couple of transient hopefuls—was born in March of 1917. She was little more than a year old when Marcus went down with a steamer on the Mississippi near Vidalia. Late at night, almost silent, nothing but the sound of bubbles like lips smacking, Marcus Denton and his pitiful luggage—his cards, his pocket watch, his dreams and aspirations for *the next big thing*—disappeared with eleven crew and sixteen guests beneath the pitch-black water. Not so much a life as a brief distraction between birth and death, events uncomfortably close to each other, his presence no more than a semicolon in between.

So Judith was raised by Evangelina, more a drunk than a mother, and when Evangelina died in May of 1937, Judith—all of twenty years old—upped and left for Whytesburg, perhaps believing that a change of location would establish the precedent for a change in fortune. That change, significantly less fortunate than she'd perhaps hoped, came in the guise of Garfield Thomasian, a shoe salesman out of Biloxi with a new station wagon and a popular line in smart cordovan wingtips. Their affair was brief and heated, fruitful in the way of Judith's immediate pregnancy, but Garfield Thomasian didn't hang around to see the results of his efforts. He was gone—gone, but not forgotten. Exhaustive attempts to locate him resulted in nothing but the discovery of a similar pattern of philandering adventures across this and several other states. Thomasian was a bad squall; he blew in, blew out, left nothing but small devastations in his wake.

Judith went the term, and when Nancy was born on the 10th of June, 1938, her mother believed that perhaps good things could come from bad. The child was beautiful and bright, as unlike the father as any betrayed mother could hope for, and things seemed to take a turn for the better.

Of Judith Denton, Gaines knew a little. Of her daughter, Nancy, he had known nothing. Not until today. Perhaps a small ghost of Whytesburg's past, only those present at the time being party to such information as rumor and hearsay could provide.

Nancy Denton's disappearance one warm evening in August of 1954 preceded Gaines's official investigatory responsibilities by two decades, and only now—the 24th of July, 1974—was Whytesburg aware of the fact that Nancy never really did go missing.

Nancy Denton, buried in the mud at the side of the river, had been here all along.

Gaines, still confused, still uncertain as to how such a thing could have happened, how a body could be preserved without deterioration to such an extent as was the case here, nevertheless understood the weight of this thing.

Thurston had possessed no doubt as to the identity of the girl.

It seemed that Judith Denton had been a single mother with a single child.

But no longer.

Now she would be a single mother with no child at all.

*

17

Gaines exited his car a half block from the Denton house and stood for a moment. He took a deep breath and considered what was ahead of him. Children went missing and children died. Didn't matter which town, which city, it was the same everywhere. Which was better—vanished or dead? If they were dead, perhaps some sense of closure could be attained. Perhaps. But if they vanished, there was always the hope that they would return. That, in itself, was enough to have you waiting for the rest of your life. Persuading yourself to just move on felt like the worst kind of betrayal, as if forgetting would consign them to history. Was this how Judith Denton had spent the last two decades? Looking from the window into the street? Imagining that one day her daughter might turn the corner and be standing right there in the yard? And what would Judith Denton fear? That she would not recognize her? That with each passing year, the daughter had grown and changed, had become a woman, and that she could walk right by her in the street and never know?

This was a strange day. A strange day indeed.

Fifteen yards from the road, Gaines met Judith's neighbor, Roy Nestor. Gaines had taken him in on a suspected B&E a couple of years before. Didn't ever come to anything, but here it didn't matter. Once you got the label, the label stuck. He had a long history of trickery and connivance. A century earlier, he'd have sold snake oil remedies to folks who had insufficient money to feed their kids. Rumor gave him a dozen post office boxes in a dozen different names, and into those boxes would come small-denomination checks for worthless items advertised in leaflets and newspapers, said items never delivered. The amounts paid were too insignificant for disgruntled and disappointed clients to chase refunds, even on principle, but those small amounts added up to handsome totals for Roy Nestor. Nestor would never find permanent work again. He was a journeyman, just as Marcus Denton had been, and Gaines had heard word of him in Wiggins, Lucedale, as far north as Poplarville, even Columbia where the I-98 met the Pearl River. He was a drinker and a fighter, forever smelled of bad armpits and stale tobacco, and irrespective of whatever money he might have swindled from people, he always looked homeless, his clothes raggedy, his shoes burst open and irreparable.

Nestor nodded at Gaines. " 'S up Sheriff?"

"Little business here, Roy. You know where Judith is at?"

The eyes. The eyes always gave it away. That immediate dimming of the light.

"Wha's happening?"

"Can't say nothing, Roy. You know that. Where's Judith at?"

Gaines took a step forward. Nestor moved to the right, and all of a sudden there was a tension and a threat in the air.

"Roy," Gaines said patiently.

"Somethin' happen?" Nestor asked. "You don't come down here unless it's bad news, eh? Never come down here to give up somethin' good, right?"

"Roy . . . please. This is personal business—"

"Personal? What could be personal that d'ain't have somethin' to do with her best friend now . . ."

"If you're her best friend, then you will let me deal with what I have to deal with here, Roy, and not be interfering."

"Did somethin' bad happen here, She'ff?"

"Roy, I'm telling you now, and I'll tell you again, this is Judith's personal business and I don't want you involved. Matters that involve her and her family—"

"Her family?"

"Roy . . . I mean it."

"You said her family, She'ff. You said her family. She ain't got no family, you know? I'm her family, you see? I'm the only—"

And then Roy Nestor stopped. His eyes widened, and he looked at Gaines with an expression that said everything that needed to be said, but he still didn't believe it.

"The girl?"

Gaines did not respond.

"You found her? You found her girl? Tell me you found her girl . . ."

Gaines said nothing, but the answer was so obvious in his eyes.

"You found her, didn't you, She'ff? You done found the girl."

Gaines nodded.

"Oh, Lord have mercy . . . Oh, Lord almighty have mercy . . ."

"I have to go and speak to Judith, Roy."

"She done for, ain't she? Tell me she ain't done for . . . Oh, this is so bad . . . It can't be anything else, can it? She's dead, ain't she?"

Once again, Gaines did not reply, but whatever words he did not utter were right there in his expression.

"Oh, man," Nestor said. "This had to happen, didn't it? This day had to come. Oh Lord, oh Lord, oh Lord . . ."

"Roy . . . I need to get by now. I don't have an ID as yet, but it looks that way, and I'm trusting you not to say a word—"

"Think I should be the one to tell her, She'ff," Nestor said, and there was something sympathetic in his expression, something so human, it was hard for Gaines to ignore it. "I knowed that girl, and I knowed Judith ever since. Man, she waited for that girl all these years. She done waited for here, thinkin' she gon' come on back, and now she gon' find out she dead. I listened to her cry too many times to let her deal with this 'un on her own."

Gaines looked at the man, his raggedy clothes, his weatherworn face, and he saw real humanity there in his eyes. Roy Nestor cared, and right now Judith Denton would perhaps need a friend more than at any other time in her life. Gaines placed his hand on Nestor's shoulder, squeezed it reassuringly. "Okay, Roy. I'm sure she would appreciate it if you were there for her. Think she's gonna need all the good people she can find right now."

Nestor shook his head slowly. He sighed deeply. "Shee-it, damned in hell we'll all be—"

Gaines frowned. "Why'd you say that?"

"Says a great deal about us when we can't take care of our own, doesn't it?"

"Does indeed, Roy."

Gaines, feeling the weight of the world on his shoulders, started walking, and Roy Nestor followed on behind.

It would come in stages, and the stages were like waves, and once the waves came, there would be nothing at all that could be done to stop them. There would be disbelief, shock, a sense of paralysis and utter terror, and then following on, close as shadows, there would be guilt, more disbelief, a vague and disorienting attempt to locate the last thing you said, the last thing you did . . . the last words that passed between you . . .

Twenty years of waiting, and all the while knowing that when the news came, it would not be good. But still believing that there might have been a chance, just a small chance, the slimmest splinter of a chance that there was a rational explanation for her disappearance, her absence for all these years, and now they would be reunited and it would be as if never a day had passed . . .

And once the mind started to get a grip on what it all meant, it was then that the pain would arrive, a pain so deep it would feel as if the world had closed its fist around you, and there would be nails and spikes and blades inside that fist, and they would be driven through you with such force.

And then it would seem that all the shattered parts of your mind had slipped their moorings, and you would be left with nothing but a vast abyss ahead of you, and you would fall in, and there would be no one beneath you and no one behind, and as you fell, there would be nothing on either side to hold on to, nothing to slow the fall, nothing to give you certainty that your drop would cease . . .

It was this that confronted Judith Denton in the moment she saw Sheriff John Gaines walking down the path toward her house, Roy Nestor walking on behind him, his head bowed, his eyes brimmed with tears and full of despair. They may as well have worn their church suits. There was a darkness about them that communicated everything without the need for words.

When Gaines arrived at the screen door, he was carrying his hat. This merely served to confirm that the message he brought was of the worst kind.

It really was as if she had been waiting on this day for twenty years.

Judith Denton smiled, a faint ghost of a smile, for she knew Sheriff Gaines. She understood his place in the scheme of things, and he understood hers, and though their places were worlds apart, he didn't take that as license to be anything less than courteous and respectful.

So Judith Denton saw John Gaines coming down toward the house, and she saw Roy Nestor, too, and she stood there for some seconds with an awkward expression on her face. The light hadn't dimmed yet. She was convincing herself it was something else, something unrelated, and despite the fact that Gaines was looking right at her, despite the fact that Roy Nestor, the very man she'd spoken to of this day so many times, was walking beside him, and despite the fact that neither of them were smiling, despite knowing that this wasn't any kind of social call . . .

Despite all these things, it was nothing less than human nature to try and convince herself that it wasn't bad news.

But she knew.

She'd known from the moment they appeared.

In her expression was everything—the simple, unfailing certainty that now she would never be short of things to regret.

And when Gaines was within ten feet of the screen door, Judith coming forward to greet him, she raised her eyebrows with a question, and the question was right there on her lips without her ever having to utter a word. It was then that Sheriff Gaines slowly shook his head, and she knew for certain. A mother would always know.

He opened the screen door, and he stood there without words. "Judith."

"Sheriff."

"We believe we may have found the body of your daughter . . ."

And then it was simply a question of whether a mistake had been made. How could they know it was her? I mean, how could they know for sure? If she herself—Judith, Nancy's own mother—could have walked by Nancy on the street and not recognized her, then how could John Gaines, a man who had never known her, be so certain that this girl they had found was her?

And then it was, how bad it could be? How had she died? How terrible had it been? And when? That same day she vanished? Or a later day? Two days, three days, a week, a year, a decade? Had she been beaten? Had she been raped . . . ?

So she asked Gaines, and her question anticipated the worst of all answers, and there was a hard edge of resignation in her eyes even before the words were uttered.

"How do you know?"

"Bob Thurston was with me . . ."

And Gaines didn't finish the statement, because he could see that moment of recognition. Bob Thurston had known Nancy, had known her well, had cared for her when she was ill, and if anyone could recognize Nancy, it would be someone like Bob Thurston.

Judith's breathing faltered. "Are you sure?" she asked. Her voice cracked, and the words seemed faint and uncertain.

Roy Nestor turned away, unable to hold her gaze.

Gaines looked down at the ground and then back at Judith.

"No," Judith said, her voice a broken-up whisper. "No, no, tell me no. For God's sake, no . . ." And she looked at her neighbor, and he still could not look back at her, and it was then that the waves came. They came fast and resolute, unerring in their accuracy, right through the heart, and they battered like fists at the door.

She seemed to fold in the middle as if a crease were already there, well marked from previous losses and disappointments. The heartbreak came, and it came with every kind of nightmare in tow, and she lowered her head as if this were the very last straw.

They tried to help her—Sheriff John Gaines and Roy Nestor—but

22

she resisted them. They followed her into the narrow wooden house, down along a corridor to the room where she had slept alone for the past twenty years. A moment of hesitation, and then she turned once more toward the parlor. And here she stood, the room no more than eight by twelve, a single window—four panes of dirty glass—a vague greasy light trying its hardest to gain entry. Beneath it sat a beaten-up chair, cotton stuffing growing through the holes in the cover, to the right a plain deal table, a two-shelf cupboard covered with netting to keep the flies out. The floor was mismatched pieces of oilcloth and linoleum, and everywhere was a feeling of despair and heartbreak.

Setting her down in the chair, Gaines paused for a moment to catch his breath.

Judith Denton looked right back at him, but he knew that she did not see him. He imagined that she was looking at the last time she'd seen Nancy, perhaps trying to convince herself that there had been some dreadful, dreadful mistake, that this was a nightmare, that any second now she would stir and wake, that she would know that her daughter was not dead, but still missing . . . and if she were missing, then there was still some small hope that one day she might return.

Better vanished or dead? Gaines asked himself again. Better to live with certainty or with hope?

But it was not a nightmare, and Judith Denton did not wake, and she felt no sense of relief.

Perhaps only then did Judith feel the full force of that news, and Gaines was on his knees before her, holding her hand while she closed up inside. The look in her eyes was now fierce and hateful, as if the world had conspired at last to take from her the only thing that mattered.

She gasped, and for a while it seemed that she would take only one breath, and somehow that single breath would be her last, and she, too, would die—right there in Gaines's arms. But she breathed again, and then again, and then she started to sob, and Gaines held her close to his chest. He felt her tears through the thin cotton of his shirt, and Judith Denton's tears felt like the bitter, black rain that had fallen as they'd exhumed her only child from that filthy, terrible grave.

Finally, through staggered breaths, through tears that would not stop, she found her voice. It was weak, a terrible, fragile sound, and though she uttered just a handful of words, those words seemed more powerful than anything Gaines had ever heard.

"Th-the day sh-she we-went miss-missing," Judith stammered. "The day she went miss-missing, I ne-never said I love you. I al-always say I love you. But not that day. It ha-had to be th-that day, didn't it? The day she disappeared . . ."

5

Gaines remembered the awareness of being alive, of waking on those rare occasions when he had clawed a handful of hours' sleep between one march and the next, between one firefight and the next, and being surprised to find himself alive. Before the war, he had taken such a thing for granted. He had taken many things for granted. He'd promised himself that afterward—*if* he made it home—he would acknowledge his survival, his *aliveness*, each and every day. But slowly, insidiously, without even realizing it, he had forgotten to make those acknowledgments. Now it was only special occasions—Thanksgiving, birthdays, Christmas—that he remembered the promise. And times of horror. He remembered the promise in times of horror. Small horrors compared to those he had survived, but horrors all the same. Perhaps he had chosen this line of work for that reason. To keep himself reminded of how sudden, how brutal, how terrible it all could be. To forever appreciate the fragility of life. How precious, and yet how terribly fragile. Of all things, however, those who came home from war were haunted by the ghosts of those who did not. At first a sense of disbelief, becoming at once a sense of responsibility to do something special, something rare and meaningful and extraordinary with their lives. Ultimately a sense of guilt that they had not and more than likely never would. What those who did not return would never know was that all you ever wanted were the small things, the narrow routines, the insignificant details of normalcy. You did not want to stand out, to be visible, to be noticed. Invisibility had engendered survival. It was against human nature to change a pattern that facilitated a future.

And now here, of all places, was a time of horror. Gaines did not know what had been done to the girl. Most of all, he did not know why. There were no questions he could answer for Judith Denton that would assuage what she was feeling. He sat with her for more than an hour, and she eventually turned away from him, buried herself into the chair as best she could, her body tight like a knot, fists clenched and pressed against her eyes, ashamed to be unable to speak, at the same time not caring who might see her.

Her vanished child was a child now dead. This much at least she knew. The details were yet to come, and Gaines didn't want rumors and assumptions stepping in where facts were needed. If Judith Denton was to be told the truth of her daughter's death, then it was only right that such a truth came from him. In such instances, the law performed a function that should not be assigned or delegated.

"Judith," he said, and he laid his hand on her shoulder. She neither flinched nor acknowledged his presence, and Gaines waited a few more minutes before he said her name again.

"Judith, I have to ask something of you now."

Gaines could feel the cool knot of anticipation in the base of his gut. His hands were sweating, his face also, and yet he could not move to retrieve his handkerchief from the pocket of his pants.

"Judith, you hear me?"

A twitch of response in her shoulder. Could have been involuntary.

"I have something I'm gonna need you to do now," he said. "I gotta take you over to the Coroner's Office . . ."

Judith Denton turned slightly. For a moment, her breathing hitched and stopped.

"You tell me what happened," she said. Her voice cracked with emotion, but beneath it was a firmness that could not be denied. "You tell me what happened to her, Sheriff Gaines. What happened to my girl?"

Gaines started to shake his head. "I can't—"

"You're the sheriff here," Judith interjected. "So don't tell me can't. You're the sheriff, and you can do whatever the hell you like. I want to know what happened to her—"

"We don't know yet," Gaines replied. "We found her down at the side of the river. She was dead. She was in the mud down there, and we had to dig her out . . ."

"How?" she asked. "How can that be? How could this happen?"

Gaines shook his head.

Judith looked at him, fixed him with an unerring gaze. "How old?" she asked.

Gaines frowned.

"How old is she, Sheriff Gaines?"

Gaines understood then. "I don't know, Judith, but Bob Thurston recognized her immediately, so she can't be much older than when she . . ."

Judith Denton was suddenly elsewhere, as if she had summoned sufficient imagination to picture her daughter. To see someone burying her perhaps, pushing her body down into the filthy, black mud . . .

"Sheriff—" Judith started, and then there was something else in her eyes, something that tore her up, because the expression on her face changed in a heartbeat from pain and grief to something else.

"D-Did th-they . . . ? Did th-they . . . ," she started, her voice catching awkwardly at the back of her throat. "Did th-they . . . ? You know wh-what I'm asking, Sheriff . . ."

"I don't know, Judith. I don't know what happened, and I won't know until the coroner does his autopsy."

Judith started shaking, pushed herself deeper into the chair once more, seemed to close herself off again from the rest of the world.

Gaines tightened his grip on her shoulder. "Like I said already, Judith, I'm gonna need you to come over to the County Coroner's Office with me. You're gonna have to be brave, as brave as you ever could be, and you're gonna have to take a look at Nancy and tell me that it's her."

Judith's eyes were rimmed red, her face contorted with anger. "Bob Thurston knows who she is!" she snapped. And then she moved suddenly, twisted her body, and turned to look up at Nestor, silent the entire time. "Bob Thurston says it was her! You can't be tellin' me that he might have made a mistake, now?" Her eyes widened, almost as if some small spark of hope had resided there all along, and he had just fanned it with his words.

Gaines shook his head solemnly. "No, Judith. You know there isn't going to be any mistake on this, but the law says that next of kin has to come down and identify the body. You know that, right?"

"I know nothin' 'cept she's dead," Judith said, such bitterness in her tone, and then she started crying again, this time with greater force, and her whole body was racked with spasms as she pulled herself in tight and tried to exclude Gaines.

"Judith . . ."

"Take Roy Nestor," she said. "Take him with you . . . He knows her as well as anyone . . ."

"Now, Judith, you know I can't do that. It has to be kin. That's the law. Has to be kin."

27

Judith's eyes flared. There was something angry and cold in her expression. "The law?" she asked. "You're down here telling me about the law? Where was the law when she was taken? I told them she'd been taken. I told them she would never run away, but did they listen? No, they didn't. Tell me about the law now, Sheriff. Where was the law when my little baby was being—"

"Judith," he said, in his voice a tone of directness and authority. "Until the truth is discovered, there is no truth. We have no indication of what happened to her." Gaines pictured the wide incision along the length of the girl's body, the rough stitching that had been employed to bind it together again. He could not tell her mother of this. Not now. Not yet. "The investigation has barely begun—"

"So what are you doing here with me? What the hell are you doing down here with me when you should be out looking for whoever did this thing?"

"Judith, I'm serious now. I have a lot of work to do on this thing. This is all that's happening for me right now, and I need to get some kind of cooperation here—"

Judith Denton faced him, and for a second Gaines believed she might throw her arms around his shoulders. She didn't. She raised her clenched fists and started beating on him, thumping on his arms, his shoulders, his chest. The woman was strong, but he did not restrain her. It was nothing more than utter desperation and loss releasing itself the only way it could.

Eventually, Gaines gripped Judith's wrists and pulled her close. She collapsed against him. He held her tight, as if to let her go was to see her vanish. He felt her tears making their way through the thin cotton of his shirt once again. He could smell the funky odor of her body, the tang of something wild and bitter in her hair, the smell of the room around them. And what he felt was hopelessness. Hopelessness and futility, because he had seen this before. He had seen it all before, and so much worse.

The horror of the tunnel complexes in the Than Khe area south of Chu Lai. Dead children, flies nesting in open mouths and hollow eye sockets, the skin dry and papery to the touch, the stomachs bloated with putrid gas. Losing his footing one time, skidding sideways like a sand surfer, arms extended for horizontal balance, Gaines had gone down a steep incline into a trench where some teenager had fallen. The weight and velocity of his descent had been sufficient to burst the boy's stomach.

Another time Gaines saw a man disappear. His name was Danny Huntsecker, and he stepped on a Claymore antipersonnel mine, and he simply disappeared. He was there, and then he was gone. This experience did not result in any philosophical realization; it did not impart some fundamental truth regarding the fragility and impermanence of man. Nothing so poetic. It merely demonstrated to Gaines that if you hurled seven hundred and fifty steel ball bearings at Danny Huntsecker with enough force, you could make him completely disappear.

He had seen worse, and he had heard of much worse.

Gaines did not understand what had happened to Nancy Denton. There were many questions to be asked and answered. When had she last been seen? Who had seen her? Where had she been going? Where had she been coming from? When had Bob Thurston said this had taken place? August of 1954? This was a twenty-year-old mystery, and Gaines knew how rapidly memories could fade in a year, let alone two decades. Most murders possessed rationale for no one but the murderer. Gaines knew this. He believed that the circumstances of Nancy Denton's death would be no different. Hers had been an unnecessary death for everyone but her killer. For her killer, there had been a great deal of point. Nancy Denton may have been murdered for who she was or what she represented. And if she'd been raped, assaulted, and if the butchery that had been performed upon her bore some relation to her kidnap and murder, then there was an even darker story to be uncovered.

And so Gaines pulled Judith Denton tight against his chest and wondered who the hell had made this world. From what he'd seen and heard, it sure didn't seem like God.

•

6

In the presence of Judith Denton, Breed County coroner Victor Powell did not divulge the details of his initial examination of Nancy's body to Sheriff Gaines. Rather, he took Gaines aside for a moment, told him that there were things that Gaines needed to know, that he should come back later when the mother had left.

"What things?" Gaines asked.

Powell shook his head, looked away for a moment, glanced at Judith, and when he turned back, the expression on his face communicated a sense of disquiet. "I'm just saying, Sheriff," he said. "I'm just saying there's things you need to know today, all right?"

"All right Victor, all right," Gaines replied. "And where's Bob?"

"He was called away. He'll be back shortly."

Gaines returned to the bench in the corridor. Judith Denton sat wringing a sodden handkerchief.

"I can't do this . . . ," she said, her voice cracking, "I can't do this, but I gotta do this . . ."

Gaines took her hand and helped her to her feet.

"I really don't think I can do this . . . Don't make me, Sheriff. Don't make me . . ."

Gaines said nothing. Her put his arm around her shoulder and turned toward Powell, who stood near a door on the right.

Powell pushed the door open and then followed them through into the morgue.

There was always a sense of surreal disconnection that removed John Gaines from such scenes. The dead were the dead. It was so clearly evident to him that the energy, the very spirit that had animated the body in life, was something separate from the body. Especially with young children who had died unexpectedly, it seemed to be the case that something remained in the vicinity. As if life had to reconcile itself to departing.

This was something he felt in the presence of Nancy Denton.

Her body had been covered with a simple white sheet. Victor Powell steeled himself. He took the sheet at its uppermost edge, and drawing it down, he revealed the face of the girl to her mother. Judith Denton's breathing stopped. Gaines waited for the hysterical rush of grief that he knew was coming, something that would pale into insignificance anything she might have expressed before . . .

"She looks the same . . ."

Judith Denton's words floated into the air, and they just hung there.

She looks the same . . .

Now that the mud had been cleaned away, Gaines saw her with such clarity.

She was a beautiful girl, her complexion and coloring more fall than winter, her dark hair swept back from her face, her eyes closed as if in sleep, her expression almost restful. Gaines did not understand how this could be. How could a body stay unchanged for twenty years? How was such a thing even possible? It was as if she had been locked in time while the entire world went on without her. Gaines imagined meeting someone from his own past, someone from two decades before, only to find that despite the passing of so many years, they had not changed at all. It provoked a feeling that he had never before experienced, and he did not like it.

He remembered how he had crouched at the top of the bank, how he had looked down at her face, how the pale, white hand had appeared from the blackness, how it had taken the strength of six men to get the mud to relinquish her, the stark and terrible image of the wound that centered her fragile frame, and now silently thanking Victor Powell for not showing the wound to the girl's mother . . .

Judith Denton's knees started to give way beneath her. Gaines held on to her with everything he possessed. Coroner Powell drew the sheet back over Nancy, and then he hurried around the edge of the gurney to help as the woman became nothing but deadweight in Gaines's hands.

Gaines felt as if he were watching the proceedings from the ceiling of the morgue. He could not hold Judith Denton anymore, and so he let her go.

Fifteen minutes later, Gaines and Judith Denton were seated on the bench in the corridor. From the car he'd brought a small silver flask, within which he kept a shot or two of bourbon. He had her drink it, held her as best he could while she cried some more, and then told her that the full examination was incomplete, that there were things he needed to know, things that could only be determined by the coroner. Without these things, it would be nigh on impossible to learn the truth of what had happened to her.

"The truth?" Judith asked. "The truth is that she is dead, Sheriff." She turned and looked at him. "So let me take her. Let me take her back where she belongs and bury her proper. Let me at least do that."

"I can't, Judith, and even if I could, I wouldn't. You're gonna have to let me do what I need to do here, and as soon as I can release her, I will."

"And if I refuse—" She stopped speaking and looked at him.

For a brief second, Gaines noticed a flash of anxiety in her eyes, as if she were afraid of what he might say or do.

"Judith," he said calmly. "I need you to help me on this. I need you to let me keep her until our work is finished. I'll help you make arrangements so things are done right. I'll find some money—"

Judith shook her head. "That is something you don't need to do," she said.

Gaines knew better than to push the point. Pride would prevent Judith Denton from ever accepting a nickel from him. "This is important enough for me to insist," he said. "I need to give the coroner the time he needs—"

"And if I don't, you can have me arrested?"

"Judith, you know I would never do such a thing."

She closed her eyes.

Gaines fell silent.

The tension between them was tangible.

"You gonna find the truth of what happened to her?" Judith asked.

"I'm going to do my best . . . That's all I can tell you. I'm gonna do everything within my power to find out what happened—"

Judith was distant for a while. "Everyone loved her," she said. "*Everyone*. And that night . . . the night she went missing . . ." She shook her head and looked down at the floor. "That was supposed to be a party. Just a party for no reason other than to have a party, but everyone was there. Michael was there, Maryanne, too, and the Wade boy. Michael had on his uniform, and he was so handsome . . ."

Judith looked back at Gaines. "I let her stay out. I let her stay out all night. She was sixteen years old, and she was a good girl. I trusted her . . ."

Gaines reached out and took her hand. He could feel the dampness of tears on her skin from where she had been clutching her handkerchief.

"You promise me—"

"You know I can't promise anything, Judith. You cannot ask me to promise anything."

" 'Cept that you'll do your best?" she asked. "You can promise me that much?"

"Yes. That much I can promise. That I'll do my best."

Judith Denton rose awkwardly, as if there were little strength in her knees.

"I'll drive you home," he said.

"I'm gonna walk, if you don't mind, Sheriff. Been inside here enough. Been inside the house, inside the car. Feel like I've been inside for twenty years, you know? Want some air. Want to walk out there by myself and have a little time."

"I understand."

Judith Denton looked down at Gaines. "I'll be expecting her home soon as you can bring her," she said. "Home is where she belongs."

"You have my word, Judith," he replied. "You have my word."

Gaines walked her to the door and watched her until she disappeared at the corner, and then he returned to the morgue.

Powell was standing over the still-shrouded body of Nancy Denton, and as Gaines entered, he drew back the entire length of the sheet and exposed the naked form of the girl.

"How can this be?" Gaines asked, still disbelieving.

"The mud," Powell replied. "I don't know a great deal about it, John, 'cept that it can happen. High salt content, low oxygen, buried deep enough to stay cold. And the fact that the mud got inside her as well. I'm sure that had something to do with it. It's something you'd have to consult a forensic archaeologist or someone about, but I've heard of bodies being preserved for hundreds of years, not just decades."

"Unbelievable," Gaines said. "This is truly unbelievable."

"The fact that you found her there is the least unbelievable thing about this," Powell said. "It gets a great deal crazier from here on. Trust me."

Gaines frowned.

"She wasn't sexually assaulted," Powell said. "I expected to find that she had been, but she hadn't. I think her hands and feet were

33

tied, but I cannot be sure. There are no signs of any real physical injury at all."

"Cause of death?" Gaines asked.

"Asphyxiation, as far as I can tell right now," Powell replied. "The hyoid bone in the throat is broken, concurrent with strangulation, but I'm not done."

Powell indicated the eighteen-inch incision down her torso. "But this is my greatest concern . . ."

"This is what you needed me to know?" Gaines asked, almost afraid to ask, aware that even he was close to his own level of tolerance.

"Yes, John, I did."

Powell leaned over the body, and then he carefully worked his fingers into the wound. Slowly, he drew the edges apart, and even as he did so, Gaines was aware that something was very wrong indeed.

"Where is her heart?" Gaines asked.

"She did not have one," Powell replied. He reached left and came back with a metal dish. In it seemed to be shreds of fabric, perhaps some kind of plant matter. And there was something else. Something that disturbed Gaines greatly.

"This came apart as I removed it," Powell said.

Gaines looked at Nancy's face. Something seemed to have changed. This was not the way she had appeared when he had entered the room with Judith. The face now seemed tight, the skin drawn, the lips pulled back against the teeth.

It was the body being influenced by the air, the change in temperature perhaps, he told himself. Nothing more than that.

Gaines closed his eyes and mouthed a few silent words.

"What?" Powell asked.

"Nothing," Gaines replied.

"You ready for this?" Powell asked.

"As I'll ever be."

"This," Powell said, indicating the few shreds of cloth in the metal dish, "is the remains of a basket."

"A what?"

"A basket. Very carefully constructed, almost spherical. Made in two halves, it was hinged on one side with wire and had a wire catch on the other. And it was made to open just like a pocket watch . . ."

Powell set the dish down on the table.

"A basket? What the hell?" Gaines started.

34

"Hold your breath, John," Powell replied, "because you ain't seen nothin' yet."

Powell took a wooden depressor and poked at a small shape to the side of the basket's remains. It seemed to uncurl, and despite its fragility, it still retained its circular shape. It was then that Gaines's eyes seemed to deceive him.

It was a snake. No question about it. An infant, its type and exact length impossible to ascertain, it was nevertheless a snake.

"Jesus Christ. What the fuck?"

"Exactly what I said," Powell interjected. "Someone strangled her, and then they opened her up, cut out her heart, and then replaced it with a snake in a basket."

Gaines didn't say a word. He simply felt a quiet sense of dread drowning every other emotion he was feeling.

7

Sometimes the mind slipped its moorings.

Gaines, standing quietly in the corridor outside the morgue, thought of Linda Newman. At first he did not know why she came to mind, but then—after a little while—he did know. It was because of the child. The child that never was.

It was 1959, and he—all of nineteen years old—met a girl in the Laundromat. As good a place as any other to meet a wife, he believed. Not like there was some wife-farm where you could go pick your own and then maybe take her back if she turned out to be a sour 'un. Her name was Linda, and she got herself all trained up in a beautician school in Baton Rouge. She came on back to Opelousas, where Gaines was living at the time, but there didn't appear to be a great demand for the things she proposed to provide. The women all wore housecoats and thick socks. They were up at five in the morning, chopping wood, firing the stove to make oatmeal for a hungover husband and a brood of kids, and such routines didn't sit so well with a bouffant and a manicure. Women like that would rather you open up another liquor store, maybe a bar or something, so their husbands would spend more nights sleeping in the garage. Lack of employment aside, John Gaines and Linda Newman figured they would make it work somehow, and they stayed together. One time in the fall of 1960, just for the hell of it, they had driven from Alexandria to Shreveport. They had shared a passion for Nabs crackers, had eaten much of the state's available supply en route. And then, in the early part of 1961, Linda got pregnant. When she was pregnant, she was crazy for frozen Milky Ways. For her, frozen Milky Ways were not so far from a religious experience.

While he was in-country, Gaines had thought about that child a lot. The child that almost was. Squatting in a foxhole, the darkness stabbing at his eyes, his mind playing tricks (for once it was dark, everyone believed in ghosts), he would make-believe that the child was alive, that he or she had made it, that Linda Newman and the child were waiting for him in Opelousas. But there had been no child, and there was no Linda Newman. Linda had miscarried, and afterwards it seemed that she could not bear to be around him, and so she'd returned to her folks in New Orleans. So many times Gaines had thought to find her, to speak to her, to try to convince her they could start over. He had imagined those conversations, practiced his lines, but they had never been delivered. Gaines had rehearsed a part he'd known he would never play, because he knew all along that it would never have worked. What had happened between them, how it had ended, had been so finite, so permanent, and they had both known it completely.

Gaines had tried so hard to think of other things, but it just kept coming back, like the taste of bad garlic, and it had made him bitter. The child he'd been denied. Seemed there was always something to remind him, and now this—this dead girl with a snake for a heart— was the most potent and powerful of all.

Linda had been gone all of thirteen years. His fourteen months in Vietnam had ended in December of 1968, and yet he was still alone, still caring for his mother, living now in Mississippi instead of Louisiana, but little, if anything, had changed.

He believed he had done the right things. However, doing the right thing was only a comfort if the result was right. There were individuals who accepted what nature had given them and others who strived against it. There were others who floated in limbo. They were waiting, it seemed, but for what? Even they did not know.

There was one God for the rich folks, one for the poor. And there were some men who spent the entirety of their lives looking for signs of forgiveness for a crime they had not committed.

Gaines, every once in a while, would still awaken in four-hour shifts. Suddenly, his eyes wide, his mind alert, a voice insisting in a hurried whisper, *Hey! Hey, Gaines! You're up*, and he would lie there, the silence of the house around him, and realize that he did not need to get up, that there was no watch to be performed tonight, that if he stepped out behind the house and stared into the darkness, he would see nothing but distance and shadows. Whatever war had existed for him was now over. Vietnam was nine and a half thousand miles away, and yet sometimes he believed it was as close as his shadow. Believed, perhaps, that it *was* his shadow. It was a mighty war, both terrible and terrifying, and back then—at twenty-seven years of age—he had been a child among children, and they had been presented with both horror and rapture in equal parts. It was said that the mind healed if given sufficient time. It did not. It merely built ever-greater defenses against the ravages of conscience and memory.

After a while you forgot what was dream and what was memory.

Above and beneath all that, John Gaines was the man he had become in Vietnam. He was a man of war. A dark and merciless and unrelenting war that took everything good from the soul and replaced it with nothing. It was hard to appreciate how little more than a year could influence and affect a human being to such a degree. But it had. There was no question that it had.

Some said they left a part of themselves in the jungles and villes and tunnels of Southeast Asia. This was not true. They left all of themselves behind. They returned as someone else, and their friends, their families, their wives and mothers and daughters, struggled to recognize them. To themselves, as well, they had become almost strangers.

Gaines had not gone the route of grad school deferment, nor the National Guard, nor the reserves; he did not cite opposition in principle, nor from some religious or ethical stance, nor from some real or imagined medical status; he did not think of running away or hiding in Canada or Mexico. On Thursday, February 9, 1967, he received his *Order to Report for Physical Exam*. He attended the exam. On Wednesday, May 10, he received his *Order to Report for Induction*. He simply read the draft notice carefully, read it once again, and then returned it to the envelope. *So that's it*, his mother had said. *Yes*, Gaines had replied. *That's it.*

Even now, looking back, he could remember the expression on her face. *I lost my husband to war*, that expression said, *and now I will lose my son*. She had been born Alice Devereau in Pointe à la Hache, Louisiana, in January of 1915. She met her husband-to-be, Edward, in 1937. Within two years, they were married. John, their only child, was born in June of 1940. When John was two, his father left for Europe. He served with the First Army, and was killed near Malmedy and Stavelot on the road to Liege, Belgium, on December 23, 1944. Alice Gaines had been all of twenty-nine years old.

So she looked at her son, two years younger than she herself had been when she'd lost her husband, and she asked him if there was any other way.

"No," John had said. "There is no other way."

Five days later, John Gaines reported for Basic Combat Training at Fort Benning, Georgia. Boots, bed, hygiene, weaponry and maintenance, C rations, first aid, land navigation, rules of war, the

Uniform Code of Military Justice, marching in ranks and parade, inspections. He graduated in July, moved on to Advanced Individual Training. He learned how to hide from people. He learned how to follow people. Then he learned how to kill them. In September, he graduated to Republic of Vietnam Training. Toward the end of the month, he took a week's leave, went home to see his mother, helped her move to Whytesburg, Mississippi, so as to be nearer an old friend, and then he shipped out. Fort Benning to Saigon, Saigon to Đà Lat, Đà Lat and onward into the Central Highlands. Two weeks' in-country orientation and training, and he was set.

Back then, back in the real history of the thing, there were smaller empires. Vietnam was a world all its own, and included the territories of Tonkin, Annam, and Cochinchina, out to Laos and Cambodge sat Siam in the west. Now it was all North and South, nothing more. Before the Second World War, the French maintained Indochinese colonies. They occupied Vietnam, Laos, and Cambodia until they were overrun by the Japanese. After the Japanese surrender, the French came back. They wanted a new French Union. Ho Chi Minh wanted complete independence. The United States supported France, but when the fortress of Dien Ben Phu fell in May of 1954, it was all over.

They should have learned then, but they did not. It would never be size or influence or money that would win a war in the jungle. It was knowledge. It was being there. It was *understanding* the land. Only the Vietnamese possessed this, and thus they would never lose.

The history of the place was important to Gaines. He had wanted to know why he was fighting. *Because your president and your country needs you to* had never been sufficient for him.

After the French defeat, they just cut the country in half where the South China Sea became the Gulf of Tonkin. North Vietnam would be governed from Hanoi by the Việt Minh. South Vietnam would be governed from Saigon. On the throne would be the French ally, Emperor Bảo Đại. The United States did not agree.

A year later, the South Vietnamese elected a new leader. Ngô Đình Diệm was a tyrant, a corrupt and dishonest man, but he was Catholic and an anticommunist, and the United States wanted to keep him in place. But then rebellion came in 1957, communists and nationalists in the south receiving their orders from the north. They coalesced, grew stronger, and three years later they became the National Liberation Front. Vietnamese communists. The Viet Cong.

These were the people that Gaines had been trained to kill.

Back in '54, Eisenhower had promised that noncommunist Indochina would never fall to the Reds. It was a matter of principle. America, the mightiest of all, had been outwitted and overthrown by a gang of sandal-wearing Russian collaborators. Eisenhower's pride had been hurt. He had defeated Nazi Germany, and yet he couldn't take out a strip of land that was half the size of Texas. Eisenhower was a Texan. Vietnam was a nothing place in the middle of nowhere. He was galled.

In November of 1963, just three weeks before Kennedy was assassinated in Dallas, South Vietnamese president Ngô Đình Diệm was murdered in an army coup. When Johnson assumed the presidency, he declared, "I am not going to lose Vietnam." August of 1964 saw a US destroyer fired upon by North Vietnamese patrol boats in the Gulf of Tonkin. Johnson launched air attacks on North Vietnamese shore installations. Johnson had a resolution-approved fistfight on his hands. Vietnam was some piece-of-shit backyard where US boys were getting their asses kicked by little yellow guys in sandals and coolie hats. Enough was enough.

By the end of '65, there were one hundred and eighty thousand American soldiers in Vietnam. By 1968, there were well over half a million. They carried orders to run offensive attacks against NLF guerrillas. Napalm rained down on Viet Cong outposts and guerrilla units in the south. Johnson went great guns. He threw more bombs at Vietnam than the combined total of all bombs hurled at Europe between '39 and '45. But this was no European engagement. The enemy the United States fought was faceless, without uniform, familiar with the terrain, its anomalies and idiosyncrasies, and thus they always possessed the upper hand. The United States had firepower, air cover, strong supply lines, an almost inexhaustible source of men, but they did not have an enemy they could see. They fought ghosts and shadows. They fought a nightmare.

And it was into this nightmare that John Gaines arrived, a twelve-month tour of duty, and it was from this arena of horror that he would bring things that would dictate and define the rest of his life. He had known that within a week.

Afterward, there would be stories. Some lavish, some exuberant, some exaggerated; others brief, succinct, to the point. Those who were not there grew tired of the telling; questioned veracity, questioned the purpose of the stories. *The reason for telling the stories is to join the seams together*, a fellow veteran once told Gaines. *To see if the past cannot belong to the present again . . . but it's like trying to stitch the sea to the sky. You know they are somehow made of the same thing, but they will always and forever be incompatible.* For Gaines, it had simply been a matter of trying to understand how the boy he had once been had become the man that he now was. The past was a different country, and if you returned, you soon realized that they spoke a language you no longer understood. War stories. If it did not seem surreal, it probably never happened. If it centered on trust and bravery and self-sacrifice, on some unquestioning loyalty to a man, a unit, a detachment, a mission, it was probably a lie. If it spoke of duty to God, to nation, to a religion, a belief, it was almost certainly a falsehood.

If it appeared unbelievable, you were safe to believe it. If you listened to the telling and even the teller seemed to doubt the story himself, then that was the one you could bet your house on.

War was a drama scripted by spite-fueled and evil children, by warped delinquents, by incarcerated madmen driven into a deep and irredeemable psychosis by the drugs and barbaric shocks of demented psychiatrists, by men with single eyes and hooks for hands and small shards of scorched glass in place of their souls.

War was a firework display for the shallow entertainment of darker gods. War cleansed men of all that was best in them. It cleansed with fire, with bullets and blades and bombs and blood. It cleansed with loss and pain, and with its own sense of unique and incommunicable disbelief engendered in all who attended the ceremony of battle. In ten thousand years, all that had changed was distance. Perhaps, eons ago, there was some small nobility in seeing the face of the man you killed, in watching the already-too-brief light extinguished, in hearing the silence as breathing halted. Now you could kill a man a mile away. Now you could release bombs through clouds and obliterate thousands.

At first you dropped the terrible fire from the sky and you believed it was purifying. In some small way, you were an emissary of right and truth and justice, perhaps of God. Later, when you saw the burned children, you understood you were simply an emissary from hell.

There were those who got their kicks herding a half-dozen sandal-footed, coolie-headed gook collaborators into a chopper and then throwing them out from a height of three hundred feet. Hands and

41

feet, a guy at each end—*Three-two-one-awaaaay*—like teenagers at the poolside. The speed of their descent just kicked the air right out of them. Gaines never heard one of them scream. Not even the kids.

A man who possessed a motivation for war was a man who hated. Hatred sourced its foundations in ignorance. Yet hatred of another was also hatred of self, for beneath all things we were the same. Agreeing to go to war did not make you wrong. It was agreeing to stay that was at fault. And the ones who went back a second time, a third time, had already lost so much of themselves, they knew they could never belong elsewhere.

There were the rationales that came afterward. The alone times when men had to justify their actions, when they had to explain to themselves why they did those terrible things.

But they did them in war. In times of war. They did not do them for love, nor for money, nor for the satisfaction of some dark and horrifying compulsion.

Outside of war, you were faced—simply—with people. Gaines believed that the vast majority of what went on in people's heads should stay in people's heads. But people carried shadows inside them, and sometimes the shadows escaped.

The death of Nancy Denton, what had been done to her, the things that Gaines had seen—this was an act performed out of some strange and terrifying vision of hell that exceeded much of what he had experienced.

He had told Judith Denton that he would do his best to find the truth of what had happened.

It went beyond that.

Someone had murdered a girl. Someone had cut out her heart and replaced it with a snake. Someone had roughly stitched her body and buried it in mud, and there that body had remained—undisturbed—for twenty years. It had taken six men four hours to bring her back.

There were questions to be asked. Many questions.

The burden of responsibility came down upon him like a wave, like the downdraft of a Huey.

He possessed his own ghosts and specters. His own phantoms. He would carry these things forever, and they would always lie heavy upon his conscience.

He did not need any more.

8

Bob Thurston appeared at Gaines's office a little after five. He apologized. He'd had to leave the autopsy to attend to a delivery at the hospital.

"It is beyond belief," Gaines said.

"Beyond disbelief," Thurston said.

"You saw the snake?"

"I did."

"Any thoughts?"

Thurston shook his head. "What is there to think? Voodoo? I don't know, John. There are some crazy, crazy people out there."

Gaines was quiet for a time, and then he said, "I saw Judith. I told her. She came and identified the body. I think it might be a good idea to go see her as soon as you can."

"I will," Thurston replied.

"And I need this kept as quiet as possible, Bob, for obvious reasons, but I know I'm whistling through a tornado on that one."

"Hell, then don't say a goddamned word to your mother, John. She'll be laying brooms across all the doorways and making us wear bundles of pig bristles . . ."

Gaines smiled sardonically. "You see some line of black humor in everything?"

"I have to," Thurston replied. "Keeps me from drinking."

"My mother will find out," Gaines said. "She'll find out from one of the neighbors."

"You better tell Caroline not to say anything."

"Caroline is a nineteen-year-old with nothing better to do than help me look after my mother. She's gonna be the first to get into it with her. I can't stop her finding out, Bob, and I can't stop the things she will do or say as a result. You know that. You know her better than anyone. Regardless, you're changing the subject . . . Fact is, we have a sixteen-year-old girl murdered, buried in the riverbank, her heart removed. Took six of us to dig her out."

"So where do you even begin on something like this?"

"I have no idea, Bob, no idea at all," Gaines replied. "My first thought is that I might be looking for a killer who is dead themselves. This is twenty years old."

"You think some of the ones who were around at the time can help you?"

"Hell, Bob, I don't even know that there is anyone around apart from the girl's mother. Right now, I don't even have a confirmed cause of death."

"You think there's anything in the voodoo idea? I mean, it sure as hell is the weirdest goddamned shit I ever heard of . . ."

"I can't discount anything," Gaines replied. "I know this kind of thing goes on. When we were kids, we used to go down to Marie Laveau's tomb and steal the pound cake that people left for Saint Expedite. Anything that involves a snake is going to be taken as a sign of Li Grand Zombi—"

"But this is Mississippi, not Louisiana—"

"Head west fifteen miles, you're in Louisiana, Bob. The influence is as strong here as anyplace between here and Baton Rouge."

"So let's just hope it was a regular psycho, eh?"

"Let's just hope. Last thing I need right now is ritual sacrifices, gris-gris ceremonies, and people turning up at your office with jimson weed poisoning."

"So I'll go see Judith Denton. I think she needs to know she's got friends right now. You?"

"I'm going to go check on my ma, and then I'll be back to see Powell. I need final COD and the autopsy report."

"Tell your ma I'll be over tomorrow."

"I will."

"You know I upped her morphine yesterday."

"I could tell," Gaines replied.

"She's rambling again?"

"In and out of it. You know how she is."

Thurston walked to the door. He hesitated, turned back. "This is a horrific thing, John. What the hell are we dealing with here? A sixteen-year-old girl, a twenty-year-old murder, a snake instead of a heart, for Christ's sake."

"I don't know, Bob . . . Don't know that I *want* to know."

"Sure you do. That's why you're doing this job. That's why we all do what we do . . . so we can know the answers to shit like this."

"Go," Gaines said. "Go see Judith. I'll speak to you later."

After Thurston had left, Gaines—sitting alone in his office—remembered an incident.

There was a grunt, name of Charles Binney. His helmet name was *Too High* on account of the fact that he was six four, maybe six five. It was a bright Tuesday morning outside of Nha Trang, near the foot of the Chu Yang Sin Mountains. There was a Vietnamese girl. Her name was not *Me Quick Fuck* or *Suck Man Root* or any of the other defamatory aliases with which such girls were christened by the members of Five Company. Her name was something like *Kwy Lao*, though perhaps with a *Q* and a handful more vowels. And Too High set his mind to impressing her by climbing a neem tree. Had Too High, arriving in-country no more than three months before, survived his brief excursion into the Southeast Asian theater of war, he would have described the young girl as *angelic*. Too High used such words because Too High was a cultured, book-reading kind of guy. It was not his height alone that singled him out, but also his intellect and vocabulary. Too High was an anachronism, always had been, and when his draft notice had arrived, his lack of resistance to military service was questioned by his younger brother. Too High had quoted Goethe: 'Unless one is committed, there is hesitancy, the chance to draw back, always ineffectiveness . . . Whatever you can do, or dream you can, begin it. Boldness has genius, magic and power in it. Begin it now.'

The following morning, Charles Binney kissed his ma, shook his father's hand, hugged his younger brother, and left for the war.

The next time they saw him, he was a stars and stripes triangled into a military tuck.

Kwy Lao had been amused by Too High's scaling of the tree, for a neem tree isn't the easiest thing in the world to climb. Spurred on by her apparent enthusiasm for this feat of daring, he attempted to climb higher and faster, even made a noise like a monkey. It was the attempted scratching of his own armpit that was his undoing. One hand seemed insufficient to bear the sudden weight of his lengthy frame, and he fell suddenly, silently, and altogether surprised. He broke his neck on impact, and the expression on his face was as calm and untroubled as a summer sky.

Five Company had possessed neither the will nor the stamina to cut an LZ for a dust off, nor to call in a Huey or a Chinook to carry Too High home. They decided to commit him to the ground then and there, and while a young man from Boise, Idaho, called Luke "Dodge" Chrysler said a few words from the Bible, Too High's body was sunk in a swamp. "Oh God, thou art my God," he murmured. "Earnestly I seek thee, my soul thirsts for thee; my flesh faints for thee, as in a dry and weary land where no water is . . ." They were the only words Luke Chrysler knew—Psalms 63, the Psalm of David when he was in the wilderness of Judah. How he knew them, and why, he could not remember, but he did. And though this in itself did not seem fitting, seeing as how they were sinking him in a swamp, it seemed better to have some words quoted than none at all.

Five Company RTO radioed a message, the message became a dispatch, the dispatch became a telegram, and then a flag. The flag was folded perfectly into something no bigger than a 9th Street Diner king-sized chili burrito, and it was delivered to the Binney household by a narrow-shouldered, pinch-faced man called Mr. Weathers.

And so Charles "Too High" Binney—who fell from a neem tree while showing off for a girl called something like Kwy Lao, a breathtakingly pretty girl, slender as a fern, her *ai do* draped over her form like a ghost—died not in battle, not with the taste of blood on his teeth; died not for valor nor country nor simply the spirit of war, but with an erection and the promise of a good lay. Such was the idiocy and reality and simplicity of war. Of course, his parents were never told such a thing, for such a thing would not have been respectful of the dead. They were told he'd been hit by a sniper while seeking refuge for his company on a bright Tuesday morning near Nha Trang at the foot of the Chu Yang Sin Mountains. His father, perhaps wishing to gain some sense of understanding, had searched out an atlas and looked for this place. He found it, right there on the tip of a country he had never even considered before, the width of his fingernail from something called *The Mouths of the Mekong*, and though he now knew where his son's body lay, it did not ease nor explain the vast gulf of sadness into which he and his wife had been swallowed. And swallowed they were, like Jonah into the whale.

Gaines remembered Binney's face, as he did all those who died around him, in front of him, behind him. They all bore the same expression. The same as Nancy Denton. An expression like an empty house. In death, bodies do things that they could never do in life. They bend, they break, they hang upside down. A booby trap in a tunnel mouth turned a solider into nothing but blood and jutting bones, as if the force of war alone could fold a human being inside out.

Gaines thought of Binney in that moment, the way his body disappeared into the swamp. He wondered then if Binney would still be the same, preserved like Nancy Denton.

In his five years of police service, Gaines had not seen such a thing as Nancy Denton. He had seen enough, of course, but nothing so macabre, nothing so unsettling.

Gaines's twelve-month tour of duty had ended in October of 1968. Back then, as had remained the case right through, if a soldier agreed to serve another six months, he could take a thirty-day R & R at the army's expense anywhere in the world. They would fly him out there, bring him back, pay him while he soaked up whatever world he'd been transported to, and then they would come and get him. Gaines did that. He didn't know why. He completed his twelve months, he survived, and yet he could not face the prospect of going home. Going home seemed more fearful than staying in-country. He took the thirty days. He asked them to fly him to Australia, and they did. He was in Melbourne for a week, did nothing but chain-smoke, drink bourbon, listen to Hendrix and Joplin. He sat in bars crowded with Seabees who had served on coastal patrol boats in the Yellow Sea and Cat Lo; with brown water sailors; with Marine Corps and SEALs; with men from the Mobile Construction Battalion; with laconic and intimidating Special Forces flattops, their jackets bearing eight or ten gold hash marks, one for each six-month tour they had served. A week, that was all, and then Gaines applied for reintegration to his platoon. He knew that if he stayed for thirty days, most of the people he knew, most of his friends, would be dead by the time he got back. The application was received; Gaines was told to see an army psychologist. The psychologist asked questions that Gaines could not answer, and then he signed the release and Gaines was packed onto a flight and expedited to a combat zone near Đắk Tô.

On the 12th of December, 1968, John Gaines was shot through the stomach in Buon Enoa, east of Ban Me Thuot. His platoon had been assigned to assist the Special Forces deployment run by 5th Group at Nha Trang. Special Forces were working "hearts and minds" on the Montagnard people, a minority peoples persecuted by the South Vietnamese. Their history of conflict with the South Vietnamese made them easy targets for Viet Cong subversion, but in exchange for their loyalty to the South, they were given military assistance and civic support. The program worked, and the Montagnard militia became enormously effective in search and destroys against VC bases and outposts.

It was during one such mission that Gaines's platoon came under heavy fire. Thirty-eight men went out, twenty-one came back, and of those twenty-one, eight were wounded. The bullet that hit Gaines had missed all vital organs. It was a through and through, but he bled heavily, and when he arrived in the field hospital outside of Đà Lat, he was in poor shape. Gaines had survived Đăk Tô in November of the previous year, the heaviest conflict since the Ia Drang Valley in 1965. Back then, the fighting had been so intense that medevacs—the KIA Travel Bureau—could not land to collect the dead and wounded. Perhaps Gaines had believed himself impregnable, unassailable, blessed with divine protection. His mother, Alice, had written to him about faith. She was a Louisiana Catholic. She believed in God, in Jesus Christ who died for our sins, but she believed also in Papa Legba, in conjure, in grimoires, in Li Grand Zombi and gris-gris. She was a complex woman, a woman of strange superstitions and intense shifts of mood, and in her letters—the few that Gaines received—she spoke of *perceiving* him, *guiding* him, *defending* him against the shadow of death. It was not until Gaines returned to Whytesburg that he understood how ill she had become, that in his absence she had been diagnosed with cancer, that she was drifting between spells of extraordinary lucidity and morphine-induced hallucination. Gaines's neighbors, Leonard and Margaret Rousseau, their daughter, Caroline—all of thirteen years old at the time—were good people, and they kept watch over her, did their utmost to assist her, but she was a difficult and ornery woman at the best of times.

Whether Gaines had *known* that there was trouble at home, or if his wounding had merely reoriented him to the realness of his own mortality, he wasn't certain. But when he was asked by an army chaplain if he wished to return to combat after his recuperation, he said no. He had completed his tour. He had fulfilled his obligation. He wanted out. He knew of his mother's cancer. Had this not been the case, he believed the army might have held him to his agreement to serve the additional six months. He was discharged honorably, and his journey—combat zone to small-town sidewalk—was all of twenty-four hours. One day he was standing amid the mud and blood of a South Vietnamese field hospital, the next he was in front of the post office in Whytesburg with his discharge papers and a check in his pocket.

Gaines did not tell his mother he had been shot. It would have served no purpose but to diminish the hardship of her own situation, and—more important—it would have invalidated the belief she possessed in her will for him to survive unharmed. She *knew* her faith had figured prominently in his return. He had survived, but he was not unharmed. None of those who returned were unharmed. As Narosky had said, *In war, there are no unwounded soldiers*.

It was during the first weeks of his return that he befriended Bob Thurston. Thurston was a good deal older than Gaines, and he would spend time with Gaines when he visited Alice. Thurston would give her morphine, and while she slept, he would sit with Gaines and listen to the war stories. Thurston became John Gaines's confidant, his confessor, most of all, his friend.

It was Thurston who advised he apply for the sheriff's department.

"You have to have structure. You have to have a schedule. You cannot spend the rest of your life smoking weed and listening to Canned Heat."

"I don't want to make any decisions until later . . ."

"Later? You mean after Alice has died? That could be years, John, seriously. She is a tough woman, and the cancer she has is not so aggressive. It will be a long battle before she gives up. She still believes she has to look after you."

So, in May of 1969, Gaines did as Thurston had advised. He was accepted immediately. He was young, single, a Vietnam veteran with a service medal and a Purple Heart. He attended the police academy in Vicksburg, graduated in November of 1969, and was assigned to the Breed County Sheriff's Department in January of 1970. In February of 1971, he was promoted to deputy sheriff, and then on October 21, 1973, the day following Nixon's Saturday Night Massacre, Whytesburg sheriff, Don Bicklow, fell down dead from a heart attack in the front hallway of his mistress's house. His mistress was a fifty-two-year-old widow who lived out near Wiggins. Taking into consideration the fact that there was an election scheduled for January of 1974, an election that Bicklow would have won without contest, Breed County Council asked Gaines to hold Bicklow's position for the intervening two months. After six weeks, no one having come forward to apply for the job, Breed Council petitioned for Gaines's permanent assignment without election.

Gaines did not contest the application, nor did the assigned representatives of the County Seat. So, at thirty-three years of age, John Gaines became Mississippi's youngest sheriff. He proved himself competent, not only in the day-to-day management of the department, but also in the small-minded politics of the thing. Seemed he had been born for the job. This was what people said. He did not speak of it, and perhaps was not fully aware of it himself, but Gaines did the job because the job was all he had. No wife, no girlfriend, no children, no father, his mother taking the long road to her grave, the routine and regularity of his existence punctuated solely by her sporadic but intense outbursts, her mutterings, her diatribes and polemics against Nixon and his cabinet, the morphine-induced hallucinations that she so vigorously believed were true. This was Gaines's life. Had been his life until now, until July 24, 1974, when the rain had uncovered a twenty-year-old murder.

One morning, no more than a week before he'd been wounded, Gaines shot a Vietnamese teenager in the face. He hadn't meant to get a head shot. He'd intended to scare him, to warn him, to cause him to flee, but the guy dropped suddenly as he fired, perhaps thinking to turn the other way. However, *why*ever, it didn't matter. Gaines triggered, the guy dropped, and he took a face shot right through the bridge of his nose and out the other side. He lay there surprised. Dead, but surprised. His eyes wide, his mouth agape, he looked like he'd been about to say something important and then had simply forgotten the necessary words.

Gaines had walked over there, looked down at the plain black shirt, the black pants, the rubber sandals, the body inside them. The dead boy was no more than eighteen or nineteen. He had been carrying a French 9mm MAT machine gun, captured by the North Vietnamese in an earlier war. He had on a belt, tucked into it a cracked leather scabbard, within the scabbard a hunting knife. He had a single grenade.

His eyes were like tight nuggets of jet. Black, depthless. And yet they burned with some profoundly bitter malice.

Gaines looked at those eyes, and all he could think of was the child he never had, of how he used to sit on the porch with Linda Newman eating ice-cream sandwiches and watching the sky get closer until it was finally dark, and the fireflies in the fields had been like agitated, earthbound stars.

Then he kicked the boy once, firmly, sharply, in the upper arm.

"Fucker," he'd said, almost under his breath, not because he resented the boy, not because the boy might have been responsible for the deaths of countless Americans, not because he disagreed with the boy's political sympathies, his loyalty to the communists, his allegiance to things that Gaines did not comprehend, but because he'd been in the way of the bullet when Gaines had pulled the trigger.

That was all he could find to hate. That the boy had been in the way.

Gaines had stood there for a moment more and then walked away, his poncho pulled tightly around him, and with the rain battering ceaselessly on his helmet, he'd eaten his breakfast out of a green Mermite tin

He'd looked out in the fog, the moist, unbreathable fog that hung over the land and through which the vagaries of the landscape took on an awful and terrifying prospect. The fog itself did not move; it was the shapes within it.

Later, when the fog cleared, the boy had gone.

That strange sense of distortion, a sense of mystery, of profound disorientation, now assaulted Gaines once more.

In closing his eyes, in trying to remember Nancy Denton's face from only a handful of hours before, he could not. He saw only the dead teenager with depthless eyes and the fog that came to retrieve him.

9

Gaines made his way back over to see Powell. Powell was not there, though he would be back before too long. Gaines just stood in the corridor and waited. After remembering Linda Newman, Charles "Too High" Binney, the VC teenager with the hole in his face, his thoughts had been quiet. He remembered a neatly stenciled legend on the side of a Jeep: *Fighting for peace is like screwing for virginity*. Why he remembered such a thing, he did not know. He smiled. He closed his eyes, and then he took a deep breath. Sometimes—even now, and for no reason—he experienced the bitter taste of salt tabs. Like sweat, like tears. No, like nothing else.

Sometimes he felt as if he'd spent his life missing the punch line, catching the last part of things, laughing not because he understood, but because everyone else was. *Get up to speed*, he kept thinking to himself. *Get with it*—another admonition.

He had never been one of the chosen few. A different world awaited the beautiful.

Sometimes resentment bled from every pore like a dark sweat. Resentment of himself, his dead father, his sick mother, of the people he had known and lost, of Linda and the child. He had believed in her—in *them*. He had found her, somehow. As if the clumsy poetry of his words had given her hope, hope that he—a spent and broken man, by all accounts—had yet somehow secured a path through the tortuous rapids and shallows of the human heart, that he had navigated a way, that he knew some means of escape, that alongside him, she would never experience the love-sick travails that appeared to befall all people. He had believed her his true north. But life happened. Life got in the way. The minuses added up, and no matter how many minuses were added, it never became a plus. Now he looked at the world as if everything before him was a little more than he could absorb, a fraction more than he could understand. And he resented it. Such an emotion infected all he touched, a virus of shadows, and some other sour-tasting bitterness. *This is not the life I envisioned or wanted . . . This is not my life, but someone else's. There has been a grave mistake. Who do I speak to about this? No one*, the world replied. *You make your bed, my friend, and you lie in it.*

"John?"

Gaines looked up. How long had he been standing there?

Powell smiled. "You okay?"

"Yes," Gaines replied. "I came back for the autopsy results."

They stood in silence for some time. The girl was laid out before them, her chest and stomach now stitched more neatly, her skin and hair washed, her hands enclosed in plastic bags, as were her feet. *To preserve any detritus or blood beneath the nails*, Powell had said. *Unlikely, and even if there is, well, the possibility of matching it to anything is unlikely to impossible. But we do what we can.*

It was the snake that held Gaines's attention.

The remnants of the small basket had been washed clean of blood and mud, the snake—now clearly identifiable as a garter—there on the table beside it. It held its own tail in its mouth. Unraveled, the snake could not have been more than a foot long, but here it was in a circle, its tail in its mouth as if ready to swallow itself.

Gaines had heard of this. Ouroboros. A symbol of the unity of all things, the cyclic nature of birth and death, of something constantly re-creating itself, of something existing with such force it cannot be extinguished.

"I have no idea," Powell said. "I don't know what it means, and I don't know what it was intended to signify. This is all lost on me."

"Was it strangulation, as you thought?" Gaines had asked him.

"Yes," Powell said. "The muscular damage around her throat and the fracture of the hyoid bone—"

"Hyoid bone," Gaines echoed. He was elsewhere. He was still thinking of Ouroboros, the snake that devours its own tail and disappears.

"The damage to her throat and clavicle was preserved, almost as if this happened a week ago. Truth is, had she not been buried in mud, well, she would be nothing but a skeleton now."

Gaines closed his eyes. He tried his best not to picture it. What she must have gone through. Perhaps the only saving grace was that she had not been raped or sexually abused. He'd seen rape victims before, girls as young as ten or twelve assaulted by the VC as revenge for Army of the Republic of Vietnam collaboration. That faraway

53

stare, the light in the eyes extinguished, the physical inertia, the apathy. The platoons left them behind. What could they do? The field hospitals couldn't take them, and there was no way the US military could provide a transportation service to the few religious missions and outposts that were scattered back behind the rear lines. This was war. This was collateral damage.

Where do I begin? This was the question in Gaines's mind. He did not voice it.

"Do you know anything of the story?" Gaines asked.

Powell shook his head. "I was transferred here just a couple of years before you. However, I did speak to Jim Hughes, and he told me that it was never reported as a murder. The girl just disappeared. That was it. People figured her for a runaway. Don Bicklow, your predecessor, was sheriff back then, or so Hughes tells me, and his deputy was a guy called George Austin. Both of them are dead now, so whatever they found out has probably gone with them."

Gaines listened to the words, but he wasn't paying attention. He was trying to find some context within which to place his thoughts.

Whytesburg had seen three murders in Gaines's four and a half years. Two had been domestics: discovered love affairs, one a cheating husband, the second a cheating wife. Leonore Franks had put a kitchen knife through her husband's chest in November of 1970. She had caught him fucking a girl called Deidra Collins, a short-order cook from Picayune. Tommy Franks was a big man, but Leonore was bigger. She waited until he was sleeping, and then she brought that blade down into his heart with all the force she could muster. Powell told Gaines that Franks wouldn't have had time to even open his eyes. It seemed no great loss to Gaines. Franks had always seemed to be too much of everything that was worthless. Infidelity was not the only way he proved himself an asshole. The man had been as crude and brash as a circus poster.

Second case was March of 1971, a man called Cyrus Capaldi, all of five foot four. He was a barber, one with a better view of himself than was warranted. He talked ceaselessly, opinions worth little more than a cent or a nickel. He wore a perpetually furtive expression, as if his purpose were to relay some sordid sexual escapade, such escapade punishable by law in thirty-nine of fifty states. *Hey, Capaldi*, Gaines wanted to say. *Why don't you shut the hell up?* But he didn't. Figured the barber would do as he was asked, but would cut the back of Gaines's hair all ragged and ornery just to get a small revenge. Anyway, Capaldi discovered his wife was screwing an itinerant carpenter called Hank Graysmith. Graysmith was not his real name, but was the name he chose to use for work and other various extracurricular activities. Cyrus poisoned his wife, Bernice, with a combination of sleeping tablets and fungicide. The fungicide had been purchased from the hardware store to treat a mysterious mold that showed around the corner posts of the veranda. Evidently, Cyrus considered that his wife was now a mold, for he used the preparation to rid himself of her once and for all. According to Cyrus, this was not the first time she had *gone out* on him.

In both of these cases, there had been no investigation. Leonore Franks had sat in her house, her hands covered in blood, until Sheriff Don Bicklow had shown up to arrest her. Cyrus Capaldi had called the sheriff himself, simply said, *It's over, Don. I done killed Bernice. She's sat here at the kitchen table with her head slumped down, and there's a white foam coming from her nose. Better come and get the both of us.* Both Cyrus Capaldi and Leonore Franks were doing life, Cyrus up at Parchman Farm, Leonore at the women's facility at Tupelo.

The third murder had been a real murder. A dismembered body in a machine at the Whytesburg Laundromat. June of 1973, two days after Gaines's thirty-third birthday, just four months before Bicklow gave himself a coronary seizure doing precisely what Tommy Franks should not have been.

There was a head, two arms, two legs, but the torso was gone. The arms and legs had been severed at the elbows and knees respectively, and thus there were five parts, each carefully wrapped in a heavy-duty polyethylene. It wasn't long before an ID was made. The victim was one Bradley Gardner, a salesman, a purveyor of sometime-necessaries, fripperies, extravagances, and wares. He was of the view that anything could be sold. Everything had a tradable value. It was simply a matter of clientele and confidence. Haircutting devices, ever-sharp razor blades, unbreakable coffee cups, socks guaranteed to last as long as your feet. Seemed to Gaines that such people as Bradley Gardner had only two functions in this world: getting drunk and sleeping it off. He was a petty criminal—nothing more, nothing less—but it seemed he had ideas above his station. Later, it transpired, Bradley Gardner was more than capable of blackmail.

Searching the burned wreckage of his trailer home, parked there on the outskirts of Whytesburg, Bicklow and Gaines had discovered the remnants of photographs. The star of these photographs, discernible only by those who might have known him, was William Hammond, the son of a wealthy local sawmill owner. Bicklow visited the elder Hammond, they shared words, the discovered photograph remnants were produced, and though Bicklow knew he would never tie the death of Bradley Gardner to the Hammond family, he nevertheless wanted them to know that he knew. Whatever the younger Hammond might have been doing in those pictures would remain unknown, but Hammond the elder was smart enough to realize that staying in Whytesburg would only exacerbate Bicklow's desire to see justice arrive in some fashion. By the end of August 1973, the Hammonds were gone—lock, stock, and barrel. Bicklow didn't ask after them, and Hammond didn't send flowers to Bicklow's funeral two months later. Whether money exchanged hands in that June meeting at the Hammond place—the kind of money that put Don Bicklow's mistress in a neat little apartment in Lyman—Gaines would never know, and he had long since reconciled himself to letting it lie. Gaines knew that if you asked questions that folks didn't want to be asked, you more than likely got answers you didn't want to hear. No need to sully Bicklow's reputation now that the man was dead. The heart attack, *in flagrante delicious*, seemed punishment enough.

So John Gaines, as a soldier, had seen more than enough death for any lifetime. As a police officer, he had seen all too little to be on firm ground with the Nancy Denton case. People would look to him—for order, for answers, for investigation, for results. This was local. There would be no external assistance. No one outside of Whytesburg would be interested in a twenty-year-old murder. The resources he possessed were the resources he could use. Richard Hagen, his deputy, and two other uniforms—Lyle Chantry and Forrest Dalton, twenty-six and twenty-four respectively. It would be the four of them, and they would have to deal with every aspect of it.

It was this simple truth that John Gaines confronted as he considered the injuries that had been inflicted upon the person of Nancy Denton. What would the law say about this? *That someone did murder the person of Nancy Grace Denton against the peace and dignity of the state of Mississippi.* What about the peace and dignity of a teenage girl? Where did that get lost in the law books?

"John?"

Gaines looked up at Powell as he drew the white sheet back over the girl.

56

"Any more questions?"

"You know who did this thing, Victor?" Gaines asked.

"No, John, I don't," Powell replied.

"Then I have no more questions."

10

It was seven o'clock. Gaines drove home to see his mother, to make a sandwich, to take a moment's respite from the insanity of the day.

When he arrived, he found his neighbor's daughter, Caroline, bringing soup to the downstairs back bedroom where Gaines's mother now spent her days.

"I'll take it," Gaines said. "You go on home."

"Thanks, John," Caroline said. "I got a date tonight. Jimmy's coming in half an hour or so. We're going to the movie theater in Bay St. Louis."

"What you gonna see?"

"Well, I wanna see *The Sugarland Express*, but Jimmy wants to see some macho thing with Clint Eastwood, *Thunder and Lightning* or something—"

Gaines smiled. *"Thunderbolt and Lightfoot."*

"Yeah, that's the one."

"I'm sure you'll get your own way," Gaines said. "Anyway, you should've called me," Gaines said. "I'd have come down sooner."

"Picture doesn't start till eight thirty. It's fine, John."

"How's she been today?"

"Asking after you, you know? Usual stuff."

"Crazy talk?"

"No more than yesterday. She's on about Nixon again, how he's the devil, an' all that other stuff she was sayin' a while back."

Gaines nodded. His mother had it in for the president. Sure he was a liar, sure he was as crooked as a country river, but Alice Gaines seemed to believe there was a special hot place in hell being saved for Tricky Dicky.

Ever since the Watergate break-in, she'd been rambling about him. Two years now. Nixon was still in the White House, and Alice Gaines was still dying of cancer. Maybe she was hanging on just to see for herself that he got his ass kicked good.

Gaines wished Caroline a good night out, told her to make sure

Jimmy didn't drink before he drove her home, that if he did drink, she was to call Gaines and he would go fetch them both.

"He won't drink," Caroline said.

"But if he does—"

"If he does, I'll call you." Caroline Rousseau smiled one more time, and then she left the house.

Gaines stood there for a moment, the tray in his hand, the soup getting cold, and he wondered what kind of world this was.

He took the soup through to his mother.

"John," she said, and she smiled. She looked well. There was some color in her cheeks. She had on *The Bob Newhart Show*, told Gaines to turn it down some.

Gaines set the tray on the dresser, rearranged the pillows behind his mother's head so she could sit and eat more comfortably, and then he put the tray in front of her. He sat on the edge of the bed. He watched her eat, as he did most evenings. This was her routine. Spend most of the day with Caroline, evening meal with her son, her waking hours filled with *The Young and the Restless*, *Columbo*, and *Barnaby Jones*. After her evening meal, Gaines would give her a sleeping tablet, and—aside from sometimes waking at three or four for help with the bathroom—she would be gone until he came in with her breakfast at six thirty. She was fifty-nine, looked seventy, but her mind—when she was lucid, when the morphine wasn't assaulting her reality with hallucinations—was as sharp and facile as it had ever been. She had been dying for six years, would go on dying for another six or ten or twelve, it seemed. She refused all treatment but the painkillers, said that things were the way they were and that was that. Bob Thurston said that she should have died within two or three years, five at most, but something kept her going.

"I think she wants to see you married," he told Gaines on one occasion. "Maybe she wants to see if you can muster up the energy to get her some grandkids."

"Not the marrying kind."

"Never done it, have you?"

"Nope."

"So how do you know it won't suit you?"

Gaines had shrugged. "I know me, and I would be a nightmare to live with. Besides, I have Ma—"

"Well, if my theory is right, once you got yourself hitched, she wouldn't hang around much longer."

"Well, Bob, you stick to your theories, and I'll stick to mine."

Thurston hadn't mentioned it again, but Caroline was in his ear on a routine basis about finding someone as well. Right now, and for the foreseeable future, it was the very least of his concerns.

"They're gonna get him, you know?" Alice said.

Gaines snapped to. "Get who, Ma?"

"Tricky Dicky."

"Why? What's he done now?"

"Same things he's always been doin'. You know. 'Cept that now they're making him hand over the tape recordings he made. The Supreme Court, that is. House Judiciary Committee will impeach the son of a bitch—"

"Ma—"

"Don't be so naive, John. He's a liar through and through. Everyone's all up in arms saying he's a good man, that he brought the war to an end, but the war isn't at an end, is it, John? There's still American soldiers out there, plenty of them, and plenty of them are going to die yet."

Gaines couldn't argue, didn't want to. He had enough on his mind without starting some political debate with his mother. Besides, she was right. The January 1973 cease-fire had held, for sure, but it was only a matter of time before the Việt Minh would come in from Laos and Cambodia, and then Saigon would fall. However, America's attention was on Nixon. He'd talked his way out of the frying pan and into the fire. Reports of the last US troops coming out of Southeast Asia at the end of March had been overshadowed by the resignation of Bob Haldeman, Nixon's chief of staff, and a whole handful of others. It was a mess. Nixon himself had as much as admitted that there had been a cover-up. The country was in limbo, everyone waiting to see whether Nixon would be impeached. Nixon *was* a crook—no doubt about it—and more than likely Chief Justice Warren Burger would get those tapes and the curtains would come down.

Alice Gaines drank her soup. John Gaines sat and watched *The Bob Newhart Show* with her, and then he fetched her sleeping tablets from the bathroom.

As she drifted away, she held his hand. "How was your day, sweetheart?" she asked.

"Same old, same old," he said.

She reached up and touched his face. "You look tired."

"I'm okay, Ma."

"You worry too much about me. You don't need to have Caroline over here day in and day out. She's a young woman now. She has things she needs to be doing. She has her own life."

"She's happy to come over, Ma, and besides, I give her some money, and if she weren't here, she'd have to go get a job, and she doesn't want to do that right now."

"She should have stayed in school."

"She can do whatever she pleases, Ma; you know that. Don't get on her about it, now. Just leave her be."

"She tells me . . ." Alice Gaines smiled wryly. She knew she was starting something that would never finish.

"Ma—"

"I'll be gone soon enough," Alice interjected, "and you're not getting any younger, and if you want children—"

"Ma—"

She squeezed her son's hand. "Enough," she said. "I'll leave you be. You want to be a bitter and lonely old man, then that's your business."

Her eyes started to droop. She inhaled deeply, exhaled slowly, and Gaines knew she was almost asleep.

"Love you, Ma," he whispered.

"Love you, Edward," she whispered back, and Gaines knew that in whatever world she inhabited when she slept, his father was there. Edward Gaines, the father that never was.

Maybe Edward was waiting for her. Maybe it would be best to just let her go. Gaines glanced at the morphine tablets in a bottle on the bedside table. He closed his eyes for a moment and then shook his head.

He rose slowly, removed the tray, drew one of the pillows out from behind his mother's head, and eased her down. She did not stir or murmur.

Gaines left the room, headed back to the kitchen to wash up and make himself a sandwich. He sat in the front room, ate slowly, drank a glass of root beer.

He thought of his father, of his mother, of what she would have to say about Nancy Denton.

One dead body was more disturbing than a hundred. One dead body was you, your friend, someone you loved, someone you just knew. A hundred dead was a featureless mass, an event, a happening, something distant and disconnected.

Gaines thought of the ones who never came home. The ones who never would. Just like Nancy Denton. Families kept looking, kept hoping, kept praying, all of them believing that if they wished hard enough, well, the wish had to come true. Not so. They did not understand that if a wish was destined to be realized, then it needed to be wished only once. Real magic was never hard work. And even if they did return, they would see that the world they'd left behind would never accept them again, would never contain them, would never be big enough or forgiving enough to absorb what they had become.

Here he was—a veteran, a casualty of war—starting a new war here in Whytesburg. A war against hidden truths. If there was one thing he knew, it was the degree of creativity and imagination that could be employed to bring a life to some unnatural end. But this? This was without precedent.

The strength of the heart had been measured—not in emotional terms, not in terms of love or passion or betrayal, for this was not possible. It had been measured in physical terms, in pounds of pressure per square inch, the force with which it could move so many gallons of blood for so many meters at such and such a speed. But the heart, irrespective of its power, was silent until fear crept in. Until panic or trauma or terror assaulted our senses, the heart went quietly about its powerful, secret business. Now Gaines believed his heart was more alive than it had been since leaving Vietnam.

Mayhem and a dark kind of magic had seemed inseparably blended as he'd looked down into the cavity of Nancy Denton's chest, as he had seen the basket, the snake that had been within it.

When you saw a blond, nineteen-year-old high school football star decapitate a fifteen-year-old Vietnamese kid and then stand there for snapshots, the head dangling from his hand by the hair, its eyes upturned, the rictus grin, the pallid hue of bloodless flesh, you knew something was wrong with the world. You never looked at people the same way again.

This was the same. The same sense of surreal and morbid fascination. The same sense of dark and terrible wonder.

Gaines closed his eyes and breathed deeply.

Seemed that we all made a deal with God. Believe, trust, have faith in His goodness, and it will all be fine. Well, hell, it wasn't fine. Never had been, never would be. It was all horror and bullshit.

Gaines truly believed—when it came to deals with God—that it sure looked like someone wasn't holding up their end of the deal.

11

The years will always erase the precise memory of a face, but they cannot erase my recollection of how beautiful Nancy Denton was.

And I was not the only one who thought Nancy Denton was the most beautiful girl in the world.

I know that everyone in Whytesburg thought she was an angel, and I think half the world would have agreed.

I remember her standing there near a turn in the road, and as soon as she saw me, she started running. I ran, too. Didn't matter whether I'd seen her an hour before or a day or a week; seeing Nancy was always the best thing.

"Hey," she said.

"Hey back."

"You ready?"

"As ever," I replied.

She twirled then, and she said, "This is my best dress for dancing. I am going to dance with Michael until the sun goes down, and then I will just keep on dancing."

I laughed with her. She looked so happy.

This was how it was. This was how it was meant to be. I believed it, but Nancy believed it more.

Before Michael Webster came home from the war, there was just me and Nancy. There was Matthias Wade, of course, and it was so very obvious that Matthias loved Nancy as much as it was possible for one person to love another. If she hadn't fallen head over heels for Michael, then maybe she would have been Matthias's girl. But—like my mom said—maybe that never would have happened, the Wades being who they were an' all. Anyway, Michael Webster did come home from the war, and everything changed.

Michael was famous before he even got off the train. We had seen his picture in the *Whytesburg Gazette*. He had a Purple Heart and some other medal that I cannot now recall the name of, and there was a party for when he arrived. It was October of 1945, and I was all of five and a half years old, but even I knew who Michael Webster was.

Michael was twenty-two years old, and every girl in Whytesburg wanted to marry him.

Sometimes, a town like this, the most interesting thing going on was the weather, and that didn't change much more than once a month. But this was a big deal. This was a special day. This was a historic event. Michael Webster came home from the war, the only member of his unit to survive, and he was Whytesburg born and bred.

He was shy and humble, and he said he hadn't done much to be such a hero, but that made people love him all the more. Seemed the more self-effacing he was, the more they built him up. It went on for weeks, it seemed. He couldn't do anything for himself. He couldn't put his hand in his pocket for anything. Everyone took care of him. Everyone wanted to be Michael Webster's friend.

Nancy was all of seven years old. I was two years behind her. We thought Michael Webster was like a movie star from Hollywood. People said he should wear his uniform all the time. People said that everyone should know what a great hero he had been. I think Michael just wanted to disappear into anonymity. I think he just wanted to be a normal person, but it seemed that no one was going to let him.

After a while, the hubbub died down.

And then Michael seemed to withdraw. He had his mother's place down at the end of Coopers Road, and he stayed there most of the time. Everyone thought he would get a job, but he didn't. Not for a long time. He seemed to want nothing but his own company. It stayed that way for four or five years, and then he started work at the machine plant west of Picayune. And then a while later, he met Nancy, really *met* her, and that was when it all changed.

Me and Nancy were already friends with the Wades by that time. It was 1950, if I remember rightly. Matthias was seventeen, Catherine was fifteen, Eugene was twelve, and Della was seven. I remember their mom as well. Her name was Lillian, and she was the most beautiful woman in America, perhaps the world. Seemed to me that some people had been personally blessed by God. Here she was, as beautiful as any magazine picture I had ever seen, and she was married to one of the richest and most powerful men in America, and she had four children, all of them kind and sweet and funny and smart.

I mean, Matthias was the eldest, but despite his age, despite his family, he never played boss. He never played that card. It was as if he had set himself to doing all he could to make us happy.

It was—at least to me—a magical time.

We played pinochle for nickels and dimes, and we played it with serious faces, like we were betting on the outcome of a capital trial or a gunfight.

I would make wisecracks, and Michael would do a John Wayne voice and say, "Well, missy, that's an awful big mouth for such a little girl."

Other times, Matthias was so darn serious, quoting lines of poetry that he'd learned in order to impress us, to impress Nancy most of all, considering himself some type of philosophical outlaw, a Frenchman perhaps, a European of indistinct origin. A sudden teenage growth spurt had stretched him unexpectedly. He seemed to forever be apologizing for his height, not with words, but with awkwardness and hesitancy, as if he imagined himself clumsy and awkward when he was in fact not. His body language was a collection of confusing signs, as if physical movement was something new to him, and he was still furiously working to get a grip on what was going on. Forever agitated, all elbows and knees and mumbled apologies. There was little he could not break or spill or damage. I imagined there would be an abundance of glue in his house, and someone—patient as a fisherman—was forever following in his wake with a sharp eye and a steady hand for delicate repair work. Matthias carried this awkwardness through his childhood and into his teens, carried it well it seemed, for awkwardness appeared to be the only thing about him still undamaged. People tried to avoid him, but could not. They gravitated toward him, magnetized into some strange, intractable orbit, perhaps no greater motivation than the simple curiosity of seeing what he could now bring to ruination by personality and presence alone.

I saw something else in him. In his eyes were a thousand secrets and always that tight-lipped tension that suggested some desperate unfulfilled urge to tell the truth and be damned. He wanted Nancy to love him as desperately as he loved her, and yet he knew she never would. His compassion was in his silence, in the strength it took not to tell. That's how I knew he was a good person. It would have been cruel to tell the truth, and so he did not.

But more than anything, Matthias's mind was full of magic, too, and he shared it equally.

Until Michael became one of us, and then everything changed a hundred times and then a hundred times more.

It was so right, but it was so wrong.

How do I know that?

Because of what happened, that's how.

But in that moment, standing there near the turn in the road, we knew nothing but excitement for the day ahead.

I remember what Nancy said as we started walking.

"I hope the summer lasts forever . . ."

That's what she said.

She was smiling, her eyes so bright and clear, and she asked me if I had to choose just one, would I fall in love with Matthias or Eugene.

I was not like Nancy. I couldn't talk about such things without feeling embarrassed.

"Oh, come on," she said. "I reckon you think about Eugene just as much as he thinks about you."

"Nancy, stop it! Really, I mean it. Stop teasing me." I felt my cheeks flush with color.

"Or maybe you want me to think that you love Eugene, when really you love Matthias."

"I don't love either of them, okay? Really. Now stop it."

She touched my arm. "I'm just playing, Maryanne. You know I am."

"Well, I don't like it," I said, but I lied. I did like it. I wanted to think about Eugene. I wanted to think about Matthias. Sometimes I made believe I was a princess and they were gallant knights, and one day they would fight a duel over me and I would marry the victor. At the same time, I knew it was just a silly dream and that neither of them loved me the way that Nancy loved Michael.

"So come on . . . let's hurry. Michael is going to meet us on Five Mile Road," Nancy said, and she grabbed my hand.

"Is everyone going to be there?" I asked. "Della and Catherine too?"

"Catherine will come only if her dad says she has to, and Della is going to be with us all summer."

"Catherine can be so bossy sometimes."

Nancy stopped dead in her tracks. "Last week, you know what she said to Matthias?"

"What?"

"She said that I was childish."

"She did not."

"She absolutely did," Nancy said. "She said I was childish and immature."

"I think she's jealous."

"Of what?"

"Of how pretty you are and that Michael loves you and doesn't love her."

"Oh, don't be silly, Maryanne."

"I'm serious, Nancy. I think she's jealous."

"Well, if she is, then she deserves to go crazy with jealousy and end up in a madhouse."

"Nancy, you can't say that! That's an awful thing to say about someone."

"I don't care, Maryanne. I am not childish and immature."

"Of course you're not, Nancy. But you can't go wishing bad things on people. You know what my ma says about that."

Nancy twirled again. "Let's not talk about Catherine. Let's talk about something else."

And then we did—about Michael, as always, about Matthias and Eugene, about how Della was going to be beautiful like her mother, about what records Matthias would bring and whether he would have ham in the picnic basket or maybe cheese from Switzerland and fresh bread and lemonade.

Nancy was always ahead of me, running a few steps, turning around, walking backward as we talked. One time she stumbled, nearly fell, and for some reason we couldn't stop laughing.

And then Michael appeared in the distance, and he raised his hand, and from that moment until we reached him, it was as if I were no longer there.

I became a ghost perhaps, which now—looking back—seems both ironic and prophetic.

Perhaps we all haunted the edges of Nancy's universe that summer. Perhaps Michael and Nancy were stars, and we were merely satellites in orbit.

She was there, and then she was gone. And though the memory of her face would fade, the memory of that day in August would haunt me for the rest of my life.

12

Gaines's first order of business on Thursday morning was to go see Lester Cobb.

Lester looked like the kind of feller who'd eat his dinner straight off of the floor. He transmitted a dense wave of stupidity, as if all who were drawn into it would find themselves making foolish utterances and inadvertent quips. Surely this could not have been the truth, but such was the profundity and abundance of Lester's ignorance that it seemed such a way. He perpetually wore a suspicious expression, as if wary of being gypped or deceived. He ran the pet store in Whytesburg, a pet store that seemed to be closed more than open, and certainly more trouble than it was worth. Gaines would get a report and send Hagen or one of the uniforms down there. Some howling and caterwauling beast was forever in back disturbing neighbors and passersby, and Lester Cobb would be dragged from his home to feed the thing or let it loose. Gaines had had words with him on three or four occasions, said he would get the Animal Welfare people in to close him down, and Cobb would stand there, his tics and twitches in full force, a nervous habit that saw him constantly finger-tipping imaginary lint from the cuffs of his jacket, and say, "Yes, sir, Sheriff Gaines. Yes, sir, indeedy." And that would be that. Cobb would feed his animals and lie low for a month or two. Gaines would see him in town, off down the street wearing that unique and extraordinary expression, as if ever alert for underhanded overtures and con tricks from strangers.

That Thursday morning was different. Gaines wanted to see Lester about snakes. He arrived and found the pet store closed, the same sign in the window as ever. *BACK IN THIRTY MINUTES. If urgent, call 224-5659.* Gaines could just imagine it. *Hey, Lester, you gotta get back here quick! It's an emergency! We need three white mice and a talking bird!*

Driving out to Cobb's house had not been on the agenda. Gaines needed to be in the office, needed to get active on the Denton killing, but the riot of barking that erupted from behind the store forced his hand. If he didn't deal with this, there would be one phone call after another about Lester's damned noisy dogs. Gaines went around back and looked over the fence. Thankfully, the hound was chained. Gaines vaulted the fence and then he stood there quiet and still until the animal settled. He approached it slowly.

"Hey, boy," Gaines said, and the dog succumbed to Gaines's tone of voice. His head went down, and his tail started wagging. He stroked the dog's head.

Gaines got in through the unlocked rear door, found a sack of dog biscuits and a bowl. He set them down in the yard, fetched a bowl of water, too, and just as he was closing up, he noticed something that caught his eye. Up near the front window, the angle of its placement catching the light through the front window, was a small aquarium. There was no water in it, and a flicker of movement within sent a shudder up Gaines's spine.

He was right. Garter snakes. Two of them. Bigger than the one found in the cavity of Nancy Denton's chest, but garters all the same. He'd seen them here before, of course, but in light of recent events, they inspired a very different reaction.

He would have to drive out and see Lester, if only to learn where Lester had gotten them from. Whytesburg was an old town, but still a town that aged only a year for every decade it existed. Maybe someone looking for a garter snake twenty years ago would look in the same places as Lester did now.

Gaines radioed Hagen from the car, said he was taking a trip over to Cobb's place, that he wouldn't be long.

"We gotta get on this Denton thing," Hagen told him.

"That's what I'm on, Richard," Gaines replied. "You heard about the snake thing, right?"

"Yeah, sure did. What in God's name is that all about, John?"

"Well, maybe God knows, but I sure as hell don't. Anyway, I got a couple of snakes down here at Cobb's place, same kinda snakes as the one we found. I'm just gonna take a moment to find out where he gets them from, is all."

The drive from Cobb's store to Cobb's house was all of ten minutes, down along the county road that ran parallel to the Pearl River. Gaines pulled up in front of the place, steeled himself for the barrage of abuse that would more than likely come his way, and he went on up to the door.

"Who's there?" Cobb shouted from within.

"Sheriff Gaines, Lester. You need to get on down to the store and sort out the hound you got tied up in the yard. He's upsettin' folk with all his hollerin' and whatever."

"I'll be there shortly."

"And I need to ask you about snakes."

There was a moment's pause and then, "Snakes?"

"Garter snakes."

"I got some if you want one."

Gaines shuddered again. He could see that dead snake, its tail in its mouth. "Want you to come on out here and talk to me civil, Lester. Don't want to spend the next five minutes shouting through your front door."

"Hang fire there a moment, Sheriff."

Gaines waited.

Cobb came to the door in dungarees and bare feet. His hair was tousled. He had an enamel mug in his hand. "You want some coffee, Sheriff? Just made it fresh."

"I'm good, thanks."

Cobb pushed open the screen door and let Gaines in.

The house—as usual—was a sty. Cobb smiled. "Cleaning woman's on vacation," he said, just as he always did.

"Garter snakes, Lester," Gaines said. "You got two in a tank in the front of the store."

"You got inside the store?"

"Went to get some biscuits for that damned noisy dog."

"Much obliged for that, Sheriff. So, the snakes. What about them?"

"Where d'you get 'em?"

"Down at the river; usual place."

"You see anyone else after snakes when you was down there?"

"Mike is down there. Don't know if he's after snakes, but he's always hangin' around, crazy old motherfucker that he is. Well, I say he's old, but he ain't much more 'an fifty or fifty-five maybe."

"Mike?"

"Yeah, Mike Webster. He fought the Japs, you know? Guadalcanal. He has some history, man. They call him the luckiest man alive. He wears the army jacket and whatever. He's always down there. Wears camouflage fuckin' paint on his face sometimes, you know? Talking to hisself most o' the time. Says he likes it down there because the devil don't like running water. Crazy, crazy son of a bitch."

Coming from you, that's something, Gaines thought, and then there was another thought, the memory of a comment Judith Denton had made. Was there a Michael? Yes, there was. And hadn't he been *in uniform* on the night that Nancy Denton had gone missing?

"And he's the only one you seen down there?"

"Only one I seen regular. Asked him one time why he was always down there and he said he was waiting for someone."

"Waiting for someone?"

" 'S what he said."

"He say who he was waiting for?"

"Nope. And I didn't ask. He ain't the sort of person you feel like you should encourage to converse, if you know what I mean. Kinda creepy. Looks at you like he's figurin' out how it would feel to wear your skin."

"How often's he down there?"

"He's been there every time I go. Last time was two days ago, three maybe. I was down there doin' some fishing, and he came along. We had a smoke. He talks a lot. Most of it I don't fucking understand. Lot of stuff about the war in Japan."

"He lived around here long?"

Lester shrugged. "Always been around, 's far as I know. He came back here after the war, I think. He told me he was in a unit in fuckin' Japan, and he was the only one who survived. And then there was that thing that happened in the factory back in whenever . . ."

"Factory? What thing?"

"Go see him, man. You go talk to him. Ask him about what happened in Japan, and then ask him about the fire in . . . hell, whenever it was. Fifty-two, I think. You go ask him about all of that. Helluva story, man, helluva story."

"What's he look like?"

"Kinda my height, sandy-colored hair, cut longish in back. Denims, army jacket, one of them bush hats like folks wear in the jungle an' all. Has a beard and whatever. Kinda like a hippy maybe, but he has the mad eyes goin' on."

Gaines couldn't think of anyone fitting that description in Whytesburg. "Where does he live, Lester?"

"Christ knows. I asked him one time, and he just said up the river a while. Was thinking he was from Poplarville, or maybe someplace in between."

"Okay, Lester, that's really appreciated. Now, you finish up your coffee and get on down to that store of yours. You got enough complaints going on, you know?"

"Hell, Sheriff, they's animals. They's gonna make a noise whatever you do with them. And them folks that complain? If they weren't complainin' about me, they'd be complainin' about someone else. That's just their nature."

Gaines said nothing. Cobb was right. *Here is a dead child in the arms of her dead mother . . . now let us speak of small and inconsequential things.*

Gaines went on back to the car. He turned the way he'd come and headed for the office. Somewhere northwest was a World War II veteran called Mike, a man who had been here forever, and Gaines needed to find him. Whytesburg was a small town, and small-town ways never seemed to change. No matter what happened, people seemed to stay put, as if distrusting and disbelieving of any wider world. In this light, it was not impossible to consider that the Michael mentioned by Judith Denton and the Michael of whom Lester Cobb spoke were one and the same person.

In Gaines's experience, there were three types of war returnees. First were those who reintegrated, neither forgetting nor remembering, those who had somehow absorbed the horror, parceled it, packed it away. They found empty spaces every once in a while, gazing into some middle distance that was neither one place nor another. They saw things that others did not see, but they did not speak of them. Partly because to speak of them was to grant them strength and longevity, partly because no one would believe them. But they held it together. They came back, and they did all they could to belong again. Gaines was such a man—still there, still fighting with memories, with conscience, but somehow *there* despite all.

The second type were those who wore their history in all that they were: still wore fatigues and flak jackets, still woke sweating in the cool half-light of dawn, aware of shapes in the fog, aware of water around their ankles, the smell of blood and cordite and the sulfurous rot of dank vegetation. They were the ones on whom you kept a watchful eye, the ones who drank alone, their few conversations scattered with references to Bouncing Betties, toe poppers, Willie Pete, 105 rounds, and napalm. They would quote aphorisms from PsyOps propaganda pamphlets as if such aphorisms were gospel. They would talk of cutting LZs for dust offs, of long-range recon patrols. They needed routine. They needed orders.

They were scared of the lonely places, the middle ground, the places between here and there, between departure and destination. They would smoke weed and get crazy-mischievous, calling random strangers from the Yellow Pages and making sinister threats. *The past always finds you out. People know what you did afore you got here. The girl survived . . . She saw what you done.* They stole restaurant napkins by the handful, motel matchbooks, even water dispenser cones. They had no use for them, but in some small way they believed they were striking a blow for the common man, the small guy, the working stiff, for those who had been betrayed by an uncaring government.

The third type were the dead. The army of the dead. Always a greater army than those who survived.

If "Mike from Poplarville," or wherever the hell he was from, with his bush hat and his *mad eyes*, was down the Pearl River, then Gaines wanted to speak with him, if for no other reason than to see what he was doing, if he knew anything of snakes, if he perhaps remembered an incident that had taken place in August of 1954 when a sixteen-year-old girl had vanished from the face of the earth.

He could not ask questions of Bicklow or Austin. Nancy Denton would remain as silent as she had been for the past twenty years. Now it was time to challenge the memories of those who had been here two decades before.

But there was something else drawing Gaines in, something he could neither define nor determine. He could not clearly picture the girl's face, despite the fact that he had seen her lying there on the mortuary slab only hours before. He could remember his father's face, Linda Newman's, the faces of Charles Binney and a host of other people who had briefly populated his life so many years before. But he could not remember Nancy, and he did not know why.

August of 1954, Gaines had been fourteen years old. McCarthyism was in its dying throes, Elvis was recording his first single, Rocky Marciano was champion of the world, and Johnson would soon be head of the Senate. The same world, but a very different world in so many ways. The subsequent twenty years had seen the assassinations of both Kennedys and Martin Luther King, the beginning of the Vietnam War, his mother's illness, the loss of Linda Newman and the child that never was, the end of so much hope.

It had also seen a body lying undiscovered and preserved in the banks of the Whytesburg River.

Perhaps Nancy—symbolically—had become the child that never was.

Perhaps he—John Gaines, latterly of the nine circles of hell—was destined not to be haunted by those he himself had killed, but by those who had been killed in his absence.

13

Sheriff Graydon McCarthy of Travis County, Mississippi, was a simple man with simple secrets, and not so many of them. He was approachable, a talker, would always share a bottle, but there were things of which he did not speak and of which you did not ask. He did not bear question of his politics. You did not ask about money, neither where it came from, nor where it went. You did not ask of the unexpected disappearance and subsequent return of his father after two years of unexplained absence. You did not ask about the night of June 16, 1959, nor a girl named Elizabeth-May Wertzel and what she swore she would never repeat to a living soul. Beyond that, if you could get Graydon McCarthy to talk, you could ask him pretty much anything.

Gaines found him at his desk in Bogalusa a little after ten that Thursday morning and was afforded the kind of courtesy that came from one man to another in the same line of work.

Coffee was brought and accepted, a cigarette was offered but declined, and Gaines sat with McCarthy making small talk until Gaines approached the subject directly.

"Mike, you say?" McCarthy asked. "Mike, Mike, Mike. War veteran. Mmmm . . ." He paused to think, to look through the window to the right of his desk and out into the forecourt of the Sheriff's Office building as if the view would assist his memory. "Can't say I do," he finally replied, "but then, this is a big county full of small towns, and I tend to keep my eyes on the bad 'uns."

"As we all do," Gaines said.

"All say the same thing when they come in here, don't they? Always desperate to tell us that they ain't bad men. Well, I say, if you ain't a bad man, then why the hell d'you keep actin' like one?" He smiled at his own smartness and lit another cigarette.

"So no one of that name with that description comes to mind? He might have a reputation. Word has it he's a pretty wild character."

"Like I said, son, it's a big county and I can't be relied upon to know everyone. Around here you find people born, schooled, working, multiplyin', getting' old, and dyin' within about a five-mile radius. Even those that leave tend to discover they don't much care for the wider world, and they come right on back. You might try the motel."

"The motel?"

"Northeast of here along 59, a handful of miles. I call it a motel. Ain't nothin' but a scattering of shacks that used to be a motel. Owned by a man called Harvey Blackburn. Drunks and hookers mainly. Always someone trying to get the place razed to the ground, but they ain't managed it yet. I'd check there. If your man's a crazy 'un, that just might be the kind of haunt he'd be hankering after."

Gaines thanked McCarthy, headed back to the car and took I-59. Follow 59 all the way to Meridian and it became I-20, took you west to Jackson and onward into Louisiana. Head the opposite way and it was no more than thirty miles to the Alabama state line, and that road would bring you right into Birmingham.

Gaines figured he knew the place McCarthy had spoken of, this scattering of rundown motel shacks set in a crescent around a gravel forecourt. It sat a quarter mile behind a derelict gas station off of the highway. Gaines followed his memory and knew where he was within minutes.

The place looked deserted, but there was music playing some-where: Hendrix maybe.

Gaines drew to a stop and got out. He stood for a while. The music played on. That was the only sound.

Ten minutes waiting and he'd had enough. He headed for the first cabin on the right, knocked on the door, got no answer. Second and third cabin on the same side provided no response either. Second one on the left got a holler from within.

"Hold up," a woman's voice called back.

"Hey there," Gaines said. "Sheriff's Office, ma'am."

There was silence for a minute or so, but just as Gaines was about to call out a second time, the door opened.

The woman was in her late twenties or early thirties. She had on worn-out jeans, a cheesecloth blouse, over it a suede vest with tassels hanging off of the front and back. Her belt was decorated with silver and turquoise ovals, like some sort of Native American Indian design. Her hair was long in back, her bangs almost in her eyes.

" 'S up?" she said.

"Looking for Mike," Gaines said.

"Lieutenant Mike?"

"He the vet?"

"Sure is."

"That'd be him, then."

"He's in the far one at the end," the woman said. She pointed at the other side of the crescent of cabins. "Whether he's in or not, I don't know, but that's where he lives."

The music had stopped. Gaines could smell grass.

" 'Preciated, ma'am," he said, and touched the brim of his hat.

The woman neither smiled nor acknowledged him. She merely closed the door.

Gaines walked back across the pitted gravel forecourt.

Gaines could smell something rank before he even arrived at Lieutenant Mike's cabin door. It was an overripe smell, beneath it the funk of rot and decay. It was obscured by joss or grass—he couldn't work out which—but it was there all right. It was a smell from his past, a smell he'd hoped never to experience again.

Gaines knocked on the door. There were sounds within.

Gaines called out. "Mike!"

"Who's that?"

"Sheriff Gaines, Whytesburg."

"Whassup?"

"Need a handful of words with you, Mike."

"Busy right now."

"Need to see you now, Mike."

The smell was becoming too much. It was sweat and filth, a stench like bad meat, something even worse beneath that.

There were more sounds within, and then the door opened a crack, and Gaines saw the man's face, the faint vestiges of black-and-green camouflage on his skin, the same greasepaint they'd used back in the jungle. In that darkened visage, Mike's eyes were white like a frightened animal.

The smell came, too, that stench of fetid rot, and Gaines took a handkerchief from his pocket and held it to his face.

He knew what he was dealing with then. Mike was in category two, those who still wore their history like a second skin. But Mike was a veteran of the Second World War, somewhere in his early- to midfifties, and thus he had carried it a great deal longer.

Somehow war was a legacy and a heritage, handed down through generations. War was the history of the world. It connected with part of the mind, with the heart, the soul perhaps, and once connected, it never fully retreated. There was no forgetting, only a practiced *un*remembering, and yet you knew—without question—that the memories could always find you.

Still, even now, six years on, Gaines would sometimes wake and think, *Where the hell am I?* It had happened when he was awake also, drifting out of some conversation, his eyes unfocused, gazing into the middle ground between somewhere and nowhere else, and then he would return, slowly, as if surfacing through dark and cloudy water, water that held the stink of human waste and death, and he would have to pretend he had heard the conversation in which he had just been engaged.

War was a holiday from reality: While you were there, it seemed as though you'd never been anywhere else; upon your return, a week felt like an hour, a year little more than a single day. Time stretched, bent, folded, collapsed; time was both ally and enemy, friend and foe; time was a sleight-of-hand parlor trick, the irony being that the recognition of its reality has been lost with the passage of itself. War changed nothing, and yet it changed everything, depending simply upon your absence or presence.

In war, a lot of people lost it. Some got it back. Lieutenant Mike—whoever the hell he was, whatever the hell he had seen—seemed to be one of those who had not.

"Do for you?" Mike asked.

"My names is Gaines. I'm the sheriff in Whytesburg."

"So you said."

"I understand you are a veteran, Mike."

Mike frowned; then he smiled. "You been out there in 'Nam, ain't you?"

"Yes, I was."

Mike grinned. "Oh man, I shoulda gone there. I really shoulda gone."

Gaines said nothing.

Mike stood there silently, looking inward at nothing for a good ten seconds, and then he seemed to snap right out of it. He grinned again. "You wanna come in? You wanna come in and have a drink or something?"

"Nothing to drink," Gaines said, "but yes, sure, I'd like to come in."

Mike stepped back and opened the door, and even as Gaines took the first step into the room, he knew. Despite the stench, the face paint, there was something else going on, and he sensed—somehow, someway—that it was inherently connected to the death of Nancy Denton. What had McCarthy said? *Even those that leave tend to discover they don't much care for the wider world, and they come right on back.*

Lieutenant Mike had carried a lot of darkness back from the war, and perhaps he had chosen Whytesburg as the place to share it with the world.

14

Everyone's war was different. Personal. Unique.

Gaines could think of it, could speak of it, could remember every detail.

Sometimes it seemed that the flares just dropped and hovered, a pale light hanging there above the ground like a ghostly multitude, the myriad dead haunting the land where they fell. And he knew the dead would always hold court, remaining long after he had departed, long after the earth and trees and sky and rivers had forgotten who he was or why he was there. It was a simple land, but its history was complex and thus never known at all, or too easily forgotten.

There were endless numbers of ways to die, both natural and man-made—malaria, gangrene, snakebites, bullets, bombs, bayonets, mortars, grenades, booby traps, staked pits, napalm, friendly fire, burial alive in the networks of tunnels that lay beneath the VC outposts, the heat, the rain, the rivers, the mudslides, the hopeless mediocrity of inadequate supply lines that gave you too little ammunition in your time of need. And tigers. Some of them had been killed by tigers. Most of all, there were those who died because of their own lack of belief that they could survive. As one NCO used to tell Gaines, *Only things that can kill you out here are faithlessness and shortness of breath.*

Most cheerful guy Gaines ever met worked in Graves Registration. He dealt with the dead from dawn to dusk and all the hours beyond. Would have seemed to be the very worst of miserable tasks, but no, apparently not. If others were dead, well, it wasn't him. That's how come he smiled so much. People expected it of him after a while. If a guy like that doing a job like this could stay cheerful, then maybe it wasn't all as bad as it seemed. Wherever you were, there were always worse places to be. Strange how consideration of a far greater hell could lift your spirits.

Gaines remembered Coleman lanterns; he remembered the Givral Restaurant on the corner of Le Loi and Tu Do.

He remembered the time a commander ordered his men to load ten or fifteen dead Viet Cong into a chopper and then drop them like so many sacks of flour into a VC-sympathetic ville. They rained down from five hundred feet, crashing through the roofs of hooches, killing animals stone dead, exploding on the ground with a noise you could hear above the whirlwind of rotor blades. "It's not psychological war," the commander had shouted. "It's just war."

He remembered a beautiful blonde attaché from the Joint US Public Affairs Office, somehow standing amid all the mayhem and carnage, head to toe in a cream linen pantsuit, her eyes bright blue, her corn-silk hair woven back from her face in a French braid, some sort of demigoddess—surreal, unbelievable, desperately, heartbreakingly, impossibly beautiful. You didn't just want to fuck her; you wanted to *make love* to her, and you wanted to make love forever. Gaines believed she should have led them into battle. The blond girl right there at the frontline, the amassed battalions and companies and units behind, the choppers flanking, the strike force and heavy bombers overhead, and she in her cream linens, her corn-silk hair rushing behind her in the downdraft, in her hand a golden spear, like some Boudicca, hurling them forward at the enemy, one mighty scream from every lung, and the war would have been over. For a good while, he dreamed of her, and then he dreamed no more.

War accepted everyone. In war, there was no racism, no bigotry, no intolerance, no division, no separation of race, color, creed, denomination, nationality, age, or gender. War would consume a five-year-old Vietnamese child who had seen nothing of life just as effortlessly and hungrily as it would consume a forty-year-old Marine Corps veteran with an insatiable thirst for dead VC.

War was crazy, but it possessed a craziness that could be understood. There were rules, and the rules were simple. Sometimes Gaines wondered if he didn't want to go back there just for a rest.

And, often, Gaines believed it had been a privilege to be so utterly, indescribably afraid. If you stayed afraid, you might make it through. That fear kept you alert; it kept your head in the game, and thus—possibly—it would enable you to keep that same head on your shoulders.

There were others who became unafraid. There were guys who became so numb to everything, they stopped looking and they stopped caring. They would walk out into gunfire with the certainty that it was all a dream.

Gaines believed that Mike Webster might be one of these men, the ones who had lost all connection to reality, the ones who had experienced emotions so far beneath and beyond actuality that they now lived in a different universe.

Gaines looked at Mike Webster, and he could see so many other men, so many who did not come back. Perhaps they returned physically, but not mentally or spiritually. They were still in-country. Would always and forever be in-country. In-country was the same, whichever war you spoke of.

It took a while for Gaines's eyes to become accustomed to the darkness within Webster's room, but when they did—when he started to pick out individual items among the shadows—he knew that Webster had slipped whatever moorings might have tethered him, and now he was elsewhere.

"Some folks, the way they think, they forever seem to come at something backward. Can't see a thing for what it is. Forever considering something ain't what it appears to be . . ."

Webster's words hung in the air for a moment, and then he laughed. He lowered himself into a deep armchair, and Gaines noticed how the stuffing protruded from holes in the arms and the headrest. It was almost identical to the chair in Judith Denton's house.

Gaines took a seat facing him—a plain wooden chair that creaked as he sat down.

"S'pose that's just the way some folks is wired, is all," Webster went on. "Sometimes everybody's looking just so damned hard, they head out and overlook the obvious, you know?"

Webster reached for a half-empty bottle of rye, uncorked it, drank from it. He wiped the lip, handed it to Gaines.

Gaines shook his head, looked down for a moment. Beneath his feet was a pale brown rug, across it a dark stain that could have been blood or mud or oil. To his right was a low table, on it a collection of books, the titles obscured but for one slim volume of poetry by Walt Whitman. Beside the books were items he recognized with vivid familiarity: army-issue knives, a compass, webbing, a single boot, two .45s, a box of shells, an empty bandolier, a water canteen.

Against the left-hand wall were stacked boxes of numerous sizes, the uppermost balanced precariously on those beneath. Draped over the corner of one was a flak jacket.

The single window had been covered with a doubled-up bedsheet, and through it the light was dim and indistinct.

The more Gaines looked, the more he saw things that he did not wish to see.

Webster was holed up in here, bedded down. He had turned a motel cabin into some kind of foxhole, and he was waiting out whatever firefight was still raging in his head.

And Gaines could smell the sweat, the fear, the paranoia, the tension. It was an all-too-familiar smell.

"Things happen, right?" Webster said.

Gaines nodded. "Right," he said.

"More bad than good, most times."

Gaines stayed silent. He figured silence was the most effective encouragement he could give for whatever Webster had to say.

It was eleven in the morning; it could have been midnight, three a.m., anytime at all, and they could have been anywhere. Felt like Whytesburg stopped at the door, almost as if it didn't want to come in.

"I was in the war before this one," Mike said. "Joined up in May of forty-two, just four days after my nineteenth birthday. Was there in Guadalcanal in November of the same year." He took another swig from the bottle. "After we secured Henderson Field, we went in, the only army battalion alongside six other marine battalions. Vandergrift had the First Marine Division. They wanted offensive actions west of the Matanikau River. Edson ran the show, and he wanted us to capture Kokumbona. Japs had their Seventeenth Army just west of Point Cruz. They were falling apart. They had been there forever. Disease was rife, they were malnourished, battle-fatigued, and we had more than five or six thousand men coming on strong. But they were merciless bastards. Fanatical. They gave us everything they had. November third, I was in a foxhole with my section. Nine of us left, all hunkered down to weather it through, and they hit us direct. Eight dead, one living." Webster smiled, almost nostalgically. "And here I am, Sheriff Gaines of Whytesburg. Knocked sideways and senseless I might be, but here I fucking am." He laughed, but there was little—if any—humor in that sound. "I seen it all, man, seen all that shit and then some. I spent weeks on point or rear cover, or maybe walking ridgelines. Never in the middle. Always visible. You know, if there was someone who was gonna get it today, well, that someone would be you. Like I said, it changes your fucking viewpoint, man."

Mike drank again. Once more he offered it to Gaines. Gaines declined.

"Sometimes you would come back from a search and destroy, and you would simply puke, and then you would cry, and then you would puke some more. You would feel neither better nor worse, just confused, cheated perhaps, like God was on no one's side. He was just fucking with everyone, you know? I feel like I've been fucked by God. Someone said that to me one time . . ."

Another pause.

Gaines could not have described how he felt. Sweat was running from his hairline and down his brow. His scalp felt electrified, as if every hair on his head was standing at attention. He felt the same as he had back then. Webster's words, his monologue, his memories . . . they brought it all back like it was yesterday.

"Most of the bad stuff happens at night," Webster said.

Gaines shuddered. Did he mean now, or back then?

"At night, you know? When the journalists and correspondents couldn't take pictures. Man, I'd see them boys come down from wherever after forty-eight hours' break, a half-dozen cameras slung around their necks like Hawaiian garlands, and there was still that distant look in their sun-bleached eyes, the look that came from watching the worst that the world could deliver through a view-finder." Webster laughed. "Present and correct, but not present and definitely not correct. Involved, but as spectator, not a participant. Even when they managed to grab a few hours' sleep in a temporary barrack somewhere, they didn't shower or shave, because they believed that if they washed the stink off of their skin, they'd be washing away their shield. War stink is camouflage; it's disguise and protection, as good as any GI flak jacket. Those boys mailed cans of film out of combat zones by the fucking bucket load, but the shots that told the truth never made the presses, right?"

Gaines nodded. He leaned back a little. The chair creaked.

Webster leaned further toward Gaines, as if trying to keep him within the circle. The smell around him was a rank blend of wet dog and whiskey.

"You ever have a friend out there, Sheriff? I mean, a real friend, someone who watched your back, someone who looked after you, someone who was always there when you were ready to blow your own brains out just to get away from the horror?"

"Yes," Gaines said. "Yes, I did."

Webster smiled. "I had a friend like that, too . . ."

Gaines could see the Highlands then, as if he had returned only yesterday. Mountainous peaks, valleys like ruptures in the earth, as if something from within, some terrible force, had split the world at its seams. The bleak expanses of open ground, ground without respite, without cover, the sudden ravines and gorges, the scattering of Montagnard villages where *the War of Hearts and Minds* was being fought to engage them as allies, not suffer them as enemies. Up there the days were so wildly hot, the nights so freakishly cold, that there was no way to acclimate. The Ia Drang battles of '65, battles that were over long before Gaines ever arrived in-country, were still a subject that evaded discussion. The Highlands were a country of the past, and the present would never find it. The reported VC dead at Đắk Tô didn't tally with the number of bodies they found. Hundreds, thousands of dead had just vanished. Where had they gone? Had the earth swallowed them? Did the earth up there just absorb its own? If ever there was a war, it had begun there. If ever it had ended, it had ended there. It was impossible to know. The Highlands were a country with no time, a country *out* of time, a country of ghosts.

He remembered late '67, a trip up to Twenty-fifth Division HQ at Cu Chi.

Gaines closed his eyes for a moment, turned his head toward the window as if following a sound, and then he smiled.

Gaines opened his eyes, looked back at Webster. He considered the fact that here was a man who had somehow survived the very same war that his own father had not. Is this how his own father would have been, had he survived? Gaines also considered the fact that he and Webster had themselves fought the same war in the same type of terrain, just twenty-five years apart.

"I spent weeks up there," Webster said. "Sometimes I wonder if I left my mind up there." He grinned. "The trees and rocks, the dirt beneath your feet . . ." His voice trailed away.

"Need to ask you about something, Mike," Gaines said, steeling himself, feeling his fingernails digging crescents into the palms of his own hands.

Webster seemed not to hear Gaines. "You know, it took me more than a year to learn how to sleep again. Back then I could baby sleep, you know? Just one moment of stillness, sitting, lying down, even leaning against a tree, and I was gone." Webster shook his head and closed his eyes. His lids seemed to come down in slow motion, like a lizard. "I knew a guy, a marine from Boise, Idaho, and he would just lie down next to the dead and find his rest there. I asked him why. He shook his head, man . . . just shook his head and said, 'You ever get to the point where you're too tired to be afraid?' You know, I never did answer that question. I figure he granted the dead some invisible shield or something. Like, he knew that the gods of war wouldn't waste their energies killing people twice, and so he would lie down there among them as that was gonna be the safest sanctuary of all . . ."

Gaines saw the intensity in Webster's eyes, as if emanating mental waves, vibrations, some sort of influence that would change the way others reacted toward him. His features were animated, his words alive. He spoke with passion and fervor, that insistent and emphatic tone reminiscent of so many Baptist preachers. But here there was no tentful of repentant sinners, merely a single man, but still Webster eulogized as if he were assigned to redeem souls otherwise lost.

"Man, I tell you . . . sometimes the only certainty was that if you were killed today, you could not be killed tomorrow. There weren't too many sure things, but that was one you could bet your house on."

"Mike," Gaines said. "I gotta ask you about something . . ."

Webster turned and looked at Gaines. Everything he did seemed to be at half speed.

"I need to ask you if you know someone called Nancy Denton."

Webster smiled. "Seems some men meet their destiny on the very road they took to avoid it." He was silent for a time. He looked directly at Gaines, and Gaines wondered whether there were tears in Mike Webster's eyes.

"You wanna ask me about Nancy Denton?"

Gaines's thoughts fell silent. His skin was cold, dry like a snake, and he felt hollow inside. Utterly, completely hollow.

"Been waiting twenty years for someone to ask me that question, Sheriff Gaines."

Gaines's chest felt like a lightbulb, a vacuum, a fragile vacuum of absolutely nothing. He felt as if he would just simply implode.

"Waiting twenty years for that one single question, but I cannot tell you anything . . ."

Gaines's intake of breath was audible.

Webster smiled knowingly. "The shit I seen, man . . . a man's flesh falling straight from the bone like all-night ribs, nothing more beyond gravity required to bring it away. Tell you this right now, that's the sort of shit no one should ever have to see."

"Nancy, Mike . . . tell me about Nancy Denton," Gaines urged.

"I can't, Sheriff. I made a promise. Too many people loved her too much. I done what I had to do, and that's all there is to the story."

It was a little after one when Gaines brought Lieutenant Michael Webster into the Sheriff's Office. Not only in the stark normalcy of the office, but also in the car on the drive over, Gaines had been aware of how dirty Webster was. His hands were gray, filth ingrained in the pores, the fingernails black, the smell of him close to unbearable. It was the sickening funk of bad meat, as if Webster himself were rotting from within. But it was not only the way Webster appeared; it was not only the smell, the things he said, the expression in his eyes; there was also a kind of haunted intensity, something that Gaines had seen all too often in war. In truth, it was the way Webster *felt*. The very presence of the man was unsettling— even when silent, even when his distant expression was directed elsewhere, Gaines could *feel* the tension around the man.

Webster said nothing on the drive over, and Gaines did not encourage him. Until Webster was in a room with a tape recorder and a second officer, Gaines didn't want to hear what he had to say about Nancy Denton.

Gaines just drove, his eyes on the road ahead, but he was so terribly aware of the man beside him. Webster was a product of war. Webster was a product of nightmares. Webster had perhaps carried some demon inside of him all the way from the foxholes of Guadalcanal and delivered it to Whytesburg.

They had dug up the body of a teenage girl, but what else had they dug up? Had they released something preternatural, some malevolent force, some specter of the past that would now forever haunt the streets and the spaces between the houses?

Gaines knew enough to understand that he could not ignore the unknown, especially in this part of the country. There were reminders everywhere that the world was not limited solely to the physical and the tangible.

As they approached the Sheriff's Office, Webster spoke for the first time since they had left the motel. "Did you find her, Sheriff Gaines? Did you find Nancy?"

"Yes, Michael, I did."

Webster closed his eyes. He made a sound as if he were deflating inside. "So she is never coming back?"

"No, Michael, she is never coming back."

Gaines pulled up ahead of the office. He started to get out, and then he realized that Webster was sobbing. He turned and looked at the man—this filthy, bedraggled man—and he watched as his chest rose and fell, as he tortured himself through whatever emotional storm he was experiencing.

After a while, a good while, he started to settle. "I knew she wouldn't," he eventually said. "Inside, deep inside, I knew it was impossible."

Gaines did not reply; he needed the man in a room with a witness and a recorder.

Webster turned and looked at Gaines. Somehow Webster's tears had made small tracks through the grime on his face. "Will I be able to see her again?" he said.

Gaines took a moment to register what Webster was saying.

"Why?" he asked. "Why would you want to see her again?"

Webster shook his head and sighed. "To see if what I did helped her in any way. To see if what I did helped her at all . . ."

15

Gaines was used to small-time, at least as far as Whytesburg's law requirements were concerned.

The predominant order of business was the drunks—the garrulous, the sentimental, and the violent. Those in the third category were the only ones who ever inhabited the cells beneath the Sheriff's Office, and that type was rare. Seemed that the wives of Whytesburg had that kind of thing under control before it ever reached the streets. Occasionally, Gaines held on to a hobo for a few hours, waiting to see if he'd figure out some way to pay the train fare he'd just skipped. Invariably he did not, and invariably said hobo was released before he stank up the place too much. One time Gaines snared a couple of paperhangers from Mobile who figured that small-town Mississippi was as good a place as any to write checks that would never cash. In truth, Gaines's clientele was ordinarily insufficiently crooked or ballsy to cheat on their tax forms or buy stolen goods, but still found it necessary to redress the balance of imagined social ills by committing pointless and negligible misdemeanors. These then consumed his days. Gaines's legacy, when he retired, would be measured in traffic violations, speeding tickets, and stern words with teenagers regarding the downside of Richards Wild Irish Rose or Ripple wine.

Whytesburg was neither ready nor able to absorb the horror of Nancy Denton and Lieutenant Michael Webster.

Gaines put Webster in a cell. The man had not confessed to anything; nor had any evidence—damning or circumstantial—been isolated or identified that could attribute the death of Nancy Denton to Webster. Regardless, the very presence of the man was sufficient to instigate a sense of agitation and disturbance in the place. Gaines had Hagen, Chantry, and Dalton take Webster's clothes from him. They gave him a pair of jeans, a white T-shirt, and a blue-and-white-striped shirt. His feet were left bare, and he was given no belt. Webster did not profess to understand what was happening, nor did he question their actions. They asked for his clothes. He stripped and handed them over. He did not complain, protest, or resist. When he stood there in his clean clothes, he seemed ageless, almost a child, the expression on his face one of bemused detachment.

Once his clothes had been bagged and tagged, Gaines went down there.

Webster was seated on the bed. Gaines stood outside the cell.

"You understand why you're here, Mike?" Gaines asked.

"Because you think I did something to Nancy Denton that I shouldn't have done."

Gaines could not argue with that.

"But I know what I know, and I see what I see," Webster went on, "and unless you knew what I knew, unless you had seen what I have seen, then there's no way to understand what I did."

"I don't think I will ever understand what you did."

Webster smiled. "Then you surprise me, Sheriff Gaines. I thought you, of all people, would appreciate what had to be done."

Gaines restrained himself from asking a direct question.

Did you kill Nancy Denton?

Did you cut open her body and remove her heart, and did you put a snake inside her and bury her in the riverbank?

A confession was needed, but on record, on tape, and preferably in the presence of a lawyer. Gaines did not wish to exhaust whatever urge Webster might have to confess in a way that could not be admissible when pressing charges and seeking arraignment.

There was silence between them for some time. Gaines could hear Webster breathing. He could feel his own heartbeat—in his chest, in his temples, in his wrists. He felt electrified, a raw tension throughout his whole body, as if his skin had been stripped and he was being doused in salt water.

He had not felt this way for six years.

"And now?" Gaines asked.

"Now?" Webster asked. He raised his eyebrows and looked directly at Gaines. His expression was clear and uncomplicated, the expression of a curious infant, an intrigued child.

"Are you not concerned about what will happen to you now?"

Webster shook his head. He smiled ruefully. "We have done too many things, Sheriff. People like you and me are consigned to some dark place. I'll say this now, and without any great concern for who hears it. If I wind up in heaven, well, I figure I'll be the first of my kind. If you follow me, then you'll be the second." He smiled, looked away for a moment. "I did what I thought was best, as we all do. Most of us, anyway. I did what I believed was the right thing to do, and I prayed that good would come of it, and I have been praying for twenty years, but I knew, you see? I knew in my heart of hearts that she would never come back to me." He closed his eyes, lowered his head. "I am sad. I am so desperately sad. She has gone, and had I chosen to go after her, then maybe we'd be together someplace now. I waited for her for twenty years, and now I am simply afraid that she was not able to wait for me."

Gaines didn't reply for a while, and then he stepped away from the bars. "You're gonna stay here for a while, Mike, and then I'm gonna have some more questions, okay?"

"Sure thing, Sheriff. I ain't fixin' to go anyplace anytime soon."

Gaines turned and headed for the stairs. He felt nauseous, light-headed. He did not understand what was happening, but he did not like how Webster made him feel. It went beyond the fact that the guy might be a child killer. It went beyond the fact that the mere presence of the man dredged up memories that Gaines had long since committed himself to forgetting. It lay in the realm of something altogether more sinister and unsettling. There was something about it that possessed undertones of the occult. The murdered girl. The heart excavated and removed. The snake in the box. The riverbank burial. It carried with it images from the stories he'd heard as a child, stories of wanga charms filled with the poisonous roots of the figure maudit tree, of voodoo queen Marie Laveau, the rituals performed behind her cottage on St. Ann Street in the French Quarter, of Li Grand Zombi and Papa Limba, of the Dahoman spirit Legba, the guardian of crossroads. If Gaines's mother got word of this, she would be in her element, her own childhood and upbringing rooted firmly in the wild collision of voodoo and Catholicism.

St. Peter, St. Peter, open the door,
I'm callin' you, come to me!
St. Peter, St. Peter, open the door,
Papa Legba, open the gate for me, Ago-e
Ativon Legba, open the gate for me;
The gate for me, papa, so that I may enter the temple,
On my way back, I shall thank you for this favor.

Gaines paused at the top of the stairwell and looked back toward the cell. Webster was immobile, seated there on the bed, his regulation blues, his bare feet, his dirty hands, his unkempt hair.

From a distance, he seemed harmless. But then, from a distance, so did the devil.

Gaines understood what would happen if word got out about Webster. He didn't know whether a lynching party would show up on the doorstep, but such a thing would not have surprised him. Sometimes the very worst solution for dealing with something like this was the only solution people could comprehend. But for this to be contained, Gaines needed a solid and sustainable case. He had nothing but a handful of words from Webster that there was a connection between himself and the girl.

I done what I had to do, and that's all there is to the story.

And then later, the things he'd said as they'd arrived at the office, when he'd asked if he could see the girl again.

Gaines would have to go down to Webster's room at the motel and search it, but for that he would need a warrant. And the likelihood of there being anything that had survived twenty years . . . unless, of course, Webster had kept some memento. Such a thing would be circumstantial, but anything that gave Gaines sufficient reason to further detain Webster would be appreciated. He would have to get a confession. That was the simplicity of it.

In those moments at Webster's motel room, in the panic he felt, the rush of alarm that assaulted his senses, his primary concern had merely been to get Webster in a cell, to hold him down, to remove any possibility of flight. Now that that had been done, he had time to think, but given the time to think, he did not know which direction to take.

Getting some kind of basic training, winding up with a certificate to prove it, well, there was a little more to policing than that. City detectives and small-town sheriffs needed the same skills. Didn't matter who or what you were investigating; the same basic tools were required. Seeing what no one else saw. Maybe just seeing the same thing but reading something different into it. That was it. That was the first thing you needed. And when everyone else had stopped looking, when everyone else has just up and quit because whatever the hell they were seeing wasn't telling them what they wanted to hear, you were the one who just kept on looking, kept asking questions, kept nagging at it until the wrong-colored thread pulled loose. There was little more required than an open mind and an inexhaustible supply of patience. And part of that ability to persevere in the face of contradiction and contrariness had to come from experience. Life experience. Experience that told you there were always truths to be found, even in the company of liars.

And despite all of this, this desire to find the truth, to do the right thing, to then spend your working hours reviled and despised by people—people who didn't know you, would never know you, not unless something happened—was harder than people imagined. And when that *something* happened, when the darkness of the world came at them with all the forces it could muster, you became the most important person in the world—friend, confidant, confessor, vigilante.

It was a strange and awkward existence, crowded with people, but lonely.

Gaines spoke briefly to Hagen. Hagen concurred. Until they had something more concrete, they could do little. A confession would give them a warrant. A warrant would give them access to Webster's room, and a thorough search might give them something substantive and physical to connect Webster and Nancy Denton. Unlikely, but always a possibility.

For some reason, however, Gaines believed that Webster *would* talk. Hadn't he said that he'd been waiting twenty years for someone to ask him the question? He had carried the guilt of whatever he'd done for two decades, and now he was ready to unburden himself, to seek forgiveness, to experience the relief that so often comes with telling the truth. If Gaines went down there right now and asked Webster what had happened, he believed Webster would just open his mouth and tell Gaines whatever he wanted to know.

But, for some reason, Gaines believed he was not ready to hear it.

He told Hagen to get busy on finding Webster a lawyer, that he was leaving to check on his mother, that he would be back soon.

Gaines did not need to see his mother. Caroline would be with her, and all would be fine. In truth, he simply wished to be out of the building, to breathe a different air than that which Michael Webster was breathing, to see something other than his own office and the basement for a brief while. He needed an interlude before he faced up to this madness again.

16

Gaines met Caroline in the kitchen of his house and knew immediately that something was awry.

"Sheriff," she said, in her voice a sense of urgency. She grabbed his sleeve and tugged it like she needed to secure his undivided attention. "I heard that some girl was killed . . ."

Gaines stayed silent. He'd known word would get out quickly, but he hadn't expected it to be quite this fast.

"Heard that someone killed her . . . killed her and put a snake inside her . . ." She shuddered visibly. "Put a dead snake in her . . . you know, her . . ." She looked awkward, embarrassed. She indicated her midriff, then lower, finally resting her hand just above her crotch.

"And who in Christ's name told you such a thing, Caroline?" Gaines asked, less amazed at the wild variation of the truth that had found its way to Caroline Rousseau than the speed at which it had happened. The Denton girl's body had been discovered only twenty-four hours earlier, and already there was rumor and hearsay on its way around Whytesburg.

"So they didn't?" she asked.

"Didn't kill her, or didn't put a dead snake up inside of her?"

"I know some girl was killed, Sheriff, but it was the snake thing . . ."

Gaines indicated left. "Sit down," he told Caroline. "Just calm yourself for a minute and let me explain the deal here."

Caroline Rousseau sat down.

Gaines sat facing her, his hands on the table, his palms together, and as he spoke, he emphasized his words with brief and emphatic gestures.

"A girl called Nancy Denton was killed, yes. Twenty years ago, okay? She was killed before you were even born. We don't know how. We don't know who did it. There was something unusual about the way in which her body was found, but she sure as hell did not have a dead snake in her vagina."

As Gaines spoke, he looked directly at Caroline. Caroline grimaced, shuddered again.

"And I would appreciate it, Caroline, if you would do everything possible to prevent such a rumor from finding its way into the collective ears of Whytesburg. More important, I don't want you discussing this with my mother . . ."

It was there in the sudden widening of the eyes, the way she raised her brows, the tension in her lips.

"You already told her," Gaines said matter-of-factly.

"I couldn't . . . I didn't . . ."

Gaines raised his right hand and Caroline fell silent. "What's done is done," he said. "I'll deal with that, but what I said about not spreading this rumor—"

"I won't say a word, Sheriff. And I'm sorry about speakin' to your mom an' everything . . ."

"It's okay, Caroline. I'll go see her now."

Gaines got up. He realized he still had on his hat. His mind was elsewhere. He never entered the house without removing his hat.

The expression was there. Alice Gaines had something on her mind and there was no way she wasn't going to be talking about it.

"Seen it before," she said as Gaines entered the room, "and the one thing that shocks me, John, is that I had to hear about it from the help and not from you."

"For Christ's sake, Ma, you can't call her that. She is not *the help*. She comes over here because she cares for you and because she likes your company."

"Don't change the subject, John. You tell me what has been going on now . . ."

"Police business, Ma, that's what's been going on."

"This dead girl, what, all of ten or twelve years old, a virgin no doubt, and someone killed her and put a snake in her . . ."

"They did not."

Alice stopped suddenly, her eyes wide. "Didn't what? Kill her?"

"No, they killed her, Ma, but they didn't do the other thing . . . and besides, she wasn't ten or twelve. She was sixteen, and I have not the faintest clue whether she was a virgin or not. Regardless, this isn't something you should be troubling yourself about. It happened in 1954, and you didn't even get here till fourteen or fifteen years later. It's none of your business, okay?"

"Shouldn't be troubling myself about? This is exactly the kind of thing I should be troubling myself about. You're my son, and you've got this kind of thing going on . . ."

"What kind of thing?"

"This ritual killing stuff. I've seen this kind of thing before . . . well, not seen it, but heard plenty about it, and this is a little more significant than just a plain old murder."

"A plain old murder?" Gaines smiled ruefully. "You mean like the plain old murders that just happen every couple of hours around here?"

Alice looked at Gaines, a look he had known since childhood, since the earliest moment of his first sarcastic retort. "We can do without the backtalk, young man."

"Ma, seriously, this is my work, and I need you to stay out of it . . ."

"Stay out of it? I'm not *in* it, John, but I'll tell you now that if someone has killed a little girl and put a snake in her . . ."

"She was not so little, and the snake was not in her vagina, okay? Where the hell that came from, I do not know, but no doubt that will be what everyone will now be thinking—"

"There is something wrong with this, John, and you know it. Wherever this damned snake might have been, there is something terribly wrong with this . . ."

"The fact that a teenage girl has been murdered, that is as wrong as it needs to get. I am investigating the murder of a teenage girl, and that is all."

His words hung in the air. He knew that he was actually investigating a great deal more than the simple murder of Nancy Denton.

And that itself was an irony, something that Gaines never believed he would hear from himself in small-town middle-American Whytesburg.

The simple murder of a girl. Was there ever such a thing?

Gaines did not want to hear any more. He left his mother's room and went back to the kitchen.

His mother was right: Irrespective of whether or not such things bore any truth, regardless of whether Gaines believed or not, it had everything to do with what other people believed. There were explanations and rationales for murders that could be comprehended—jealousy, revenge, financial gain, crimes of passion, acts of hatred and bigotry and racism. But this? This was in a territory all its own. Here was the zone inhabited by serial killers, sadists, sex-and-death torture freaks. Those who killed for its own

96

sake. Those who sought out victims by appearance or physical type, those who killed strangers for no other reason than some imagined but nevertheless very real motive. And if they could kill for such incredible reasons, they could sure as hell open up a body, replace a heart with a snake in a box, and stitch it back up. This was perhaps in the realms of hoodoo and religious ritual, and Gaines's first thought in considering this was whether Webster had acted alone, or if he was part of a group. The Klan was still down here, would always be down here as far as Gaines could see. There were lynchings and murders. Hell, those three civil rights workers had been killed up near Meridian, and that was just ten years before. That had been the White Citizens' Council, but the Neshoba County deputy who arrested the three kids and kept them in his jail until the murder squad could be organized was Klan. The car was driven into Bogue Chitto swamp and set on fire, and once the three boys had been beaten half to death and shot, their bodies had been buried in an earthen dam. Regardless of the manner of death—shooting, stabbing, hanging, choking—a murder was still a murder, and a riverbank was not so different from an earth dam. The national uproar had driven Lyndon Johnson to threaten Hoover with political reprisals if he didn't send the FBI down there. Hoover conceded. The Feds went in. They even had navy divers searching for those three bodies, and in the process they discovered a further seven dead blacks whose disappearances had gone unnoticed by the rest of the country. And even when the bodies were found, even when the murderers were named and arrested, Mississippi refused to prosecute them for murder. So now? Was this Klan? Was this some bizarre ritual enacted by white supremacists? Couldn't be. Had it been Klan or Council then Nancy Denton would have been a black girl. No, this was something different. This was something that Lieutenant Michael Webster needed to explain, and he needed to explain it now.

Before leaving the house, Gaines went back and spoke to his mother. "I need you to do whatever's needed to let this go no further. Do not call anyone, Ma. Don't discuss this with Caroline any more. I am serious. Right now this is a murder, plain and simple, and I have to deal with it just as it is. People are superstitious, always have been and always will be, and I need to contain this right now."

"You can't contain such things, John. Seriously, things like this do not belong to any world you're familiar with—"

"Ma, enough, okay?"

She looked at him maternally, almost sympathetically. She looked at him with the same expression she'd worn when she'd tried to explain why his father was never coming home.

17

Whytesburg Sheriff's Office, representative office of the entire Breed County Police Department, provided four basement cells, two on the left, two on the right, with a walkway between them wide enough to prevent prisoner contact. At the end of the room, an inclined vent allowed a ghost of light and fresh air into the space. Regardless, the basement had always suffered from an ever-present odor of damp mustiness that did not change season to season. In the summer it smelled rotten, in the winter merely aged and decayed. A brick wall separated each adjacent pair, the remaining two sides of each merely bars. There was no privacy, no solitary confinement. These were designed for nothing but temporary holding.

Gaines arrived at the office, and even before he started down the steps to the basement cells, he could hear Webster's voice.

". . . must not break our bonds of affection. The mystic chords of memory, stretching from every battlefield and patriot grave, to every living heart and hearthstone, all over this broad land, will yet swell the chorus of the Union when again touched, as surely they will be, by the better angels of our nature . . . We must not be enemies. Though passion may have strained, it must not break our bonds . . ."

Hagen was down there, exasperated and angry.

"Over and over again, he's been saying this," he told Gaines. "Guy's fucking crazy."

"It's Lincoln," Gaines said. "He's quoting Abraham Lincoln."

Gaines approached the cell. He stood inches from the bars and looked directly at Webster.

After a moment, Gaines started speaking, merely echoed precisely what Webster was saying. They went through it twice, and then Webster fell silent. He smiled, nodded at Gaines.

"Sheriff," he said.

"You think that girl was one of the better angels, Michael?"

"Everyone thought she was an angel, Sheriff."

"I figure she might very well have been, you know?"

Webster shrugged, at once noncommittally, and then he glanced away, looked down, and when he looked back, there seemed to be tears in his eyes. What was this? Remorse?

"You hungry, Michael?"

"Not 'specially."

"You eaten anything today?"

Webster shook his head.

"I'm gonna send out for some sandwiches. I'm gonna come on in there with you and we can talk, and then we can have some sandwiches. Sound okay to you?"

"Sure thing, Sheriff."

"What do you like?"

"Oh, anything you got. Ham on rye, cheese, whatever's easy."

Gaines turned and nodded at Hagen. Hagen gave the cell keys to Gaines and then headed for the stairwell.

"Bring some Coke, as well," Gaines called out, and then—turning back to Webster—asked, "Or do you want root beer?"

"Coke is good," Webster replied.

Hagen looked back at Gaines, the expression on his face like, *What, all of a sudden I'm a waiter?*

Gaines paused until he heard the door close at the top of the stairwell, and then he took out his gun, laid it on the floor out of arm's reach from the cell, and unlocked the door.

Webster just stayed right where he was, seated there on the bunk, his feet bare, his hands beneath his thighs, but Gaines was alert for any movement, attuned to the slightest shift in Webster's position. That same sense returned. Gaines could smell the funk of the water-logged riverbank, the smell of the girl as she surfaced, the smell of her in the morgue as she lay there with her torso unlaced.

Gaines could picture Victor Powell's face as the snake emerged from the box, its tail in its mouth.

Hesitating for just a moment, Gaines then closed the cell door behind him. It remained ajar, unlocked, but Gaines positioned himself on the edge of the bunk so he could merely stand and block Webster if Webster attempted to run.

There was silence between them for a moment, and then Gaines spoke.

"So you wanna tell me about Nancy Denton, Michael?"

Webster was looking toward the inclined vent, at the vague light that crept on through, at the motes of dust dancing and shifting perpetually.

"I just don't know what to say, Sheriff," Webster replied.

"Just tell me whatever you can . . . whatever you want to tell me . . ."

"Well, I don't know what it is, aside from a terrible thing an' all. Her being dead like that and what was done to her—"

"Done to her?"

"The way she was killed, you know? She was strangled. She was held down and the life was strangled right out of her."

"Right," Gaines said. So consumed had he been by the fact that her heart had been removed that he had failed to appreciate what she must have gone through before she died. She had been strangled to death. Someone—and it certainly seemed that Michael Webster was the primary candidate in that moment—had put their hands around her pale throat and choked her. They had looked right into her eyes, a fragile teenage girl, and had not let go until she had gasped her final, tortured breath. Sixteen years old. It was no life at all. Jesus Christ.

Gaines felt a sudden hatred for Webster. A intense feeling overcame him, a sense of righteous outrage, a feeling that this business would be resolved right here, right now if he also put his hands around Webster's throat and choked the last of his sick life right out of him.

Gaines closed his eyes for just a moment. He breathed deeply. He tried to center himself.

"It's a terrible, terrible business," Webster said. "Somethin' like that done to a young girl. How do you deal with something like that, Sheriff?"

Webster looked at Gaines.

Gaines didn't speak.

"I mean, we saw some things out there," Webster went on. "We saw the worst of all of it out there. Kids all blown to hell an' back. People decapitated, people run through with knives and machetes. People smashed up in pieces and spread all through the trees, right? We seen all of it and then some, but there's little I can remember that compares to Nancy Denton . . . seein' her lyin' there, not a movement, not a sound . . ."

Webster's voice trailed away.

Gaines was struggling to comprehend how someone could do such a thing and then speak of it with such distance. Was this what war had done to Lieutenant Michael Webster? Was this the legacy of Guadalcanal for this man? For America? Surely not, for Gaines himself had seen the very things of which Webster spoke and yet he was not compelled to strangle a child, to cut out her heart, to defile her body in such a way and then bury it in mud. No, this was not the war; this was just the man.

"So you want to tell me how it happened, Michael?" Gaines repeated.

Webster shook his head. "I don't want to say nothin'."

Gaines turned at the sound of the door opening at the top of the stairs. Hagen came down with sandwiches, bottles of Coke. Gaines went out through the door and collected them. He returned to the cell, set the sandwiches on the bunk, handed a bottle to Webster, and then started eating.

Webster followed suit, neither of them speaking, Webster looking in the direction of the vent, Gaines looking at his shoes, every once in a while glancing at the man beside him.

When they were done, Gaines took the bottles out and placed them near the wall on the far side. He went back to the cell and sat down.

"We saw the lightning and that was the guns," Webster suddenly said, "and then we heard the thunder and that was the big guns . . . and then we heard the rain falling and that was the blood falling . . . and when we came to get in the crops, it was dead men that we reaped . . ."

Gaines frowned.

"Harriet Tubman said that," Webster explained. "And there were two guys on the radio back in sixty-seven, guys called Gragni and Rado, and they said that the draft was white people sending black people to fight yellow people to protect the country they stole from red people." He smiled. "It was a different war, but it was the same war."

Gaines nodded. "I heard that."

"You know what Hemingway said?" Webster asked.

"No, Mike, what did he say?"

"Never think that war, no matter how necessary, nor how justified, is not a crime. That's what he said."

"Right."

"But war is war, right? War is about two groups of people who know they might die, and they go anyway. They go because they believe in something, because they think something is important enough to fight for."

"Except for the draft."

"Even the draft," Webster said. "There were plenty of people who didn't go, plenty who dodged it, went to Canada and whatever. Conscientious objection an' all that." Webster smiled. "But that's not the point here, is it? The point here is that Nancy Denton wasn't in no war. She wasn't in no army. She wasn't fighting for anything except her own life. And it was taken anyway, wasn't it? Her life was taken anyway, and what the hell did she ever do to anyone?"

"I don't know, Mike. Why don't you tell me what she did?"

Webster looked at Gaines. His expression was one of confusion. "What did she do? It wasn't what she did, Sheriff; it was who she was. Bright, pretty, funny, kind. That's who she was, and that's why she had to die like that? Everyone loved her, but this time she was loved too much . . ."

"Loving someone too much means you have to kill them? Is that it? Because you don't want anyone else to have them?"

"Christ almighty knows, Sheriff. Hell, maybe it was just to feel what it was like to strangle a girl like that."

"Is that what happened?"

"Well, it's what I think, is all," Webster said. "You just asked me what I thought an' I told you."

"Was there a ritual of some kind? Is that why she was killed?"

Webster frowned, and for a moment he looked vexed. "How the hell do you think I know that?" he asked. "You think if I knew I wouldn't tell you?"

"I don't know, Mike," Gaines replied. "I don't know anything about you. You could be an honest man; you could be a liar. I just know that I have a dead sixteen-year-old girl and a lot of people waiting for an explanation."

"Sixteen. That's no time at all. That ain't any kind of a life, is it, Sheriff?" Webster replied, echoing Gaines's own thoughts from just moments before.

"No, Mike, it isn't."

Webster whistled through his teeth. "Sixteen years old. Jesus Christ almighty."

"Does that change the way you feel about her?" Gaines asked.

Webster didn't speak for a moment. He looked away toward the vent and then back at Gaines. "Change the way I feel about her?"

"Thinking about her being sixteen."

"Would it have made a difference if she was fourteen, or fifteen maybe? Hell no, she would still be nothing but a child, Sheriff. You think if she was a year or two older it would have been any less worse?"

"No, Mike, I don't."

"Well, what the hell you askin' me that for, then?"

"I'm just trying to understand why someone would do this to a girl like Nancy Denton, is all. I'm just trying to understand—"

"Same as me. I'm tryin' to understand, too. Hell, why does anyone do anything crazy? Because they're crazy, that's why. Why do people start wars? Why do people murder other people? Why do people up and marry some girl and then get tired of her and beat her half to death and throw her out the car into the fucking road? I don't know why, Sheriff. Seems to me you'd be the better one to answer that question, wouldn't you say?"

"I don't understand it, Mike . . . no better than you."

Webster smiled wryly. "Then if you don't get it an' I don't get it, I'd say we're screwed."

Gaines was quiet, and then the need to know overcame his training and his common sense. "Tell me what happened, Mike."

" 'Tain't complicated. Happened not half a mile from where I live. She was just there, just right there in a shack at the side of the road. Just lying there in the doorway. Picked her up and took her back to my place. Did what I could there, and then I buried her near running water."

"Why running water, Mike?"

" 'S what my friend said to do."

"Friend? What friend?"

"Friend I had back then. Al Warren was his name."

"*Was* his name?"

Webster shook his head. "He didn't make it back. He died out there. He was like a brother to me. Hard to explain that, but when you're in a unit together, when you fight together, when you are engaged in looking after someone else's life day after day, something happens. It's closer than brothers, you know? Like it's something spiritual. He was the smartest man I ever knew. No, not the smartest; he was the wisest. He was like a Buddhist or something. He was like a religious guy, but not like going to church and sayin' prayers and whatever. He was true religion, like it was something he had a mission to do. A mission for the truth, you know?"

"I don't understand, Michael. Your friend in the war told you to bury Nancy Denton in the riverbank?"

"He told me a lot of things, Sheriff. All about the magic. He told me who to trust and who not to trust. It was because of him I made the deal, and the deal I made has got me where I am now. I knew it would happen, and I knew I'd have to make the payback. I just didn't know when."

"The payback?"

"For getting out of there. For getting through the war despite the fact that everyone around me, everyone I knew, was blown to shit that day. I made a deal for that, and just to prove to me that the deal was good, that thing happened in fifty-two, and it was the same thing all over again. That's when they started calling me the luckiest man alive." Webster shook his head resignedly, and then he looked through Gaines as if Gaines were not there at all. "They didn't understand that I was already dead. Had been dead ever since the moment I made that deal."

"I don't understand, Michael. What deal? What payback? What happened in fifty-two?"

Michael shook his head. "It doesn't matter now, does it? She's gone. She's dead. She ain't never comin' back. Whatever I did to help her after she was dead, it all counts for shit now, doesn't it?"

Webster turned and looked at Gaines directly. This time Gaines believed that Mike was really seeing him. Webster's eyes were filled with tears, his skin pale, and a fine sweat varnished his brow. He looked sick, upset, agitated. "Just trying to do whatever I could to get her through this thing. I read stuff afterward, you know? Trying to understand what I'd done. Trying to understand the deal I'd made, if there was any way out of it. Well, I found out one thing for sure. There ain't no way out of a deal like that. I was raised in Louisiana, out in Baton Rouge, and I heard what Al was saying, 'cause he was out of Louisiana, too, and later on, afterward, I read all about that stuff, and I figured there had to be some truth in some of it. That's the way it goes when you're raised out that way . . ."

Gaines heard the words, words he had heard before, and the memories came back, images from his own childhood, the things he had seen, and he knew what Webster was talking about.

"But when she didn't come back, I figured maybe it was because of the deal I'd made. And then I figured that maybe I just had to be patient and never say a damned word about it, because saying anything about it would have ruined any hope that it would work . . ."

He shook his head, lowered his chin to his chest, and for a moment Gaines believed the man was crying again.

When he spoke, his voice was barely a whisper.

"But it didn't work, did it? She didn't come back. You found her all this time later, and now all I can hope for is that she made it through to the other side and she's safe somewhere, someplace where she don't hurt no more . . ."

But she did come back, Gaines thought. She was preserved perfectly, looked the same as she had twenty years before.

"But why, Mike?" he asked. "Why do what you did to her after killing her so brutally?"

Webster's eyes widened. "What?" he asked, in his voice a tone of disbelief and incredulity. "What the hell are you talking about? I didn't kill her. Is that what you think I did? Jesus Christ, no, I didn't kill her. I found her dead, Sheriff . . . found her dead in the doorway of that shack by the side of the road and just tried to help her the best way I knew how . . ."

18

Gaines could only listen to so much. He knew he was dealing with a crazy man, and whatever chords might have struck with him, it was still delusion and insanity.

Gaines did not want to question Webster further, not until a lawyer was there, not until they could get this on tape. He did ask Webster one other question, however, and that was the location of where Webster had found Nancy Denton. Where he *said* he'd found her. The location was a half mile or so from the motel where Webster lived. Gaines took Hagen with him and drove out there. He just stood at the side of the road and tried to imagine what had happened twenty years before. If ever there had been a shack there, it was long since gone. Perhaps if they tore up the undergrowth, they could find the footprint of it, but Gaines wasn't about to do such a thing.

Gaines and Hagen then drove on out to Bogalusa, only to learn that Sheriff Graydon McCarthy was off shift. A couple of questions and they found him in a bar up on Wintergreen. He was sitting in the corner with another man, the pair of them watching a pickup band rehearsing a set for a visiting singer. Above their heads, right there on the wall, was a sign.

Bar Tabs Available
Terms & Conditions Apply*
*$1,000 Deposit Required

"Didn't think I'd be seein' you so soon," McCarthy said.

"Looks like maybe we got our man," Gaines said.

"Good to hear it."

"Need to coordinate this with you."

"Understand that, Sheriff," McCarthy said, "but this here is my brother, come on down from Hattiesburg to see a little music with me. We don't get to see each other much these days, but we do like a bit o' country music." McCarthy nodded at the band. "This here shower o' half-wits are strangling a couple of classics, but we got Mary May Coates arrivin' sooner or later, and she's an old-time star, a real class act." McCarthy smiled. "You could stay and have a drink with us, sociable like, and then we could deal with this mess in the morning."

"Thank you, Sheriff McCarthy, but I gotta get back. All I need is your sanction on taking this case. The guy we got lives out in that motel place you spoke of, so, in truth, that makes the arrest itself a Travis County matter. However, the girl was from Whytesburg. Her ma still lives there, and that makes it Breed County. I wanna take this thing, Sheriff, but I'm more than likely gonna be back and forth in Travis checking up on things and getting myself involved in other people's business, if you know what I mean."

McCarthy set down his glass. He leaned forward, rested his hands flat on the table. His expression was serious, almost foreboding.

"You're tellin' me that you wanna take a murder case off my hands? You want to take a case from Travis and just move it all over to Whytesburg and leave me with nothin' to do?"

"I don't mean this disrespectfully, Sheriff—"

McCarthy grinned—high, wide, and handsome. "Hell, son, I'm just yankin' your chain. You go on and take all the cases from Travis you can carry, and when you're done with them, you can come on back and take some more."

Gaines nodded. "'Preciated, Sheriff." He stood up, extended his hand to McCarthy's brother. "Pleasure to meet you, sir." They shook hands. "Sheriff," Gaines added, replacing his hat and touching the brim.

Gaines headed back to the door, found Hagen standing beside the car watching an overweight woman in full country singer regalia—rhinestones, knee-high maroon leather boots, a mountain of blond curls—as she maneuvered her way out of a station wagon.

"Miss Mary May Coates, I believe," Gaines said.

The woman turned, beamed at Gaines.

"Think you'll find yourself an enthusiastic crowd tonight, ma'am."

"Why, honey, that's mighty sweet of you," she crooned.

Gaines got in the car, and Hagen headed around and got in the passenger side. They pulled away sharply, left a wide crescent in the gravel of the forecourt behind them.

"He all right?" Hagen asked.

"It's our case," Gaines replied. "Because he doesn't want it, first and foremost, but mainly because we do."

Back at the Whytesburg office, Gaines headed on down to see Webster. Webster was sleeping, snoring lightly, the expression on his face one of a man seemingly untroubled by anything.

Gaines woke him.

Webster rubbed his eyes, sat up, stretched his neck from side to side.

"Mike, I have to get straight what you're telling me here. You're telling me that you found Nancy Denton dead in a shack at the side of the road.

Webster nodded. "Yes, I am."

"And the things that were done to her . . . before she was buried?"

"I just did what I had to do," Webster replied. "To help her through, you know? Just to help her through."

"And she was already dead? This is what you're telling me?"

Webster looked hurt. "I cannot believe you would think I was capable of killing Nancy—"

Gaines was silent for a moment—taking it all in, trying not to picture this man sweating over the body of Nancy Denton, the strength it must have taken to cut through her chest, the removal of her heart . . . and as far as the snake was concerned, he could not even bring himself to mention it.

"I need to look in your room, Mike. I can fuck around for a day getting a warrant, or you can give me permission to go look in your room."

"Go look," Webster said. "I ain't hiding nothin' from you."

"You'll sign something to that effect, that you gave me permission to search your room, your belongings, everything?"

"Sure I will."

"Good enough," Gaines said, and then he turned to walk away.

"Sheriff?"

Gaines hesitated, turned back to look at Webster.

"After you're done searchin' my place, can I see Nancy?"

Gaines didn't reply. He took a deep breath. He exhaled slowly. He walked as quickly as he could to the stairwell and left the basement.

19

As Graydon McCarthy had said, the motel was owned by one Harvey Blackburn. Harvey was easily found, again in the nearest bar, and Gaines explained the situation as far as Webster was concerned.

Blackburn was a drunk, was drunk when Gaines found him, would be drunk for the rest of the night. From Gaines's first impression, the man was a chiseler and a thief. Somehow or other, he'd wound up owning the property—a dozen or so falling-apart motel rooms built in a crescent, the neon sign in the center driveway, now broken down and out of action, a small office to the right. This was the kind of place that had been in its prime in the mid-fifties, a simple, clean stopover joint for interstate travelers, some headed south to New Orleans, others north to Jackson, perhaps even Memphis. There would have been a catalog of house rules, a wedge of pages with a hole punched through the upper-left-hand corner and hung from a nail behind the door of each cabin. *No smoking in the bed. No milk to be left in the room upon vacating. No music. No dancing. No loud talking after nine p.m.* On it would go—item by item—until it seemed that whatever brief sojourn might be endured there would involve nothing more than standing silent and immobile in the corner of the room, your unpacked suitcase ready for collection at the door, your shod feet encased in polythene bags to prevent inadvertent marks on the carpet or scuffs on the baseboard.

Now Blackburn charged by the hour, the day, the week, the year, whatever you liked. He catered to all and sundry.

Gaines knew that whatever Blackburn told him, there would always be some other story hiding just beneath the surface. He was curious as to how such a small man could bear such a burden of secrets.

Gaines told Blackburn that Webster's motel cabin was a crime scene, that it was to be treated as such. There would be no entry, not even for Blackburn, and he—Sheriff Gaines of Whytesburg—would be overall responsible for any and all matters that related to the investigation.

He asked Blackburn how long Webster had lived there.

"A year," Blackburn said. "Maybe a year and a half."

Gaines didn't wait for questions, and it seemed Blackburn didn't have any. Blackburn seemed like a man well practiced in keeping his mouth shut tight, just in case he opened it and the truth inadvertently fell out.

Gaines told Hagen to call in to the office, to get Lyle Chantry and Forrest Dalton out there. Every resident of the motel needed to be questioned, their particulars taken. Gaines wanted to know—first and foremost—if any of these people had known about this. Had Webster ever spoken to anyone of these twenty-year-old events?

Chantry and Dalton arrived. Gaines gave Hagen the responsibility of overseeing the actions there, the canvassing of the neighbors, the collection of whatever information they could glean about Webster himself, about his comings and goings during his residence at the motel. Lester Cobb had said that Webster was upstream regularly, but had Webster been seen in the proximity of the buried body? Did he make a habit of returning to the scene of the crime?

Hagen produced the release document. "I typed this up," he said. "Get Webster to sign it soon as you can."

Gaines read it through, folded it, and tucked it into his pocket, and with Hagen and the deputies then organized, Gaines steeled himself for the task at hand. He would search the room, the bathroom, the front and rear of the cabin.

Once again, he covered his face, and once again he entered Lieutenant Michael Webster's motel cabin, the first room of which was dark, unsettling, and stank like rotten meat.

Gaines switched on the lights, and it was only then—in the glare of two stark and shadeless bulbs—that he appreciated the level of filth and chaos that had consumed Webster's cabin. It was said that the state of a man's living space was a reflection of his state of mind. Gaines's own quarters were somewhat stark, an evident lack of personal touches, but he lived with his mother, cared for her there, and thus had considered all things from her perspective and for her comfort. When she died, *if* she ever died, then her things would go. Gaines would not want to live with constant reminders of her presence. And then the house would be empty and he would have to start over.

But here? Here was something beyond all comprehension. In the darkness of the unlit room, those minutes when he had first spoken with Webster, his attention had been on Webster. Now Webster was not present, the room no longer dark, and Gaines could see the reasons for the unbearable funk of the place. To the right was a small kitchenette and eating area, and it was here that the vast majority of the garbage was concentrated. Takeout food boxes, a half-eaten pie, trash bags spilling over with mold-infested waste, dirty plates, articles of unwashed clothing, a heap of skin mags, clothes, shoes, boxes of ammo, three handguns, a rusted bandolier, napsacks, a suitcase full of 45-rpm records, many of them broken. Amid this bedlam were ashtrays piled high with the roaches of joints, a couple of plastic bags of weed, twists of paper, within which was amphetamine sulfate. And then Gaines found a grocery sack filled with prescription medication bottles, many of them bearing names that were not Webster's. Uppers, downers, everything imaginable, a concoction of which would have killed any man of regular constitution. Webster was able to stand, to talk, to act, but his mind, his imagination, his rationale, had to be utterly fucked.

Gaines found a heap of clothes in the corner of the room. Using the tip of his pen, he lifted the pants, held them up, saw the thick, dried mud that traveled as far as the knees. He gagged, felt the tension in his throat fighting against the urge to just puke, to just let it out, to release the entire physical reaction to this terrible, terrible thing. But Gaines held it down.

He dropped the pants, headed back to the car for some bags, returned with a pair of gloves as well. Carefully, trying to ensure that none of the dried mud fell away, he bagged the pants, a shirt, a pair of boots. If this mud could be identified as the same mud from the riverbank, then it would corroborate Cobb's statement that he had seen Webster there. It was of no great consequence, of course. So Webster liked to go looking for garter snakes. So Webster took a walk by the river every once in a while. Perhaps, Gaines thought, he himself was looking for nothing more than any small certainty he could find amid the ocean of uncertainties that faced him. He put the bags in the trunk of his car, and then he took a few moments to breathe deeply, to gather his thoughts, to steady his nerves before he searched further.

He stood for a while, almost as if he believed that he could become acclimated and insensate to the smell. He could not, and he would not, and he knew he was merely postponing the inevitable.

He maneuvered his way through the garbage to the back of the room. Here were the boxes he had seen behind Webster. There were a good half dozen, and he lifted down the first and started looking through it. At first, Gaines had the impression that here was nothing but a mountain of random newspaper clippings, but then a certain pattern seemed to emerge. Fires, collapsed buildings, mining disasters, floods, storms, hurricanes, typhoons, ships lost at sea, car crashes, train wrecks, bridges dropping into ravines and rivers, forest fires, farming accidents and gas explosions. On it went, both natural disasters and man-made calamities. The common thread, sometimes so obvious from images of individuals being carried from the ruins of some building, other times revealed in the third or fourth paragraphs, were the survivors. Sometimes one, sometimes two or three, but always a small number in relation to those who had lost their lives. And the clippings had been collected from newspapers right across the country, not only local but national, covering everything from the *Los Angeles Times* and the *Washington Post* to the *Boise City News* and the *Charleston Post and Courier*. The boxes were dated in sequential years, starting as far back as Christmas of 1945 and running all the way to the present. Gaines counted six boxes, each box covering five years, the last box having started in 1970 and still incomplete. If nothing else, Webster had been obsessive in his organization. He had underlined the number of survivors in each case, and where they had been mentioned, he had underlined their names.

What this meant, Gaines could not even begin to conceive, but it had to represent something.

And then Gaines had it. The reference Webster had made to his section in Guadalcanal.

November third, I was in a foxhole with my section. Nine of us left, all hunkered down to weather it through, and they hit us direct. Eight dead, one living.

And after that, what he had said about making a deal. How he had made some kind of deal. And then something had happened in 1952, and they had started calling him the luckiest man alive. Who were they? People in general, or some specific people?

And he had gone on to say that he had been dead already, dead ever since the moment he'd made the deal.

What was this deal? A deal to survive the war? And with whom?

Such a thing had to exist solely in Webster's deranged mind. Did he believe he had made a deal with some divine or arcane force and thus had survived Guadalcanal while everyone else in his section had been killed? And what was this thing in '52? Had he murdered Nancy Denton and performed some bizarre ritual on her as some kind of payback for the life he'd been given? Is that what Michael Webster actually believed?

Gaines was even more uncertain than when he had left the office. He started to put the newspaper clippings back where he'd taken them from, careful not to disturb their original order, and it was then that he found the Bible. Battered, dog-eared, the leather cracked in places, it seemed not only old, but neglected. Flicking through it for any marker or inserts, of which there were none, he noticed the occasional underlined passage. Inside the front cover was a handwritten scrawl. *This helped me. E.* Who was E? Right now it was of no great concern. Maybe it was a war buddy of Webster's, someone from the VA perhaps. As Gaines stacked the boxes once more, he found the photo album. It was there, down against the baseboard, and he nearly missed it. But something drew him to it, and even as he opened it up to look at the first picture, he hoped that here he would find something more than circumstantial evidence and the ramblings of a crazy man to connect Michael Webster to Nancy Denton.

In the pictures she was alive. So utterly alive. She seemed always to be smiling, and when she was not smiling, she was laughing. There were images of her with three or four others, the same faces appearing time and again. There was no mistaking the presence of Lieutenant Michael Webster, sometimes in his own clothes, sometimes in uniform, and in these pictures there was no mistaking the familiarity and affection that seemed to exist between Webster the killer and Nancy the victim. Wasn't it the case that more than eighty percent of murders were perpetrated by people who were known to the victim? The others that recurred constantly included a girl who seemed a year or two younger than Nancy, two young men who bore similarities enough to be related, and every once in a while a much younger girl. A crowd of childhood friends, it seemed, and their images looked back at Gaines from the monochrome snapshots of years gone by, and he wondered what had really happened on the August night in 1954 that saw Nancy Denton dead.

Gaines took the album and the Bible to the car. He put them in the trunk. He closed up Webster's room and drove back to the office.

Once there, Gaines instructed Hagen to secure everything in the evidence room, itself little more than a store cupboard with a lock, but it sufficed for those very rare occasions when Whytesburg needed somewhere to secure items of significance or value.

Gaines then called Dalton out at the motel.

"We got anything?" he asked.

"Not a great deal, Sheriff. They're all saying the same thing. Quiet guy. Kept himself to himself. Hardly ever saw him. Kind of intense. Apart from that, squat."

"I reckoned that would be the case. So finish up there, and then get back here."

There was a moment's pause.

"What is it, Forrest?"

"Figured we'd maybe be done for the night. We're already a couple of hours over shift hours, Sheriff . . ."

"Have a sixteen year-old-girl here, Officer Dalton. Sixteen years old. Don't much care that it happened twenty years ago, but I have a whacko in the basement who sawed her pretty much in two. You got a choice. You can either come back here and keep an eye on him, or you can go out and spend the night consoling her mother."

"Yes," Dalton replied. "Understood, Sheriff. Sorry about that. I'll see you at the office."

20

Gaines went on down to the basement to see Webster. He found him there on the bunk, outside the door a plate with a couple of fried pork chops and some rice and beans. Webster hadn't touched it.

Gaines recognized the expression on Webster's face. It was called the thousand-yard stare. In Gaines's experience, mostly those he had known at the VA, all veterans had it at one time or another—the odd moment, perhaps a week apart, growing ever more infrequent as the months elapsed. Seems that Webster had it almost all the time. Once again, the man seemed to possess the ability to look right *through* Gaines, and he did it with such intensity that Gaines felt like nothing at all. It really was that intense. If Webster had just reached out in that moment, Gaines knew Webster's fingers would touch him and then pass right on through.

"Michael?" Gaines said.

A faint smile crossed Webster's lips.

Gaines had also seen that smile before—the haunted, guilty survivor's smile—at the VA, at the Veterans Hospital up in Jackson, in the awkward silence of the Demobilization Center as those who had served their tours were processed out of a war and back into a world that neither could, nor would ever, understand. But above that smile were the eyes. Nineteen- and twenty-year-olds with a look in their eyes they should not have possessed until they reached their forties. Perhaps they still believed they wouldn't make it, that their lives could be taken at any moment, so they thought it best to assume such expressions now while they still had a chance. Cynical, bitter, world-weary, battle-fatigued, hardened in so many ways, save those ways that were useful in any other life.

Webster looked like that, as did Gaines, but Gaines knew he was still fighting against it, still escaping from it, and one day he perhaps would.

"Sheriff," Webster said.

"Mike . . . I need you to tell me what happened to her heart."

116

Webster closed his eyes, opened them again, almost in slow motion. "It went into a box, Sheriff. A box that could not be broken by root nor animal nor lightning nor rain. That was what needed to be done. Four yards east, twelve yards north from where the body was planted under . . ."

"Planted under?"

"Want something to grow, well, you gotta plant it under, right?"

Gaines was silent for a moment. "You put her heart in a box."

"I did."

"What kind of box did you use, Mike?"

"I used a strong metal box that had belonged to my father, and I emptied out the nails and screws, and I wrapped Nancy's heart in cloth, and I tied the cloth tight, and then I buried the box, like I said."

"Four east, twelve north from where you buried her body."

" 'S right."

Gaines turned and walked to the base of the stairwell. He turned and looked back at Webster. Webster was gone again—into the thousand-yard stare, into whatever world existed behind those dark and distant eyes.

Back upstairs, he told Hagen to load the car with as many torches as he could find.

"And get sawhorses, crime-scene tape, rope as well."

Hagen complied without questioning their purpose. Perhaps he had now reconciled himself to the fact that from here it would likely get worse rather than better.

Gaines checked with Barbara Jacobs if there were any outstanding messages, learned there were none, and then he headed out front to the car. What it was that alerted him, he did not know, but before he reached reception, he was aware that trouble had arrived.

Gaines had been anticipating the inevitable appearance of ex–deputy sheriff Eddie Holland, alongside him his sidekick, Nate Ross, one-time legal eagle around these parts, now nothing more than a retired lawyer with too much time and money. Even when he'd worked under Don Bicklow, Holland had been contrariwise. Always against the grain of things, sometimes stating opinions simply because they countered the consensus. Disagreeable for disagreements' sake. Whichever ways considered, something of an asshole. However, he had mellowed with age, it seemed, and though he spent a good deal too much attention concerning himself with the affairs of others, Gaines did not dislike him. He did not dislike either of them, truth be known, but they always had too much to say when he had too little time to listen. Ross had been a very successful attorney, at first a public defender, then owning and managing his own practice, and then, finally, he had become a state prosecutor. Maybe he had tired of listening to his clients' lies and bullshit and decided that jail was a better place for them. Once retired, he started looking for someplace to drown his sorrows and relieve his boredom. He used to live up in some fancy place in Hattiesburg, but then his wife died, and the three kids they'd wrestled into adulthood apparently felt there was no need to come home now that their mother had passed. Ross had rattled around the empty halls and emptier rooms for a handful of months and then sold the place for three times more than he'd paid. New money from the North was buying into the appearance of old-South wealth and style, and some stationery and office supplies tycoon had snapped up the Ross mansion. Gaines had seen the place one time—reputedly bought with money earned from prosecuting black people for things that had never happened or had been perpetrated by whites—and it looked like a three-tier wedding cake. So Nate Ross came to Whytesburg, had arrived back in the fall of 1970, just a few months after Gaines had graduated from Vicksburg and taken the job in Breed County. The sorrows Nate Ross was trying to drown still weren't dead. They had some brave pair of lungs, or maybe some secret supply of oxygen unbeknownst to Ross. Regardless, he kept sluicing down those sorrows with good, hard liquor in the hope that he'd wake up happier tomorrow.

Holland and Ross were rarely apart, both widowed, both lonely, both a great deal more interested in other people's affairs than was healthy. The ex-cop and the ex-lawyer, minds set on interfering and getting involved, had somehow gotten word about Webster and had come down to see what was happening.

"Nate," Gaines said, "and Ed. Well, what a great pleasure it is to see you pair."

Ross was a good ten feet from Gaines, but Gaines could smell the liquor.

"Don't bullshit us, Sheriff," Holland said, grinning broadly. "We're the last people in the world you want to see, and that doesn't just count for this evening."

Gaines paused. Inside, he just counted to ten.

One.

"Seems we got ourselves a situation here . . . ," Ross said.

Two, three.

"A little bit of a situation, wouldn't you say?"

Four, five.

"Seems to me we have a responsibility to ensure that everything—"

Six, seven.

"—is done right and proper."

Eight, nine.

"Wouldn't want you making a mess of such an important case as this, would we, Sheriff?"

Ten.

"We're doing just fine here, gentlemen," Gaines said. "We have everything under control . . ."

"You sure now?" Holland asked. "Don't seem that Whytesburg's had such a case for as long as I can recall . . . not only a murder, but the butchering of a young girl—"

"Now, where d'you go and hear such a thing?" Gaines asked, knowing full well that Victor Powell would have told his wife, who would then have told her friends, and before lunchtime half the folks of Whytesburg would have been fully apprised of the situation.

"Honestly," Gaines went on, "I don't know that there are two more advised and responsible people in this town, and I'd have thought that such a responsibility, you with your police experience, Ed, and you, Nate, being so legally educated and wise, would feel nothing less than the full burden of care in such a matter."

Neither Holland nor Ross said a word. They looked at each other, then back at Gaines.

Gaines leaned closer, the confidant, acknowledging both Holland and Ross as equals, if not superiors.

"If I can't rely on you guys to manage this business with confidentiality and discretion, then who can I rely on? Place like this, Whytesburg, depends upon its elders to keep order, to make sure that rumor doesn't find its way where it shouldn't."

Once again, Holland looked at Ross, and Ross looked back at Holland.

"Now, I know you weren't deputy when this Denton girl went missing, Ed, and you, Nate . . . well, you were up at your practice in Hattiesburg, far as I know. You are probably not aware of the original circumstances of her disappearance, and Don Bicklow and

George Austin are both long gone. So that leaves me to ask questions of those who *were* here and those who *were* involved. So, unless you were here, or unless you were involved, then I don't know that I can ask anything of you but the exercising of your sense of duty in setting a good example around and about. I will be speaking to you both, because I believe that you may know some things of value to this case, but we're not doing that tonight. So, as far as the here and now is concerned, I have matters to attend to with some urgency. I know that you both appreciate the situation I am dealing with far better than anyone else here, maybe even better than me. I am the sheriff, and I gotta deal with this thing, but I want to know that I can count on you for assistance and advice if I should so need it."

"Of course, Sheriff," Holland blurted, taken aback perhaps by the level of confidence that was being expressed in his abilities and position.

"Without question," Ross added. "Without any question at all."

"Well, that makes me feel a great deal better," Gaines said, and he shook their hands. "Now, I really do need to impress upon you the need to maintain some sense of order on this thing, gentlemen. I know all too well how many folks around here value your opinion, and I want you to use that opinion as wisely as you can. Let's keep this thing localized, shall we? Let's keep this problem a Whytesburg problem, and with both of you on my side, I'm sure we can deal with it quite capably ourselves. We wouldn't want the whole county coming on down here to have a lynching party, now, would we?"

Gaines didn't wait for a response. He gripped Ross's shoulder, squeezed it assuredly, and then left the building.

When he looked back, they were still standing there—looked like they didn't know Tuesday from Sunday, nor any of the days in between—and Gaines smiled to himself.

Sometimes the only way to deal with Ross and Holland was to grant them the importance they so earnestly believed they deserved. Truth was, he was perhaps granting them no more importance than they *did* deserve. They were good people, people used to working hard and getting things done, and retirement didn't suit such folks.

Hagen joined Gaines. He had loaded the trunk with everything Gaines had asked for.

"Where we going?" Hagen asked.

"Back to where we found her body and then a little way off."

"What're we looking for?"

"Her heart, Richard. We're looking for her heart."

Hagen just looked at Gaines.

"Seems I'm gonna spend this week looking at the faces of folks who don't believe what I'm saying to them."

Hagen—wide-eyed—just nodded. He opened the driver's-side door and climbed in.

Gaines got in the passenger side, the car pulled away, and neither of them spoke for a good ten minutes.

"You get him to sign that release document?" Hagen asked.

"Oh hell, I forgot," Gaines said. He reached into his pocket and found the paper that Hagen had given him.

"He needs to sign it, John."

"Soon as I get back," Gaines replied.

Silence filled the car again.

Gaines did not know if finding Nancy Denton's heart—whatever might remain of it—would be worse than discovering nothing at all. Finding that poor girl's heart precisely four yards east and twelve yards north of the point where they had wrestled her frail and broken body from the black filth of the riverbank would merely confirm that they were dealing with something far darker than Gaines had feared.

The things you witnessed in war tied your nerves in knots, tied and twisted them so damned tight they would never unravel, not with a hundred, not with a thousand years of living. And if the living brought you such things as this—things that were equal to the horrors Gaines had seen, things that were carried from the very heart of war itself into an unsuspecting, fragile small-town America—then what hope did he have of becoming fully human again? Scant hope at best, and perhaps it was this of which Gaines was most afraid.

21

Sometimes Gaines liked to drink a glass of whiskey, but it gave him an upset liver and a bad stomach, and thus the bad outweighed the good. That night he drank as if it was the final hour of R & R, that he—the GI round eye—was heading back to the front come daybreak.

When he was at war, he knew it was the worst place he had ever been, the worst place he would *ever* be. Such an awareness did something to the mind, the emotions, the very spirit of a man. It blunted him, rendered him insensate, as if the upper and lower registers of his humanness had been cauterized. Just as he would now no longer experience any real depth of fear, so he would be immune to joy, to elation, to the sometimes giddy rush of pleasure that came from simple things. A child would smile, and he would see an eight-year-old facedown in a pool of muddy, stinking water, the back of its head blown away. A bright bouquet of flowers, and he would see not only the bursting hearts and lingering tails of magnesium flares but the zip and crash of tracers, and in his ears would be the thump and rumble of mortar fire. Like the devil's firework show. The sounds of 105s and 155s were relentless, as if they were counting off the seconds. It was deafening, interminable, but—back then—hearing that sound at least meant you were still alive.

And there was the smell. The smell of things burning. The unmistakable stench of chemical fires in wet vegetation. And bodies. Like scorched hair and rotted pork. Gaines knew the mind did not pick favorites, did not prefer one recollection over another. Some days he could recall the warm aroma of fresh popcorn, the ghost of some long-forgotten and too-brief childhood. But that was always fleeting—there, and then gone. The darker sense memories lingered for hours, and it was at such times that he began to worry for the stability of his own mind. He too was fragile, and he wondered how long it would be before the seams began their inevitable and irreparable divide.

And afterward, after he had returned home, luck became important, fate even, because there was no logical reason for having survived the war. Why had one man died and another lived?

There was no delineation or marker identifying those who would see home and those who would not. Did not matter where you had come from, whether you were born army, a volunteer, or a draftee. When it came, it came. It did not matter if you were loved or despised, whether you attended church for faith or simply to steal from the charity box, whether you worshipped your mother or cursed her blind, whether you lied and swindled, blasphemed, whether you reveled in each and every one of the seven deadly sins or adhered to the letter of each commandment as a point of personal law. War possessed no prejudice, no predetermination, no preference. War would take you as you were, no questions asked.

Why? How were such matters decided? And who did the deciding?

It was such questions that invaded the normalcy and routine of his life. It was such questions that he tried not to ask himself.

But then there were moments: moments of self-doubt, moments when he questioned his own humanity, moments when he questioned the human race itself, the things of which men were made, the things that drove them, their purposes, their aspirations, their rationale. Surely war was invented by man, and if man could invent war, then was there no level to which he could not stoop?

Gaines did not believe Webster, not for a moment. He could see the man with his hands around Nancy Denton's throat. He could see the man choking the life out of the poor, defenseless, beautiful teenager. Perhaps Webster had earned a taste for killing in Guadalcanal, and he had needed to satiate that taste any way he could. Gaines did not believe that Webster had found a dead girl in a shack by the side of the road. He had taken her there, and he had taken her there to kill her.

They found the heart. The girl's heart. Or they found what Gaines could only assume had once been her heart. Four yards east, twelve yards north, just as Webster had told them. It looked like a small, dark knot of something, like a fragment of wood, a chunk of dried leather, and even as they opened the metal box within which it had been contained, there was a certainty that it would stand no physical contact. It was nothing more than dust, in truth, and whatever cloth it might have been wrapped in was gossamer-thin, again little more than a memory of what it had once been, and the box itself, once sturdy, once capable of carrying nails and bolts and screws and suchlike, was rusted and frail, and it came apart in pieces as Gaines and Hagen tried to rescue it from the earth.

The simple truth was that they had followed Webster's directions, and they had found something that could have been a sixteen-year-old girl's heart in a metal box. Irrespective of the fact that it was no longer a heart at all, it *was* something, and it was where Webster had said it would be. That was all that Gaines had needed to confirm his worst fears and his most assured suspicions.

Standing there, his breath coming hard and fast, not only from the physical exertion of digging, but also the mental stress of what was happening, Gaines believed that the only mind he possessed was broken. Sometimes his certainty of this was intense, and it burned with the luminescence, the intensity, the smell of a heat tab beneath a makeshift stove.

Other times he believed he was the only who'd returned sane.

When he closed his eyes, he could still see the dead. He could see the pieces of the dead. He could see heaps of blood-soaked fatigues and flak jackets outside the makeshift triage tent. Almost as if to say, *Hey boys, if the NVA don't get getcha, we'll finish the job pronto right here and now!*

Only at such times could people look at one another and say all that needed to be said without uttering a single word.

Gaines possessed that same feeling then—right there in Whytesburg—as he and Hagen dug into the wet ground. They did not speak as they worked, and they did not speak when they found what they'd hoped they would not find.

The earth had given up Nancy Denton, and now it had given up her heart. The earth was a living thing, a thing with memory, with history, and releasing its secrets would perhaps permit the escape of other things, other darknesses, other memories that would have been best left buried.

What were they doing here? Were they bringing out the dead, and alongside them, the very madness that killed them in the first place?

And what would happen if they took Nancy Denton right now, carried her back to the river, and returned her to the grave that Webster had given her? Would the world return to how it had been before they found her? Was it better to hide what had happened all those years before? Was it better to let the dead go on being dead, to let the truth die with Michael Webster, to release Whytesburg from the ghosts it never knew it had?

Gaines was disturbed. He was cold, distracted, upset. Nevertheless, he went on with the business in front of him. He directed Hagen to put sawhorses around the scene. Together they roped it and taped it. Hagen took a dozen or more photographs from every angle, and each time the flash popped, Gaines started. Even when he knew the flash was coming, he still started. They took what they could of the box, the cloth within, the memory of a young girl's heart, and they bagged it as carefully as they could. Hagen sat in the passenger seat with this strange cargo in his lap. He looked straight ahead, almost as if to look at the remnants directly was to somehow be cursed.

Hagen closed his eyes when the engine started, and he did not open them again until he and Gaines had reached the office.

Gaines and Hagen filled out paperwork, and then Gaines called Victor Powell. Powell told Gaines to meet him at the Coroner's Office, to bring everything he had found. When Powell took these things from him, thanked Gaines, and put them in the same room as Nancy Denton's body, it was late. Gaines looked exhausted, and Powell told him so.

"Go home now," he said. "You need to rest, my friend, before you collapse."

Gaines nodded. Powell was right. He went home. He looked in on his mother. She was out for the count. He closed her door silently, returned to the kitchen, and then he took the bottle of whiskey from the cupboard and he started drinking.

For an hour he tried to feel something other than the horror, and then for an hour he tried to feel nothing at all.

And then he lay down on his bed and closed his eyes.

Gaines knows he is dreaming, but he cannot bring himself awake. He stands in a secluded area, somehow clear of vegetation, yet around him and over him is the shroud and the canopy and the wilderness of impenetrable jungle. A thin and insubstantial light seeps into the fug as a misty, malodorous haze. He is not alone. Of this much he is certain. He is being watched, and whoever is watching him is as patient as Job. Gaines knows he has been there for some time—hours, perhaps days—and yet whoever is stalking him has made no attempt to challenge him. And yet Gaines knows this is what they wish to do. What they *need* to do. This is war, and if you are not an ally, a comrade, a friend, then you are an enemy. There is no middle ground.

Gaines understands then that it is he who needs to move first.

And so he does.

He is seated cross-legged, and he seems to grow from the ground effortlessly. He is naked. His body is dark with mud and blood and black-and-green, and his eyes are stark white against his visage. His hair is glued back against his scalp, and he feels like something from one of his own nightmares. He is outside himself, and he can see himself, and he is terrifying.

In the distance he can hear CH-47s. They are mounted with 20x102 mike-mike Vulcans. He can hear them as certainly as he can hear his own heart. Or can he?

Perhaps he is hearing nothing but the rush and chatter of his pulse, the blood in his veins, the sound of his pores opening in the warm moisture-drenched air.

And then he folds into the vegetation and the jungle swallows him. He understands that he has vanished from view and the watcher cannot see him and does not know where he has gone. Gaines flits from tree to tree, from shadow to shadow, and before he knows it, he is standing behind the watcher, and the watcher has become his prey. The watcher turns and holds out his hands, his eyes wide beneath the shadow of his coolie hat, and somehow Gaines has his rifle before him, the bayonet affixed, and he lunges forward with that blade. The steel punches through outstretched hands, the wounds in the pale flesh of the palms like stigmata, and everything is silent but for the ripping of flesh and the sound of the blood against the ground, against the trees, against his own face. His enemy falls, and he—Gaines—is over him like a wild thing. He has his knife in his hand, and he is hacking and sawing furiously. When he is done, he sees that he has made a ragged series of incisions from the throat to the navel, and suddenly—opening up, as if a zipper had been drawn—the snakes unfold and tumble out, dozens of them, all sizes and colors, and beneath the shadow of the coolie hat is the face of Nancy Denton, a taut smile, a bared-teeth rictus grin, and all the darkness and hatred of the war is there within her eyes.

And then Gaines woke.

He did not wake sweating. He did not lurch awkwardly from the mattress—heaving, retching, his mouth bitter with the imagined taste of blood, his nerves taut, his heart thundering.

When he woke, he was calm, and though he remembered vividly each fragmented second of the nightmare, though he saw every scene in slow motion as he replayed it, he did not torture himself with questions of significance.

He just lay there, and he remembered how it was to be beside someone.

Linda Newman, mother of the child that never was.

He had dreamed such dreams before, a long time ago. For a year or so following his return, the nightmares—vivid and terrifying—would throw him violently from the bed, and he would wake suddenly, startled, enraged even. He had tracked enemies in the boonies, and when he had found them, he had killed them. Often—possessing no discernible weapon, no gun, no blade—he had killed them with his hands.

Reason enough to sleep alone.

He did not wish to wake beside a corpse, their unnecessary and inexplicable death founded somewhere within a nightmare.

And then the dreams had stopped.

There had been times he'd wished for the dreams to return, terrible though they were, just so he could wake and realize that he was no longer there.

Now the girl had invaded his thoughts, his emotions, his mind.

Nancy Denton had joined the cast of characters—those who had died beside him, those he had killed, the dead he had seen lying in the mud.

It was four in the morning. Gaines rose and sluiced his face with cold water. He did not feel sick, despite the whiskey he had drunk. He knew he would not sleep again, and yet he lay down on the mattress and tugged the covers over him. Perhaps the last few hours before daylight would serve no purpose other than to delay the continuing and inevitable confrontation of Nancy Denton's pointless and terrible death. As was always the case with murder, it resulted, ordinarily, in the death of both victim and perpetrator, one by the hand of a killer, the other by the hand of the state.

As Gaines closed his eyes against the gathering light, there was an echo in his mind—half-remembered, half-forgotten. Something that Webster had said, something about finding Nancy in a shack, just lying there in the doorway, and how he had buried her near running water.

Why running water? Why had he buried her near running water? The question presented no immediate answer, and Gaines dismissed it from his mind. It was a detail, a simple detail, and there were so many other questions that begged to be answered first.

22

Even now, if I close my eyes and think as hard as I can, I can remember the feeling of sun on my face.

I can feel that warmth against my skin. I can smell the grass, the flowers in the field. I can hear birds somewhere in the distance.

I went down there with Nancy, and Michael took her hand for just a moment. He smiled at her and then at me, and we turned and started walking.

I know that when Nancy was with Michael, she saw little but him, but Michael was never like that. Michael had a heart the size of a house, and he made everyone feel special. That was just his way. He didn't try. It came naturally.

Nancy was laughing. She was so excited, she could barely speak, but she spoke anyway. After just a few words, Michael started laughing and told her, "Slow down, Nance. Slow down there."

Michael was all of thirty or thirty-one years old, and Nancy was going on sixteen. Though it seemed strange that two people could be so far apart in years, it did not seem strange to anyone who knew them. He never did lay a hand on her. If nothing else, Michael was a true gentleman. You could see that in his eyes, in the way he permitted Nancy to kiss him on the cheek every once in a while and nothing more than that. He behaved like her older brother. That sounds weird, but that's the only way I can tell it. He wasn't her father, nor her uncle, nothing like that. He was like a cousin maybe, someone close, but not too close. He had just made a decision. Nancy was the girl for him. This was the woman with whom he planned to spend the rest of his life, and if he had to wait a while for her to become that woman, then so be it. For Michael, Nancy was worth a thousand years of waiting, no question about it.

And Nancy knew too. Maybe she had known from the first moment he stepped off the train that day in 1945.

But when we were together—me and Matthias, Nancy and Michael—it was as if we were all the same age. Catherine came along sometimes—but only when her father told her to keep an eye on us. Eugene and Della floated around the edges of our little world, and sometimes they were involved and sometimes they were not. But no one frowned on our friendship. Perhaps folks believed Michael was a good influence on these rowdy, troublemaking teenagers. We were all from different families, different backgrounds. Nancy's mom didn't have two quarters in the same place at the same time. My mom was just as ordinary as ordinary people could be, and yet none of it mattered. Matthias's family had more money than anyone could spend in a dozen lifetimes, and yet he dressed the same as us and he talked the same as us, and only when he brought down the old Victrola and the records, only when he turned up with a picnic hamper for us to share by the river, was it obvious that he had more than we did. Age was not a barrier, nor was money or possessions or what name we were given. We were just getting on with living the best way we knew how, and it wasn't complicated.

I remember those years—just a couple of them—that seemed to last forever. It was as if the sun shone each and every day, and it shone for us. And even when it rained and was cold, there was a warmth in friendship and fellowship that defied the elements. I know I look back with rose-colored glasses—we always do when we recall our childhood—but we really did seem to be blessed with something special. Me and Nancy and Michael and the Wade clan, as we used to call them. The best times. The very best times we could ever have wished for.

And that day was really no different from so many others that we had shared.

We chattered as we walked. We talked of what we would do, where we would go, if Eugene would come out this time or if he would stay home and read like he seemed to do so much these days.

We did not talk about Lillian Wade. She had died back at the end of 1952, and no one said her name. Everyone tried not to think about her, because it had been an awful, frightening thing.

I asked my mother one time why someone so rich and young and beautiful had died, and she shook her head and said, "No one knows why, Maryanne. Maybe being so rich and young and beautiful all at the same time is more than the human heart can bear," and then she never spoke of it again.

I had heard rumors that she had taken her own life. I did not know if it was true, and I wasn't about to go asking her children.

Maybe having to wake up and look at Earl Wade every day—that scary face he sometimes had—finally killed her.

I remember when it happened. I remember how me and Nancy were on our own for weeks. Lillian Wade died in October of 1952, and we saw Michael infrequently until after that Christmas. Even though the Wades were about as Whytesburg as the Rockefellers, everyone was stunned by the news. I heard she was a *drinker*, but that meant nothing to me. I liked to drink—soda, water, orange juice, pretty much everything. I figured it was maybe a polite way of saying something else entirely. But it wasn't until the spring of 1953 that we saw Matthias and Catherine and Della and Eugene again, at least for any length of time. Then—slowly, but surely—things started to come right again. Except for Eugene. Eugene was still Eugene, but he was like a quieter version. He still laughed, but he never laughed for long. He still smiled, but the smile seemed more an effort than a pleasure. He never really talked to me directly about his mother, but he made reference to her often. He was fifteen years old by then, and I think he took it the worst of all of them. He always had his books with him, and every once in a while I'd see him drift a little, but he'd always come back, you know? He was still Eugene, however, and Eugene was just a little older than me. If I had to be honest, which I would never have been, I would have said that of the two of them—Matthias and Eugene—I loved Eugene just that little bit more. There was something sensitive and artistic about him. Whereas Matthias had to force himself to learn poems to impress Nancy, Eugene just knew them. He talked about things he'd read and films he'd seen, and he was always the one who brought the best records to play.

But that day, that Thursday in August of 1954, thoughts of Lillian Wade and what had really happened were the furthest thing from all our minds, it seemed.

We walked a little way toward the Five Mile Road, and then Michael told us that we were going to wait there for Matthias and the others.

"Where are we going?" I asked him.

"Everywhere and nowhere," he said. He lit a cigarette then, and—just like always—Nancy asked him for one.

"Not a prayer, Miss Nancy Denton," he replied, just as he always did.

It was a game—and a silly one at that—but there were so many such games between Nancy and Michael, and no matter how many times they played them, they never seemed to tire of it.

We heard them before we saw them. They came on bikes—all four of them. Eugene and Della had lollipop sticks wired to their spokes, and the noise they made was like a thousand children clattering sticks along a picket fence.

It was a sight to behold—Della and Eugene and Matthias cater-wauling over the hill, hollering like fire sirens, whooping and squawking like banshees. And then there was Catherine some way behind, and you could just tell from the way she looked that she had been sent as supervisor yet again. Catherine would escape as soon as she could. She would return to the house alone and get back to whatever it was that Catherine Wade got back to. She was younger than Matthias, but still there was always something of the boy in Matthias. My ma told me that girls grow up faster, as if that were something to be grateful for. Seemed sad that anyone would be better by having less of their childhood.

And then it was all noise and laughter and wisecracks and bottles of soda being shaken and sprayed, and Della with her hair soaking wet and sticky and Michael just standing there watching over us all like the grown-up that he was.

"The river," Matthias said. "We have to go to the river."

Eugene was laughing like a mad thing. It was good to see him laugh. It made me happy.

"Come on, then," Catherine said. "If we're headed that way, then let's get going."

"You don't have to stay, Catherine," Michael said. "I can take it from here."

"But my father—"

"Is off at one of the factories, I am sure," Michael interjected, "And will be none the wiser unless someone tells him. You go off and enjoy your day. I'll look after this lot."

Catherine reached out and touched his shoulder. Nancy didn't see her; otherwise Catherine would have gotten an icy look.

"Thanks, Michael," Catherine said. "That's really kind of you."

"It's nothing," he said, and then he turned and started off toward the river.

Catherine took her bike and headed back the way she'd come.

Nancy ran after Michael, and then me and the others went after her.

I walked with Matthias and Della. Eugene was up ahead a little way. He kept glancing back at us, almost as if he wanted to make sure that we didn't drag behind.

I smiled at him. He smiled back. I felt the color rise in my cheeks.

He was such a handsome boy. He had these deep, dark eyes, and the line of his mouth was just like his mother's. If he'd been a girl, he would have been so beautiful. I remember thinking that, and though it seemed such a strange thought, it also seemed to make perfect sense.

"You didn't bring the record player?" I asked Matthias.

"I'll go back and get it later," he said. "We have food, though. We made a great picnic, didn't we, Della?"

"Apart from stinky boiled eggs," she said, and she wrinkled her nose.

"That's funny," Eugene said, "because those eggs said the same thing about you."

She stuck her tongue out.

Eugene did the same, crossed his eyes, and Matthias sighed and shook his head like they had already tried his patience sufficiently for one day.

And then we were at the river, and Nancy was already ankle deep in the cool water. Michael was seated against the trunk of a tree, and he smoked his cigarette and watched us as we shed our shoes and socks and went on down there.

Eugene said how he would catch a fish with his bare hands and we'd eat it for lunch.

"You'd no more catch a fish with your bare hands than catch a ride on a moon rocket!" Della shouted, and he splashed her once, twice, and it was all downhill from there.

Had Catherine been there, she would have had words to say, but Michael just watched us, laughing at our foolishness, and it seemed like the happiness we felt somehow reached him in a way that he needed. Looking back, maybe it reminded him of a time before the war, before everything that happened to him out there, and it was somehow *healing* for him.

Half an hour later, five drenched troublemakers stumbled up the bank and lay on the grass in their sodden clothes, but the sun was high by then, and it seemed like no time at all before we were dry.

That was what was different. *That* was the thing that seemed so strange. Time was flexible, almost liquid. When I wanted it to go quickly, it went slowly. When I wanted it to drag its heels, it ran full tilt to the finish line.

"So, where's this fish?" I asked Eugene.

"I nearly had him . . . I did, really," he said, but he was kidding me, and I pushed him.

He grabbed my hand to stop himself falling, and even when he righted himself, he didn't let go. Just for a moment, a moment while the world waited, he held my hand and looked at me. I felt my heart go *bump*, and even though I should have been embarrassed, I was not.

"I will get you a fish, Maryanne," he said. "One day, I will get you a fish . . . I promise . . ."

And then the moment was gone. He released my hand, and like a record slowed down on the turntable that suddenly resumes its speed, the world caught up with us and everything came to life once more.

I glanced around, expecting to see Della and Matthias and Nancy looking at us, but they were elsewhere, laughing among themselves, oblivious to what had happened.

And then it was as if nothing had happened. We were all together again, Michael telling us to stay in the sun until our clothes dried off.

The morning became the afternoon, and Eugene and Matthias brought the picnic baskets from their bikes. We sat out beneath the canopy of a tree and unpacked everything. Michael told Della he would give her fifty cents if she ate a boiled egg, but she would not.

"They smell *so* bad," she said. "I can't bear the thought at all."

So Michael ate three. He had his cheeks all full of boiled egg, and Della couldn't even look at him.

Michael laughed so much, he nearly choked.

"*So* disgusting," Della said. And then she looked at Nancy like a disapproving aunt and said, "Such a disgusting man, Nancy."

And Michael nearly choked again, because Della was so serious, and she said it like she really meant it.

After we were done eating, we lay on the grass, and Michael made up stories about a man so tall he could reach the stars from the sky and put them inside his hat. He carried some in his vest and some in his shoes, and one special star he kept tucked behind his ear in case of emergencies. And he used the stars to light the way for lonely travelers and ships lost at sea, and sometimes he used them to help people find what they were looking for. It was a beautiful story, but ever such a little bit sad, and now I can't remember how it ended.

I just remember that when he was done we were all quiet, and it seemed like an eternity before anyone said a word.

And when someone spoke, it was Della, and she said that she wanted to dance.

Matthias said he could take the picnic baskets back and fetch the record player. Della said she didn't want to go home, but we could all see how exhausted she was. She was barely able to stand.

"I'll come too," Eugene said, and I didn't know whether he was leaving to make Della feel better, or leaving because he didn't want to be with us anymore. It could have been either. Eugene was both considerate and lonely, compassionate and a little sad. He was sensitive, it seemed, to all things and all people. The death of his mother had caught him unaware, kicked him off balance, understandably of course, and the quiet moments that swallowed him seemed to swallow him whole.

Eugene looked at me. Perhaps he saw that flash of disappointment in my eyes.

He mouthed something. Was it *Sorry?*

My imagination, I guess.

Eugene no more loved me than I loved . . . well, I don't know what.

I tried to smile, but there was a lump in my throat. Perhaps there was a premonition there, a sense that not only was I saying goodbye for the evening, but that I was saying goodbye to something a whole lot more significant. It was only August, the second week, and summer stretched out ahead of us like some endless road. We would just keep on walking toward that sunset, but that sun would never really set, and it would always be hazy and warm and beautiful, and beneath everything there would be the sense that here we were witnessing the best time of our collective lives. It could never be better than this. Better than this was not possible.

But this moment was a punctuation mark, a hesitation, a scratch on the record.

I watched Eugene as he took Della's hand and started toward the bikes. Della looked back and smiled. She gave a little wave, as if to let us know that even though she could not stay, she wished she could stay more than anything in the world . . .

I raised my hand. I looked away, and then they were gone.

Michael said we'd walk down to the field at the end of Five Mile Road, the last field before the trees started, and we would meet Matthias there.

And so we walked—Michael and Nancy up ahead, me trailing behind, pushing my bike, already feeling the weariness of the day in my heart and in my bones. Evening was threatening the horizon. The cicadas were warming up for their nightly performance. We all knew the day would soon be closing, but no one wanted to think about that.

I had so wanted to dance with Eugene. I had so hoped he would ask me. I had already decided that I would wait for two songs, and if

135

he didn't ask me, then I would ask him. But he had gone home, and I would have to dance with Matthias, and though I didn't mind, it was not what I had wished for.

I had felt so bold and brave. Maybe it was seeing how Nancy looked at Michael and wishing that one day I would be able to love someone that much. I would have to feel bold and brave another day. And there would be other days just like this one. I believed that then. I really believed it.

It seemed that living could not have been easier or better or more fun.

It seemed to me that being fourteen years old was the best thing in the world, and I never wanted it to end.

It would end, of course. I knew that. But had I known *how* it would end, I would have run a thousand miles from that riverbank at a hundred miles an hour, and I would have kept on running until I burst right open and fell stone dead to the ground.

But I did not know, and so I stayed right there and kept on smiling as wide as wide could be.

There is no way you could have known, they say, but you do not believe them. You believe you *could* have known and you *should* have known.

Ignorance is bliss, they say, but only in the moment.

Ever after, what you did not know is the greatest single burden the human heart can bear.

23

Caroline arrived at seven. She did not ask about Gaines's mother; nor did she ask about the Denton girl. The words Gaines had shared with her had served to quiet her on the subject, at least to Gaines himself, though he knew she would be sharing rumors and hearsay with friends, with her own parents, with the townsfolk she knew. There was nothing Gaines could do about it. All he wished for was the official charge, arraignment, bail application and refusal, and then Webster would be shipped up to Hattiesburg, maybe Jackson, to wait on remand while the rest of the investigation was pursued. Gaines was optimistic that such a sequence of events would be rapid and straightforward. There was more than sufficient circumstantial evidence to warrant the charge and arraignment, and there was no doubt in Gaines's mind that Mississippi attorney general, Jack Kidd, would move very swiftly. Such a case would be reviewed at circuit court level here in Whytesburg by Judge Marvin Wallace, and Wallace would drive on down from Purvis to hear it as soon as Gaines needed him. The trial itself, however, would go up to the county seat at Branford to be heard by Judge Frederick Otis. Wallace wouldn't give bail, and Otis wouldn't give anything at all. Otis was as tough as they came, way past the point of no return on anything resembling *the new attitude* toward criminals. It had begun in the early sixties, the viewpoint that men should first be considered men and only secondly as lying, murdering, cheating scum. A political and ethical shift, perhaps best exemplified by the official closure of Alcatraz by Robert Kennedy, the viewpoint being that people who perpetrated such crimes as rape and murder were victims themselves, that rehabilitation was a more humane consideration when it came to confronting the grim and terrible truth of who these people really were. Gaines did not possess a viewpoint worth mentioning. He fulfilled his legal requirement as an officer of the law and left such decisions to the lawyers and the courts. His sole duty was to deliver Lieutenant Michael Webster into the hands of the attorney general of the state, and his job would be done until he was called to testify. Kidd would waste no time in jury selection; he would bear no laxity in the defense preparation; Kidd would want Webster tried, sentenced, and on up to Vicksburg as soon as was realistically possible. Such a case would be inflammatory and volatile. Had Nancy Denton been a black girl, it would have been a different matter, but she was not. She had been white and pretty and vulnerable and sixteen. She had been strangled and butchered. The crime had been perpetrated twenty years before, but Webster would hang for it, and Mississippi would hang him as slowly as was possible.

His mood notwithstanding, Gaines felt it right to share a few words with Caroline. He asked her about the date.

"Got my own way," she said. "We saw *The Sugarland Express*."

"Doesn't surprise me in the slightest," Gaines said.

"That's mean," she said. "I'm very considerate. Why do you have to say a thing like that?"

"You're a girl," Gaines replied, smiling. "Ultimately, whichever way you look at it, you always get your own way."

"And you're basing this on your vast personal experience with the female sex, I suppose?"

"Now who's mean, eh?"

"You know me. I give as good as I get."

"Anyway, you had a good time."

"And you, sir, are changing the subject."

Gaines audibly sighed. "Seriously, Caroline, I am not having another conversation with you about my love life."

"Wouldn't say there was enough of a love life to have a conversation about," she retorted.

"My, my, we do have our claws sharpened today, don't we, young lady?"

"Hell, John, even my mom asks about you. She says it's not normal for a man of your age to be single for so long. She says she has a friend—"

"Enough now," Gaines replied. "I am not having your mom set me up on a blind date with some fifty-three-year-old widow from Biloxi."

"She's not a fifty-three-year-old widow, and she's not from Biloxi. She's less than forty, and she looks like Jane Fonda."

"Does she, now?"

"She does."

"Well, if she's less than forty and looks like Jane Fonda, what the

138

hell is she doing single and getting set up on a blind date by your mom?"

"You are an ass, John Gaines. Sometimes you are such an ass."

"Watch your mouth, or I'll have you arrested."

Caroline smiled. She shook her head resignedly, once more disappointed with the lack of enthusiasm Gaines demonstrated for her mother's matchmaking efforts.

"One day I will get you out on a date with someone, John."

"I am sure you will, Caroline. Like I said, girls always get their own way in the end. Now I have to go to work. Call me if you need me."

Caroline went in to see Alice. Gaines collected his hat and headed out to the car.

Gaines was into the office at ten past eight. He found Hagen and Victor Powell in the lobby. Powell wore the church-suit expression.

"What you delivered last night . . . ," Powell started. He looked at Hagen, as if for moral support.

"Far as I'm concerned, we've got enough to get him charged and arraigned," Gaines said.

"Wallace will do that here?" Hagen asked.

"Wallace will do the arraignment and the post-indictment, but the trial will go on up to Otis at Branford," Gaines replied.

"You think he'll plead?" Powell asked, a nod toward the stairwell that led down to the basement.

Gaines shrugged. "We shall see."

"Well, let's get it done, then," Hagen said. "No reason to wait."

"I'm gonna go speak to him awhile," Gaines said. "I'm gonna tell him what we're doing, see if he has anything to say. I'd like to know if he's going to enter a plea. You call Wallace in Purvis, let him know we're going to need him in a little while, and get a public defender down here as well. Try Tom Whittall, and if he's not available, get Ken Howard."

"He hasn't asked for one yet," Hagen said.

"He hasn't been charged yet," Gaines replied. "Regardless, I want someone down here."

"Will do," Hagen replied. He turned and headed toward his own office.

"Helluva mess you got here," Powell said.

"We got what we got," Gaines replied. "I just need it to go by the book, no problems, and Webster out of here as soon as possible.

Right now, there seems to be a lot less noise than I anticipated, but I'm expecting trouble."

"Couldn't blame anyone," Powell ventured. "There's people here who knew her. Her ma still lives here, for Christ's sake. It's gonna be a big deal, no two ways about it. Right now, the only thing that Webster's got going for him is that he's white and a war vet. He'd have been a black fella, then they'd have burned this place down to get to him."

"You don't think I know that?" Gaines asked, a rhetorical question.

"Well, rather you than me," Powell said. They shook hands. Powell left. Gaines went to check on Hagen. Hagen had spoken with Wallace but had failed to reach either Whittall or Howard.

"Keep trying," Gaines said. "Go out there if needs be. I want at least one of them here when we charge him."

Gaines left the office, headed back across reception, and took the stairs down to the basement.

24

Webster still possessed the thousand-yard stare, but now he wore a faint smile on his lips.

He did not verbally acknowledge Gaines's appearance at the cell bars, but Gaines knew Webster was aware of him.

"I went to your room," Gaines said.

Webster nodded but did not speak. He continued to look right through Gaines.

"I found newspaper clippings . . . and I found a Bible and an album of pictures . . ." Gaines paused. "Pictures of you and Nancy Denton and some other people."

"There is something I did not tell you," Webster said.

Gaines stayed silent.

"After I found her, I knew I had to do something. After it was done, I told Matthias what had happened. He agreed with me that it would never work if I said a word about what had happened."

Webster turned and looked at Gaines. His expression was one of compassion and understanding, almost as if he were now detailing some selfless act of kindness he had performed.

"Who?"

"Matthias Wade."

"Matthias Wade? You're talking about *the* Wade family?"

"He knows all about this, Sheriff. He told me never to say a word, but now she has been found, and now you know the truth, so I cannot keep our secret any longer . . ."

Gaines, leaning there against the bars, closed his eyes. He felt the cool metal against the side of his face. He felt a fist of tension in his chest, a sense of disturbance and agitation in his lower gut, and he knew he was dealing with something far beyond his experience. Michael Webster, for whatever reason, however it might have happened, was completely insane. Yet, in that moment, his expression was as blank and untroubled as a cloudless sky.

There seemed to be no connection between what he believed he had done and what he had in fact done. In his own mind, he had been kind, compassionate, humane. In reality, he had perpetrated the very worst kind of horror against a teenage girl.

"Speak to Matthias if you can," Webster said. "He will explain these things far better than I can." Webster looked up at Gaines. "We were always together. Me and Matthias, Maryanne and Nancy. Catherine was there. Eugene, too. Everyone loved her, but I think Matthias loved her the most . . ."

Gaines recalled the images in the photo album he'd found. Was that who those people were? The Wades as children? Was that the next angle on this thing, that Michael Webster and Nancy Denton had been friends with the Wades all those years ago?

This, very simply, opened up another world entirely. The Wades were a dynasty, a Southern institution. More than just landowners, they were businessmen, industrialists, and politicians. Michael Webster was a broken-down, crazy war veteran, and whatever connection he believed he still had with the Wades was more than likely some internal creation, a figment of Webster's dark and troubled imagination, some alter ego carried somewhere within his psyche that answered questions, rationalized his actions, provided explanations for what he was doing and what he had done.

However, if Michael Webster and Matthias Wade had been complicit in the death of Nancy Denton, that was a can of worms that needed to be opened.

"I went out to where you told me, and we found the remains of a metal box, just as you said we would," Gaines continued. "We are now going to charge you with first-degree murder, and we are going to get you arraigned before Judge Wallace. More than likely, they will ship you off to Hattiesburg or Jackson while the investigation proceeds. I imagine they will want a psych evaluation done as well, just to determine whether or not you are in a fit mental state to face these charges in court."

Webster nodded as if he understood precisely what Gaines was saying, though the expression in his eyes suggested he was in some other world entirely.

Gaines crouched down, his hands around the bars, and he looked through the gap at Webster.

Webster held his gaze as Gaines spoke.

"I need to know if you understand what's happening here, Mike," Gaines said. "Twenty years ago, a sixteen-year-old girl called Nancy Denton was strangled, mutilated, and buried. You did these things to her. You took her from her family, from her mother, and you did these things to her, and now you have to face the consequences of what you did." Gaines paused. There was nothing, not a flicker in Webster's eyes.

"Are you listening to me, Mike? Can you hear what I am saying?" Webster nodded. Just once. A dip of the head, nothing more.

"If you get a psych eval and they say you're crazy, then you will spend the rest of your life in some state psychiatric facility. If they say you're not crazy, and they say that you were aware of what you were doing, then you will be jailed for life. Do you understand?"

Webster leaned forward. He rested his elbows on his knees and steepled his fingers together.

"We have seen things that others could never imagine, Sheriff. Not even in their wildest nightmares. More beyond even that. Such things should not be witnessed by men, but then men created all of this, so why should they be excluded from seeing it? You cannot bear a burden like that in any regular life. We survived, perhaps. We did not die, but we might as well have. The people that we were when we shipped out were not the people we were when we returned. You arrive home and everyone and everything has changed. People you've known your entire life are unfamiliar and yet familiar. Their expressions, their voices, their attitudes, they are all different. And then you see that they didn't change at all. You did. And those you figured knew you the best seemed to be the ones who recognized you the least. Like something else had assumed possession of your body while you were away." Webster nodded as if imparting some profound truth. "We will always be irregular. We will always be outsiders. We will never belong again."

He cleared his throat, and then he smiled as if remembering some past moment of happiness. "Sometimes you'd see lights in the trees, haunting the ground, you know? Like ghosts that were afraid of heights. Flares and gunshots fireworking out into the blue-black sky. And the rain . . . that monsoon rain coming down like lead shot, painful, finding you through flak jackets and shirts and vests, even through your skin, like needles into the marrow of your bones. And you could still hear movement out there, and you know without thinking whether it's Jap or grunt. And after a while it feels like you have never been anywhere else and you will never be anyplace else. There is no before; there is no afterward; there is just where you are and what you are doing." Webster paused, opened his eyes. They were tear-filled. "You come home, Sheriff, and you think the world you knew no longer exists. But it does. The world is just the same,

143

but you see it differently because you are no longer the same. Now you see everything in a different light. You understand that life and death are inconsequential, that there is the physical and there is the spiritual, and they come apart and they are different, and they are not one and the same at all." A single tear rolled down Webster's cheek. "I found her, Sheriff. I found her there by the side of the road after it was all done, and I was right back there, right back in the war. But this time I could do something to help, and though it wasn't much, it was something. I did the best I could, and if that was wrong and I have to go to prison for what I did, then so be it. That is what I am telling you, and I really haven't anything else to say."

And Gaines, watching Webster, listening to every word he uttered, had nothing to say either.

He stood up, took a deep breath, and then walked to the stairwell. He did not look back at the man. He could not bring himself to. There was too much truth among the madness, and he could not let it take hold of his thoughts.

25

Ken Howard had arrived by the time Gaines came up from the basement. Hagen had already gotten him up to speed.

"Wallace'll see him as soon as we're ready," Howard said. "He'll want this off his hands as fast as he can. I would too. Fucking nightmare. Jesus, it hardly bears thinking of . . . that poor girl." He shook his head. "I may be a public defender, but sometimes I wanna do as little as possible to interrupt the prosecution." He shook his head resignedly. "So give me all you've got. I'll get it written up for Jack Kidd, and let's see if we can't get the crazy son of a bitch out of your cells as fast as possible."

"That'd be appreciated," Gaines said.

"You okay, Sheriff?" Hagen asked. "You sick or something?"

Gaines felt left of center, but no more than he would have expected considering what he was dealing with. "I'm all right," he said. "Too long in the company of a crazy man."

"I can take care of the paperwork with Ken," Hagen said. "Give us a couple of hours, and then we'll get back together again and see if there's anything else we need."

"Sure," Gaines replied. "I'll do that."

"Hagen here says you got some more evidence . . . some photos or something?"

"Circumstantial," Gaines replied. "Pictures of Webster, the girl, a whole crowd of other people when they were younger. I need to start finding out who they all were. Those are the people that need to answer questions. I also have a bunch of muddy clothes, for what good it'll do me. I don't know why I bothered bringing them, but they're here anyway."

"Good 'nough. You deal with that. Hagen can let you know if we've got any questions." Howard headed toward the offices behind reception, Hagen on his heels

Gaines hesitated for a minute and then fetched the photo album from the evidence room. He took it to his office, asked Barbara to get him some coffee, and then he sat poring over the images for a good hour. First of all, there was Michael Webster. Beside him, right there in his shadow, was Nancy Denton. They were unmistakable. In some of the photos, he was in uniform. He was a handsome man, and the attraction between him and Nancy was undeniable, irrespective of their age difference. In their orbit, present in most of the pictures—sometimes alone, other times in twos and threes—were five others, at least three of whom Gaines believed to be related. These had to be the Wades. They ranged between the oldest—another good-looking young man, blond-haired, a strong jawline, perhaps late teens or early twenties—all the way down to a pretty brunette girl whose age Gaines couldn't guess. The young man was more than likely Matthias, the others his siblings. But it was Nancy who always drew Gaines's eye. So bold, so bright, so beautiful, this was not the fragile and pale specter that lay on Powell's mortuary slab. This was a girl so full of life, she just seemed to burst out from every image.

Gaines called Barbara into the office, asked her to get the album over to Hagen's brother, Ralph.

"These people here, all seven of them . . . I need him to take photos of these pictures, enlarge them, and get me seven head shots, four by five at least. Tell him to choose the ones that give the best full-face images, okay?"

"By when?"

"Soon as he can do it. Thanks, Barbara."

After she'd left, Gaines sat for a while amid his own thoughts. He felt he should stay, but there was little he could do that Hagen would not do just as well. Simply stated, if all went according to protocol, Webster would be away from here within hours.

He decided to go home—just to check on his ma, just to change the scenery for a little while. He drove slowly, put some music on the radio, turned it off after just a moment. There was a tension in his neck, his shoulders, the length of his back, and he knew it would not dissipate without a good night's sleep. The previous night had been restless, fitful. He had dreamed. He remembered some small sense of what had taken place in that dream, but it was vague and indistinct. The girl had been there. That much he knew. Until this case was done with, until he'd had some time away from Webster and all that this entailed, he believed that the girl would stay with him.

And then he thought of Matthias Wade. Had Webster actually spoken to Matthias Wade? Was there a second person involved in what had happened to Nancy Denton? Had Matthias Wade been an accomplice in this murder, or was this some other figment of Webster's wild imagination? And who was Maryanne mentioned now by not only Judith Denton, but Webster as well? Was she some part of this, too? Were Matthias Wade and this Maryanne among the people in the picture album? Soon enough he would have pictures he could show people. He would ask Eddie Holland. Eddie had been in Whytesburg his entire life, and Gaines felt sure he would be able to identify some, if not all, of the kids in the album.

It was as he drove that the first fragile thread of doubt started to wind itself around his conviction. He tried to let it go, but it had snagged his attention like a fishhook. Until then, he had not doubted that Webster was not only crazy, but also a liar. Any human being capable of doing what had been done to Nancy Denton was no doubt capable of killing her in the first place. In fact, the strangulation—especially from a man with a military background, a man trained to kill, a man *experienced* with killing—was nothing compared to the dissection of the torso, the removal of the heart, the subsequent bizarre ritual performed. It was medieval in its brutality.

So why was he now considering that Webster might not be lying? That he had not strangled the girl? The answer was simple. The photographs. That was all there was, yet those images communicated something wordlessly, yet so clearly. The way he looked at her. The way she looked at him. The *tension* that seemed to exist between Nancy Denton and Michael Webster, even in those flat twenty-year-old monochrome snapshots.

That was how this seed of doubt had been planted, and that seed was drawing light and moisture from somewhere.

But no, Webster was insane. Psych evaluations would be done. Men with a far greater understanding of the vagaries and vicissitudes of the human mind would ask adroit questions of Webster and determine that he was as far gone as it was possible to go. He had to be. To have done what he'd done, he *had* to be. And besides, all that immediately concerned Gaines was the securing of Webster someplace other than the Whytesburg Sheriff's Office basement. The case itself would unravel over the coming days and weeks, and if there were other people involved, well, Gaines would get to them as and when that was needed.

However, Webster's words still haunted him.

I did the best I could, and if that was wrong and now I have to pay for what I did, then so be it.

And the expression in his eyes, that sense of wonder, that sense of desperate hope that this terrible, terrible act had been of some benefit.

It was incomprehensible that anyone could have thought such in a way, but Webster did, and he seemed convinced of his own rightness.

Gaines drew to a stop against the curb and got out of the car. He walked on up to the house and called for his ma from the hallway.

"Back here," she said, and Gaines was surprised to hear her voice from the kitchen.

"What are you doing up?" he asked her. "Where's Caroline?"

Alice Gaines looked at her son like he'd cussed in church. "You think I'm gonna spend every waking hour of whatever time I have left lying in that sickbed? Lose the use of my legs, I would. I'm feeling okay, John. I'm feeling all right this morning. Just wanted to get up for a little while and check that the world was doing okay without me."

"What are you doing?" he asked. "Making some tea? Let me do that for you."

"How about you let me make you some tea? How about that for a change, eh?"

Gaines nodded. "Sure, if you're okay."

"You just sit down. I'm fine here. Took one of them pain pills that Bob Thurston keeps leaving for me, and I'm feeling all energetic and sprightly." She smiled, reached out and touched her son's cheek with the palm of her hand.

"So, what's happening with your man?"

"He's gonna be arraigned this morning, and then they'll take him on up to Jackson or Hattiesburg, I should think."

"He have anything new to say for himself?"

"Nope, same old crazy stuff, aside from something about the Wades. Seems he and Matthias Wade were friends all those years ago."

"Is that so?" Alice said, and she turned to look at her son.

"What?"

"Is your man saying that Matthias Wade was involved in this terrible thing?"

"He's said a lot of things, Ma. Most of them don't make the slightest bit of sense. He says that Matthias Wade knew of what had happened, that he told him not to say anything. That's all he's said so far."

Alice shook her head. She closed her eyes for a moment.

Gaines frowned. "Do you know Matthias Wade?"

"Oh, I don't know him, John. I know *of* him. A great many people know *of* him, and that's about the same number of people who wish they didn't."

"Why do people wish they didn't know him?"

"It's the whole family, John. They're not good people. They're bad people, crazy people. They have always been surrounded by tragedy, and most of it I can guarantee they have created for themselves. Like the terrible thing that happened to Earl Wade's wife. No one says it out loud, but that poor woman drank herself to death. I know she did. Lord knows what that did to those kids, watching their mother in that state. Anyway, be that as it may, it was Matthias, the eldest boy, that I thought of when you told me what had happened to that little girl here . . ."

"Why? Why would you think of him in connection with Nancy Denton?"

"Because of what happened back in Louisiana. It happened a long, long time ago, and it may have nothing to do with anything, but when you told me what happened here, I couldn't help but think of it."

"Louisiana? The Wades are from Louisiana?"

"You go look them up, John. Morgan City, 1968. There's a great many people who know a great deal more than I do about the Wades. This all happened back in the early part of sixty-eight. You were gone to the war. And besides, Morgan City can't be much more than a hundred miles or so from where we're sat right now. Word travels, and people like the Wades have a way of getting their stories heard by whoever wants to hear such things."

"So what happened?" Gaines asked.

"Couple of girls were killed, John. That's all I know for sure."

Gaines looked at his mother, eyes wide. "And you didn't think to mention this to me yesterday?"

She smiled. "It was a long time ago, John. Six years. A different city, a different state. I thought of it, and then I didn't think of it. Besides, I didn't want to be putting ideas into your head that didn't belong there."

"So what are you saying? You think Matthias Wade killed a couple of girls in Morgan City six years ago?"

149

"I'm not saying anything, John. At least nothing I can be certain of. Let's just say that there are folks who think he did a great deal more than that, John . . . a great deal more than just kill them."

Gaines leaned back in his chair. He looked at his mother, the way she just stared back at him, and he could feel such a tension in that small kitchen, the very same kind of tension he'd experienced as he'd driven Webster to the Sheriff's Office.

Matthias Wade was someone with a history, it seemed. Michael Webster said that he'd told someone about what he'd done back then, twenty years before, and that person was Matthias Wade.

From the moment Nancy Denton's body had come up out of that black filth, from the moment Gaines had seen that cross-stitch pattern running the length of her torso, he had known that something terribly wrong had taken place in Whytesburg. He wondered then how much worse than his imagination it really was.

Perhaps there was a truth in letting the dead lie where they were, never to be disturbed, never to be woken. What had he started here? What had he brought back to Whytesburg? What had he released?

"You go ask folks in Morgan City," Alice Gaines said. "You go ask them about the Wade family . . ."

26

Gaines went out to the front hall as the phone rang. It was Hagen.

"We have a problem," he said. "Ken has been on the phone with the AG, and the AG says we don't have enough to hold Webster—"

"What the hell are you talking about?"

"Whatever he told you doesn't count as a confession. There was no lawyer present when he spoke to you. The things we dug up are circumstantial, irrespective of the fact that he told us where to dig, at least according to Kidd. And the release document might not even count for much either."

Gaines felt his stomach drop.

Hagen must have sensed it.

"John . . . tell me you didn't forget."

Gaines opened his mouth to speak, but the moment of hesitation was sufficient to give Hagen his answer.

"Really?"

"Richard . . . I had it in my pocket. I meant to—"

"Then we're screwed for whatever we took from the motel, as well. Jesus Christ, John . . ."

"But Webster still gave me his permission to search the room—"

"He's saying he didn't."

"What?"

"What I said, John. Webster says he never spoke to you about going into his room. He says he never gave you permission."

"Are you serious? Are you fucking serious?"

"Serious as it gets, John. Ken Howard started to get everything together. He called the state attorney general's office, spoke to Kidd himself, explained what we had, what we didn't have, and that was the first question Kidd asked. I told him we had a signed release document, but he said that any PD could overturn that based on Webster's state of mind. Now I have to tell him that we don't even have that. Kidd also asked whether Webster had been given any opportunity to make any calls for his own defense lawyer. I had to tell him that he hadn't made any calls that I knew of. Kidd said that Webster needed to be given his phone call, and he made it. Spoke to someone called Wade. You know any lawyer called Wade?"

Gaines couldn't speak for a moment. "You're kidding me," he said. "Oh, you have to be fucking kidding me, Richard . . ."

"What? You know this guy?"

"And then what happened? Is that when he said he hadn't given me permission to search his room?"

"After the phone call? Er, well, yes, I suppose so. I didn't think the two were related. I had to give him the call, and then when Ken Howard went back to Kidd and started explaining about the evidence, that's when the thing came up about the warrant. Kidd asked which judge had signed the search warrant—Wallace here in Whytesburg or Otis in Branford—and we had to tell him that there wasn't a warrant and that you'd brought that photo album and the clothes in from Webster's motel room. Kidd asked us to check with Webster if you'd discussed that with him, whether you could go in the room and take stuff, just as a backup to the document I said he'd signed, and Webster said no, that he hadn't said any such thing. We went back to Jack Kidd, and he said that the document more than likely wouldn't hold water, that anything you took was now inadmissible, and that we didn't have enough to hold Webster for more than another couple of hours. He said we had to release him once the twenty-four hours were up. He also said you should retract the murder charge. You can't charge him for the same thing twice, and right now there's no way any judge would arraign him on what evidence we actually have. I checked the book, John, and Webster was brought in here just after one yesterday afternoon. It's now eleven. We have two hours to come up with something solid, or we gotta let him go."

Gaines could not believe his own forgetfulness and stupidity. Kidd would have words with him—he knew that much—and they would not be encouraging.

"I'm on my way," Gaines said.

Gaines went back to the kitchen, told his mother he'd see her later, and he left the house. She called after him, asked him what was going on, but he didn't stop to explain.

Webster was seated in precisely the same place as he had been when Gaines had last seen him. Nothing about the man had changed, except there was something in his eyes, something that spoke of defiance perhaps. Maybe Gaines was misreading everything he was seeing based on what he now knew, but there was certainly a change in the man's demeanor and attitude.

"Tell me about Matthias Wade, Mike," Gaines said.

"What about him?" Webster asked.

"Who is he? How do you know him?"

"Who is he?" Webster echoed. "He's just a guy, just a man like you or me. How do I know him? I know a lot of people. I know people who know people. I met him a good while back."

"And you just spoke to him on the telephone, right? Deputy Hagen told you that you could make a phone call, and you called Matthias Wade?"

"I called Matthias, yes."

"Why him? Why did you call him, Mike?"

Webster shrugged. "Loneliness, maybe. Because he's my friend. It gets pretty quiet down here on your own, Sheriff."

"And this is the same Matthias Wade that you knew twenty years ago, the one who knew what happened to Nancy Denton, right?"

"Sure, it's the same Matthias Wade. There's only one Matthias Wade."

"And what about your motel room?"

"What about it?"

"You told me I could go on in there and make a search—"

"I think you're mistaken, Sheriff. I don't recall ever saying such a thing—"

"What the hell are you talking about? I asked you. I remember asking you clear and simple, Webster. You said I could go on in there and make a search—"

Webster said nothing immediately, and then he looked unerringly at Gaines. "Did I sign anything to say you could?"

"Wade told you to say this, didn't he? He told you to say you'd given no permission for the search, didn't he? Where the hell is he, Webster? Where the hell is this Matthias Wade?"

"Right now? I have no idea where he is, Sheriff."

Gaines stepped back from the bars. He was enraged, incensed, could barely control the anger that he felt. He had been stupid; there was no question about it. He had intended to have Webster sign the paper, had even carried it in his pocket, but in his eagerness to discover what was in that motel room, he had let it slip his mind.

Now everything that he had done was undone.

Gaines looked at his watch. It was twenty minutes after eleven.

One hour and forty minutes, and there would be little he could do aside from release Webster and begin the investigation over again.

Gaines left the basement, went back to his office, and called the state attorney general, Jack Kidd. He was on hold for a good six or seven minutes before Kidd came on the line.

"Hey, Sheriff Gaines," Kidd said. "I hear you done fucked the dog on this 'un."

"Seems that way, sir."

"Ain't a lot I can do to help you, son. I heard what happened down there, and there's no one more sorry about that son of a bitch walking out on you than me. As you know, I got three girls myself. Okay, so they're all growed up and whatever, causin' their own brand of trouble on a daily basis, but it ain't so long ago that they were young 'uns like your Nancy Denton. It's a sad state of affairs when the law steps in to stop you getting justice, but that's the way it is, and that's more than likely the way it's always gonna be—"

"But—"

"But nothin', son. You done an illegal search and seizure. Better to have sealed that place up tight, put some of them deputies and whatever you got down there around the place, and then get that warrant. Goin' on in there, regardless of what Webster might or might not have said, was never a good course of action. Hell, even if he'd signed up a permission slip like your deputy told me he done, that wouldn't have stood for a great deal in my court. From the sound of it, even the dumbest PD coulda gotten that discredited because of the man's mental state. And now I hear you didn't even get that paper signed. You gotta do this shit by the book. You know that. And this thing about some box buried someplace with the girl's heart in it? Jesus, I never did hear of such a thing. But you done dug that up as well, I hear. Should've got him to tell you where it was on tape. Shoulda got someone in that there office with you to corroborate your report, son." Kidd cleared his throat just as Gaines started to respond. "And frankly, Sheriff Gaines," Kidd went on, "I figured you smart as a whip, but you just proved yourself as dumb as the rest o' them rednecks you got down there."

"You're telling me there is nothing—absolutely nothing—we can do to hold on to Webster?"

"Well, Hagen tells me he said he done cut up the girl, but he didn't kill her, right?"

"That's right."

"So right now he could be charged with removing evidence from a crime scene, destruction of evidence, for that's what she was, you see, little more than evidence of a murder. He could be charged with them two, but you done messed it up with this illegal search. Hell, man, I've even had Ken Howard on the phone telling me my job, and he's the guy who's supposed to be defending your boy! Bottom line, son, is that the law is the law, and whether we like it or not, we have got to charge him with something else and hope to hell he doesn't make bail, or we gotta let him go. Whichever way you decide, you got about two hours to do it."

Gaines was left speechless.

"So?" Kidd said. "Whaddya wanna do, son?"

"Pull the murder charge, charge him with destruction of evidence, obstructing an ongoing investigation—"

"That will fly like a fuckin' dodo, that one will. Nancy Denton's murder wasn't even discovered when he took the body. There was no *ongoing* investigation. Do like I said. Charge him with removing evidence from a crime scene and destruction of said evidence. That's what you got. Who you got down there on circuit? Wallace?"

"Yes, I have Wallace on circuit, but I got Otis for Branford County."

"Wallace is as sharp as Otis. If Wallace can find a way to hold him without bail, all well and good, but I doubt it. Those are misdemeanors, because the nature of the original crime does not influence the severity of the removal or destruction charges, you see?" Kidd exhaled audibly. "Shee-it, Gaines, you really done fucked the dog."

"I know it. I don't need to keep hearing it."

"Well, maybe you do, son, just to make sure you keep your damned wits about you and don't pull some dumbass stunt like this again."

"Yes, sir."

"Now, go disappear whatever paperwork you had on the first-degree charge, and get some new paperwork on the lines for the removal and destruction. Get Wallace out of whatever watering hole he's in and tell him to call me if he has any questions."

"Will do."

"And, Gaines?"

"Yes?"

"Use your head and not your heart on this stuff, will you? I know how big a deal this is for you folks. I don't even remember the last time Whytesburg had a murder, and I don't think you've ever had anything as bad as this, even when old lover boy Don Bicklow was running the show. It's a tough one. I get that. But the tougher they are, the more you gotta color inside the lines. People get emotional, son, especially when it comes to dead kids, and you gotta be real careful what you say and do. Otherwise you wind up with Webster back on the street and a lynch mob on your hands. You understand me?"

"Yes, sir, I do."

"Well, good. Now, go hustle up that paperwork and let's see if we can't keep the crazy son of a bitch off the streets for a little while longer. Sure as hell he's been free and easy for twenty-some-odd years, but that don't mean we have to give the crazy motherfucker another day of liberty if we can help it."

Kidd hung up.

Gaines followed suit. He stood there for a while, felt the speed and force of his own heart in his chest. Kidd was right. He had pulled a dumbass stunt. He had let his emotional reaction to the whole thing override his senses.

Gaines went back out front and called for Hagen. He told him what was needed on the paperwork. Hagen got going, and Gaines started calling around for Judge Marvin Wallace.

27

At 1:45 p.m. on the afternoon of Friday, July 26, 1974, Michael Anthony Webster, ex-lieutenant, US Infantry, appeared before Judge Marvin Wallace, Whytesburg Circuit Court, to face two charges, first that he did remove evidence from the scene of a crime, said evidence being the body of Nancy Grace Denton, and second that he did inflict destruction and damage against said evidence, such being the person of Nancy Grace Denton.

Webster was handcuffed on each side, to his left Officer Lyle Chantry, to his right Officer Forrest Dalton. He stood immobile and implacable as the charges were read out, and when Wallace asked Howard if the defendant wished to plead, Howard merely said, "At this time, the defendant wishes to plead no contest to both charges." Webster had decided to leave his options open as to a guilty or not guilty plea. Perhaps he was hoping for a deal from the DA.

"Prisoner is held over in custody," Wallace said. "Bail is set at five thousand dollars."

Howard stepped forward. "Your honor, I have to ask that the prisoner be released on his own recognizance. He is a decorated war veteran and has no prior convictions in this or any other state. I do not consider that he is a flight risk."

"Understood, Counsel, and your comments are noted. However, due to the severity of this crime, I am setting bail at five thousand dollars." The gavel came down. The discussion was over.

Howard glanced at Gaines. Gaines knew that Howard had had no choice but to contest Wallace's ruling. A failure to contest could be considered tantamount to inadequate defense representation at some later appeal hearing.

Webster didn't say a word, and only when Chantry and Dalton started moving did he move with them.

They took him back across to the Sheriff's Office.

Wallace stopped Gaines as Gaines was leaving the courtroom. "That bail amount was the highest I could set," Wallace explained.

"I tried to get it higher, but there was no additional justification. Anyway, I think someone like Webster has as much chance of raising five grand as he does fifty."

Gaines thanked Wallace and headed back to the office to check that Webster was safe and secure in the basement.

Once again, Webster was silent and immobile.

Gaines did not want to speak to him, didn't want to see him. He returned to his office.

Hagen was there. He had an anxious expression on his face.

"What?"

"Someone is here to pay Webster's bail."

Gaines sighed resignedly. "Let me guess. Matthias Wade, right?"

"In reception. He says he has the money to pay Webster's bail right now."

"You have got to be fucking kidding me," Gaines said, his dismay evident in his voice. "This is some kind of fucking stunt . . ."

He stepped around Hagen, headed for the door, then hesitated and turned back. "Find out something for me, would you? Morgan City, Louisiana. Check which parish it is. Get hold of the sheriff there and tell him I need to see him."

"Will do," Hagen said.

Gaines went across the building to reception. As he approached the desk, a man stood up and smiled at him.

Immediately there was recognition. Gaines had been right. This was the eldest of the Wades from the pictures in the photo album. The blond hair had grayed, but that jawline was unmistakable.

"Sheriff Gaines," he said. "My name is Matthias Wade, and I am here to assist my friend Lieutenant Webster. I understand that his bail has been set at five thousand dollars . . ."

Wade was not a tall man, perhaps no more than five seven or eight. At first there seemed nothing specific or extraordinary about his appearance. He was dressed casually—an open-necked shirt, a plain sport jacket, a pair of dark blue slacks. He was in his early forties, Gaines guessed, clean-shaven, his features forgettable, ordinary. His eyes were blue-green, and to any outside observer, he would have seemed relaxed, unhurried, friendly, even extending his hand in greeting as Gaines cleared the desk and stood in front of him.

Gaines did not shake the man's hand.

Wade paid the absence of courtesy no mind. "So," he said, "how do we do this?"

Gaines smiled awkwardly, more disbelief than dismay. "Seriously, you are here to pay Webster's bail?"

"Sure I am," Wade said, and there—in his tone—were the last vestiges of New Orleans. This man was as Louisianan as Gaines, but he had lost the greater part of his accent somewhere along the road.

"You are what to him? His friend? His counselor?"

"I am just a businessman, Sheriff Gaines. I have a number of small businesses here and there, but I am also a good citizen, a hard worker, and I like to think of myself as somewhat of a philanthropist. Seems to me that when a man has some good fortune in his life, he carries a responsibility to share that fortune with those less fortunate."

"And Webster is one of these less fortunates?"

"Michael Webster is a war veteran, as I believe you are, Sheriff. He seems to have been given a raw deal, wouldn't you say? Some men seem to be able to integrate themselves back into society. Take yourself, for example. You served your country at war, and now you are home and you are continuing to serve your country. You are perhaps made of stronger stuff than Lieutenant Webster. Some men are just a little more fragile than others, you know?"

"You're telling me that *he* is the victim here? Are you fucking crazy?"

"Oh, I am saying nothing of the sort, Sheriff. I am well aware that a heinous crime has been perpetrated here, that some poor girl was abused and murdered, but this was all twenty years ago. Memories might be long, but evidence is short-lived for the main part. I just think that Michael Webster is incapable of establishing any kind of stable ground for his own defense, and I would like to think I am assisting him with his constitutional right to fair representation when it comes to his day in court."

"This is just bullshit, if you don't mind me saying, Mr. Wade. This is just the most extraordinary bullshit I have ever heard. I have a killer in my basement, plain and simple. And even if he was not directly and solely responsible for her death, he was certainly responsible for what was done to her after she was dead." Gaines stopped. "But, then again, I don't need to detail what he did to her, do I, Mr. Wade?"

Wade frowned. "I'm sorry, Sheriff. I don't think I understand what you mean."

"He says he told you. All those years ago, he told you what

he'd done, and so, according to your friend, you are as guilty of withholding this as he is . . . ?"

Wade smiled. Then he started laughing. "I think Lieutenant Webster is even more fragile in his mind than I understood him to be. Or perhaps it was just a simple misunderstanding, much the same kind of misunderstanding as you and he had when you thought he'd given you permission to search his motel room . . ."

Wade let the statement hang in the air.

Gaines had no response.

"So," Wade said eventually, "who wants my five thousand dollars?"

28

Before and after combat there was fear. During combat there was only adrenaline. It seemed that the two were mutually exclusive—one could not exist in the presence of the other. Other emotions did not register or apply. It was only later, much later, that anger, hatred, disbelief, horror, wonder, and awe overtook everything else. It was only later that mental and emotional reactions impinged upon the physical, that hands shook uncontrollably, that nervous twitches assaulted muscles. Gaines was familiar with this delayed response, and though he did not feel anything so overpowering as that, he did feel rage and dismay as he watched Michael Webster leaving the Sheriff's Office with Matthias Wade.

He knew it would be no time at all before Judith Denton got word of what had happened. The thought of facing her, of trying to explain himself, how he had failed her, how he had failed Nancy . . .

It was five minutes past three on the afternoon of Friday, July 26th, and Gaines watched silently as Matthias Wade walked Webster to a plain sedan parked outside the office. Where they were going, Gaines did not know. Neither Webster nor Wade had to tell him. Perhaps Wade would take Webster to his own house. Perhaps Gaines would not see either of them again.

Had Gaines applied the letter of the law, Webster would more than likely still be in the basement, if not there then en route to Jackson or Hattiesburg to be remanded until trial. If Gaines had acted according to standard protocol, then some of the things that Webster had told him would be on tape, Ken Howard would have been present, and bail would never have been granted. But Gaines had acted impulsively, without due consideration, and now Webster was going to leave nothing more than a trail of dust behind him as he was chauffeured out of Gaines's custody.

Gaines turned away from the swiftly vanishing sedan and went back to his office.

Hagen was waiting there for him. "Morgan City is St. Mary

Parish," he said. "I spoke to the deputy, and he said that the sheriff wouldn't be back until about five."

"His name?" Gaines asked.

"Sheriff is Dennis Young. Deputy is Garrett Ryan."

"I'm going over there," Gaines said. "It's about a hundred or so miles. I'll be there by the time he gets back from wherever he is."

"You want I should come with you?"

"No, you stay here."

"Judith Denton's gonna turn up, ain't she?"

"I reckon so."

"What do I tell her?"

"You tell her whatever you think she can stand to hear, Richard. I don't know what to say. I fucked it up, and now Webster is out on the street and we have no way of keeping tabs on him."

"And what's the deal with this Wade character? You know anything about him?"

"Nothing 'cept rumor an' hearsay. That's why I want to go on up and see Sheriff Young in Morgan."

Hagen sighed audibly. "Jesus, this is a hell of a mess, ain't it?"

"As good as any I've seen before," Gaines replied.

Hagen left the office. Gaines called home, was relieved when he got Caroline instead of his ma.

"Gonna be late tonight, more than likely," Gaines said. "Have to go on out to see someone. You got any plans for later that I'm upsetting?"

"No, I'm good, John," Caroline replied.

"Appreciated, sweetheart. Don't know what I'd do without you."

"You'd cope, I'm sure," Caroline said. "Safe travels."

Gaines hung up, fetched his hat down from the stand behind the door, headed on out to the car, and aimed it west toward Slidell.

Crow-wise, it was little more than a hundred and fifty clicks to Morgan City. Use the bridge, it was heading for 180. The other route—I-12 from Slidell to Hammond, south on 55, cutting through the outskirts of New Orleans and turning west again toward Morgan—wasn't significantly greater. Gaines decided to bypass the bridge and go around the northeast route. Perhaps the traffic through the center of New Orleans would be fine, but he didn't want to risk it.

It was ten after five by the time Gaines pulled up in front of the St.

Mary Parish Sheriff's Office on Bayonard Street. Against a broken-yolk sunset, the office was lit up bright and bold like Fenway Park. Beside it was an expanse of waste ground, across it a collection of rusted machinery—large, awkward insects now weakened by time and weather, unable to resist the wild suffocation of vines scrawled all around them like indecipherable calligraphy. A yappy, discourteous dog chained to a tractor tire argued with Gaines as he crossed from his car to the main entrance.

Sheriff Dennis Young was not the man Gaines expected. Had Gaines been asked what he expected, he wouldn't have been precise, but Young was not it. Maybe he expected some kind of old-school Huey Long character, one of those who figured the world should solely be plantations, all of them run as fiefdoms by people such as himself. To Gaines, Young looked like the sort of person who'd never had friends, more than likely never would. Not meanness, but wound up so tight that no one would ever get under his skin. Most people believed there was room enough in their lives for a host of visitors and a handful of permanents. The impression Young gave was that there was room enough for himself and himself alone. Aloneness was not necessarily loneliness, but as far as quality of life was concerned, it seemed to Gaines that such an existence was a handful of small change instead of a fistful of bills.

Sheriff Dennis Young, the better part of sixty, a good head taller than Gaines, looked directly at Gaines as Gaines entered the room. Young's expression was almost a threat, but his eyes seemed to carry a weight of sadness. Looked like a man who not only remembered the past, but longed to live there. He reminded Gaines of the hard-faced, bitter police veteran with whom he'd first been partnered. That man, the first day they met, had shook Gaines's hand roughly, slapped him on the shoulder, and said, "Well, hell, son, let's get you out there and see if we can't get you shot at or blown to kingdom come, eh?"

"Do for you?" Young asked.

"I'm Sheriff John Gaines, Breed County, Mississippi—"

"I know who you is, son. 'Parently, one of your people called here and said you was on the way. Who you is ain't what I asked."

"I'm here about Matthias Wade."

Young slowed down then. Had Gaines not been as intent, had he not been so aware of Young's every move, he perhaps would not have noticed it. There was a definite and tangible shift in atmosphere in that room.

163

"He's been around and about again, has he?"

"Yes, sir, he has."

Young smiled knowingly. He seemed to relax a mite, barely noticeable, but relax he did.

"He was always one for getting on and about into other folks' business."

"He's getting involved over in Breed County," Gaines said.

"Tell me what he's been saying."

"Not what he says, but what he's done. I had a guy called Michael Webster on a possible first-degree. World War Two veteran, crazy as a shithouse rat. Looks like he strangled a teenage girl down there a while back, and there was a fuck-up with a warrant and he was given bail. Wade came down and paid up the bail and took him away just three or four hours ago. Paid all of five thousand dollars."

"Did he, now?"

"Yes, Sheriff, he did."

Young nodded, and then he smiled. "The name's Dennis, son, just Dennis. After all, we is family, is we not?"

Gaines nodded respectfully. Maybe Young wasn't so impregnable after all.

"And you have a question for me, right?" Young prompted. "And I'm wonderin' if it has something to do with what happened back here in sixty-eight."

"That's right," Gaines said.

"What did you hear?"

"Nothing much. Word has it that some girls were killed."

Young smiled resignedly. "Oh, there is more than a word, my friend. We think he killed two little girls. Personally, I would stake my life on it. But it don't seem my life has a great deal of weight against the lack of evidence. What actually happened back then, and what we think happened, well, that's where the disagreements start, and to this day they have not ended. All we got right now is Matthias Wade walking the streets a free man, two little girls dead, and not an ounce of justice to share between them."

"Can you tell me about it?"

"I can tell you what I know," Young said. "Two girls, one ten, the other twelve, found strangled . . . left in a shack someplace out in the middle of no place special. Only thing that linked them to the Wades was that both girls were daughters of Wade-family employees. That was the thing, you see? It was such a fragile link, and there was nothing substantive we could use to bring Matthias

164

Wade in. He was—what?—maybe thirty-five years old at the time. He wasn't some clueless punk. He was a smart man, Sheriff Gaines, and more than likely still is."

"So what made you think he was responsible for the killings?"

"Some people you think are bad," Young said. "But there's some people you *know* are bad. He's one of them. Can smell his kind from a mile and a half away. Pompous asshole, telling us what we can and can't say to him. Son of a bitch. I know he killed those girls. I had him in here for two hours, and he talked himself around the countryside, saying how he didn't know squat about nothin', but I could read it in his eyes and the dark sack of shadows he has in place of a soul."

Young shook his head and sighed. "God didn't make many of them like that, but the ones he did make are awful bad." He paused to light a cigarette. "So tell me what you got over there in Breed." He leaned forward, his eyes all fired up bright with interest.

"Girl of sixteen years old, found buried in a riverbank. She'd been there for twenty years. Was a disappearance back in fifty-four, only come to light now, so to speak. Had her heart cut out, in her chest a wicker basket with a snake inside. She'd been strangled and then butchered postmortem."

"Jesus Christ almighty," Young said, and he whistled through his teeth. "What the hell kind of madness is that?"

"What happened to the two girls here?" Gaines asked.

"I can show you the files, my friend. You can look at the pictures, too. However, sounds like we had ourselves a church picnic compared to what you're dealing with."

"There are others who think that Wade was responsible for the deaths of these two girls?"

"I am not alone in my conviction, Sheriff. Whole heap of people don't see it could have been any other way. Wade is the baddest kind of son of a bitch I've ever had the misfortune of dealing with." Young shook his head. "Most folks is simple. Even the crooks and the crazies. You know what they're gonna say before they even set themselves down to the table. That's the thing that makes most of this job pretty straightforward. Someone gets killed around here, well, there's pretty much gonna be only two or three that coulda done it. Even with the housebreaking an' all that, you get some folks' place robbed, and a day later you got some dumbass son of a bitch tryin' to sell their shit in a bar three blocks from home. It ain't complicated because most people ain't complicated. But then there's others. Others who is intricate. Others who are a different kind of animal altogether. You just can't predict what they're thinking, nor what will pass their lips. And even when they do say it, well, it's just as likely gonna mean something different than how it sounds. Wade is a devious creature. He don't pretty much say nothin' 'cept if it's a lie. Easiest way to know if he's lying is to look see if his lips are moving. If his lips are moving, he's delivering up some kind of bullshit, and that's a fact. Those girls of ours, Anna-Louise Mayhew and Dorothy McCormick, went missing within three days of each other back in January of sixty-eight. They were both found together less than a week after Dorothy disappeared . . . Well, you can read the files and look at the pictures, and then you can tell me what kind of human being it is that can strangle little kids like that."

"And Wade was your only suspect?"

"Only suspect then, only suspect now. He was local, you see. Ran a whole heap of companies down around these parts, and after it happened, he got real busy quieting everyone down about it, newspapers suddenly deciding they weren't going to run the story and this sort of thing. And here we are six years down the line, and the likelihood of proving anything against him grows more impossible with every passing day. He has connections, you see? He has family down here, and the Wades are a family that will do whatever it takes not to have their name sullied by the taint of such things."

"I didn't get it at first, but these are *the* Wades, aren't they?"

"Only ones I know. More money than is decent. Sugar and cotton and crawfish and rice and soybeans and whatever the hell else they fancy. You look under the porch of a Wade house and you find everyone from the bank owners and the real estate folks to the governor hiding there. That family's been backhanding support to pretty much every political official that suits their business for five generations."

"And there was a picture album in Webster's room. Photographs of Webster with Wade and our victim, a girl called Nancy Denton. There are pictures of the other Wade kids, as well. And there was another girl that Webster mentioned, a girl called Maryanne?"

Young shook his head. "Can't help you there, son."

"So the question now is how come Matthias Wade would pay five grand to bail Webster out. Is he helping out an old friend, or . . ." Gaines stopped and looked at Young.

"That's a question beggin' for an answer," Young said. "But if I know Matthias Wade, you'll wind up askin' yourself a load more questions that don't belong, and you'll still walk away with nothing."

"You think I could take a look at those files?"

"Sure you can, son." Young leaned forward and lifted the phone. "Marcie, Get me them files on Mayhew and McCormick, would you? Bring 'em on in here for me."

Young set down the receiver. He lit another cigarette and smoked it in silence. It was no more than a minute before Marcie came in bearing an armful of dossiers.

She put them on Young's desk, backed up, and left the room.

There was no similarity in appearance between either girl and the other, or either girl and Nancy Denton. Young slid out the pictures one by one, and there was nothing that needed to be explained.

Both girls had been strangled. Bruising was evident around the base of their throats.

The more Gaines looked at the pictures, the more he noticed a strangeness around the eyes.

"Eyebrows," Young said quietly. "We think they were blindfolded with a heavy adhesive tape, and when the tape was removed, most of the eyebrow came with it."

Gaines looked at the rest of the pictures. He wanted to feel so much. He wanted to be shocked, enraged, upset, but he was not. Had he not seen what had been done to Nancy Denton, had he not been still submerged beneath the weight of conscience for his procedural omission, he might have been objective enough to suffer the expected emotions. But he was not. He had seen it all, if not here, then in war, and he just felt numb.

"And there really was nothing of any substance, evidence-wise, against Matthias Wade?" Gaines asked.

"No, nothing at all. Circumstantial stuff. The fact that both girls were daughters of Wade-family employees. Tire tracks near the bodies that were produced by the same brand of tires as could be found on one of Wade's many cars. It was a brief 'Yes, you did,' 'No, I didn't' back and forth, and then Wade got some heavyweight legal counsel in from Jackson, and that was the end of that. He was cooperative, polite, didn't give us any trouble, answered every question we asked him, gave us nothing to hang anything on, and then he upped and left without so much as a fingerprint to follow up on."

"But you really believe he did it," Gaines said. "You *really* believe he murdered these two girls."

"I don't believe anything, son. I *know* it. Either he strangled those girls with his own hands, or he was accomplice to it. Whichever way it went down, he knows what happened back then, and he ain't sayin' a word."

"Well, he's gotten himself involved with another dead girl now," Gaines said.

"Sure as hell looks that way," Young said. "And if you can nail him for that, then I would owe you a mountain of gratitude. Nothin' would give me greater pleasure than to see that son of a bitch brought to justice for something."

Gaines was quiet for a time, his attention still fixed on the display of pictures before him. "Would it be okay if I just sat somewhere for a while and made some notes about these cases?" he asked.

Young started to get up. "You just take whatever notes you like, son. In fact, you can take those files with you, back on up to Whytesburg. If you're gonna be followin' up on this, then better to have the original documents and pictures and whatnot. When you're done, you bring 'em on back here, okay?"

"That's very much appreciated."

"What'll be more appreciated is seein' that bastard pay for what he's done."

"I won't be long," Gaines said.

"You have all the time you need. I got a bunch of things to do. You let Marcie know if you need any help."

Young headed for the door, paused to grip Gaines's shoulder. "Good luck, son. Not that I believe in luck, but good luck anyway. Wade is a devious son of a bitch, like I said, and he's got more money than Croesus behind him. Maybe you're gonna see something I didn't and get him this time. Whatever the hell we think he's been doing, I can guarantee he's been doing a lot worse. That's the nature of this one. Too much money, too much time on his hands, and the devil makes plenty of work for idle hands, as they say."

"I appreciate your time, Sheriff," Gaines said.

"No problem. If you need more of it, you just let me know."

Young left the room.

Gaines sat there for a while, and then he started in on the first murder. Anna-Louise Mayhew, all of ten years old, left to visit with a girlfriend on the morning on Wednesday, January 3, 1968, found eight days later in St. Mary Parish, strangled and cast aside like an unwanted rag doll.

29

It was past ten by the time Gaines reached home. He shared no more than half a dozen words with Caroline before she left, checked on his ma, and then sat alone in the kitchen with Dennis Young's case files and his notes in front of him.

He had not seen Young again before leaving St. Mary Parish, but Marcie—Young's secretary and receptionist—had passed on a message.

"He told me to tell you that whatever you need, just call him or come on over."

Gaines had thanked her, told her to thank Young for him.

"A dreadful case," Marcie had commented. "Can't bear to think how it must haunt their families."

That was the thought that had assaulted Gaines's defenses with the greatest effectiveness.

A child that never was.

A child that was and then was taken away.

They were not the same thing, but they were close.

There were so many things he had wanted to feel back then, so many things he had wanted to say to Linda, but he had been little more than stunned and silent. Her pregnancy had heralded the beginning of a new life, a different kind of life, a life they had talked about, planned together, imagined as real. It had become real, and then it had been obliterated by one single, simple act of fate. Perhaps their child had never been destined to exist as anything other than a dream.

Gaines could remember the moment he had learned, the call that had come from the hospital where Linda had been rushed—unbeknownst to him—on that spring afternoon in 1961. She had been at work. He had seen her that very morning. Everything had been fine. Everything had been the same as every other day.

He was in the kitchen. He was drying dishes. He had the radio on, and they were playing "What a Difference a Day Makes" by Dinah Washington.

And then the call came.

He had asked them, "What's happened? Is everything okay?"

"You should come to the hospital, Mr. Gaines," the voice at the other end of the line had repeated. "Just come to the hospital now."

And he had gone, driving like a madman, knowing in his bones and in his heart that something terrible had happened.

And when he arrived, it was as if no one knew who he was or why he was there, and he had to ask three different people for help before a nurse finally asked him, "Are you Linda Newman's husband?"

And he had said, "Yes . . . not her husband, no . . . but yes, I am here to see her."

And the nurse had said, "She's in the ward on the left. Sorry for your loss."

"Loss?" he asked.

And the nurse had looked at him and realized what she'd said, that he hadn't known, that he didn't know. Her expression was ashen and troubled, and she turned and hurried away without another word.

Gaines had gone down there, to the ward on the left, and Linda was sitting upright, her back against the wall, the look in her eyes one of utter defeat.

He had approached her, and it seemed an age before she realized he was there, and then she said, "Oh, John . . . John . . ." And the tears had come like a wave.

Thinking of it in that moment, Gaines could feel the emotion swelling in his chest, but whatever depth of loss he might have experienced as a result of Linda's miscarriage was merely a thousandth of what the families of Anna-Louise Mayhew and Dorothy McCormick must have felt and must still feel. A thousandth of what Judith Denton was going through right this very moment.

Perhaps there was some small mitigation of pain to be derived from justice in such a case. To see the guilty brought to account for their crimes would at least have resolved some aspect of uncertainty and wonder. But here? Perhaps to have known that Matthias Wade had been suspected, questioned, and then to have seen him walk away without any further resolution would have been worse than no one being suspected at all. To carry the burden of knowledge and yet to be impotent, to see that knowledge denied and refuted by the continued presence of the man . . .

Can't bear to think how it must haunt their families.

And Judith Denton. She had lost her only child, and not through illness or accident, not through misfortune or misadventure, but by the hands of some unknown assailant, someone who simply put their hands around the girl's throat and choked her until she was dead. What must that do to a parent? What must that do to a human being?

The weight of grief and guilt and conscience would be unbearable.

How could I have protected her? What could I have done differently? Why didn't I drive her to the friend's house? Why did I let her walk out alone?

How could I bear a child, raise them, feed them, guide them through all the pitfalls and obstacles of life, and then lose them in a moment?

"We are not gods," Lieutenant Wilson used to tell Gaines. "We are just men. We are grown-up enough now to see that happy-ever-afters occur only in fairy tales. The young believe that bad will be balanced out by the good, and they imagine there are enough years ahead of them to see this happen. The old, having lived all those years, now see it's the other way around. If there is a God, then he is cruel and bitter and fickle, and men—made in his image—are equally cruel and bitter and fickle. Shit happens, and it happens all the time, and it keeps on happening, and most of the time there is no explanation for it. Life is random and unpredictable, and it doesn't stop coming at you. If you try to stop it, it will just crush you. If you slow down enough to try to understand it all, it will swallow you whole. Best you can do is understand as much of it as possible while you keep running."

Maybe Lieutenant Wilson, sideshow philosopher that he was, slowed down to try and see things better and the bullet that killed him caught up.

Gaines did not know, did not profess to know. Not just about Webster, not just about Wade, not about Nancy Denton and the two girls from St. Mary Parish, but most everything. He did not pretend to know anything. He did not know why his mother was sick and yet did not die. He did not know why Michael Webster had cut open Nancy Denton's chest and replaced her heart with a snake. He did not know what he could say or do that would lessen the sense of guilt and stupidity he felt for removing evidence from Webster's motel room without a damned warrant.

All he knew—*all* he knew—was that he needed to pick Webster up again in the morning, get him into an interview room once more, and have him say enough to justify Judge Wallace signing a warrant to search that motel room again. There had to be something else there, some aspect of incriminating evidence that could be brought to bear upon Webster, something that would tie him up with a charge, an arraignment, a trial date. Or perhaps Webster could be made to say something again, but this time on tape, in the presence of Ken Howard, in the presence of any damned person.

And Wade? Matthias Wade was an entirely different game altogether. If there was some way to tie Wade in with the Denton killing, then perhaps the Mayhew-McCormick double murder could be revisited.

There had to be some connection. There had to be. If not, then why the hell would someone like Matthias Wade be willing to pay five thousand dollars to get Michael Webster out of jail? It went beyond one old friend helping another. Gaines was sure of that.

Had Webster been telling the truth? Had he merely found the girl at the side of the road, and—in some warped and delusory reality—imagined that opening up her chest, removing her heart, and replacing it with a snake would somehow serve a purpose? Webster had said that he *had known what to do*. Those had been Webster's words. How had he known what to do? From Al Warren, the man who had been there for him in Guadalcanal?

Had Webster merely been the means by which Nancy Denton's body could be disposed of? Had Matthias Wade told Michael Webster where to find the body, what to do with it, where to bury it? And had this ritualistic performance been undertaken merely to confuse and confound the issue, to create the appearance that there was something more sinister and arcane going on beyond the abduction and murder of a teenage girl?

Was this all a game of smoke and mirrors, the entire thing played out by Matthias Wade and his unwitting confederate, Michael Webster?

These were the questions that plagued Gaines. His mind grew tired, his eyes gritty, and every time he closed them, he saw those same images—the discarded bodies of the two Morgan City girls, now not only on the kitchen table before him, but also there behind his eyelids.

Gaines went for the bottle of bourbon on top of the refrigerator. He drank two inches neat, felt the raw burning in his chest, and knew it would help him close down, if only for a few hours.

He did not know what would transpire next, but in his wildest imagination, he could not have anticipated that which woke him merely four and a half hours later. And that, in truth, was not the worst of it. There was a great deal more to come, and John Gaines, sheriff of Breed County, he who had seen the nine circles of hell, started to believe that the war had followed him home.

30

The filth and mud beneath the waterlogged wood, the smell of smoke and charred earth and all that this brought to mind was nothing in the face of what was revealed as the blackened timbers of Lieutenant Michael Webster's motel room were hauled away by the fire chief, his deputy, and the other attending officers of the Breed County Fire Service

They hauled away those timbers with ropes affixed to the rear of the fire truck, and those timbers snapped and released clouds of hot ash and sparks skyward.

It was close to dawn, and the sky was flat and bleak with a low ceiling and almost without color at all. The trees were like scrimshaw etchings, indistinct and fragile, like pictures incompletely developed in a tray of solution.

It was a monochrome world, and John Gaines stood aside from the fray near the adjacent cabin, and when he touched the wooden wall of that cabin, he could still feel the heat of the fire that had been extinguished.

Webster's cabin was little more than a shadowed footprint of its former self, and Gaines knew what they would find within.

The fire chief's name was Frank Morgan, and it was Morgan who came to Gaines with the news. "He's in there," he said. "Well, *who* it is might be difficult to establish, but that's Vic Powell's job, not mine."

"Burned beyond recognition?" Gaines asked.

"Decapitated beyond recognition, more like, and he ain't got his left hand neither," Morgan replied.

"Seriously?" Gaines asked. "They cut off his head and one of his hands?"

"Sure did."

"Jesus Christ, what the fuck is this?" Gaines said, dismayed and confused, almost disbelieving his own ears. In a matter of no time at all, Whytesburg had become the kind of place one read about in inflammatory and melodramatic novels.

Now Gaines would no longer need to concern himself with what additional evidence might be found in that motel room. Regardless of what was discovered, Webster would no longer be the primary target of his investigation.

Gaines did not doubt for a second that the headless cadaver in the ashes of the fire was Webster. The only thing that now needed to be determined was who had killed the man, and—more important—why.

Matthias Wade stood right there on the horizon of Gaines's thoughts, but perhaps that was too obvious. Had Matthias Wade killed Nancy Denton and then used Webster as the cleanup guy? And if so, why the thing with the heart and the snake and the wicker basket? What the hell was that all about? Wade had bailed Webster out, and this was the result. Would someone such as Wade dirty his own hands in such a manner? More than likely not, Gaines believed. But then Wade had enough money to cover any expenses incurred in such a situation. Was that what had happened here? Had Wade paid someone else to get rid of Webster and thus pre-empt any possibility that Webster would implicate Wade in the Denton killing? And why remove the head and hand? To delay identification of the body? To make a point? If so, what message was Wade trying to send? Was this some other kind of ritual, like the snake in the box?

Gaines was adrift. There were no bearings here, no context within which he could place this thing.

Now he had two dead and fewer answers than those with which he'd started. At least with Webster alive, there had been some direct, tangible link to the Denton girl, even if Webster himself hadn't been solely responsible for her murder. Now, with Webster dead, it was—essentially—a new investigation.

The only name on the page was Matthias Wade, and Wade was protected by money, by influence, by social position, by reputation. There would be no stopping by for a few words just to clear up a couple of outstanding questions. Now Gaines would need something concrete and incontrovertible to even get onto the porch of the Wade house.

Gaines walked back to his car. He stood there for a while and watched as the body was brought out of the ashes and laid down on the ground. Powell had been called. He would arrive shortly. But Gaines did not want any discussion with him. Not now, not at this moment. What he wanted to do was see Judith Denton. He wanted to tell her that Michael Webster was dead. He wanted Judith to know that Webster had suffered his own retribution for the part he'd played in the desecration of Nancy's body, irrespective of whether or not he'd been responsible for her murder. He also wanted to ask her about this *Maryanne* and where she might be found.

Gaines left word with Frank Morgan that he could be reached through the office if Powell needed him.

"Tell him all I need now is an ID on the body and anything he can tell me about how the head and hand were removed."

"Will do," Morgan replied.

Gaines drove away. It was a little after six in the morning, Saturday, the twenty-seventh, and he believed that delivering this news to Nancy Denton's mother would somehow lessen the burden of guilt he carried for his mishandling of the Webster search and seizure.

31

John Gaines stood for a while on the porch. The screen was open, the inner door unlocked, but he did not enter. It was still early, the sky barely bleached of darkness. He guessed Judith was still asleep.

He knocked one more time, waited a minute longer, and then walked around behind the property.

There had been a fire out there as well, a small one for sure, but still a fire. Looked like she'd been burning clothes. A melted plastic chair seemed to grow from the ground. What must have once been a doll, nothing left but half the face, one eye watching Gaines unerringly.

Surely Judith Denton had not burned all her daughter's clothes and toys? Would she do that? Keep them for twenty years in the belief that the girl would return, and now—aware of what had really happened—destroy them all? Desperate, grief-stricken, unable to bear seeing such reminders of her now-dead daughter, had she dragged everything out into the yard and set it afire?

Gaines's thoughts darkened.

This did not bode well.

He backed up, went up the rear steps, and found the door unlocked.

Stepping into the walkway that opened into the kitchen, Gaines was overcome with a sense of real dread. He knew something was wrong. He could not ascribe that feeling to anything but intuition, but he knew that something was wrong.

Gaines found Judith in the front room of the house. She had on her widow's weeds. Her complexion was pallid and milky, the kind of complexion acquired from spending daylight hours in darkness. The expression she wore was one of open admission, as if prepared to accept culpability for anything of which she might be accused.

Gaines knew one thing for sure. There wasn't anything to see around dead folk. Whatever was in there—whatever *élan*, whatever *animé*—was gone in the moment of dying. As if the door had

178

opened and the shock of death just propelled them away. Didn't matter how long you stared into the eyes of a corpse, the light was good and gone.

Gaines did not wonder about the nature of Judith Denton's death. He did not inspect the pill bottle that sat on the table beside her chair. Such things were merely details. He did find a note, and on it was printed just ten words, and they said all that needed to be said.

If I go now, maybe I will catch her up.

Gaines knew that despite the fact that all human beings were made of the same parts, none were put together the same way. Maybe the glue was different; maybe the seams were in different places. Different people, faced with the same circumstances, saw entirely different situations. Responsibility was nothing more than that which each individual considered the best response to any of those given situations. Judith Denton had lost her daughter. There was no husband, no other child to care for, perhaps no parents alive. There was no reason to stay, or perhaps—more accurately—there was far greater rationale and reason in trying to follow her daughter to whatever might be waiting for her.

Seemed to Gaines that you could always run out of things to laugh about, but things to make you cry? Hell, they just kept on coming.

Seemed like all the madness of the world had been rushing at him for as long as he could recall.

He had tried to hide, but he was shit out of luck on that front.

There were things that aged you a decade in an afternoon, if not physically, then mentally, emotionally, spiritually.

These were such things—three dead in as many days. A child, a suspected killer, a mother.

Gaines did not believe that there was murder here. He believed that what appeared to have happened was precisely what had happened. Overcome with grief and loss, Judith Denton had burned her daughter's clothes and then taken her own life by overdose. Or perhaps she had burned the clothes and then—overwhelmed by the guilt of what she had done to the memory of her daughter—had considered that the only option she had was to follow her and say sorry. Sorry for destroying your things, sorry for challenging your memory, but—most of all—sorry for failing to protect you against the vagaries and vicissitudes of this terrible life.

Here was real humanity, Gaines thought. Among the lost and fallen, among the disillusioned and forgotten. Among the ones who did not make it.

Maybe some people wanted to die simply because they were so damned tired of trying to stay alive.

"Oh, for Christ's sake, Judith . . . why didn't you come and talk to me?" Gaines said out loud, but he knew that even if she had, it would have changed nothing. Perhaps he might have said something that delayed the inevitable, but that would be all that would have happened.

Just as in war, if your time was up, then it was up. Sometimes you got postponed by an hour or two, but that was all.

Gaines walked to the front of the house and opened the door. He crossed the path, reached his car, radioed Barbara Jacobs at the desk, told her to find Bob Thurston and get him over to the Denton house.

"When you're done, call Victor Powell and tell him we got another body to collect."

Barbara—an unquestioning sense of discretion and professionalism in all she did—simply said, "Judith?". To which Gaines replied, "Yes, Judith."

"Oh Lord almighty," Barbara said, her voice almost a whisper.

"Think He's been absent around here for a few days, wouldn't you say?" Gaines said.

Barbara did not rise to the comment, but merely said, "I'll get Bob over there right away."

Gaines smoked a cigarette while he waited. He returned to the yard, once again surveyed the charred earth, the few remaining fragments of child's clothes and playthings. This was it now. This was all that was left of the Denton family line. It had ended here.

Still, Nancy's body and the box that had held her heart were at the morgue. Now Judith would join them alongside the headless corpse of Lieutenant Michael Webster.

There would be no great desire to see this investigation go any further. Gaines could imagine—even now—the conversations that would take place. Webster had killed the girl. He got his just deserts. No one could cry for a man like that. Gaines should just let it go. The truth had died with Webster, and it was best left that way.

But Gaines could not leave it that way. Not at all. Not simply because of his official duty, but more a sense of personal obligation to Nancy and her mother to find out what had really happened.

And if this investigation indicated beyond all reasonable doubt that Michael Webster had acted alone, that he had strangled Nancy, that he had desecrated her body as part of some bizarre ritual, then so be it. But if there was some indication that another person had been involved—someone such as Matthias Wade—then Gaines would not let it go until the truth was out. He *could* not. It was against his nature, against his own dictate and integrity, and right now—faced with this madness—it seemed that these commodities were all he possessed. Someone had perpetrated a dark and terrible wrong here, and that someone needed to be identified.

Then, and only then, could it all be laid to rest.

If it was Wade—if he had been complicit in the murder of Nancy Denton, in the killing of Michael Webster, perhaps also in the murders of Anna-Louise Mayhew and Dorothy McCormick—then it would be his life for theirs, and there was no other way to see it.

As had been said so many times in Vietnam, sometimes you just had to kill people to show them the error of their ways.

Gaines went back into the house. He sat with Judith Denton until he heard Bob Thurston's car pull up outside. He knew she'd spent the last twenty years alone, and—crazy though it was—it now seemed right to stay with her as long as he could.

32

Thurston made a preliminary examination and signed the certificate of death.

"Every indication of a self-administered drug overdose," he told Gaines.

"What did she take?"

"No question there. It's Seconal. I prescribed it for her to help her sleep."

"When?"

"She came to see me on Thursday evening."

"You think she planned this and just said she was not sleeping?"

Thurston shrugged his shoulders. "I have no way of knowing, John. She'd just lost her daughter; she looked exhausted, utterly devastated. I know that in such situations, people lose their appetites and cannot sleep, and those two factors contribute greatly to the depth of depression they fall into. More often than not, a couple nights of good sleep give them sufficient strength to carry on and get through it."

"I understand," Gaines said.

"So Vic is en route?"

Gaines nodded. "He has a headless Michael Webster to get to the morgue, and then he will come get Judith."

"You think Webster killed Nancy?"

"I don't know, Bob," Gaines said. "I thought I was sure, but now I'm not."

"So who?"

"I have ideas," Gaines said, "but nothing substantial or evidenced."

"Heard Matthias Wade bailed Webster out."

"You heard right."

"You think—"

Gaines shook his head. "It's best not to think. It's best just to look, to see what's there, what's not there, and try and figure out the bit that's missing."

"You know there was a case back in—"

"I already went out there last night," Gaines interjected. "I spoke to Dennis Young. He showed me the pictures and the case files."

"They never got anyone for that, far as I recall, but I heard rumor that Matthias Wade had been in their sights."

"So Young told me."

Thurston shook his head. "They say an apple doesn't fall far from the tree, but if ever you wanted proof of that, you'd only have only to look as far as Matthias and Wade Senior."

"You know the father?"

"Sure, as much as it's possible to know someone like that. They live in a different world, John. The money they have, the political influence, the businesses they own. Matthias is just one of four, far as I know, two sons, two daughters, but the father is ever-present, lives in some huge place between here and Morgan City. Don't know where the other kids are, but Matthias has always lived with the father. He's the oldest, will inherit the lion's share of everything, I should imagine."

"Wade Senior's name?"

"Earl."

"And the mother?"

"Lillian. Long since dead. She was an alcoholic. It's all predictable stuff, John. Heard Earl Wade had mellowed in recent years, but I find that hard to believe. As a younger man, he was a great deal more active in managing his businesses. Got himself involved in politics for a while. There was even talk of him running for governor, but that never came to anything. Anyway, that's all history, but whatever is said, and whatever can be said about the Wades, they are a real honest-to-God Southern dynasty."

"Well, Matthias is the only one I've met, and he looks like five and a half feet of stiff shit in a handmade suit."

Thurston laughed, and then he stopped as suddenly as he'd started. Perhaps he'd forgotten where he was for a moment, seated right there in Judith Denton's kitchen while her dead body sat no more than ten feet away.

"I better be going," he said. "You okay here until Vic arrives?"

"Sure am," Gaines replied.

"Well, let's hope that this is the end of it," Thurston said when he reached the door.

"Somehow I don't think it is," Gaines replied, but Thurston did not acknowledge the comment.

Gaines heard the front door open and close. He heard Thurston's car start and then pull away.

Gaines was left in silence in the Denton kitchen. He thought about Earl and Matthias Wade, about the alcoholic wife, the two girls found in January of 1968, and considered the fact that he had been in Vietnam for only three months when those little girls lost their lives.

Whichever side of the world you were on, there was always some kind of crazy bullshit going down. Wars of race, of religion, of territory, of political agenda, even wars within the minds of madmen, compelled to do truly terrible things to other human beings with no logical reason at all.

There was no acceptance, no reconciliation, no explanation. Until man understood his own mind, there would never be freedom from such things.

Plato had been right. Only the dead had seen the end of war.

The small war that now occupied Gaines's thoughts raged on, and the Dentons and Michael Webster were the only ones out of it for good.

33

Judith Denton's body was transferred to the morgue by Victor Powell a little after noon. From initial indications, it appeared that she'd been dead for approximately twelve hours.

"Midnight, one, maybe two in the morning," Powell told Gaines. "I'll give you a more accurate time once I've done the autopsy."

Powell hesitated. There was an unspoken question on his lips. "Did she know that Webster was being released?"

Gaines shook his head. "I don't know, Victor."

"I heard about the thing with the warrant," Powell went on. "We make mistakes, John. We're human. Mistakes are often what we do best. You can't beat yourself up about it."

Gaines did not reply, and they did not speak again. Gaines merely watched Powell drive away in the long white car, and he wondered if there would be further dead before the truth of Nancy Denton's killing was revealed. *If* it was ever revealed.

Gaines headed back to the office. He took the Morgan City files from his desk and put them in the evidence locker. He spoke to Hagen, told him to chase up the Webster findings.

"And you?" Hagen asked.

"I'm going to visit with Matthias Wade."

"On what basis, John?"

"Oh, just a social call. I thought we might perhaps have watermelon juleps on the veranda."

Hagen smiled sarcastically. "I doubt he'll give you the time of day."

"We shall see."

The Wade estate went as far as Gaines could see both left and right. Somewhere close to two thirty, he stood in front of the main gates and looked down a driveway that snaked away between groves of trees shrouded in Spanish moss, a dense curtain of foliage that made the house itself invisible. Gaines did not know what parish he was in, perhaps St. Mary's, maybe now St. Martin's. The site seemed to follow the curve of the Atchafalaya River away from Morgan City. To the west was New Iberia, to the right was Donaldsonville, and Gaines would not have been surprised to learn that the Wades owned every acre of land in between.

At the gate there seemed to be no means by which visitors could make their presence known, but it was not long before someone appeared from among the trees to the right and walked toward the entrance.

The man was well built in the upper body, a bull neck, a blunt and brutal fist of a face, the range of expressions spanning little breadth beyond anger, obstinacy, and displeasure. He wore a permanent scowl, as if anyone appearing at the gate was interrupting something of great importance.

He did not speak. He just looked through the bars at Gaines and raised his eyebrows.

"I need to speak to Mr. Wade," Gaines said.

"Which one?" the man asked.

"Matthias."

"And who are you?"

"Sheriff John Gaines."

The man didn't nod, didn't acknowledge; he simply turned and walked the way he'd come and disappeared into the trees.

Four, five minutes passed, and then the gates started opening.

Gaines hurried back to his car, started the engine, drove slowly through the gates, and headed along the drive.

Past the first bend, and then the same man appeared from between the overhanging boughs. He stared at Gaines for a moment, and then he raised his hand and pointed to his right.

The Wade house itself came into view in stages. It must have spanned a good hundred or hundred and twenty yards, but parts of it were obscured behind further trees, and down to the left there was a separate arrangement of smaller buildings that were fashioned in the same architectural style but were evidently a good deal younger than the main house.

On the second floor was a balcony that ran the length of the entire facade, and it was in the center of this that Gaines saw Matthias Wade. Wade stood immobile for just a moment, and then he turned and reentered the house. As Gaines drew his car to a halt in front of the main steps, Wade appeared at their head. He had on a cream-colored suit, an open-necked shirt, and a sun hat despite the coolness of the day. He seemed relaxed, at ease, and Gaines was very much aware of the fact that this was Wade territory and he was nothing more than a guest. He had no right to be here save the courtesy and favor of the host.

Gaines killed the engine. He got out of the car and walked toward the steps.

"Sheriff," Wade said. He came down the steps and extended his hand.

This time Gaines felt it best to respond appropriately. "Mr. Wade," he said, and they shook.

"Do for you?"

"Just a house call, Mr. Wade. Just wanted to ask you about the events that might have followed your bail payment yesterday."

"Mr. Webster is dead, I understand," Wade said.

"Yes, he is. His motel room was burned to the ground, and he was inside."

"You're sure it was him?" Wade asked.

"Why do you ask that?"

"Word is that his head and his hand were missing."

"Is that so?"

"Yes, that's what I heard, Sheriff."

"From whom, might I ask?"

Wade waved the question away as insignificant. "Just around, you know?"

"I don't know that I do know, Mr. Wade."

Wade smiled. He seemed to be enjoying himself. "Maybe you'd be better off spending your time someplace you're welcome, eh, Sheriff?"

"I'm not welcome here, Mr. Wade?"

Wade shrugged. His eyes smiled, but his mouth didn't. "Perhaps welcome is too strong a word. Maybe you should be spending your time with people who can answer your questions . . . people who can tell you something you don't already know."

"I believe you know a number of things that I don't know, Mr. Wade."

Gaines didn't wait for Wade to respond.

"You know where you took Mr. Webster after he left the Sheriff's Office at three in the afternoon yesterday. You were, as far as I can tell, one of the last people to see him alive. You also know why you were willing to pay five thousand dollars to get him out of jail . . ."

"Perhaps, in truth, I am nothing more than a concerned citizen, Sheriff."

"How so?"

"Perhaps I am one of those people who have become somewhat dismayed by the apparent lack of justice that seems available for the common man. Perhaps I felt that justice would best be served by letting fate take its course as far as Lieutenant Michael Webster was concerned. Perhaps there are folks in Whytesburg who think that an eye for an eye is still the best kind of justice."

"You think he was killed by someone for what he did to Nancy Denton?"

Wade took a packet of cigarettes from his jacket pocket and lit one. He did not offer one to Gaines. "I am not trying to second-guess you, Sheriff, but it might be worth looking into that as a possibility."

"You know that Nancy Denton's mother is dead."

Wade didn't flinch. There seemed to be no reaction at all. He looked directly at Gaines, smoke issuing from his nostrils, and said, "No, I did not know that."

"Suicide," Gaines said. "As far as we can tell right now."

"Would make sense."

"How so?"

"Lost her daughter in such terrible circumstances, no husband, overwhelmed with grief . . . Seems that suicide would be very much at the forefront of her mind. People don't commit suicide when they're at their best, Sheriff."

Gaines didn't rise to the sarcastic bait. He was doing his utmost to maintain his objectivity and patience. There was nothing to suggest Matthias Wade had anything to do with the deaths of Nancy Denton or Michael Webster. The only thing that connected Wade to any of it was the fact that he and Webster had known each other for many years and Wade had paid Webster's bail. How well they had known each other, Gaines did not know. And how well each of them had really known Nancy Denton was also uncertain. The dynamics of their relationship all those years ago were still a mystery to Gaines. Webster had been so much older than all of them. If Matthias Wade was now in his early forties, he would still have been ten years younger than Webster back in '54 and a good five years older than Nancy. But they had acted like equals—at least that was the impression from the pictures he had seen. It was as if all seven of them—Webster, Nancy, the four Wade children, and this unidentified Maryanne—had been oblivious to all accepted social parameters. Neither age nor the Wades' position in the community had seemed an obstacle to their respective friendships. Had Nancy's death therefore been precipitated by nothing more complex than jealousy? Had Matthias Wade actually killed her because he couldn't have her?

Gaines had already decided not to speak of the photo album to Wade. If Wade knew of its existence, then perhaps he had wished it to burn in the fire. If he was unaware of it, then Gaines would keep that card close to his chest as long as possible. Perhaps Wade had bailed Webster out for the very reason he suggested: to give the people of Whytesburg a chance to see justice done in their own way. Webster's behavior could easily have swung him an insanity plea, and what would have happened then? Five or six years in the fruit farm, a few chats with some anal-fixated shrink, and then he'd be back home and able to implicate Wade. But then again, if Wade was involved in the Nancy Denton murder, and Webster had known of this, why had Wade not killed Webster back then? Because there was nothing to connect Wade to the girl's death? Because the only evidence that existed would identify Webster as her killer, and Wade wanted him alive to take the fall if it ever came to light? No, that made no sense. The simplest thing to do would have been to dispose of Webster way back when, get him out of the picture altogether. In that way, people would have put the Denton murder to rest. In the absence of answers, any answers would do. People wanted closure, and Webster's death would have given them that, just as it would give them closure now. There were few people who would be happy to hear that John Gaines was pressing for further details on the Denton case, especially now that Judith was dead. There were too many questions, too few answers, and though Wade might not have had all of them, he had a handful, for sure. If nothing else, Gaines was certain of that.

"And then there's always the possibility that Judith was the one who exacted revenge on Webster," Wade added. "And then she killed herself as she could not face the possibility of going to prison for murder."

"A woman alone? And she removed Webster's hand and decapitated him?"

"Maybe she had a friend to help her."

"I think that's very unlikely, Mr. Wade. Did you even know Judith Denton?"

"No, sir, I did not." Wade made a small performance of looking at his watch. "So is that all, Sheriff?"

"You still haven't answered my question, Mr. Wade."

"And what question would that be?"

"What happened after you left the Sheriff's Office yesterday afternoon? Where did you take Webster?"

"I took him to a bar, Sheriff. I took him to a bar called Blues and Beers outside of Whytesburg."

Gaines knew the place, a rundown dive where most of the drugs available in Whytesburg could be sourced.

"And what time was that?"

"Oh, I don't know. Maybe three thirty, three forty-five. I don't remember the exact time we left your office."

"It was five after three."

"Then it must have been about three thirty. Your office to the bar is no more than twenty minutes or so."

"And how was Webster?"

Wade smiled. "Talkative, but most of the stuff he said was nonsense to me. He seemed a bit crazy, you know?"

Gaines looked down at his shoes. He knew that Wade was lying. The lie was right there in his eyes, as obvious as those military spokesmen who smiled all too easily and told the press corps how the United States was winning the war in Vietnam.

"And you left him at the bar and you didn't see him again?"

"That's right, Sheriff."

"And your whereabouts for the remainder of the day?"

"You're asking me if I have an alibi, Sheriff?"

"I am, sir."

Wade smiled, and in that expression was an air of condescension and dismissal. "I was here, Sheriff. Ask my father; ask the help. Ask whoever you want."

"And you're not going to give me any explanation as to why you were willing to risk five thousand dollars to bail him out of jail?"

"You just don't seem to be able to accept the simplest answer to that question, do you? Why can't you just consider the possibility that I might be a social-minded citizen, like I said before?"

"Because it doesn't make sense, sir, and it doesn't ring true. I think you're holding something back here, Mr. Wade. I really do."

Wade dropped the cigarette butt and lit a second. He inhaled deeply, held the smoke for a while, and then sighed. "You seem defeated, Sheriff."

"Frustrated perhaps, not defeated."

"Frustrated by the lack of answers you're getting?"

"Frustrated by the apparent unwillingness of those who know the truth to do anything more than try and hide it."

"You know what they say?"

"They? Who's they?"

"Folks in general, I s'pose."

"No, why don't you tell me what folks in general say?"

"They say the real strength of a man is in recognizing when he's beat."

Gaines smiled, almost to himself. "Guess I must be a weak man, then, Mr. Wade."

"You said it, Sheriff. You said it."

"I did."

"Well, it's been good chatting with you, Sheriff, but I have things to do."

"As do I," Gaines replied.

"Until we meet again—which, I hope, won't be for a long time and will be under more favorable circumstances." Wade turned toward the house.

"Something here is awry, Mr. Wade," Gaines said. "I know it, and you sure as hell know it, and I want you to understand that whichever way this goes, you'll not get away with it."

Wade smiled patiently. "You think not?" He took a moment to straighten a crease in the sleeve of his jacket. "Well, Sheriff Gaines, you just watch real careful while I do exactly that."

34

Gaines believed that the fundamental difference between the good and the bad was one of self-interest. There were those who made choices that incorporated a consideration of others and those who made choices that did not.

The meeting with Wade had disturbed him greatly. He was certain that Wade knew a great deal more than he was saying and yet had set himself to defy Gaines. Whytesburg had three dead, and Gaines was none the wiser regarding the circumstances of any of them. Even the possibility that Judith Denton's suicide was more than just suicide loomed large on the horizon of his fears. A distraught woman—discovering that her daughter was dead, had in fact been dead for twenty years while she'd yet lived with the distant hope of her eventual return—could so easily have been convinced to take her own life. Matthias Wade had said he did not know Judith Denton, yet if he had spent so many years of his childhood as Nancy's friend, how could he have *not* known her? And he had also commented that suicide might very well have been at the forefront of Judith's mind. Why would he have ventured such an opinion when not called for? It was an old legal adage that offense was the best form of defense. Was Wade preempting any possibility that he might be accused of facilitating or encouraging Judith Denton's suicide by remarking upon the possibility of it to Gaines?

The predominant omission now prevalent in Gaines's mind was knowledge of the Wades as a family. He knew *of* them, but not *about* them, and he knew precisely where to start asking questions. Once he had some kind of background on them, then he would best get busy looking into the original disappearance of Nancy Denton. He told Hagen to dig up any reports that might have existed from the time.

"Ahead of you on that one," Hagen told Gaines. "I already looked. Apparently, she was last seen on the evening of Thursday, August 12, 1954. Sixteen years old at the time, best friends with someone called Maryanne Benedict, and the pair of them used to hang around with Webster and the Wade children. I say children, but Matthias was twenty-one at the time. There were four in all—Matthias, Catherine, Eugene, and Della, the last three eighteen, sixteen, and ten respectively. There aren't any reports, not as such anyway, because there was never really an investigation. But there are a few notes that Bicklow made. He questioned all of them, also Judith, a couple of other folks who knew her, but it was assumed that she was a runaway. No indications of foul play. Nothing like that."

"So who is this Maryanne Benedict?"

"Not a great deal to go on as yet. I called up Jim Hughes. He says he vaguely remembers her but didn't know her too well. Knew the parents, but they moved away a good while back. Maryanne was an only child, a couple of years younger than Nancy, according to the notes."

"So if she's alive, she'd be—what?—early thirties."

"Right. Thirty-four, if she was fourteen when Nancy disappeared."

"Well, you get on to tracking her down," Gaines said. "Least of all, she might want to know that two of her childhood friends are dead, and she might be able to give us something else on the Denton girl's disappearance."

Hagen left. Gaines started calling around to locate Eddie Holland. Holland, predictably, was at Nate Ross's place down on Coopers Road. Gaines asked if he could come over and speak with them. Ross seemed all too eager to receive Gaines, and Gaines knew why. There was something going on that was a great deal more interesting than the weather, and Nate Ross would be first in line to get involved.

Gaines felt it was a visit worth making. For all their bluff and bravado, Ross and Holland were good people. They were lonely; that was all. Lonely without careers, lonely without wives. They talked too much, they held court too often, voiced too many unwanted opinions, but every town in the South had their own Ross and Holland, that was for sure. They drank too much. That was obvious from the get-go. Gaines knew the pattern. At first you waited until dark before the first drink, and then dark became sunset became dusk became twilight, and finally there was no waiting at all. If you were awake, you were drunk, and it stayed that way until the drink carried you down through the closing of your life.

Perhaps that was the way he himself would go, the way that his predecessor—Don Bicklow—would have gone, had he not fucked himself into an early grave with a fifty-two-year-old widow out near Wiggins.

Ross's house was old-style South, the balustrades, the balcony out front, the veranda and porch. Ross was there at the screen door as Gaines pulled up, and Eddie Holland was right behind him.

"Gentlemen," Gaines said, removing his hat and leaving it on the passenger seat of the car.

"Sheriff," Nate Ross replied, and he came down the steps to meet Gaines.

Once greetings were exchanged, Gaines followed them into the house, was directed to the kitchen, where Holland had a pot of coffee on the stove.

It did not pass Gaines by that Holland put a splash of bourbon in each cup before it was delivered to the table. Such was the way of things in Nate Ross's house.

"So, how can we assist you, Sheriff?" Eddie Holland said as he took a seat facing Gaines.

"Information," Gaines said.

"About?"

"Well, there's one area where I know you can help me and one area you might not be able to help me, and that's why I'm here."

"Shoot," Ross said.

"This you won't know about so much, Nate, but back in August of 1954, a girl went missing—"

"Nancy Denton," Holland said.

"Right. And now we've found her. And I believed that Mike Webster was responsible for her killing, but now I'm not so sure. I wanted to find out all I could about the original disappearance from Judith, but—"

"She committed suicide," Ross interjected.

"And Webster is dead as well," Gaines went on, unsurprised that Ross already knew about Judith. "And so here I am, dealing with a twenty-year-old runaway case that wasn't really a runaway, a dead mother, a dead primary suspect, and I don't know shit about what the hell is going on . . ."

"Except that Matthias Wade is gonna be involved, one way or another," Holland said. "Because he paid Webster's bail, and all of a sudden Webster is burned to hell without his head and his hand in a motel cabin out toward Bogalusa."

"Which brings me to my second area of questions," Gaines said, also unsurprised that Holland would have mentioned Wade's name so readily, or that he knew of Webster's unfortunate and distressing end. Holland had been around a long time. Whytesburg was a small town. There was little that stayed secret in such places.

"The Wades," Gaines said, matter-of-factly. "That's what I want to know about."

"And what do you want to know about the Wades?" Ross asked.

"Anything you've got, Nate. That would be a start."

Nate Ross shrugged. He sipped his loaded coffee, nodded at Holland, and Holland refreshed the brew with a mite more spirit. He advanced the bottle to Gaines, but Gaines declined.

"Ed'll know more about the family as a whole, being from here an' all. But Earl? Earl Wade must be all of seventy-five or eighty by now. Hardheaded son of a bitch, business-wise, at least. Had some dealings with him back in the early fifties, some property and land he was interested in up in Hattiesburg. The deal didn't go through eventually, but he was ballbreaker, I'll tell you."

"His wife?" Gaines asked.

"His wife was Lillian Tresselt," Holland said. "A good ten or fifteen years younger than him. They had four kids, as far as I recall, Matthias being the eldest. He's the one who'll inherit the businesses and the estate when the old man finally gives up the ghost."

"His wife *was* Lillian Tresselt?"

"Yeah, was," Ross went on. "She drank herself to death. In fact, she died around the same time as I was working on that Hattiesburg thing, so that must have been getting toward the end of fifty-two. Of course, it was never reported that she drank herself to death, but she did. She was famous for her drunken performances at the parties that Wade used to throw."

"And their kids?" Gaines had out his notebook, started writing things down.

"Matthias is the eldest," Holland said. "Then there's Catherine, Eugene, then Della. As far as I know, Catherine is still married, has a family up in Tupelo. I think her husband's a lawyer."

"Yes, he is," Ross said. "I know that because I met a guy a while back who was on some other realty deal with Wade. He told me that the eldest daughter's fiancé was studying up for the law and was gonna be handling all of the Wade work when he finally got his practice."

"His name?" Gaines asked.

Ross shook his head, looked at Holland.

"I don't recall," Holland said.

"So the next one?"

"Next one is Eugene, and he's about as far from the old man as you could get. Isn't he an artist or something, an actor maybe?"

"Musician," Holland said. "Lives in Memphis, last I heard. He'd be maybe mid-thirties or so. Guitar player, I think. Singer, too. Can't say as I've ever heard the name Eugene Wade on the wireless, so maybe he ain't doin' so good."

"Could use a stage name," Ross said. "Lot of them kind do that sort of thing. Use a false name an' all, the musicians and the TV folk and whoever . . ."

"So Eugene isn't like his father?" Gaines prompted, steering the discussion away from bohemian lifestyle choices and back to the matter at hand.

"Hell no," Holland said. "Earl is a businessman through and through. Everything is money and influence and power and politics an' all that. Eugene was the odd one in the bunch, the one that didn't make sense. And after his mother died, well, I don't know what was going through his mind, but he spent a good deal of time in church. Lookin' for answers, maybe. Tryin' to figure out why his ma died an' all that."

"Any possibility he wasn't Earl's child?"

Neither Ross nor Holland responded, and then Ross leaned forward and said, "Hell, son, this is the South. Anything's possible, right?"

"So after Eugene?"

"There was Della," Holland said, "and if ever there was a girl who took after her mother, it was Della Wade. She was one pretty girl, let me tell you, and I can imagine she is one pretty young woman."

"You know where she's at?"

"Last I heard, she was still at the Wade house, but that was a good while back, a year at least, and it's not something I've been keepin' tabs on, you know?"

"Nate?"

"Couldn't tell you, Sheriff. Didn't know her, didn't really know any of them by face. Just knew the name, a little of the business dealings. Not like Ed here. Ed is Whytesburg, whereas I'm Hattiesburg."

"So, to Nancy Denton," Gaines said.

"I wasn't deputy back then," Holland said. "Deputy back then was George Austin, but he died in sixty-seven, and that's when I took over. Don Bicklow was sheriff, as you know. But regardless, there wasn't a hell of a lot to talk about. Everyone figured she was a runaway. She was spirited girl, John, a firecracker, you know? It was before I was in the department. I was away a lot of the time, traveling around and about, selling shoes and tires and whatnot, but I remember them kids all together. Her and Matthias, the other Wades, Michael Webster when he came back from the war, and Maryanne Benedict—"

"That was the other one I wanted to ask you about," Gaines interjected. "The Benedict girl."

"Lives in Gulfport," Holland said. "And I know that because her father and I were friends a long while back. Her parents are both dead now, but I have always kept tabs on her. Haven't spoken to her since . . . oh, I don't know, Christmas maybe, but last time I did, she was still down there."

"Married? Kids?"

"Nope, never did marry," Holland said. "Strange. Always seemed like she'd make just the best mother."

"You have an address for her?"

"Sure do," Holland said. "Lives on Hester Road in Gulfport."

"Knew it would be a worthwhile trip out here," Gaines said.

"Hell, Sheriff, places like this, everyone knows everyone, and they're all in and out of one another's business, right?"

"Seems a shame such familiarity comes up most useful when someone gets themselves killed," Gaines said.

"Never a truer word," Ross replied.

"I'll be off to see her, then." Gaines drained his coffee cup, appreciated the warm bloom of liquor in his chest, and rose from his chair. "I don't doubt I'll be back with more questions at some point."

"Look forward to it, Sheriff," Ross said, and walked Gaines out to the porch.

Gaines called Hagen from the car before he'd even left Nate Ross's driveway.

"I'm off to see this Maryanne Benedict. Got her address from Eddie."

"I was checking on her, too. Got an address. Hester Road in Gulfport, right?"

"Jeez, Richard, I figure I might as well just go home and let you do all the work. Seems you're better at it than me."

"I didn't want to be the one to raise that point, John, but . . ."

Gaines laughed, hung up the radio, started the engine, and pulled away.

35

For some reason, Gaines thought of his father as he drove the thirty or so miles to Gulfport.

It was late afternoon, the day had cooled somewhat, some song had come on the radio, and he had gotten to thinking about the man, about what life might have been like for him and his mother had Edward Gaines returned from the war instead of losing his life somewhere along the road near Malmedy and Stavelot two days before Christmas, 1944.

Gaines had been four years old at the time, could recall nothing personal about him, save the fact that, for some brief while, there had been someone other than his mother in the house. A presence, that was all. Just a fatherly presence.

From what his mother had told him, Edward Gaines was a tough man. Awkward, opinionated, as if he'd set himself to stand at some angle contrary to the world and weather whatever came. Alice said that he was the kind of man who believed that abstinence and self-denial were somehow the roads to health and good humor. His was not and never would be a life of comforts, and though she sensed that sometimes he would long for such things and feel an ache of absence in his bones, he would never accede to such temptations. To succumb would be to admit defeat. To what, he did not know nor care. It would simply be defeat, and this was something he never wished to have said of him. But he provided for his wife and then his son, and though he did not squander what little money they had on fripperies and such, he did ensure that there was always sufficient of what was needed. And then the war came, the same year that he and Alice were married, and Edward Gaines watched the drama unfold with a weather eye. He knew it would ultimately turn toward the Pacific, toward the need for America to engage in this struggle, and when that need came, he was one of the first in line. So he went, and he survived for thirteen or fourteen months, and then it was all done.

Gaines had looked for Malmedy on a map one time. It was in a province called Liège in Belgium. It was infamous during the Battle of the Bulge, for here the SS had murdered eighty-four American prisoners. And then—during that fateful week in December of 1944, despite the fact that the area was under US control—it had been relentlessly bombed by US forces. Two hundred civilians were killed. The number of American soldiers who lost their lives was not revealed by the Department of Defense.

Gaines did not want to believe that his father had been killed by a bomb made at the Elwood Ordnance Plant in Illinois. He did not want to know if the explosive that blew him to pieces had been manufactured by E.I. du Pont or Sanderson and Porter or the United States Rubber Company. He did not want details. He wanted to believe that his father had died doing whatever he considered was the right thing to do—for himself, for his family, for his country. It was that simple.

And why he thought of him then, as he drove along 10 toward Lyman and then took the south turning to Gulfport, he did not know. Perhaps it was this talk of dying, of childhood friends, of people who went missing and never returned.

Or perhaps none of these things.

Perhaps it was nothing more than some deep-rooted sense of aloneness that invaded his thoughts and emotions every once in a while.

Like when he thought of Linda and the child that never was.

He wondered where she was now, what she was doing, if she had married, raised a family, whether she ever thought of him.

Did a distant memory of John Gaines invade her thoughts in those quiet times, the times that the world briefly stopped and there was space between the minutes?

Maybe, Gaines thought, once this thing was done, once he knew the truth of what had really happened that night in August of 1954, he would take some time away from the horrors of the world—those that he remembered from his own war experiences, those that he was now witnessing—and look at the possibility of remedying the sense of aloneness that seemed to be growing ever more noticeable. Maybe Bob Thurston was right. Maybe Alice would hang on in there until she believed her son would be okay without her. She was, if nothing else, the personification of maternal instinct. That's the only way she could be described, as if she knew that her place on this earth was to care for everyone who fell within her circle of influence. Caring was something of which she would never grow tired. Caring for others seemed not to drain her, but to revive her, as if her heart were a battery that absorbed all those thank-yous and converted them into whatever energy was needed to go on. Maybe it was now time to let her go. Such a thought did not instill a sense of guilt in Gaines, but rather a sense of relief, if not for himself then for his mother. She was in pain—he knew that—and almost constantly. How much pain, he did not know, and she would never do anything but her best to hide it. Again, that was borne out of her consideration for him. She should have married again. She should have had more children. Twenty-nine years old when she lost her one and only husband, and she had then spent the rest of her life alone. Had she felt that marrying again would be a betrayal of Edward's memory? Had she believed that to take another husband, to have had more children, would somehow have caused difficulty for her son? There would be an explanation for her choice, of course, but just as Gaines was unaware of it, so he too believed that Alice might herself be unaware. There was no explaining his own decision to remain single, but remain so he did.

It was with the vague aftermath of these thoughts still in his mind that Gaines arrived in Gulfport. It was a little after five, and he pulled to the curb on the central drag and asked a passerby for directions to Hester Street. It was no more than three blocks, and Gaines decided to walk. He went on down there, hat in hand, and he stood for a while on the sidewalk in front of Maryanne Benedict's house. It was a simple home—white plank board–built, a short veranda that spanned merely the facade, beneath each window a box containing flowers in various colors.

Gaines's hesitation was evident in his manner as he approached, and before he even reached the screen, the inner door opened and he saw Maryanne Benedict.

For a moment, all thoughts stopped. Later, he could not identify what it was about her that struck him so forcibly, but Maryanne Benedict possessed something undeniable and unforgettable in the way that she appeared, there in the doorway of her own small house on Hester Road. Something that defied easy description. She was not a beautiful woman, not in any classically accepted sense. Her features were defined, but shadowed, simple but strangely elegant. She looked through the mesh of the screen door, and—had Gaines thought of it—he again would have defined that look as a thousand-yard stare. But it was not. It was something beyond that.

The outer door swung open, and she remained silent until Gaines had reached the lower steps that led up to the veranda.

"You have good manners or bad news," she said, "or both."

Gaines smiled awkwardly. He looked down at the hat in his hand. "Perhaps the first," he replied. "Definitely the second."

"Well, both my folks are dead and I'm an only child. I never married, have no kids, and so it's a neighbor or a friend or someone you think I care about."

"Nancy Denton," Gaines said, and in that second he saw a change of expression so sudden, so dramatic, that he could say nothing further.

He remembered delivering the news to Judith. *Your daughter is dead. Your only child, the one you have been waiting for these past twenty years, is dead.*

In some way, a way that Gaines could not understand, this felt even worse.

Maryanne Benedict seemed to lean against the frame of the door for support. A brief sound escaped her lips. A whimper. A cry of repressed astonishment and disbelief.

Gaines walked up the steps toward her, held out his hand to assist her, but she waved him back. Gaines just stood there in silence, not knowing where to look but unable to avert his eyes from the woman.

Standing closer now, he felt awkward, ashamed, embarrassed to have been the one to bring news that would create such an effect, but unable to move, unable to think of any words that might alleviate the distress that Maryanne Benedict was evidently experiencing.

She was first to speak, standing straight and looking back into the house. "I need to get inside," she said, her voice cracking. "I need to sit down . . ."

She left the door open wide, and Gaines could do nothing but follow her.

Inside, the house was much as it had appeared from the street. Neat, orderly, precise. The furnishings were feminine but functional, nothing too embellished or decorative. It seemed Spartan to Gaines, almost unlived in, and in some strange way reminiscent of his own quarters. There was nothing there that really communicated anything of Maryanne Benedict's personality—no photographs, no trinkets, no paintings on the walls.

She walked back through the house to the kitchen, Gaines following on behind her.

She turned suddenly. "Some tea," she said. "We will have tea."

Gaines didn't reply.

Maryanne filled the kettle, set it on the stove, busied herself with a teapot, cups, saucers.

"I am sorry to be the one to bring this news," Gaines said, and for some strange reason, his voice sounded strong and definite.

"You will tell me what happened," Maryanne said, without turning around.

"I'll tell you what I can," Gaines replied.

She nodded.

"There is something else—"

And this time she did turn around, and her expression was alive and anticipatory, her eyes bright, rimmed with tears, the muscles in her jawline twitching visibly. Everything was there—every feeling, every thought and emotion and fear—and she was using every single last line of defense to hold it all inside.

"Michael . . . ," Gaines said.

"Michael," she echoed.

"Michael Webster."

"Yes, yes, I know Michael . . . I know of Michael. What about Michael . . . ? Did you tell him, as well?"

Gaines nodded. "I did, Ms. Benedict, yes."

"And is he okay? What did he say? Oh my God, I can't even begin to imagine what he—"

"Michael is dead as well, Miss Benedict."

The last line went down. The depth of pain that seemed to fill that small kitchen as Maryanne Benedict broke down was greater than anything Gaines had before witnessed.

She dropped a cup into the sink. It somehow did not break.

Gaines was there to hold Maryanne Benedict. She seemed to fold in half—mentally, spiritually, just like Judith—and she sobbed uncontrollably for as long a time as Gaines had ever known.

36

The sun was nearing the horizon. Gaines was aware of this as he sat at the kitchen table.

For a long while the woman said nothing at all, merely glancing at Gaines, her eyes swollen, her mouth forming words that never reached him, as if she were holding some conversation with Nancy, perhaps with Michael, perhaps with someone else entirely.

Gaines remained silent. He felt it best not to interrupt whatever internal monologue was taking place. People dealt with such things in their own ways, and Gaines believed himself more than capable of sitting there as long as was needed. For some reason, he did not feel awkward in the presence of Maryanne Benedict. Perhaps this was due to nothing more than his own emotional exhaustion. He was not fighting anymore. The deaths of Nancy, Michael Webster, and Judith Denton seemed to have bleached his mind of thoughts. He anticipated everything now, as if nothing at all could surprise him. Like Vietnam. Be ready for anything. Run for three days, stand still for four. Move at a moment's notice; go back the way you came—all of it without explanation as to why.

Eventually, Maryanne Benedict seemed to wind down. Gaines could feel it in the silence between them.

"I am sorry," she said, and her voice was a whisper.

"You have nothing to be sorry for, Miss Benedict."

A faint smile flickered across her lips, as if it amused her to be called *Miss Benedict*, but she did not correct Gaines.

"It must be awful for you," she went on, "having to do this . . ."

Gaines looked at her. He had yet to tell her about Judith Denton's suicide. Would there be a better time than now?

"I am sorry about what happened to your friends," Gaines said. "I understand that you and Nancy and Michael were very close when you were younger."

Again that faint smile, and then Maryanne looked away toward the window and seemed lost for some minutes.

"When you were children," Gaines added.

"We were all close," she said. She looked back at Gaines. "I was fourteen when Nancy disappeared. She was sixteen. Matthias was all grown-up too, but it never felt like we were anything but the same age. Della was ten, soon to be eleven. Eugene was a couple of years older than me, and Catherine was a month or so away from her nineteenth birthday. And Michael? Michael was thirty-one." She shook her head. "It seems strange now to consider such a thing, but at the time it didn't seem strange at all. He didn't seem that much older than us, either. It wasn't like that. It wasn't like there was any difference between us at all, but now . . ." Her voice trailed away. "He was twice her age, wasn't he?"

Gaines said nothing.

"And there was Matthias . . . ," she said quietly.

"I have spoken to Matthias."

"You have?"

"Yes."

"And . . ."

Gaines shifted in the chair. He had to tell her what had happened, but he did not want to.

"Tell me, Sheriff. I don't know that you can be the bearer of any worse news than you've already been . . ."

Gaines's expression gave him away.

"Oh," she said, in her response the sound of despair.

"Nancy . . . Nancy was found buried, Miss Benedict . . . buried in the riverbank in Whytesburg. Appeared she had been there for twenty years . . ."

"Oh," Maryanne said again, but it was an involuntary reaction, an unintentional sound, and she looked as surprised as Gaines to hear her own voice.

"That's not all," Gaines went on.

Maryanne's eyes widened, perhaps in anticipation, perhaps in disbelief that the news could be any worse.

"It seems she had been . . . well, she had been strangled. That was the cause of death, you see? She was strangled . . ." Gaines's voice faded. He did not want to say *butchered*. He did not want to tell her that. He wanted only to tell Maryanne Benedict only that her childhood friend had been strangled, not that she had been violated so terribly. He was thankful then—perhaps more than ever—that Nancy had not been raped. He could recall memories of such things. Those girls in Vietnam—those children—seemed to have had whatever internal light that animated their thoughts and feelings just snuffed out. Somebody was home, but everything was in darkness. Some of them committed suicide. Once he had seen a girl no more than twelve snatch a sidearm and just shoot herself in the head. He had seen it with his own eyes. She was kneeling before she was dead, still kneeling afterward, eyes still open, still gazing into some vague middle distance where resided her innocence and childlike naïveté, perhaps the belief that she could survive this terrible war, that she could come through the other end of this and have a future. But no, someone had mercilessly snatched away such a belief and with it had gone any reason she might have possessed to go on living. No, whatever horrors he was bringing to Maryanne Benedict's door, at least he was not bringing that.

He had to tell her the next thing, but tell her so she understood that Nancy was already dead when it happened.

"After she was dead . . . after she was dead, it . . ."

"What, Sheriff? After she was dead, what?"

"She was cut open, Miss Benedict . . . She was cut open down the length of her torso, and her heart was removed . . ."

Maryanne Benedict covered her mouth with her hand. "Oh my God," she said. "Oh, Lord almighty . . ."

"Some kind of ritual perhaps. We don't know yet. We don't understand what really happened . . . the circumstances, you know? All we have is what her body tells us, and her body tells us that some sort of ritual was performed . . ."

"Her heart? Someone took out her heart?"

"Yes," Gaines replied. "Someone took out her heart." He looked away.

"What else?" she said, interpreting that look for what it was.

"Something was put in its place," he said. "Someone replaced her heart with a snake . . ."

Maryanne Benedict's reaction was not as Gaines had expected. A hysterical response? An exclamation of utter disbelief? What had he anticipated? Certainly not the silent lowering of the head, the way she closed her eyes, the way her hands came together as if in prayer. Certainly not the sound of her breathing deeply as if trying to focus everything at once, trying to pull everything together and prevent herself from unraveling at the seams right before his eyes.

And if Gaines was surprised at her absence of reaction, then he was even further surprised by what she said next.

"Did Michael do that to her?"

Gaines couldn't hide his expression.

Maryanne looked at him, her eyes tortured with something indefinable. "Did Michael do that to her . . . this thing?"

"We think so," Gaines said.

"Did he commit suicide?"

Gaines shook his head. "He was murdered . . ."

Maryanne lowered her head, and when she looked up, her brow was furrowed, her eyes intense. "What? He was *murdered*?"

"Yes," Gaines said. "He was decapitated and his left hand was removed. His body was left in the room where he lived, and it was burned to the ground."

Maryanne started to get up, using the table to support herself as she tried to stand, but her knees gave way and she sat in the chair heavily.

Gaines knew there was no good time for this. He had told her of Nancy, of Michael, and now the truth about Judith Denton needed to be confronted.

"And Judith Denton, Nancy's mother . . . she committed suicide." Gaines cleared his throat. His voice sounded calm, almost too calm, and quiet, as if she would have to struggle to hear him. "In the early hours of this morning," Gaines went on. "She took an overdose of sleeping tablets, and she died . . ."

"Nothing to live for now," Maryanne said. "At last she found out that Nancy would never be coming home, and there was nothing to live for . . ."

"Yes, I believe so."

Maryanne leaned back. She inhaled deeply, exhaled again, closed her eyes once more, and sat there immobile for a good minute or two.

Eventually, seeming to surface from her reverie, she opened her eyes and looked unerringly at Gaines. "I do not believe that Michael Webster murdered Nancy Denton," she said. "He loved her. He loved her with everything he had. She was in love with him, as well. He was a strong man, a patient man, and he told her that he would wait five years, ten years, whatever was needed. They loved each other so much, but nothing ever happened between them of a . . . you know, of a sexual nature. It wasn't like that at all. Michael was our soldier. He was our protector and defender. He would never have let any harm come to me or Nancy, and he loved Nancy unquestioningly. He was utterly devoted to her, and she to him, and that was just the way it was. They were meant to be together, but something happened, and she was born fifteen years too late. There was always going to be that gap between them, but they knew what they had, and it didn't matter. He would never have killed her . . ." Maryanne looked away toward the window and then looked back at Gaines. "No, he could not have done that, Sheriff Gaines."

"Did you know anything about this before today?" Gaines asked.

She shook her head. "No, of course I didn't know."

"Did he say anything, do anything . . . ?"

Maryanne was silent for some time, and then she cleared her throat. "We fell apart after she was gone. Before that, we were always together. Every moment we could spend together, we did. That was who we were. And then she disappeared, and we didn't see one another for a long time. I haven't seen Matthias for fifteen years, perhaps more. Michael I last saw maybe three or four years ago, but I couldn't bring myself to speak to him. I did ask him once if he knew what had happened, if he had any idea at all. This was a long time ago, maybe twelve or thirteen years, and all he said was that he could not speak of it, but he was still waiting. He said that if he broke his vow of silence, it would all come to nothing . . ." She paused, breathed deeply. "I didn't understand what he meant then, and I don't understand it now. Michael said he was still waiting for her, and he didn't say anything else."

Gaines leaned back. He reached for his hat there on the table, fingered the brim nervously.

Maryanne Benedict held Gaines with an intense and penetrating gaze. "Do you have any idea what he might have meant?"

"No idea at all, Miss Benedict."

"So the question, now that we know she is dead, is who did kill her? If Michael didn't kill her, then who did?"

Gaines didn't reply. He did not know the answer to that question either. He did not wish to voice his suspicions or enter into any discussion with Maryanne Benedict until she began that discussion. He was determined not to lead her.

"You have your suspicions, Sheriff?" she asked.

Gaines shook his head.

"Not even Matthias?"

Gaines hesitated. Once again, he tried to give away nothing in his expression. Evidently he failed.

"Matthias is a law unto himself," Maryanne said.

"Why do you say that?"

"People with money always are."

"You know him well?"

"No," she said matter-of-factly. "I knew him, at least to some degree, when we were younger, but we were never that close. I spent more time with Eugene than I did with Matthias. But Nancy was my closest friend. Nancy was like my sister . . . ."

"I can imagine how difficult—"

"Can you, Sheriff?"

Gaines looked at her. "Yes, Miss Benedict, I can."

She looked down at the floor, then looked at her hands on the table as if they belonged to someone else. "Three dead . . . two murders, one suicide, all in a matter of days . . ."

"All in a matter of twenty years," Gaines said. "Nancy died the night she disappeared, or very soon thereafter."

"How do you even comprehend this? How do you deal with something like this? I mean, there's no point of reference. There's no context . . ."

"What do you think happened that night, Miss Benedict?"

"To Nancy? I think she was taken by someone . . ." She paused. "Was she . . . you know, was she sexually . . . ?"

"No," Gaines said. "She was not raped. She was strangled, and her heart was cut out, but she was not raped."

Maryanne lowered her head. Her entire body seemed to diminish in size as she exhaled. "It is just too unbearable to imagine . . . ," she whispered.

"So what do you think happened?" Gaines prompted.

For a while, Maryanne Benedict said nothing. Gaines did not interrupt the silence in that room. She had to absorb and come to terms with what he was telling her in her own way. There was no way to speed up the process, no way to circumvent whatever was going on in her mind. She looked away several times—to the floor, toward the window—but she was not looking *at* anything present or tangible. She was looking with her mind's eye, recalling events, situations, words exchanged, perhaps ideas that she had considered during the previous two decades. "I think she was taken by someone," she eventually said. Her voice was measured, controlled, precise. "Now you have told me that she was strangled . . . I don't know . . . Perhaps Michael found her dead and then, for some reason known only to him, he did this terrible thing to her body . . ." Maryanne shook her head. "Michael had his dark side, like everyone. He survived the war, you know?"

"I heard about that . . . in Guadalcanal, the only surviving member of his unit."

"The luckiest man alive," Maryanne interjected.

"He said that," Gaines replied. "Lester Cobb said it, too. What does that mean?"

"Means what it says," Maryanne replied. "He survived the war, and then he survived the thing that happened at the factory in 1952. That's when he started to believe he was protected . . ."

"Protected?"

Maryanne smiled. It was a sad and resigned smile. "I never made that tea," she said. "You want some?"

37

Gaines watched her as she went about the business of preparing tea.

She didn't say a word as she recovered the kettle from the sink, filled it, set it atop the stove, lit the gas. She fussed with leaves and cups, and she stood for a while gazing through the small window that overlooked the yard. She was alone within whatever world she inhabited, internally and externally it seemed, and Gaines—despite feeling the sense of emptiness around her—withheld himself from saying or doing anything to interrupt that aloneness.

Eventually, she turned and looked at Gaines, her hands behind her on the edge of the sink, her head down, but her eyes fixed on him.

"To think . . . all these years, and it ends like this. There hasn't been a single day when I haven't thought of her. Of Nancy, you know? Twenty years. I knew she was dead, but I didn't know how, and I didn't know why. I hoped she wasn't, of course, but I knew it was hopeless. She wasn't a runaway. Everyone said she was a runaway, but they didn't know her, and they didn't understand her relationship with Michael. All she talked about was reaching eighteen and marrying Michael. And Matthias was jealous as hell, but he loved her enough to understand that she had made her decision." Maryanne smiled, a memory right there in her eyes. "I asked Matthias one time if he thought that Michael was too old for Nancy, and he said that there was about one year more between Michael and Nancy as there was between his own mom and dad. He didn't answer the question, but I could tell what he meant. He did not have an easy relationship with his parents, and I think that was down to the fact that his parents did not have an easy relationship with each other. Matthias believed that he was right for Nancy and that no one else was."

Maryanne turned back to the worktop and poured tea. She brought the cups to the table, set one in front of Gaines, and took her seat once more.

"Me and Nancy, Michael and Matthias. I cannot think of one of us without seeing all of us together."

"But there were others, right?"

"Sure there were, but they weren't part of us in the same way. They were there, of course, but—" She left the statement unfinished.

Gaines let the silence hang between them for a moment, just to ensure that she wasn't going to start talking again, and then he said, "And you now have nothing to do with Matthias Wade? Nothing at all?"

She shook her head. "Like I said, I haven't seen him for a decade and a half, perhaps more."

"Did he know Judith?"

"Nancy's mother? Yes, of course he did."

Gaines cast his mind back to the conversation he'd had with Wade, the fact that Wade had said he did not know Judith Denton. The comment he'd made could be interpreted as a denial of any knowledge of her, or—as was perhaps the case here—a simple statement to the effect that he did not *know* her. She was an acquaintance from many years ago, the mother of a childhood friend, and nothing more significant.

"You were going to tell me about what happened in 1952," Gaines prompted.

"Yes, I was," Maryanne replied. She hesitated, looking at him then as if with some sense of apologetic resignation, as if she would now share with him something of the awkward, broken tangle of her life, and she knew it would unsettle him.

Gaines thought to tell her that nothing would now surprise him, that he had seen and heard it all, the very worst the world could offer up—not only in Vietnam, but here in this small-town catastrophe—but he remained silent.

"There was a machine plant west of Picayune," she said, "east of the Pearl River. They built it there because of the water supply, but that didn't serve them so well when it was really needed. The plant is not there now, for obvious reasons." She smiled awkwardly. "For reasons that will become obvious when I tell you what happened. The plant was originally built by another family, many decades ago, back at the end of the eighteen hundreds, I think. Anyway, it was a business that changed hands, changed purpose, was turned over to munitions manufacturing during the war, and when the war was over and munitions were no longer required, the Wades bought it.

212

Matthias's father was forever buying up other businesses, even ones that didn't make any money. It was as if he just set his mind to owning as much as he could, regardless of its real value. Anyway, they made ball bearings, springs, axels for vehicles and such. Other things as well, metal trays for prison food, enamel cups, everything. It was a small business, maybe a hundred or a hundred and fifty men worked there, but it was prosperous. And Matthias got Michael a job there. Usually, they only took on people who were already skilled, but Matthias had influence, of course, and he arranged for Michael to get an apprenticeship there. And Michael kept to his word, and he showed up, and he learned how to do whatever was needed, and he was a good employee. He always worked hard; he wasn't late; he did overtime. It was like he had spent all these years doing nothing after the war, and then finally he had something to throw himself into."

Maryanne looked up at Gaines, perhaps lost somewhere in her recollection and then remembering Gaines's presence in front of her. She smiled. "It wasn't a hugely important purpose, of course, but it was a purpose. It was a reason to get up in the morning, and he seized it. And he had money then, of course, and he insisted on paying for things and buying things for Nancy and me. One Christmas, we were all invited to the Wade house for their Christmas Eve party, and Michael bought dresses for both of us from a store in Biloxi. Silk dresses, yellow and pink, and flowers, too, and we went up there to the big house and felt like we were in *Gone with the Wind*."

Maryanne laughed softly. It was a beautiful sound.

"He was always like that then. Generous, kind, patient. We all loved him, but whereas he cared for me and Matthias and the others greatly, he loved only Nancy. Anyway, it was June of 1952. Michael would have been in his late twenties by then, and Nancy, she would have been . . . well, yes, it was just three or four days before her fourteenth birthday. I remember now. We had a party planned, just something simple, but considering what happened, we had to cancel it. Anyway, it was June, and everything was fine, everything was normal, and then we got word that there had been a terrible fire at the plant. It wasn't the whole plant, because each section had its own building, if you like. Auto things were made in one factory, metal pressings in another, enamel goods in another, you know? Anyway, by this time, Michael was one of the foremen in the building where they cast things in iron or steel or whatever. They had these huge containers of sand, because they used sand to make the molds for some of the things they manufactured. They were like enormous wooden barrels, but raised up about six feet high, and they held tons and tons of sand. So, there was a fire somewhere in the back of the building, and there were maybe twenty-five or thirty men working in that building. Once the fire got a grip, there were a number of them trapped in one section of the building. What happened was that the wooden legs of these sand barrels gave way, and these things came over and created this obstacle between one part of the building and the next. There were a number of men behind this great mountain of sand. The sand was scorching hot, and they couldn't climb over it and they couldn't get around it. So Michael took half a dozen other men, and they went outside the building from the other end. They took digger trucks and some kind of wagon and they drove those trucks into the back wall again and again until they breached it, and they made an escape route for the men who had been trapped inside. But not all of them came out, and Michael figured they must have been overcome by smoke or something. The fire department had arrived by then, and because the summer had been so hot, the river was low, and they couldn't get the water up as fast as they needed it. Anyway, Michael took a team of firemen in to show them where these workers were trapped, and they disappeared into the smoke and not one of them came out. Not the workers who'd been left behind, not the firemen. Just Michael. The roof came down, and then the back wall collapsed, and the firemen and the workers were trapped in there and they died. Somehow Michael came out. And, after what had happened in the war, that's when he became known as the luckiest man alive."

Gaines had watched her talking the entire time. The more she spoke, the more alive she appeared to become. As if to recount this terrible tragedy had somehow reminded her of not only her own mortality, but also her own *aliveness*. There was something truly captivating about the woman, as if something inside her was alight and yet hidden behind the shadows of the past. Past experience had buried who she was, and in speaking of these things, perhaps some small avenue of escape had become visible.

"And Michael?" Gaines asked.

"He withdrew to a degree, just as he had after his return from the war. We still spent time together, and he was still as much in love with Nancy as he'd ever been, but something had changed. It wasn't even identifiable. It wasn't something you could put your finger on.

He wasn't crazy. He didn't act crazy. Nothing like that. It was like there was only seventy-five percent of him there, whereas before there had been a hundred. And then, after Nancy's disappearance two years later . . . well, that's when he really started to display signs of the lonely, crazy man he became. After that, I hardly ever saw him. I didn't want to see him. When I did see him, he spoke about how he was a curse on everyone around him, about how he had made a pact with the devil, about how his own life had been spared twice, but that the price he now had to pay was the sacrifice of the one person he truly loved. It was too much to listen to him. It overwhelmed you. It was scary, terrifying, you know? It was obsessive."

"And he stopped seeing you and Matthias completely after Nancy's disappearance?"

"As best he could. He told me that he didn't dare spend time with us. That if we stayed together, then we would go the same way as his friends in Guadalcanal, the same way as the people he worked with in Picayune, the same as Nancy. He believed that he was protecting us by becoming reclusive, by never seeing us, by staying away."

"And you were all with her the night she disappeared, right?"

Maryanne smiled. "Yes, and that was the last time I saw her. It was the last time we were all together in the same place at the same time."

"So what happened that night?"

"Nothing happened, Sheriff. Nothing at all. It was the same as so many other times that we had been together. It was a summer evening, August, 1954. We were in the field. We had the old record player from Matthias's house. Catherine had left much earlier, and then when Matthias went back to get the record player, he took Eugene and Della with him. Then there was just the four of us in the field at the end of Five Mile Road near the trees, and we played music and we danced. And then Michael and Nancy went into the trees, and she never came out again."

"And the police?"

Maryanne shrugged. "They found nothing. No sign at all. Don Bicklow was the sheriff at the time. George Austin was his deputy. They asked around; they spoke to Michael, to Matthias, to all three of us, and we didn't know what had happened."

"What did Michael tell them?"

"That they had gone into the trees together, that it was dark, that they had gotten separated but that he could still hear her singing.

And then it went quiet, and he couldn't hear her anymore. He went looking, and he called out for her. He got no answer, and he thought that maybe she was just hiding from him, that she would suddenly jump out from behind a tree to scare him, but she never did. Then he came out to the field again, and I was there with Matthias, and Michael figured she would be with us. She wasn't, and so Michael and Matthias sent me home, and they went into the trees again to look for her, and after about an hour, they still hadn't found her and they went to the Sheriff's Office."

"And when Michael and Matthias went back into the trees, did they search together, or did they split up?"

Maryanne shook her head. "I have no idea."

"And Don Bicklow figured she was a runaway, and that was the end of it, right?"

"Seemed so, but now we know different. Now we know that Michael found her body, and then he did what he did . . ."

"We think that Michael found her body," Gaines said. "We cannot be sure what really happened from the evidence we have." Gaines leaned forward and looked at Maryanne directly. "What do *you* think really happened, Miss Benedict?"

Maryanne smiled. "Miss Benedict? No one calls me Miss Benedict, Sheriff Gaines. I am an institution here. I am the crazy lady who lives alone with cats and flowers and memories. I am just Maryanne."

Gaines nodded. "Maryanne," he said. "What do you believe really happened that night?"

She looked away toward the window, back to the sink, the stove, the wall behind Gaines. Never once did she look at him directly as she considered her thoughts.

"I agreed with what a lot of people said at the time, Sheriff Gaines," she eventually replied.

"And what did people say?"

"That the devil came to Whytesburg to collect on Michael's debt."

38

Gaines believed in crazy.

In war, truth was the first casualty. So said Aeschylus. Gaines did not agree with Aeschylus. In war, sanity went first, and crazy followed in right after to take its place.

As crazy as the handful of survivors who made it out of the NVA assault of Lang Vei in February of '68.

As crazy as the nineteen-year-old lance corporal telling you that you were lucky to be going someplace that had a lower-than-average kill rate.

Gaines remembered someone telling him that the Marine Corps was earning its reputation as the most efficient and effective means of killing young Americans ever devised.

A dead marine cost eighteen thousand dollars.

Someone else, maybe like a spec 4 from Special Forces, cost a good deal more.

So yes, Gaines knew all about crazy.

Despite the fact that he had not been there in Khe Sanh at the end of '67, he knew that Khe Sanh was really was the beginning of the end. The NVA had the US encampment surrounded—the 304th division lay to the south, the 320th to the east; northwest was 325C, northeast was B, and a fifth unidentified division waited patiently across the Laotian border. The NVA were using routes along foothills bridging Laos and Vietnam, routes that had been used by the Viet Minh in the 1940s. They understood the war. They understood the weather. They understood the country. This was their territory.

In April and May of '67, additional forces that had been deployed to keep Khe Sanh secure engaged with NVA battalions holding hills 881 North and 881 South. The 1st and 3rd Battalions of 26th Marines were rotated through the firebase.

In the Terrace Bar of the Continental, in the L'Amiral Restaurant, the Danang Press Center, in the daily forty-five minute briefings in the Saigon press rooms, endless parallels were drawn between the 1954 French defeat at Dien Bien Phu and what was happening in

Khe Sanh. Fortune was against the United States. America had challenged fate, and fate would not be challenged lightly. Special Forces had moved in in '62 and built their defense lines over the remains of the French bunkers. The French had lost there, and so would the Americans. Monsoons favored the NVA. Air observation and cover were impossible to maintain. Khe Sanh was encircled. All evacuation routes, including Route 9, were NVA held. Everyone was going to die. The war was going to be lost. That was where you found real crazy. Soldiers on their way out found themselves unable to leave. Their tours were over, and they could not go home.

Only in war did people understand war.

And then—finally—when bad news was coming in from Hue, Danang, Qui Nhơn, Khe Sanh, Buôn Ma Thụt, Saigon, from every fucking place, that was when people really started to lose it. That was when they realized that the entire fucking thing had been pointless. The administration already knew it was over. The VC had the embassy, they had Cholon. Tan Son Nhut was burning to the ground. Convoys of trucks were coming from Phu Bai with replacements. So many had been lost in all the shit going down south of the Perfume River, and the rain was heavy, and the mud was everywhere, and Gaines could remember standing at the side of the road and watching that convoy of vehicles coming in. He saw the faces of the grunts, and he knew what they were seeing. They saw their own deaths. Some of them were there for the very first time and yet somehow they understood that this was where they were going to die. Everyone knew the end was coming, but the war machine was too dumb and too arrogant to cry *uncle*. Those boys were going to see a handful of hours, a day perhaps, and then they'd be shipped back in body bags while another five hundred fresh ones were convoyed in. It was like delivering targets to an amusement park shooting gallery. Gaines had been with the Marines of 2/5 when they gained the central south bank, and he saw the graves. Five thousand graves of all those the NVA had executed.

There was a Hotel Company, a Sierra Company, an India Company, a Foxtrot Company. No Charlie Company. That would have been too much irony for anyone to bear. It just started Alpha, Bravo, Delta, like the first three acts of some ironic Greek tragedy. And in every company there was always *the one*. He walked between bullets; hell, the guy could even walk between raindrops in monsoon season, to hear his fellows speak of him. He was the one who always survived, who went in first, came out last, never a scratch. A million near misses and almosts, bullets close enough to feel the sharp breeze and hear the whistle, but never a hit, as if God had some other divine intent and the war was just a movie to sit through so he could say he'd been there.

And every day the kind of sights that opened one eye wide in shock and caused the other to rapid-fire blink in disbelief.

That drove you crazy.

That was what crazy was all about.

And that's what Michael Webster had carried in his heart and his soul all the way from Southeast Asia, and that's what he had delivered, unexpectedly perhaps, unintentionally, to Whytesburg.

And that kind of crazy was contagious. Perhaps airborne, perhaps absorbed through the pores of the skin, but insidious, malignant, consuming.

Maryanne Benedict had it, and perhaps Matthias Wade too.

Nancy Denton had escaped early.

What had they uncovered? Really, what had they dug up out of that riverbank? Gaines could not believe that it was simply the preserved body of a teenage girl. They had opened a door, a portal, a window into some other place, some other reality, and through that aperture had come something strong enough and malevolent enough to poison the very air they breathed. They were all infected. The town was infected. And there was no way to put it back where they had found it.

John Gaines sat alone with these thoughts in his car, and he wondered if he was going crazy, too. He was just a little way down the street from Maryanne Benedict's house, but he could have been a thousand miles away.

It seemed to be a closed circle now, much like the snake itself. It had swallowed its own tail and would finally disappear.

Gaines started the car. He headed back to Whytesburg. By the time he arrived home, it would be close to eight, maybe a little after. He'd had enough. He would spend some time with his ma, perhaps watch a little TV, try to get a decent night's sleep. He would address this tomorrow, Sunday, and see if there wasn't some thread left somewhere that he could follow.

What had happened that night in August of 1954 was, in truth, less important than what had happened to Michael Webster. If Webster had in fact been responsible for Nancy's death, then there was nothing further to investigate. The killer had found his own justice, albeit two decades after the fact. The killer of Webster, however, was—in all probability—somewhere close, and Gaines believed it was Wade. Had Webster and Matthias Wade searched those woods together that night? No one but Wade knew, and he was not talking. If they had searched separately, then either one could have strangled Nancy without the other knowing. And if Wade had been her killer and Webster had known this, why had Webster maintained his silence? And why did Wade wait for twenty years to kill Webster, knowing all the while that Webster could tell the truth of what happened?

Gaines's head was filled with thoughts, images, bizarre ideas, and none of it made sense. In the final analysis, all that mattered was the identity of Nancy Denton's killer, the identity of Michael Webster's killer, and Gaines could not escape from the intuitive certainty that they were one and the same person: Matthias Wade.

Irrespective of what Gaines might believe, however, he had nothing of a probative nature with which to pursue an investigation of Wade. Wade had paid Michael Webster's bail, had driven him away from the Sheriff's Office, and that was that.

If Gaines discovered nothing else of significance, then the investigation—to all intents and purposes—was over.

That troubled him more than anything else: the simple fact that whoever had done these things might never be called to account.

But tonight, just for a few hours perhaps, he *had* to let it go. He had to rest his mind from the ever-nagging insistence of these mysteries. He had to devote some time to his mother, to her needs and wants. He had neglected her these past days, and that needed to be remedied.

Gaines turned on the radio. He turned it up loud. He found a music station somewhere out of Mobile. He forced himself to hear the song. He tried hard not to picture Maryanne Benedict's face as she'd told him that the devil had come to Whytesburg.

39

Yes, childhood was a time of magic, but perhaps the magic came at a price.

People do bad things, and then they run away from reminders. They move towns, change states, sometimes even countries. But conscience is an internal country, and guilt is a town you can never leave, and that's just part of being human. No matter how you change the landscape, there'll always be someone or something that reminds you of the worst you've ever done. What was it that we did that made this happen? I didn't know then, and I don't know now.

It was a special time, but it ended with a strange and inexplicable tragedy that no one could comprehend.

But that day, that afternoon, that evening seemed like all the others.

Dusk approached; the sun kissed the tops of the trees, and we could hear Matthias returning with the record player even before we saw him.

Matthias had changed his shirt and combed his hair, and as he set up the player and started winding it, he glanced at me.

He knew that I would have to dance with him, and yet I sensed something else. More than before, I was aware of how pleased he was that Eugene was not there to vie with him for my attention. I felt awkward, and then I dismissed it. This was Matthias. This was my friend Matthias. Nothing would happen here unless I wanted it to, unless I agreed to it. How naive I was, for never once did I consider that what would happen might involve Michael and Nancy.

Matthias put on a record. It was "Cry" by Johnnie Ray, and then he played "Why Don't You Believe Me?" by Joni James. I danced with him, and I could feel how close he was. I think he must have been wearing some of his father's cologne, because he smelled sweet, like lavender maybe, or violets.

I danced with Matthias for a little while, and then I was content to just lie down in the cool grass and watch Michael and Nancy.

I felt warm and sleepy and so utterly alive.

Matthias sat right there beside me, and I could feel his hand against my leg, and even though I was aware of how close we were, I did not want to move.

Nancy was perfect. Michael said one time that they left the gates of heaven open for a moment, and an angel escaped. She seemed like that to me that night, more than any other night, and it was as if her feet never touched the ground as she danced with her soldier, her Michael, the handsomest and bravest man in Whytesburg.

But there was something else present, too, though I could never have defined it.

Perhaps I knew the end was on its way. Perhaps I knew in my heart that here was a night that I would recall for the rest of my life. When I became an old lady, sitting somewhere on a stoop, perhaps rocking in a chair on a veranda somewhere, I would cast my mind back and relive this evening, this night. But I would not remember it for the sunshine or the picnic hamper or the music we played that evening, or the way Nancy danced with Michael, her with her bare feet on his shoes, the way he held her at a gentle distance, never too close, never too near, as if he understood and respected the simple fact that she was not yet the woman he could love with anything but his heart and mind. No, I would not remember it for those things, but for something altogether different. Something terrible and awful, something that struck right through my heart like an iron nail, a nail that would lodge there and spread its rust into my blood for the rest of my life.

It should have all been so right, and yet it was all so very wrong.

Love may be blind. It may be quiet. It may rage like a torrent or howl like a storm. It may begin lives and end them. It may have the power to extinguish the sun, to stop the sea, to illuminate the deepest of all shadows. It may be the torch that lights the way to redemption, to salvation, to freedom. It may do all these things. But regardless of its power, it is something we will never truly understand. We do not know why we feel this thing for someone. We just know we need to be near them, beside them, to feel the touch of their hand, the brush of their lips against our cheek, the smell of them, the sensation of their fingers in our hair, the realness of who they are, and know that they will forever find a home in our heart. We need this, but we do not comprehend it.

But loss. We understand loss. Loss is simple. It is perfect in its simplicity.

They were there, and then they were gone.

That is all there is to say.

I could feel their love—the love so effortlessly shared by Michael Webster and Nancy Denton—and it was pure and simple and perfect.

It should have stayed that way forever, but nothing lasts forever, does it?

At least nothing like love.

40

His mother was well enough. She had slept much of the day. She told him that Caroline had brought her some supper, and now all she wanted to do was sleep some more.

Gaines sat with her for a good hour, listened to her talk of Nixon yet again, what a dreadful man he was, how he had lied his way into office, how he was now attempting to lie his way out of any responsibility for what he had done. "He will fall," she said, "but it is just a matter of how many others he will take with him when he goes."

Gaines listened, but he did not pay a great deal of mind to the significance of what she was saying. In that moment, the machinations of Nixon's tentative hold on power were the least of his concerns. When it came to politics, Gaines agreed with Eugene McCarthy, that it was nothing more than a game for those smart enough to understand it and yet dumb enough to think it was important.

It was nearing ten by the time Alice Gaines finally wound down and drifted to sleep.

Gaines left her room and went to the kitchen. He fetched down the bottle of bourbon, a clean glass, took some ice from the freezer. He sat in silence, drinking a little, thinking a lot, considering the facts that within one day he had discovered the decapitated body of Michael Webster in the burned-out shell of his motel room, the dead body of Nancy's mother, and had spoken to both Matthias Wade and Maryanne Benedict. One day. So much in so little time. He remembered a quote from Wendell Holmes, how a man's mind, once stretched by an idea, never again regained its original dimensions. That had applied in war, but it applied here as well. Whatever may have happened twenty years before, and whatever was happening now, irrespective of whether Gaines believed in these undertones of cabalistic and occult influence, they were still present, still in force, and they needed to be understood.

And then, finally, Gaines's mind slowed down too. Perhaps it was the whiskey, perhaps the sheer mental and physical exhaustion of what had occurred, but he knew that if he lay down, he would sleep, and he wanted to sleep so very badly.

Gaines left the half-empty glass, the melting ice cubes, the bottle of bourbon. He went through to his room, shuffled off his clothes, and collapsed into bed. He breathed deeply—once, twice—and then he was gone, his thoughts extinguished like lights.

And within moments, they came. Both of them.

The girl comes first and then her mother, both Nancy and Judith Denton, and they stand at the door of his room, a pale light within each of them, and they beckon him. They don't speak, but everything they wish to communicate is in their eyes, their expressions, their outstretched hands.

He does not wish to go, but he knows he has to.

He follows them, seems to pass right through them, and yet when he steps beyond the threshold of the door, they are still ahead of him.

The rich cloying decay of rank vegetation fills his nostrils.

Once again, as if this sound is now an inherent and integral part of his very being, he can hear the distant chatter of CH-47s, the crack and whip and drumroll of the 105 howitzers and the Vulcans, behind that Charlie's 51 cals and the 82mm mortars. But it is all so very distant this time, so deeply lost in the sound of his own heart, his own breathing, the rush of blood though his veins and arteries, that he has to strain to hear it. He wonders if in fact those sounds do not come from without, but from within.

They fold into the vegetation, and the jungle swallows them, and he is swallowed also, and he understands that he has vanished from view and that no one but Nancy and Judith can see him, and no one will ever find them.

He does not wish to be here.

He calls out to them, asks them to slow down, to stop, to tell him what they can.

Who killed you, Nancy?

Was it Michael?

Was it Matthias?

What happened to you all those years ago?

He hears nothing now but the sweep of foliage as they flit through it—appearing, disappearing, the indistinct trace of laughter as they vanish ahead of him once more.

Eventually he tires. He cannot follow them any more. He sits on the damp earth, the moisture seeping through the seat and legs of his pants almost immediately. He smells blood. He knows it is blood, and he feels the warmth of the blood as it seeps up through the dirt, through the roots and undergrowth, and yet he does not care anymore. Perhaps this is all the blood that he has seen spilled in his life, and wherever he hesitates, wherever he pauses, it will seek him out and remind him of his past.

Michael is there. He sits facing Gaines, cross-legged, his head and his hands attached to his body, and he speaks so quietly that Gaines cannot understand a word he is saying.

Louder, he says. *Speak louder, Michael.*

But Michael just goes on and on, his voice like a whisper, incessant, too fast to be anything other than a torrent of unintelligible words, and Gaines feels the frustration and desperation of this thing in every pore of his being.

And then he hears a single word. Clear, precise, defined, unmistakable.

Goodbye.

A word from reality that has somehow found its way into his dreams.

And he knows. Even in sleep, he knows.

He knows the time has finally come.

John Gaines opened his eyes and lay there for some time. How long, he did not know. It could have been merely a handful of minutes, perhaps half an hour, maybe more.

He knew what had happened, and yet he struggled to absorb it.

Gaines had not imagined it would be this way.

He had imagined a hundred different scenarios, but not this one.

He had believed he would be there, always there, that he would be the last one to whom she spoke, that she would hold his hand, that there would be final words exchanged, a final gentle admonishment to marry, to raise up a family, to be a father. Be like your father, she would say, if in that way alone, be like your father.

But not this.

Not waking in the cool half-light of nascent dawn with a deep and profound certainty that this had finally happened, and without him.

He rose slowly. He dressed in jeans and a T-shirt. He glanced at the clock. It was 4:15 a.m.

He stood at the window for a while. There was a flicker of light in the back field behind the house, perhaps a hundred or so yards away. He paid it no mind. His mind was elsewhere, perhaps looking for her, trying to sense her presence, trying to register some vague awareness that she was still with him.

There was nothing.

Gaines stepped into the bathroom and sluiced his face with cold water. He held the towel against his skin for a long time, and he felt the emotion rising in his chest.

He set down the towel, turned back, and left his room.

He stopped at her door, and with his fingers upon the handle, he paused for some moments. There was silence everywhere, even within, everything but his heart, but it did not race. It did not fight within his chest. It merely swelled with something indefinably sad and powerful and deep.

He opened the door.

The scent of lavender was in the room. He was aware of that. He hesitated in the doorway, and then he closed the door behind him, almost as if to exclude the rest of the world from this very private moment.

He did not know how it was to be irretrievably alone, and yet now he was.

It was just him—John Gaines—and no one else.

He stepped closer to the bed, and he could see her. Her eyes were closed. She appeared to be sleeping, and yet there was no sound at all. The blankets that covered her did not gently rise and fall. The lids did not flicker. She did not murmur words known only to her dream self. She was gone. Her body was there, but she had left.

Gaines stepped closer, sat on the edge of the bed, took her hand, and held it.

Some slight vestige of warmth remained in her skin, and yet Gaines was certain that, whatever *élan* or soul or spirit had occupied this body, it had left. She looked like Alice Gaines, and yet she was not Alice Gaines. This was Alice Gaines's body, but that was all it was. Alice herself was not present.

For some reason Gaines felt the need to kneel. He did so, there at the side of the bed, and he placed his hands together, steepled his fingers, rested his face on the edge of the mattress, his cheek to the blanket, his eyes directed toward his mother's face.

Why had he not seen this coming? Was it always meant to be this way? That he would not have any prediction at all? That there would be no sudden and noticeable decline? That she would fight to go on living even as she knew the end had come?

He wanted to cry, but he could not. Not now. Not here.

He needed to call Bob Thurston. He needed to deal with the official aspects of her death.

He rose to his feet once more. He looked down at her, leaned to kiss her forehead, to whisper *I love you*, and then he hesitated, closed his eyes, felt the salt sting of tears, the taut knot of grief in his chest, his throat, and he uttered a single, whispered word—"Goodbye"— and turned once more to leave the room.

Standing in the hallway, the receiver in his hand, he felt awkward about waking Thurston, but there was no choice.

The phone was answered within moments, and Bob Thurston's slurred voice greeted him.

All Gaines said was, "Bob, it's John . . ."

Thurston replied, "I'll be there right away."

He was there right away, or so it seemed, but when Gaines glanced at the clock, it was nearing five thirty a.m. More than an hour had passed, though had he been asked, he would have said that he'd stepped across the threshold of his mother's room no more than ten minutes earlier.

Thurston attended to Alice Gaines alone. He took her body temperature, made notes, recorded the estimated time of death on the certificate, signed it, tucked it away in his case, and joined Gaines in the kitchen.

Gaines had made coffee, asked Thurston if he wanted some.

Thurston said yes, that would be much appreciated.

"I am surprised," Gaines said. "Not greatly, but a little."

"That it wasn't more dramatic?"

"Yes."

"Better this way, John. She passed in her sleep. She would not have known anything at all."

Gaines stopped filling the cup. "You believe that? That we're just a body and a brain, that there's no separate awareness?"

"I don't know, John."

"I do. I think she is still alive. She, herself, not my mother, because my mother was a physical personality as well, but whatever force of life animated my mother's body is still alive. Whatever awareness gives us life is still there . . ."

Gaines finished pouring the coffee, brought it to the table for Thurston, and sat down.

Thurston did not respond to Gaines's comments, and there was silence between them for some time.

"I will get Vic Powell over here," Thurston eventually said.

"I can call the Coroner's Office," Gaines said.

"Let me deal with it," Thurston replied. "I want to deal with it, John."

"Okay," Gaines said. He closed his hands around his coffee cup as if to draw warmth from it.

"You will not be able to avoid a service and a memorial, John," Thurston said. "Too many people knew her, and too many loved her. You are going to have to accept that you will not grieve alone."

"I know."

"So what can I do?"

Gaines shook his head. "Nothing." He looked at Thurston, his gaze unerring. "I am okay, Bob. I think I am okay."

"Well, you know I am here, whatever's going on, alright?"

"Yes, I know. Appreciated."

"I'll call Victor Powell," Thurston said. "I'll deal with all of that. You need to organize her funeral. Maybe not today, but soon."

"I can deal with it."

Thurston rose. "Do you want me to say nothing? Do you want to tell people yourself?"

"No, you tell whoever, Bob. It's not an issue."

"I just wondered if you wanted some time alone. If I tell people, you'll be overwhelmed with visitors."

"That is inevitable, Bob. It happens now, or it happens tomorrow or the next day. Best just to deal with it." Gaines smiled weakly. "You cannot postpone life, and you can't postpone dying either, right?"

"Seems not," Thurston replied.

Gaines stayed in the kitchen while Thurston used the phone in the hall. His conversation with Coroner Powell was hushed, respectful, brief.

Gaines stood near the back-facing window and looked toward the horizon. His attention was again caught by the brief flicker of light out there in the field, but again he dismissed it.

"He'll be here soon," Thurston said as he came back into the room. "He'll take her to the mortuary, and then we'll arrange for the undertaker to prepare her for burial. Have you thought . . . ?"

"My father was buried in Europe," Gaines said, "but he had a family plot in Baton Rouge. She wanted to be buried there."

"Understood. Then best to contact whoever you need to. But tomorrow. That can wait until tomorrow."

"It's Sunday," Gaines said. "It will have to wait until tomorrow."

"I'll stay with you until Victor gets here, then," Thurston said.

"No, Bob, it's okay. You go on back home. Go have breakfast with your family. I just need a little time alone with her before she goes."

Thurston nodded understandingly. He walked toward Gaines, and for a moment they just looked at each other.

Gaines held out his hand. They shook.

"Thanks for all you did for her, Bob."

"I wish I could have done more."

"Don't we all?" Gaines replied.

And then Bob Thurston gathered up his things and was gone, and John Gaines returned to the window and watched for a little while as the sun rose across the fields, and he tried to empty his mind of everything, but could not.

In that moment, he knew that there was nothing left in him of the child he'd once been. His mother had kept that part of him alive, the small reminiscences and anecdotes, the reminders of barefoot summers, the stories of the father he had never known.

Now it was all gone. Gone for good.

A ray of sunlight, bright and precise enough to be solid, and yet within it the constant motion of dust particles, broke through the kitchen window.

John Gaines reached out his hand toward it. The motes swarmed and danced around his fingers.

He closed his eyes. He inhaled deeply, exhaled once more, and tried to recall the last words he had shared with his mother.

There was nothing there at all, as if she—in leaving—had taken with her the very last memory that he'd possessed.

41

It nagged at his thoughts. The light in the field.

He could not see it now, but he had seen it earlier, believed it to be nothing more than something reflective catching the rays of the rising sun. A discarded bottle. A tin can. But it had flickered before dawn. He had seen something out there in the back field before the sun even rose, and so it could not have been what he thought it was.

Victor Powell came. He was quiet and methodical, and he went about his business and did not ask questions of Gaines until he and Gaines had taken Alice out on the gurney and into the back of the vehicle. And then they came inside once more. Gaines sat at the kitchen table, and Powell stood for a while in silence before he spoke.

"I met your mother on the first day she arrived here," he said. "It was the spring of 1968. You were on your way to Vietnam, far as I recall."

Gaines looked up at Powell. All he could think of was the fact that his mother would now be in the morgue alongside the Dentons and Michael Webster. That and the light in the field. He had looked for it, but it had gone. Later he would walk out there and see what he could find.

"What was it like?"

Gaines frowned, shook his head. "What was *what* like?"

"The war? In Vietnam?"

"The war?" Gaines asked, almost of himself. "I should imagine it was like any other war, Victor. The strange thing is that since this has happened, since we found Nancy, it has been in my thoughts far more than ever."

Powell merely nodded, as if understanding that there was no appropriate acknowledgment for Gaines's comment.

"I thought a great deal of your mother, John," he said. "I am really sorry she's passed, but it was inevitable."

"It's inevitable for all of us."

Powell stepped forward, took the chair facing Gaines. "Was there anything specific that you didn't have a chance to say to her?"

Gaines didn't reply.

"I mean, I have often found that not everything has been said . . . everything that needed to be said, and sometimes it is just best to say it. Say it out loud. Say it like they can still hear it."

"I understand," Gaines replied, and then he slowly shook his head. "There is nothing that didn't get said."

Powell reached out and closed his hand over Gaines's. "I am taking her now. You let me know of the arrangements, and if you wish to see her again . . ."

"I will, and thanks, Victor. Thank you for being her friend."

Powell rose slowly. He put on his hat, walked to the door, looked back once more at Gaines, and then left.

Gaines listened to the sound of the mortuary wagon as it pulled away, and then there were voices outside, those of Caroline and her parents, Leonard and Margaret. They came in from the back yard, and when Caroline saw Gaines she rushed towards him and started to cry.

Gaines just looked back at Margaret and Leonard, their faces like lost dogs, and he closed his eyes. He held Caroline tight as she sobbed, and he could smell juniper in her hair, and he was reminded of a girl he once knew from Fort Morgan, Alabama, but he could not remember her name.

It seemed that they stayed that way for some small eternity, and then Margaret pulled Caroline away from him. They all sat, and Margaret made coffee, and Caroline started talking. Once she started talking, it seemed that she did not want to stop, for to stop would mean silence, and it was always in the silence that her grief returned to fill the vacuum.

They talked among themselves then—Margaret and Leonard and Caroline—and Gaines listened, as if eavesdropping on a conversation that had nothing to do with him. He was thankful for their presence, for the decision that Margaret made to make eggs, to feed him, for had they not been there, he would have eaten nothing.

He did eat, surprising even himself, and quietly, as if in slow motion, he seemed to return, inch by inch, to some semblance of the real world, to the reality that necessitated funeral arrangements, a memorial service, the transportation of his mother's body out to Baton Rouge, Louisiana, to be buried in the plot that was always meant to welcome his father.

It seemed then, strangely, that Alice had been yet another victim of this sequence of events that had begun with the discovery of Nancy Denton.

Gaines was struck with the oddest thought: that Alice had gone after Nancy, after Webster, too, to find them, to ask them, to resolve the mystery for herself.

Do the dead commune with the dead?

Is that how it worked?

And then—once more—the sense of chill and dread that invaded his whole body when he asked himself what they had unleashed in Whytesburg.

He did not pursue that thought. He let it go. He tried to listen to the Rousseaus. He tried to stay right there in the kitchen with his neighbors and be the person he was supposed to be at such a time.

It was not long before Bob Thurston returned, and then came Eddie Holland and Nate Ross, and shortly thereafter Richard Hagen arrived from the Sheriff's Office, Lyle Chantry and Forrest Dalton in tow, and soon the house was filled with voices and noise. No one seemed to notice when Gaines slipped away to his mother's room, drew a chair to the edge of the bed, and sat there with his eyes closed, the tears welling behind, the anguish and pain in his chest too much to bear now, the words that he wanted to say vanished somewhere forever.

It was Thurston who came to find him, and he stood there with his hand on Gaines's shoulder, and he said nothing as Gaines sobbed. When Gaines could cry no more, he just waited with him until he had gathered himself together again, and then they left the room and returned to the kitchen.

Hagen had gone, as had Dalton, Chantry, Ross, and Holland. Margaret and Leonard were back home, but Caroline had stayed. So it was that the three of them—Alice Gaines's son, her doctor, her caregiver—sat in that kitchen and spoke of other things, things that bore no relevance to the death of Alice, things that were meaningless and irrelevant in the face of what had happened, but—at such a time—were perhaps the best things of which to speak.

Gaines understood that it would be weeks, months, before he even began to appreciate the meaning of this. It was said that each anniversary and special occasion needed to pass at least once—a full turn of the calendar—before you could begin to accommodate such a change. Only then, as he contemplated this, did Gaines appreciate some small aspect of what Judith Denton had suffered. Death, at least in a physical sense, was all encompassing and final. There was no coming back. There was no chance of circumstances conspiring to present some other outcome. But Nancy's disappearance for all of twenty years? The sense of hope, growing ever weaker with each passing year and yet somehow kept alive by the sheer will of her mother, was then dashed to pieces. Judith Denton's suicide demonstrated that she had continued to survive solely and only because of her hope. And when that hope had gone, well, there was no reason to continue.

Gaines always imagined that Alice had hung in there for one reason—to see him find someone, to see him married, perhaps start a family, to give herself the certainty that her son would be cared for. But perhaps it had not been that at all. Perhaps she had finally resigned herself to the fact that the only way to get her son to do anything along that line was to show him how deep and profound real loneliness could be. She was all he had, and with her gone, well, perhaps his necessity would rise to the point where he did something about it.

He did not know, and for now it did not matter.

It was late afternoon by the time Bob Thurston and Caroline Rousseau bade their farewells, Caroline with the reminder that she and her folks were only next door, that Gaines should come across and eat with them if he felt like it.

He thanked her, thanked Thurston for his time, his concern, his friendship, and then he watched them leave the house, Caroline turning left, Thurston driving away toward the center of town and home.

Gaines stood there for a while. The evening was warm, a good deal of moisture in the air, and he went back inside to pour himself a drink.

It was as he raised the glass to his lips that he remembered the light in the field. He smiled to himself. Why did this thing engage his attention so much? Surely it was nothing.

He set the glass down, left the house by the back door, and stood on the veranda. He looked out toward the point where he had seen it.

There was no reason for any sense of disquiet or unease, but as he tried to identify the precise spot, he was aware that the air seemed cooler, an almost electric tension present in the atmosphere. He passed it off as merely imagination. It had been a terrible day, a day filled with awkward, inexplicable emotions, a day of guilt and sadness and pain and heartbreak, a day that presented him with a future that he neither understood, nor cared to understand.

He went on looking, ever more aware of the fact that something—what, he did not know—did not feel right. In truth, something felt very wrong indeed.

The entirety of his world seemed nothing less than surreal, as if here he had found some middle ground between what was real and what was simply imagination.

Sheriff John Gaines considered the possibility that he had never returned from the nine levels of hell, that somewhere he had slipped through a gap in time and space, and everything that had happened, everything that was happening, was merely a creation of his own darkest thoughts and fears. Or maybe he had in fact returned, but in returning he had carried the nine levels with him, bearing them gently, bearing them undisturbed and complete, and here—in this small Mississippi town—he had delivered them for all to see.

Perhaps Maryanne Benedict had been right in one sense.

Perhaps the devil had in fact come to Whytesburg, but it was he—John Gaines—who had opened the door.

42

The sun had not yet set, and the air was warm and filled with moisture, and Gaines started down the short flight of steps and headed for the horizon.

At least here, he had believed, unlike in war, the night was some slight and brief reprieve from the darkness of the day. But no, the darkness followed whoever it chose to follow, and it found you wherever you were.

Gaines went out across the yard behind the house, through the low gate at the end, across the rutted, foot-worn walkway that passed left and right to adjacent properties, and he descended the small incline into the field. The simple action of placing one foot before the other took some concentration and effort. He had felt this before, his boots waterlogged, thigh-deep in dirty water, his rifle held high, his eyes peeled for the slightest movement, his ears attuned for the briefest suggestion of anomalous sound. It became a state of mind, that degree of sensitivity, and if you did not recognize the difference between recon and rest, then you started to hear many more words than were spoken, began to receive messages that were never meant at all. Even the voices that belonged to the ghosts of your past knew that the best way to be heard was to whisper. And once you gave them space on the stage, they never left.

Gaines walked, one foot after the other, one step, a second, a third, and he felt the weight of all that he was confronting. At one point, he merely stopped and looked back toward the house, a house he had known for all the years since his return, a house that had come to represent his life with his mother.

It was hard to fathom, hard to absorb, harder to comprehend. The closest he had ever come to such a wide and strange spectrum of emotions was the loss of Linda Newman. But she was not dead, merely departed. He had seen men die in war—brutally, tragically, suddenly, and in ways that no human being should ever have to witness—but, in the main, they had been men he did not know. Their names yes, sometimes their occupations before the draft, but little else. They were there, and then they were gone. Linda was different, a thousand times different, and then the loss of his mother was a hundred thousand times beyond even that. There was no means by which he could measure the extent of his sadness. Perhaps when people grieve, they do not grieve for the loss of what has passed but the loss of what might have been. They grieve for a future that will never be.

Gaines sat on the ground. He did not know why. After a while, he remembered where he had been going, the fact that going there—to find out what had caught his attention in the field—was something he had started simply to have something to do. He got up, brushed down his pants, and carried on walking.

He did not know how long he had paused, at first to look back at the house, then to sit in the dirt, but the sun had lowered and the shadows had lengthened.

Not all things needed to be rationalized or explained. Gaines believed his mother was attuned to things beyond the immediately corporeal and tangible. She had said little of this, but she believed it. If others believed something so strongly that they could then act upon those beliefs, did that not make them as real as any other beliefs? Who said that one belief was more valid and believable than another?

Gaines realized he had stopped walking again. He had taken no more than three or four steps, and he had come to a stop once more. He smiled to himself, a fleeting consideration of his own indecisiveness, and then he moved once more.

Surely he must have reached the point from where the flickering light had come.

And then he had another thought, and the thought seemed to swallow up every other thought in one simple go. What if it had not been a physical light? What if it had been something else entirely? What if he had seen the light of life? Seriously, what if he had experienced some bizarre and surreal perception of something beyond the physical? What if such things *could* be perceived? Was there a life force that, in leaving the body, could remain for a while and could be seen, literally *seen* with the eyes?

Gaines shuddered. Was a ghost nothing more than the soul of a person, sometimes remaining for some time after the event of death, perhaps with some intent to communicate what had been left unsaid?

Had he seen his mother out here in the field? Was that what had happened? Had only he been able to see her?

It was this thought that underpinned every accepted reality, every certainty possessed about the nature of life and death for centuries—that the very essence of man was a spiritual thing—and he wrestled with that thought right until the moment that he came upon the thing that had winked and flickered at him through the darkness.

Clearly visible beneath the thick rivulets of melted wax was a dismembered hand.

Gaines had read of such things, had seen representations and images. He had heard of *Petit Albert*, but how he had heard of it, he could not recall. Perhaps it had been something of which his mother had spoken. Perhaps it was something there within the woof and warp of New Orleans history and heritage and folklore and rumor.

The image was undeniable and surreal, both horrific and somehow, strangely, expected.

Perhaps this was nothing more than a catalyst, the single thing that tipped him over the edge of his internal defenses, but he felt those defenses yielding. He felt the tension unraveling in his chest—a combination of despair and grief, of loss and horror, within this some kind of bone-deep certainty that he had brought this upon himself—even brought it upon the whole town of Whytesburg—by failing to hold Webster, by failing to keep him alive, but most of all for bringing Nancy Denton back from that stinking, black grave.

And it was then that Gaines cried again, but really cried, not like a man who'd lost his mother, but like a man who'd lost everything.

Gaines knelt down in the dirt, his knees in the furrows of the fields, and he sobbed until his chest was racked with pain, and through his tear-filled eyes he looked at Michael Webster's dismembered hand—for he knew without doubt that this was all it could be—the skin caked with melted wax, the last vestige of the candle burned down to nothing. He remembered how that light had flickered while his mother lay dead, and he wondered what terrible nightmare had been unleashed in Whytesburg that had opened a twenty-year-old grave and put a Hand of Glory out here in the darkness for him to find.

And he knew that Webster's head would be buried somewhere close, though what he would find beyond that he did not know.

Gaines did not believe that this was some arcane and occult conjuration. This was merely violence and some perverse desire to frighten Gaines more than he was already frightened.

Michael Webster had left the Sheriff's Office with Matthias Wade. Matthias Wade knew something of this, and it was a great deal more than he had already said. Gaines was certain that Wade knew the truth of Nancy Denton, that he knew the truth of Webster, and that such truths were the only thing that would relieve the terrible pressure that Gaines felt all around him. It was as if such a revelation would open the only door that was needed, the door through which could pass the dreadful horrors that had befallen Whytesburg these past few days.

It was a long time before Gaines rose to his feet, and when he did, he walked back to the house and called Richard Hagen. He told him to bring sawhorses and crime-scene tape, torches, a shovel, and to call Victor Powell and tell him to get out there also.

Hagen didn't ask questions. Perhaps he, too, did not want to know what John Gaines had found. Perhaps he, too, believed that the worst had already been witnessed.

On the back steps of the house, John Gaines waited patiently for the arrival of his deputy and the coroner.

In that moment, the world seemed very small indeed, claustrophobic with shadows and whispered voices, and Gaines believed that his mother's voice was among those that he heard, and she was telling him to leave.

43

It was a task of careful excavation—to retain as much physical evidence as they could. Powell assisted too, and it was Powell who said what Gaines had hoped he would not hear.

"There is something buried here."

Powell's voice was calm and measured, and yet Gaines could hear that edge of agitated disturbance beneath it. Powell was uneasy, as was Hagen, as was Gaines himself. It was dark, and they worked by flashlight, and the constant movement of shadows around them added nothing but further disquiet to the already tense atmosphere.

Gaines and Hagen held their lights steady as Powell worked his fingers around the edges of what had had found.

"Some sort of canvas," Powell said. "Something wrapped in canvas, I think."

He dug further, Hagen assisting then, until it was nothing less than obvious what they had found. They carefully eased back the edges of the wrapping, and the features were unmistakable.

"Webster's head," Powell said, and he looked up at Gaines.

Gaines directed his flashlight, and for a moment it seemed that Michael Webster had been buried up to his neck, only his head protruding from the dirt. He looked back at Gaines with blank and lifeless eyes. Gaines knew that he would never be able to blanch his mind of such a grotesque and strange image.

Their work was swift then, almost as if they wanted to be engaged in the task for as brief a time as possible. Preserving as much integrity as they could in the surrounding earth, they lifted the decapitated head from the ground and set it aside on some plastic sheeting that Hagen had brought from the trunk of the car. They would need to take pictures now, not wait until morning, so Gaines dispatched Hagen to get more lights, to bring the camera and flashbulbs from the office, and they would do the best they could.

After Hagen's departure, Gaines and Powell stood back from the scene.

There was a tense and awkward silence between them for some

minutes, and then Powell broke the deadlock with, "So, serious business or bullshit designed to scare you?"

Gaines shook his head. "It's never what you believe, but what others believe."

"But what do you believe?"

Gaines smiled resignedly. "I am a Louisianan. I was raised in New Orleans. This kind of thing has been there all through my life. Alice believed in it, and she saw things that she couldn't even begin to explain, but . . ." He shook his head. "I am the eternal skeptic."

"And it's supposed to mean what?"

"The thing with the hand? It's called a Hand of Glory. As far as I can recall, it's supposed to be the dried and pickled hand of a hanged man. Usually the left hand, the sinister, unless the man was hanged for murder, in which case it's the hand that he used to commit the murder. And fat is taken from the body and mixed with virgin wax and sesame oil to make a candle, and his hair is used for a wick. Whoever makes it is supposed to be able to render any person motionless and open any door. But I don't think this is anything but a message."

"And the message is what? That you should stay away? That you'll be next to get your head buried in a field?"

"Maybe."

"Any thoughts?"

"I'm pretty sure now that Webster did not kill Nancy. That he found her, just as he said. Why he did the thing with her heart, maybe we'll never know. Now I'm starting to think that whoever killed Nancy also killed Michael and did this too. Or someone paid someone to do it."

"Wade?"

"That's what I'm thinking."

"But you have nothing on him."

"Right."

"Except that he was the one who bailed Webster out, and he was the last person to see him."

"Absolutely, yes. But I cannot arrest him for paying bail or giving the man a ride."

"So what do you do when you have nothing probative?"

"You make something."

"Meaning?"

Gaines turned at the sound of Hagen returning in the black-and-white.

"Right now? Hell, I don't know. I need to get this out of here. I need to organize my mother's funeral. I need to . . ." Gaines sighed audibly.

Victor Powell put his hand on Gaines's shoulder.

"Maybe you should call State."

"Maybe I will," Gaines replied.

Hagen pulled up five yards away and got out of the car. Within minutes, they had erected lights, hooked them up to the car battery, and flooded the scene. From a distance, a bright ghost of illumination hovered in the field behind Gaines's house, and Gaines busied himself taking shots of the dismembered hand, the hole in which the head had been buried, the head itself, the surrounding furrows where footprints had flattened the dirt.

Soon they were done, and Hagen and Gaines returned the lights to the car while Powell gently lifted the head and hand into separate containers and put them in the trunk of his vehicle.

"Don't know what else I'll be able to tell you aside from what we already know," he told Gaines as he readied himself to leave.

"I'm not interested in what happened anymore," Gaines replied. "Just who did it and why."

"What I said earlier, about calling someone in State. I meant it. I don't know about you, but I sure as hell feel out of my depth. With everything else that's happened and with what you have to deal with personally . . ."

"No decisions until tomorrow," Gaines said.

"Well, anything I can do, just let me know."

Gaines thanked Powell, watched as he drove away, and stood there looking at the hole where they had found Webster's head.

He could not help but be reminded of the pictures he had seen in Dennis Young's office in St. Mary Parish, the shallow graves where Anna-Louise Mayhew and Dorothy McCormick had been found.

The crime and the circumstances were very different, but the feeling was very much the same.

Or perhaps it was simply a case of wanting it to be Matthias Wade because there was no one else.

"You gonna be okay?" Hagen asked. "You want me to stay?"

"No, you go on home," Gaines said. "I'm not very good company right now."

"Hey, if you want me to stay—"

"I'll be better alone," Gaines said. "Seriously."

"Well, my door's open, and if you want somewhere else to sleep, you know?"

"Thanks, Richard. I'll be fine."

Hagen hesitated for a moment, and then he nodded. He turned and walked to the car, started it up, and drove away.

After a minute or so, there was nothing—no light but a slim rind of moon above the trees, no sound but for cicadas and a cool breeze that ruffled leaves and carried a vague haunt of music from somewhere west—and John Gaines, once again, sat in the dirt of the field behind his house. Cross-legged, his head down, his hands clasped behind, his elbows on his knees, he rocked gently back and forth. He tried to picture all their faces—Nancy Denton in '54, the little girls from '68, Michael and Judith and his mother. He believed they could see him, every single one of them, as if the mere devotion of his attention to the circumstances and manner of their deaths brought them back to life, if not in this world, then in some other.

Gaines could not believe that a human being was simply a body. There was so much more to it than that. As far as voodoo was concerned, he did not know what he believed or what *to* believe. He believed in murder, however, and murder had been perpetrated in this time and place, also in Morgan City in 1968, also in the woods or down by the river in 1954.

And he believed that Matthias Wade was a liar, if only from the viewpoint that there were things he was not saying, and without some of those things—Gaines felt sure—the truth of what had taken place here would never be known.

At last he rose to his feet, and with the weight of the world on his shoulders, Gaines made his way back to the house. He stood once again on the veranda, looking toward the trees, the narrow rind of moon, the sky beyond, and he wondered if that truth would ever be revealed.

He would bury his mother, he would say his goodbyes, and then— whatever it took—he would dedicate himself to this task, if not for Webster and Nancy, then for the girls in '68, and if not for them, then for himself. To leave this unresolved did not bear consideration.

And no, he would not call the State Troopers, nor the FBI. He would do this alone. Not out of pride or the concern that his reputation would be harmed, but because he did not wish to share with anyone the satisfaction of walking Matthias Wade into court.

Also, in truth, he knew that there would be disciplinary action for his mishandling of the Webster search. He would face the music for that, of course, but he would face it when the investigation was over. And it would not be a matter of trying to placate anyone with a solved case, but merely that at this juncture he could not afford to be distracted.

On the day of his mother's death, someone has invaded his thoughts with an act of cruelty and horror. Instead of giving him time to grieve, to let go, to be the best son he could be at such a time, his attention had been snatched from her by this terrible thing. It had become a personal issue, he had been delivered a personal message, and if this was the way it was going to be, then so be it.

If Matthias Wade wanted a war, then Gaines could bring a war.

It was that simple.

44

It was Wednesday, the day of the funeral, before Gaines became aware that he had no real recollection of Monday or Tuesday. All that occupied his mind was a radio report he had heard in passing the day before, something to the effect that the *executive privilege* presented by Nixon's advisers as a means by which he could withhold the last of the Oval Office tapes had been deemed as *not absolute* by Chief Justice Warren Burger. Nixon would have to give them up. The House judiciary had voted twenty-seven to eleven in favor of impeachment. Alice had been right. Nixon had lied his way into a corner, and he didn't seem able to lie himself out. All that Gaines could think of was the simple fact that she had missed seeing the man take a fall.

This thought seemed to occupy his mind during the service. The small plank-board Whytesburg First Methodist Church could not have contained more people. The ceremony itself was brief, almost perfunctory. Victor Powell spoke, as did Bob Thurston, and Caroline Rousseau cried as she read a poem by Emily Dickinson.

Gaines did not speak. Those things he wished to say about his mother he had already said to her, and he was not a religious man. The minister, a man Gaines barely knew, a man who had visited his mother no more than twice in all her years of illness, was respectful but distant. Once the service was done, they all trooped out to the front of the building, and here his mother's coffin was laid inside a hearse for the long drive to Baton Rouge.

Gaines followed in his own car, and he followed alone. He left Whytesburg behind, and it was as if he were leaving his past. He knew he would return, of course, but there was something symbolic in what was happening. One man departed; another man would come back. A man with a different viewpoint, a different purpose, a different rationale. That was how Gaines imagined it, for throughout the journey, his thoughts were no longer occupied by the downfall of Richard Nixon but by determining the truth of these most recent events. If Matthias Wade was responsible for these killings, then Wade would be finished either by the hand of the state or some other means. Three young girls and a war veteran were dead, and there was a price to be paid.

Gaines oversaw the interment, and while he stood there alongside the cemetery caretaker, behind him the two men responsible for seeing his mother's coffin into its final resting place, it did not go unacknowledged that Baton Rouge was also the birthplace and home of Michael Webster.

Everything was done by noon, and Gaines took an early lunch in a diner not far from the cemetery. He did not want to go back to Whytesburg, not immediately, and he decided to stay overnight. He found a motel a handful of miles down I-10, watched TV, drank himself to sleep, woke with a terrible thirst and a pounding head. It was Thursday, the first of August, and he decided to simply follow 10 through New Orleans and then head back up to Whytesburg across the bridge. He took some breakfast, just a couple of warm rolls and some black coffee and then began the hundred-or-so-mile drive. The day was warm, and with the windows down, he could smell the salt air as the northwesterly breeze carried it in from the coast. Beneath it was the bayou funk, the rank and brackish ghost of waterlogged trees, of rotting corduroy roads navigated through swampland and undergrowth. It was the smell of his childhood, and not without some sense of nostalgia and affection did he recall the years he'd spent in this very part of the country. He was thirty-four years old, had left Louisiana just seven years earlier, and yet felt as if he'd been gone for more than a lifetime. So much had intervened, and though he had spent merely fourteen months at war, that also felt like a hundred times more when he considered the significance and import of what he had witnessed and experienced there.

But it seemed that Whytesburg had been the setting for the greatest tragedies of all. The loss of his mother now stood front and center in his life, and would for a great while to come. He did not feel the *alone* yet, but he knew that the feeling would come. There was a point where aloneness became loneliness, and though some seemed to deal with this well, Gaines knew he would not. Too much time in solitude and he would turn inward among his own thoughts, just as Michael Webster had done. Not completely lost, but somehow sufficiently detached and disconnected from reality to preclude the chance for any genuine well-being, and if such internalization continued for too long, perhaps there would be no recovery. He would inhabit a world of his own creating, populated by the darkness he still carried from the war, the darkness occasioned by most recent events, all of it overshadowed by the fact that he was the very last of the Gaines line, and there would be no more. It was with this self-awareness that he had joined the sheriff's department post-demobilization. Without a structure of some fashion, there would have been little enough to support him.

Gaines had thought to stop over in New Orleans, but he did not dare. He drove on through, made a brief stop outside of Slidell to get some lunch, and was back on the road to Whytesburg within twenty minutes.

He called in first to see Powell, found him alone in the office at the rear of the building.

"As I thought, there's not a great deal more that I can tell you. Webster's head and his left hand were severed relatively cleanly. An ax, perhaps a machete or a heavy knife."

Gaines sat quiet for a time, and then he said, "The Wade sister, Della. Do you know her?"

Powell shrugged his shoulders. "I know *of* her, but I wouldn't say I know her."

"She lives with the father and Matthias, right?"

"As far as I'm aware, yes." Powell leaned forward. "Why? What you looking at?"

"Getting some kind of inside line on that family."

"You really think this is the work of Matthias Wade."

"I do."

"Except for the fact that he has nothing to do with any of it, save that he knew Nancy Denton when he was a kid and he paid out Webster's bail."

"I know that, Victor."

"I mean, I'm not supposing to tell you your business, John, but it seems like you're chasing the longest of long shots. And besides, those people have more money than they know what to do with. You go after Matthias Wade, and you'll just find yourself surrounded by a horde of fancy-ass lawyers from Jackson, and you won't get a word in edgeways."

"Which is why I'm not going after Matthias Wade."

"But you're gonna go after his sister."

"I just want to talk to her, that's all."

"That's not the way Matthias is going to see it, and who's to say that she's going to be willing to talk to you anyway?"

"She might not be, but what the hell else am I going to do? Regardless of Nancy Denton's murder, I have Michael Webster's killing to deal with. Even if we forget what happened twenty years ago, I can't overlook a headless body in a burned-out motel cabin."

"I'm not saying to overlook it, John. Of course not. I'm just advising you not to go charging in on the Wades, accusations flying all over the place. They have enough influence to make you disappear without a second thought."

"Like they made Nancy and Michael disappear?"

"John, seriously, you're talking first-degree murder here," Powell said. "You're talking a life sentence here. Say that Matthias Wade is responsible for killing Nancy Denton and that he then killed Webster to prevent Webster from talking, you think he'll stop at anything to protect his own life? Sooner or later, that old man is going on his way, and then Matthias controls everything that the Wade family owns. It would take just the tiniest percentage of what he has in his checking account to make you vanish from the face of the earth without a single trace."

Gaines smiled sardonically. "That can go both ways, Victor, but it wouldn't cost me anything to make him vanish."

"I didn't hear that," Powell said.

"That's because I didn't say it."

"Okay, so I'm not going to stop you from trying to talk to her, but how do you do that without Matthias knowing?"

"Well, she must have her own life. I'm sure she doesn't spend every waking hour locked up in that house. She must go out; she must know people."

"Well, I haven't a clue who knows them, who doesn't, where they go, what they do. Maybe check with Bob Thurston; see if he knows who the family doctor is. Maybe he can tell you something about their comings and goings."

Gaines's first thought had been to check with Nate Ross and Eddie Holland. There was little they did not know, and questions along that line would be more discreet than any kind of official action. To ask the Wade doctor for anything at all would require some kind of warrant, as records and personal details would be confidential.

"I'll start looking around," Gaines said as he rose from his chair.

"And how are you doing?" Powell asked. "Everything went fine in Baton Rouge?"

"It hasn't reached me yet," Gaines replied. "Not fully. I think I have to get through a few more days without her to even realize she's not there anymore."

"She was one hell of a woman, John, no doubt about it. Like I said, if there is anything I can do—"

Gaines thanked Powell. They shook hands. Gaines left the building and headed back over to Nate Ross's place on Coopers Road. Eddie Holland was evident in his absence, but Nate Ross was all too willing to welcome Gaines in and offer him a drink.

Gaines accepted, took delivery of a significantly loaded glass of W.L. Weller, and the pair of them sat in Ross's kitchen in silence until Ross asked after Gaines's well-being.

"I'll be fine," Gaines said. "I just said to Vic Powell that I have to get through a few more days of being alone to really get that she's not here."

"Know where that's at," Ross replied. "Took me a year, maybe two, to finally accept that my wife had passed. Every room seems too big, every day is too long, and it's always so damned quiet. Half the reason I have Eddie Holland around here all the time is 'cause he makes so much noise."

Gaines smiled. "Which begs the question, where is he?"

Ross smiled back, but knowingly. "Take a guess."

"Hell, Nate, I haven't a clue."

"Maybe Gulfport."

"Gulfport?"

"Sure thing. He gets a call from Maryanne Benedict yesterday. They were on the phone for half an hour. Seems your visit stirred her up some, and she was asking about Michael Webster, about the Denton girl, and about you."

"Me?"

Ross shrugged. "Don't ask me why she'd be interested in a broken-down deadbeat like you, but she was."

"And you didn't think to tell me about this?"

"Hell, John, you were dealing with everything else, with your mother, going out to Baton Rouge. I was gonna tell you, but maybe later today."

"Tell Eddie that I want to know what she said when he gets back."

"About you?"

"Yeah sure, Nate. That really is at the forefront of my attention right now."

Ross raised his hand in a placatory fashion. "I'm just baiting you.

I'm not serious." He sipped his drink, cleared his throat. "So what brings you out here again?"

"Della Wade."

"What about her?"

"You say she still lives up at the Wade house?"

"Last time I heard, yes."

"I want to know everything you can tell me about her."

"What have you heard?"

"Nothing, Nate. That's just the point."

"Well, she was a wild one, John, and she has been corralled by that family and brought back into line, but there's a streak in that one that'll never get tamed, no matter how long you lock her up."

"Wild? How?"

"Well, there were a few years while she was in her twenties that she was forever causing some kind of trouble. Drugs, the whole bohemian lifestyle thing in New Orleans. I can only presume she was hanging out with the brother, the musician, Eugene. But then she got herself in some serious shit and Daddy had to bail her out. He brought her back here, and here she's been ever since."

"What serious shit?"

"Blowing the family fortune on Lord knows what. Parties, gambling, got herself pregnant on two separate occasions by two different guys. Aborted both times. Involved with women, you know, sexually and everything. Got in with a crowd of small-time crooks, one of whom ripped her off for about ten grand, which means that he ripped off old man Wade for ten grand. Anyway, she's been back home for a good while now, and they have her on a short leash."

"She goes out?"

"I would think so, yes, but you're asking me specifics about something that I really don't know one hell of a lot about. If you want the inside scoop on Della Wade, then you need to talk to a man called Clifton Regis."

"And who the hell is Clifton Regis?"

"He's the guy who's rumored to have taken her for ten grand, but only for a short while."

"Meaning?"

"Meaning that Della Wade got ten grand out of old man Wade, gave it to Regis, and then went back for more. Wade figured out what was going on, or maybe Matthias did, and as far as I know, that ten grand went back where it had come from pretty damned fast."

"When was this?"

"This was just before they clipped her wings, maybe a coupla years ago. I don't recall exactly."

"But he's not going to know the ins and outs of Della Wade's life if he hasn't seen her recently."

"No, but he can tell you a great deal more about her than I can, and maybe that will give you an inside line on getting to her."

"And why would he know anything about her . . . I mean, wasn't he just trying to take her money?"

"No, not as far as I understand. What I heard, they were planning on getting away together. What happened in the end, I don't know."

"You know where he lives?"

"Used to live in Lyman, but whether he's still there or not is anyone's guess."

"Appreciated, Nate." Gaines got up to leave. He lifted his glass, drained it, turned toward the door. Reaching it, he paused, turned back, and added, "And tell Eddie that anything he got from Maryanne Benedict, anything of any use, would be appreciated, too."

"Sure will, John," Ross replied. "And you take care now. Always been my way to have as little to do with the Wades as I could, and I advise that course of action for you as well."

"I'll bear that in mind, Nate."

45

Friday morning, Gaines set to work finding Clifton Regis, and it proved to be a great deal easier than he'd anticipated. One call to the Lyman Sheriff's Office, another to the County Records Bureau, and he had him located. However, Gaines's task did not stay so straightforward. First and foremost, Clifton Regis was a colored man. That was the first difficulty. The second difficulty was that Regis was mid a three-to-five for burglary, and they had him up at Parchman Farm, all of two hundred and fifty miles northwest in Sunflower County.

It had taken no more than half an hour to track him down, but Gaines—seated there at his desk, the notepad in front of him where he had scrawled the man's details—spent twice that time figuring on how best to tackle this obstacle.

Being colored, Regis would more than likely be unwilling to countenance a visit from a white sheriff. Such a thing would become quickly known, and Regis would not fare well as a result. Discussions with law enforcement officials meant only two things— further charges, or deals being made. In either case, the prisoner would request legal counsel be in attendance. Gaines did not want any third party present at his intended conversation with Regis. And if Gaines did not go into Parchman in an official capacity, then there would be no reason for him to go in.

Gaines could now understand Wade Senior's desire to have Della under his wing. The Wades were staunch Southerners, and their affiliation with Klan was inevitable, directly or indirectly, visibly or not. Nothing overt, nothing obvious, but financial support had surely made its way from some of those Wade-owned businesses into the hands and pockets of pro-segregation activists. So having Della Wade involved with the coloreds would have been out of the question, and to have his daughter scammed by Clifton Regis would have been an insult of the most personal nature. What had Nate Ross said—that the ten grand went back from where it had come pretty damned fast? Gaines could imagine the conversation that had taken place between Regis and a couple of Wade's people. No kind of conversation at all, in truth. It was a miracle, in fact, that Regis was even alive to tell the story. And then the recalcitrant and troublesome Della had been returned to the fold, appropriately admonished by her father, perhaps Matthias, and there she had stayed. If it was in fact true that Della was maintaining a relationship with Regis, then Gaines hoped that some sour taste of resentment had remained on Della Wade's lips, the kind of resentment that would see her wanting to inflict some vengeance on her father and her elder brother. But then Gaines could have it all wrong. Della could be the sweetest kind of girl imaginable, led astray by an ill-intentioned men, seduced into a life of drugs and debauchery, an unwitting pawn in their game. Perhaps the ten grand had merely been a precursor, something to test the water, and Regis's intent had been to fleece the family for a great deal more. Anyway, whoever she was and whatever might have happened, the man she'd been involved with was no longer involved. He was up at Parchman, and Parchman was not a good place to be, regardless of who you were.

Parchman was the oldest prison in the state, the only one capable of providing maximum-security detention. Until the Supreme Court suspension, it was also the home for Mississippi's death row facility, Unit 17. Up there in the delta, the Farm covered the better part of twenty thousand acres, and due to its location and the inhospitality of its surround, it needed no great and mighty walls to house its inmates. And then there were the Freedom Riders. That was a history all its own. Back at the start of '61, a host of civil rights activists, both coloreds and whites, came to the South to test the desegregation of public properties and facilities. Within six months, more than one hundred and fifty had been arrested, convicted, and jailed in Parchman. Those activists were given the worst treatment possible, everything from issued clothes being several sizes too small to no mail. The food was barely edible, strong black coffee, grits, and blackstrap molasses for breakfast, beans and pork gristle for lunch, the same again for dinner, only cold. Freedom Riders were permitted one shower a week. Governor Barnett went down there a few times to enforce these conditions. The prisoners began singing. They sang their hearts out. Deputy Tyson, the man responsible for their containment, took away their mattresses and bug screens. They kept on singing. The cells were flooded, but still they went on. Eventually Tyson yielded, unable to maintain such harsh treatment. Most of the Freedom Riders were bailed out within the subsequent month. Then came the big civil rights violation lawsuit of 1972. Gaines could remember it capturing the headlines week after week. Four Parchman inmates brought a suit against the prison superintendent in federal district court, citing instances of murders, rapes, and beatings. But, as in all things, change came slowly and resentfully. Parchman was still Parchman, more than likely always would be, and whatever legacy it carried, it carried that legacy in the very earth upon which it stood. Parchman was still divided by race, and Gaines couldn't see it changing within his lifetime, if ever. You didn't need to say you were Klan to be Klan. You didn't need to shout the Klan call-to-arms as you beat a colored man half to death with a Black Annie. Penitentiary inspectors and independent observers spoke of significant improvements at Parchman, but they saw only what the vested interests wanted them to see, and those reports were based on temporary and artificial showcase facilities. Parchman was the size of a town, several towns in fact, and those things that they wished to hide were more than amply hidden.

The problem of how to get in there and see Regis was considerable, and it preyed on Gaines's mind for a while. The natural paranoia of the penitentiary governor and his deputies precluded any real possibility of negotiating an official visit. They would suspect that this was nothing more than further outside interference. Even after the *Gates v. Collier* case, Parchman was still believed to be running the penal farm system that was supposed to have been disbanded. Camp B, the main colored camp, previously up near Lambert in Quitman County, had been demolished, and all prisoners were now concentrated within the Parchman facility itself. Most areas had no guard towers, no cell blocks, no walls. There were merely double fences of concertina wire and high gun towers overlooking the compounds and barrack units. Local farmers and construction outfits used prison labor, unauthorized, unreported, and the governor and his lackeys took a hefty commission. Such arrangements were integral to the woof and warp of penitentiaries the country over, but not every penitentiary had been subjected to the legal scrutiny that Parchman had undergone. Hence, penitentiary officials were alert for covert inspections, unannounced visits, unwanted attention. But then, perhaps that very paranoia was the thing that would most assist Gaines. Corruption loved company, for it served to justify and vindicate itself. Criminals spent time with criminals because it confirmed their slanted view of the world. If a straightforward appeal to the responsible deputy in charge of visitations didn't work out, then a suggestion of recompense might do the job. If Gaines then proved to be a fifth columnist, well, he would have ruled out any hope of reporting what he saw to his seniors due to the simple fact that he had bribed his way in there.

Gaines took a hundred bucks from the office petty cash fund, that fund provided for so generously by those who chose to pay on-the-spot speeding fines instead of opting for a ticket and a court appearance. He told Hagen where he was going and why.

"Best of luck to you," was Hagen's response. "If you get in there, you're a better man than me."

"Oh, I don't doubt I'll get in there," Gaines said, "but whether I get to see who I'm after is a different matter entirely."

Gaines went home to change out of his uniform. He left his gun behind, but took his ID and the hundred bucks. It was a little after eleven by the time he left the house, and he had a three- or four-hour drive ahead of him.

En route he tried to find some framework within which to put the previous nine days. Inside of little more than a week, the entirety of his life had been upended and scattered on the ground. That was how it felt. And then someone had come along and kicked through every part of his existence as if looking for something they believed was there. Truth was, there was nothing there. Not anymore. Now there was no family. There was just an empty house and a great deal of silence.

Perhaps that was the reason he felt so driven to speak to Clifton Regis, to find a way to get to Della Wade, to find out from Eddie Holland the reason for his visit to Maryanne Benedict in Gulfport. Not because he truly cared, but because he had to have something with which to fill his mind, to occupy his thoughts, to make the hours pass. Time was not a healer, not at all. It was merely the means by which ever-greater psychological and emotional defenses were erected against the ravages of conscience and memory. He felt guilty, but why? For his mother? She had been ill for a long time. Her death had been inevitable. He had lost count of the number of conversations he'd had with Bob Thurston, the questions he'd asked about what he could do to help her, what possible treatments there were. Save pain management, which she steadfastly refused to commit to, there was little else that could have been done. And there was nothing he had withheld from her. There were no words that he had wished he'd said. She had known he loved her. She had always known that. So no, he did not feel guilty about some omission relating to his mother. So what else was there? For the fact that both Judith Denton and Michael Webster were dead, even after the discovery of Nancy's body? As far as they were concerned, he had been appointed to protect and serve, as he had all Whytesburg's residents, and he had failed in both responsibilities. But what could he have done? He could not have predicted Judith's suicide, and he was not able to stand watch over everyone. And then there was the illegal search of Webster's motel cabin, the fact that he'd had no one else present when he interviewed the man, the fact that he'd failed to secure immediate PD representation for Webster. Kidd had been right when he'd said that Gaines had allowed his emotions to get in the way. That was a serious omission on Gaines's part, and he knew it. He could neither evade nor escape that sense of having failed. It nagged at him relentlessly.

He could see so clearly where he had let his heart rule his head, but there was something else, something he could not identify. He was deeply troubled—mentally and emotionally—and he knew that the sense of unease would only grow with time. The discovery of Webster's hand and head were a blind. This was not some occult trial performed to prevent him from seeing the truth. It was an attempt to scare him.

This was the work of someone calculating and precise in their intentions. It could only be Wade. It *had* to be Wade. There was no one else to consider. Yet, even as Gaines recalled his conversation with Matthias Wade, he also understood that there was nothing but intuition to support his viewpoint. It wasn't even intuition, but a simple hunch, a wish for it to be Wade, a desire to see that smug expression wiped from his face.

What he lacked was any real information about these people, and that was where Della came in, and to get to Della, he needed Regis, and to get to Regis, he had to make it all the way to Parchman Farm and then get inside.

Gaines tried to stop thinking as he drove. He turned on the radio. He found a station out of Mobile playing music he recalled from Vietnam—Janis Joplin, Hendrix, Canned Heat. Usually he would turn it off, the memories too dark and intense, but this time he let it play, and for some reason he found it comforting. If nothing else, it reminded him that a part of his life was over, a part that he never wished to see again. He had made it through. He had come out the other side—damaged, but still intact—and that was a great deal more than could be said for so many thousands of others.

Perhaps he had survived to do this, and this alone. Perhaps, in some fatalistic way, he had walked away from the war only to uncover the truths of Whytesburg. A twenty-year-old ghost had returned. That ghost was haunting the streets and sidewalks. It had changed the tone and atmosphere of the town. It had changed people's attitudes. He sensed that people believed him responsible for unearthing so much more than the body of Nancy Denton, as if he had opened a door into some other plane, some other reality, and something dark and terrible had found its way into their world. He wondered about the number of people who wished he'd let it all be just as it was. No one need ever have known. The girl could have been spirited away into another grave, Judith Denton would still be alive, as would Michael Webster, and—for those who believed in something preternatural—there was also the possibility that Alice might still be alive, too. Whatever had happened, there was a ghost, and until the ghost was finally laid to rest, it would keep on haunting them.

And then Gaines understood the source of that nagging sense of guilt. Guilty for surviving. Guilty for being one of the few who made it home. Why him? Why had he made it? And that guilt would only resolve and become stronger the longer he remained distant and disengaged. Surely it was the foremost responsibility of those who were still alive to actually *live*. He had been in hiding for four years, hiding behind his mother's illness, hiding behind a uniform, behind rules and regulations, behind official protocol, schedules, duty rosters, and bureaucracy. Who did he know? Who did he *really* know? Who was his best friend? Bob Thurston? Victor Powell? Richard Hagen? They were acquaintances, work colleagues, nothing more. How many times had Hagen asked him to come over for a barbecue, to spend time with his family? How many times had he been invited to Thanksgiving dinners, even Christmas? Always his excuses had been the same: his mother's health, his work commitments. *Take a day off; you deserve it. Well, the invitation extends to your mother as well, John, and she seems to be doing just fine right now. I'm sure she'd like to get out of the house, even if only for a few hours.* But no, he had always evaded those questions, and when directly asked, he had avoided any real explanation. Truth was, he had survived Vietnam and yet had continued to live life in some sort of irreducibly minimalist fashion. He had tried his utmost to experience the least of everything. That was the way it seemed right now. Alice was gone. The barrier was down. There was nothing that he could now employ to defend himself from facing reality. Perhaps he was more damaged than he believed. Perhaps the effects of the war had taken a far greater toll than he'd imagined.

If this was right, then he was in trouble. If this was right, then perhaps this unfounded and ill-advised commitment to uncover the truth of Matthias Wade's involvement in these recent events, regardless of whether or not he *was* involved, was a way for Gaines to justify his continuing existence. If he could not live for himself, he could live for his mother, and if he could not live for her, then he could live for the memory of Nancy Denton. She had not died in battle. She had died to satisfy some dark and horrific purpose. That was no reason to die. Nancy Denton should still be alive. She should be a mother, a woman with a career, a family, a life. But all these things had been taken from her before she'd even had a chance to see out her teens. Denial of this kind was surely the cruelest of all. The world did not favor the weak and vulnerable. Nancy had been vulnerable, perhaps weak as well, but such things did not justify her murder. She was no longer here to name names and see justice done, so those who were perhaps stronger and less vulnerable needed to stand in her place.

Approaching Hattiesburg, Gaines determined that whatever had taken place all those years ago could never remain unpunished.

46

There at the intersection of Route 49 West and Highway 32, Gaines found the less-than-imposing entrance to Parchman Farm. What was at first evident was the complete lack of an external fence, an absence of trees, just an endless vista of flat scrubland. There was nowhere to hide. Even if you broke free from the chain gang, even if you managed to escape from the work team or detention unit, there was no place to go. It was a desert, little more than that, and its bleakness and desolation seemed more ominous and threatening than any dense facade of monolithic granite walls. Gaines turned and drove through a simple plank-board gateway. Overhead the sign read *Mississippi State Penitentiary*, and he pulled up alongside a small wooden office. Exiting his car, he went up and knocked on the window. The window opened, a face appeared, and an elderly man with a glass right eye looked at him askance and asked him his business.

"Sheriff John Gaines, Whytesburg, Breed County, come on up here in the hope of speaking to one of your inmates."

"You got a name for him?"

"Clifton Regis."

"Appointment?"

"Nope."

"He a colored fella?"

"He is, yes."

"He is solitary?"

"Not that I'm aware of."

"Well, he'll be out on the chain gang, then."

"Time they finish?"

The old man squinted at his pocket watch. "It's just after half past three now, and they'll work until eight. Unless you got yourself an appointment, then you've got a wait on your hands."

"Where do I find the people who arrange appointments?" Gaines asked.

"Oh, you just keep on drivin', son, and then you drive some

more. Straight road. Don't go nowhere but the horizon. Maybe four, five miles, and then on the left you'll see a sign that says *Administrative Buildings*, and you hang a right there. You'll come to a huddle of small offices, and you go on up there and ask for Ted McNamara. You can see if he'll give you the time o' day, but you sure as hell woulda been wise to call up and arrange this before comin' on out here."

Gaines thanked the man, got back in his car and drove on.

En route, he passed the working teams, lines of men chained together at the ankles pitching rocks into buckets, erecting fence posts, turning fields over by hand. Some of them sang; some of them did not. The whites were separated from the blacks, yet all of them wore the same striped pants and jackets, and those that had no jackets wore blue shirts with *MSP* emblazoned on the back in white letters.

The work seemed ceaseless, repetitive, mind-numbing, and physically strenuous. Out here you would get nothing but lean like a hunting dog. But there was nowhere to run, just nowhere at all. Wherever you looked, there was just the same absence of anything definable. No landmarks, no trees, no ridged banks behind which to hide or seek respite from the sun. And the wardens were mounted on horseback, armed with Springfield .30-06s, sidearms, and bull-whips. Gaines figured any one of them could run down a man in a heartbeat, bring him to the ground with a nudge from the horse's flank, and it would all be over. Then it would be a halfway-to-senseless beating with Black Annie and thirty days in the hole. Parchman Farm had earned its reputation. It was not somewhere you wanted to wind up.

Gaines found the administrative office complex, a scattering of no more than half a dozen clapboard buildings, just where the old man had told him. He asked after Ted McNamara, found him pretty much as he expected—rail-thin, his skin the color of parchment and aged the same way, an expression that spoke of a fundamental and perpetual mistrust of all persons, said mistrust not completely unfounded due to his line of work.

"Well, son, you gotta have one of them visiting authorization chitties," was McNamara's response to Gaines's reason for being up there at the Farm.

McNamara's office was one of the clapboard sheds, two narrow windows, a desk, two chairs, a filing cabinet, a fan that moved the air around lethargically and yet did nothing to cool it. McNamara chained smokes one after the other, and the room hung with a pall of fug that limited Gaines's vision. It was yet another experience in a long concatenation of such experiences, each of them seemingly more surreal than the last.

"I have a murdered child," Gaines said.

"I could list a few hundred murdered children, each of them the result of the kind of handiwork they favor up here."

"Murdered twenty years ago, and no one was ever arrested or charged."

McNamara nodded. "And you think this Clifton Regis fella had something to do with it?"

"No, it's not that simple. Regis knows someone, and I need to speak to that someone, and I think Regis might be my way in."

"You know what'll happen if I bring Regis off his chain and get him down here for you?"

Gaines raised his eyebrows questioningly.

"The others'll take a dark slant on it. They'll figure him for fessin' up on somethin' that's none of our business. More 'an likely get hisself a beatin', or maybe someone'll sharpen up a toothbrush and put it in his back while he's takin' a shower."

"Is there some way it could be done that wouldn't result in such a situation?"

"Why, 'cause you care what happens to him after you've discovered what you wanna know and gone on your way?"

"Sure, of course. He shouldn't have to suffer for something he's not guilty of."

"Well, that's the one thing you can be sure of out here, Sheriff Gaines. They's all guilty of so much more than what we got 'em for. Seems to me that justice has a way of findin' folk, even when they least expect it. Hell, even the ones that got railroaded and is here on a bullshit testimony is guilty of more than adequate for us to keep 'em till they croak."

Gaines said nothing for a moment, and then he leaned forward. "I understand that this is irregular, Mr. McNamara, and I appreciate that it is additional work for you and your staff, and I wouldn't expect such a burden of labor to be covered by the taxpayers of Sunflower County, if you know what I mean."

McNamara smiled. It was the kind of smile you'd get from a snake.

"So, let me get you straight here, Sheriff Gaines. You're tryin' to bribe me to violate penitentiary rules and regulations, to allow you to come down here, take a man off the chain, get him into an interview room, and let you ask him however many questions you like, and then go on your way and leave him to the hounds and the wolves . . . Is that what we got happenin' here?"

Gaines didn't avert his gaze. "Not so much a bribe, Mr. McNamara, more a willingness to help carry the administrative cost of such a thing."

"Well, down here, Sheriff Gaines, we call a nigger a nigger, a white a white, and there don't happen to anything resembling a shade of gray. Are you offerin' me a bribe, or am I mistaken?"

Gaines still could not look away. McNamara had him cornered, and if Gaines lied, he would be as transparent as glass.

"You're not mistaken, Mr. McNamara."

McNamara smiled, but with his lips, not his eyes. It was the cruelest smile Gaines believed he'd ever seen.

"Well, good 'nough, Sheriff Gaines. That's the kind of language I understand. If we're gonna be straight with each other, then we're gonna be straight. None of this bullshit fancy footwork. The fee for what you require of me is fifty bucks. That's twenty-five dollars for finding the boy and bringing him someplace for you to speak with him, the other twenty-five for finding some way to make sure he don't get hisself stabbed in the yard tomorrow morning."

Gaines took the money from his pocket. He kept it beneath the edge of the table. If McNamara saw he had a hundred bucks, the price would go up, no doubt about it.

Gaines folded the notes and passed them over to McNamara. They went into McNamara's desk drawer, and then he rose, ground out the half-smoked cigarette, and told Gaines to go back to his car, to pull out onto the main road, and then wait for McNamara to come out in his vehicle.

"You follow me on up to Unit 26, and then you're gonna wait there until I find this boy and bring him down to you. Then we'll get you a room someplace where you won't be disturbed. Maybe I'll put you in the chapel, huh? Some of these lowlifes professed to findin' Jesus someplace out in them fields, took it upon themselves to build a chapel a few years back. Ain't much of anythin', to tell you the truth, and ain't much used now 'cept when some of these fellas first come in. They get such a shock to the system; they think they's in hell an' figure that prayin' might be a good 'nough way to make it different. They can pray all they like; it only gets worse."

McNamara opened the door. Gaines walked to his car, pulled back out onto the main road, and waited for McNamara to come out after him in one of the official MSP pickup trucks.

They drove for another mile, maybe a mile and a half, and then— seemingly out of nowhere—another complex of low-slung white-painted buildings appeared out of the landscape, as if they had just grown from the dust and dry air.

McNamara pulled over. Gaines parked behind the pickup, and McNamara came around to the driver's-side window.

"You stay here. I'll check what gang he's on and then go fetch him. Anyone asks what you're doing here, just lie, all right, son?"

Gaines nodded.

McNamara drove away once more, and Gaines was left stranded in the middle of the Mississippi delta, a half-dozen miles from the highway, no valid reason for being there, and he wondered whether he would ever see Ted McNamara again.

47

If Ted McNamara was precisely as Gaines had imagined, Clifton Regis was not.

Despite the fact that he wore regulation stripes, that he had been out on a chain gang for pretty much the entire day, he somehow managed to look anything other than browbeaten and disheveled. He was a tall man, a good three or four inches over Gaines, and aside from a fine scar running the length of his left nostril and ending a quarter inch beneath his left eye, his face was unmarked. His hair was close-cropped, nothing more than a shadow, and only when Gaines extended his hand and Regis took it, did Gaines realize that the pinky and ring fingers were missing from Regis's right hand.

It was like shaking the hand of a small child, and it was unnerving.

Regis said nothing at all as he sat down. McNamara had in fact given them use of the chapel, though the term *chapel* was applied in the very loosest sense of the word. It was a shack, constructed—it seemed—not only from random sections of wood and offcuts, but also heavy branches and sawn logs. The floor was wood in places, oilcloth in others, and in the corners the dry earth beneath was visible. The roof was corrugated iron, rusted in the main, punched through with fist-sized holes, and it was solely through the gaps in the walls and the roof that any light entered. Thus John Gaines, here on a wild mission to find something that seemed impossible, and Clifton Regis, thankful perhaps for nothing more than an hour away from the work party, sat on a rickety wooden bench in the gloom of a makeshift building on Parchman Farm and looked at each other in awkward silence for a little while.

"You know who I am?" Gaines eventually asked.

"I know you're law," Regis said, and—yet again—Regis surprised Gaines with his diction and accent. He was almost accentless, if such a thing were possible.

"Any idea why I might have asked to see you?"

Regis shrugged. "Only three or four reasons the law comes out to see people like me," Regis replied. "You think I've done something which I haven't, you think I know someone who's done something they didn't do, you want me to find out something from someone in here about something they didn't do, or you brought me a reprieve and a pardon from the governor." Regis smiled sardonically. "I'm guessin' we can rule out the last one, right?"

"We can rule out all of them," Gaines said.

Regis's expression changed then, noticeably so, and not for the good. He slid a little farther away on the bench and eyed Gaines suspiciously.

"I have to level with you, Clifton," Gaines said. "Otherwise this is all bullshit."

"You got smokes?" Regis asked.

Gaines took a pack from his shirt pocket, handed them over. Regis withdrew one and Gaines lit it for him. He set his Zippo there on the packet as an open invitation for Regis to just help himself.

"I want to talk to you about Della Wade."

The reaction was immediate and astonishing. Regis seemed to visibly pale, as if the blood was being drawn downward from his face. He seemed nervous. He looked away, shook his head, turned back to Gaines.

"I been here seventeen months, sir," Regis said. "Took me a year to forget what she looked like, another three or four to forget why I loved her, and I just started working on convincing myself that I lost my fingers some other way. Now you show up and spoil it all." Regis switched his cigarette from his right to his left and then held up his right hand for Gaines to see. "That, sir, is my constant reminder of Della Wade and her crazy-ass family."

"Heard word that you took ten thousand dollars from Earl Wade."

"Is that so? Well, that's precisely what I'd expect you to have heard."

"Not the truth?"

"About as far from the truth as you could hope to get and then some."

"So, the truth is what?"

Regis dropped his half-smoked cigarette on the ground, put his foot on it, took another from the pack and lit it with Gaines's Zippo. It was simply nervousness, something with which to be momentarily distracted.

"I *have* to talk to you?" Regis asked.

Gaines shook his head. "No, you don't have to talk to me."

"Then give me a good reason why I should."

"Because I have a dead girl with her heart missing, a dead war veteran with his head and his hand cut off, and I think both of these things are connected, and I think both of these things have something to do with the Wades."

Regis looked at Gaines for some time, as if his mind was simply trying to absorb the information he'd just been given.

Finally, he cleared his throat and said, "And you think you can touch the Wades?"

"I can try."

Regis smiled, started to laugh. "Then you have bigger balls than me, sir. However, you do have one thing that I don't."

"I am the law."

Regis laughed again. "Shit, no. You think the law has any authority or influence over people like the Wades? No, the thing you have that I don't is your color. Being a colored man, see, everyone knows we are lying before we even say a word."

"Things are changing—"

"Tell the Freedom Riders that. Tell the niggers they got swinging from trees south of here every Saturday night. You go looking for the Wades, you're gonna find yourself in a whole heap of Klan trouble, my friend, and the fact that you're a white sheriff won't count for much of anything, believe me. They might not hang you literally, but they'll hang you some other way. I guarantee it."

"So what was the deal with you and Della?"

"Romeo and Juliet."

Gaines frowned.

"I loved her, man, and she loved me, and that's all there was to it. If I was some white fella out of Mobile with a daddy and a plantation then I wouldn't be here. She and I would be married, and around about now we'd have gotten ourselves a handful of kids and I'd be talkin' with Mr. Matthias Wade about how there might be an opening somewhere within one of his companies, seein' as how I was like family an' all."

"And the money?"

"Was her money, sir. That ten thousand dollars was her money, and her money alone, and she got it for me, and she gave it to me, and it was how we was gonna get away from that damned crazy family and go disappear somewhere and start over. That was the plan."

266

"Her money?"

"Hers by law and by birthright and by anything else that's supposed to be meaningful, but that brother of hers got involved. He found us together, and he took her back."

"And he cut your fingers off?"

Regis shook his head. "Someone like Matthias Wade doesn't do his own business. No, he had a fella with him, and he got me sat down quiet while Matthias gave me a talkin' to."

"And he said what?"

"He said that he didn't believe I had stolen the money, that he knew Della was deluded, maybe a little crazy, and that she had somehow gotten it into her mind that she loved me, but such a thing was not possible, me bein' a black fella an' all, and so he was going to give me a choice. Either he was going to report me to the police and have me arrested for raping Della and then stealing the money, or he was going to take away my livelihood."

"I don't understand," Gaines interjected. "Your livelihood?"

"You think I'm a thief? You think I've always been in trouble with the law? No, sir. I was a musician. I am a guitar player. That's how I met Della in the first place. I used to know her brother, Eugene, down in some of them blues and jazz joints in New Orleans, and she came on down to see him and that was that. One look at her and it was all over."

"So he cut your fingers off?"

"Well, he had his fella cut my fingers off. It was either that, or twenty-five to thirty up here, and that was something I could never have done. I get myself out of here, I can learn to play guitar again, missing two fingers or not. That gypsy fella in France did it, right?"

Gaines reached for a cigarette himself, lit it, inhaled, closed his eyes for a moment, and wondered where he would next take this conversation.

"So you want Matthias, or you want the old man?" Regis asked.

"Matthias," Gaines replied. "I think Matthias killed a girl twenty years ago, and I think he killed another man just recently."

"And I am sure he got a few of my kind with the old Saturday-night necktie parties, as well."

"So how do I get to Della?" Gaines asked. "That's what I need to do. I need to get to Della. As far as I can see, she is the only one who might be able to help me."

Regis shook his head. "You don't get to her," he said. "That's the point."

267

"When did you meet her?"

"Late summer of seventy-two."

"In New Orleans?"

"Right."

"And you started dating?"

Regis laughed. "If that's what you want to call it, yes."

"How soon after you met her?"

"Right away, the same night. It was like that. I saw her, she saw me, and we was done for."

"And how long did the relationship go on until she gave you the money?"

"Four, five months. She would come down to New Orleans every weekend with the pretense of seeing Eugene, but she was coming to see me. Far as I could tell, she didn't have a great deal to do with Eugene. Never had. But Eugene knew what was going on. I think Eugene feels the same way about his family as Della does. He stays out of their business, and they stay out of his. He has his music and his church, and he pretty much keeps himself to himself. Live and let live, you know?"

"And Eugene had no problem with you being with her?"

"You've met Eugene?"

"No, I haven't."

Regis smiled. "No, Eugene never had a problem with us."

"And she brought the money, when?"

"Twenty-first of December."

"And Matthias came to see you how soon after?"

"Two days."

"The twenty-third."

"Right."

"And he gave you your choice."

"He sure did."

"And then when were you arrested for this thing here?"

"Arrested at the end of January 1973, held over, tried, sentenced, shipped up here in March of the same year, and, like I said, been here all of the seventeen months since."

"And you did the burglary you got this three-to-five for?"

"Never burgled anyplace in my life."

Gaines frowned and shook his head. "But—"

"But what, Sheriff? You know how this goes. We all look the same. We all do the same things. We're all guilty of the same shit, so it don't matter which ones they throw in jail. I agree it was a little stretch to have me climbing walls and breaking windows and whatever, having lost two of my fingers only a month beforehand, but hell, what does a detail like that count for when you have the kind of public defenders we get assigned to us?"

"You think Matthias Wade had any part in getting you sent up here?"

"Seems like it would be a good way for him to get me a couple hundred miles away from Della, doesn't it?"

"Sure does," Gaines replied.

"So what now?" Regis asked.

"Like I said, I need to get to Della. I need to ask her some things."

"And you think she'll say enough for you to be able to get something on her brother for these killings you spoke of?"

"That's the plan."

"You don't have a prayer, sir, not a single, solitary prayer. Della would no more turn her brother in to the law than she would . . . well hell, I don't know what. But you're just wishin' on some kinda wild dream there."

"You could testify that he threatened you, that he was there when this man cut your fingers off."

"For what? What the hell have you been smokin'? Jeez, do you have even the faintest idea who you're dealin' with? Even if something like that got a charge, you'd have three hundred lawyers and the judge hisself swearing they was home with Matthias Wade as their dinner guest at precisely the moment I got my fingers removed."

"You know who this man was who was with him?"

"No idea. Just one of Wade's people. There's no end of people who'll do that kind of work for someone like him."

"If I could get a message to her for you, would that be something—"

"Man, if you could get a message to her, that would be just unfucking-believable."

"You want to get her back, right?"

Clifton Regis looked at Gaines then, and the expression in his eyes was one of such desperate hope that it was all Gaines could do to remain implacable. However, beneath that hope was a sense of exhausted resignation. Gaines did not so much see it, as *feel* it around the man.

"You ever been in love, Sheriff Gaines?"

Gaines felt himself sigh inside. He remembered Linda Newman. "One time," he replied, "but that was a long time ago."

"Doesn't matter how long ago it was. It's still gonna make you feel the same."

"You think she still loves you?" Gaines asked.

"If I believed she didn't, then there'd be no point going on. That's what I tell myself, you know? But sometimes I believe I just have to accept that she's gone for good—"

"But bringing down Matthias Wade gives you a chance of seeing her and finding out whether there is some hope you could be together again."

"Bringing down Matthias Wade? Like I said, I think you are dreamin'. You bring him down, then you're gonna have to bring down a great deal more than just him. They're all living out of each other's pockets. The lawyers, the judges, the rich folks, they're all working for one another, and that's one hell of a lot of people. All that stuff I said, how I've been working as hard as I can to forget her . . . that's just because I know there'll never be a hope that we'll be together again."

"Unless he's gone, right?"

"Maybe. Maybe then there's a chance."

"But you'll help me?"

Regis shrugged. "Help you? How the hell could I help you?"

"You can start by writing a letter to Della Wade to tell her that she should meet with me. If I can get it to her, then there's a chance she might trust me enough to tell me something that will help. If she feels for you the way you feel for her, then how can she not talk to me?"

"And how the hell you gonna get a letter to Della without Matthias finding out about it?"

"I think there might be someone who'll help me," Gaines said, "someone that Matthias won't refuse entry to that house."

"Well, you get me a pen and some paper and I'll write your letter," Regis said, "but this goes down wrong and they end up comin' after me, then I'm gonna be comin' after you, you understand?"

"I don't doubt it, Clifton," Gaines replied.

"This is a bad scene you got yourself involved in, man, a real bad scene. Maybe the Wades ain't as bad as they get down here, but they're pretty damned bad. You know the kind of shit these Klan people do when they get let off the leash, right?"

"I do, sure, though we ain't had a great deal of it in Breed County while I've been there."

"Well, people like Matthias Wade are not so dumb as to be shitting on their own porch, are they? More 'an likely they take whoever over the state line into Louisiana and run their hunting trips there."

Gaines had heard of such things, the Klan abducting some unsuspecting colored, driving them across state lines into some area outside of town, and then a half dozen or more good ol' boys would hunt them down like a safari. Dogs, trucks, a whole bellyful of liquor for every man, and they would make a night of it. End up with some guy stripped, beaten, lynched, one time even crucified. Maybe the civil rights movement got a say-so in Memphis or Atlanta, but in the backwoods of Mississippi and Alabama they hadn't even heard of such a thing. For such people, civil rights meant the right to civilize a neighborhood or a town, and the only way to do that was to rout out and get rid of the coloreds.

Gaines got up. "I'm gonna get some paper and a pen, and you write me a letter for Della, and I give you my word I will do everything I can to get it to her. Only way Matthias will find out is if she then gives it to him herself."

"I don't see her doin' that," Regis replied. "Not in a hundred lifetimes."

"You cannot be sure," Gaines replied. "People's minds can get turned awful fast. You haven't seen her for the better part of two years, and she's been right there in that family all this time, listening to whatever Matthias Wade has to say about the way of things. This goes to hell, and both you and I are in it neck-deep."

"Well, sir, you didn't know Della, and if you think there is anything even remotely similar between her and Matthias, then you're gonna have to look again. Doesn't make sense to me Matthias and Della are even in the same family."

"So you're sure?"

"You get me the paper there, Sheriff Gaines. You'll get your letter. You get it to Della, and we'll see what the hell happens, eh?"

48

Clifton Regis wrote the letter. He insisted that Gaines read it. Gaines said that whatever business existed between him and Della Wade was their business alone, but Regis made it a condition.

"I want you to understand what this means to me," he said. "I want you to appreciate how significant this thing is, because that'll make me feel like you will try your hardest to get this to her without her brother finding out."

"So read me the letter," Gaines said.

Regis cleared his throat, looked at Gaines with that wide-eyed hopefulness, and then started.

"D. Got a chance here to get you a letter, so I'm taking it. A man came to see me. He's a sheriff from Whytesburg called John Gaines, and he told me that M is maybe in some trouble down there. I know you feel the same way about M as me, and I know that you get why I'm here. I am also hoping that what we had in New Orleans is still alive and that you are waiting for me. I need you to know that everything that has happened between us means as much now as it did back then and that I will do anything to be with you again. I want you to talk to this man, and I want you to tell him what you know. I want you to help him if you can, so that we have a chance to be together again. That's why I want you to do this. If you cannot do this, or you have decided that we cannot be together, then I need you to tell me so I can make my decisions. And if you cannot help this man or you are not willing to talk to him, then just burn this letter and do not let M see it. Not for my sake, but because I know he will get mad and hurt you if he thinks that we are in contact. Somehow, some way, I think we can be together again. That is what I live for. I just want to see you again, to hold you, to tell you how much I love you. I wish every day that you feel the same. I believe in my heart that you do. Love you forever. C."

Gaines merely nodded in acknowledgment. Then he took the

letter from Regis, folded it, tucked it into his shirt pocket, and got up.

They shook hands again, and Gaines thanked Regis for his time and his help.

"You gonna be okay when you go back?" Gaines asked.

"Back into population? Sure, why'd you ask?"

"McNamara said that maybe you'd get some trouble for being out here talking to the law."

"Hey, they're gonna believe whatever I tell 'em. I don't get no trouble from these guys. I can take care of myself."

"Good to hear it."

"One other thing," Regis said.

"Yes?"

"You get her that letter, you find out what she says about me, whether she's waiting for me, and you gotta let me know somehow, okay?"

"Yes," Gaines replied. "I can do that for sure."

"You got family, Sheriff Gaines?"

"No, Clifton, I don't."

"Well, good enough."

Gaines frowned.

"I'd be more worried for you if you had a wife and some little 'uns to mourn you. You step all over Matthias Wade's toes and he ain't gonna take a polite apology. He's gonna take your head."

"Well, he did that already to someone else, and I think it's about time he got some retribution."

Regis got up, and the pair of them walked to the makeshift door.

"So you really think he killed some girl?" Regis asked.

"I do. At first I thought it was someone else, and now I think it was Matthias."

"And you said something about her heart?"

Gaines nodded. "Yes. She was sixteen, a pretty, bright teenage girl, and someone strangled her and then cut out her heart."

Regis's expression was suddenly one of intense curiosity. "That is a very strange thing to do, Sheriff."

Gaines smiled sardonically. "Cutting her heart out was nothing compared to what they did next—"

"Which was?"

"You won't believe me, but in place of her heart they put a wicker basket—"

"With a snake inside," Regis said, and he looked down at the

273

ground. It was not a question; it was a statement. Regis's entire body language changed. It seemed as if a great weight had been lowered down onto his shoulders.

"How did you—"

Regis looked up. "They did a revival, Sheriff Gaines. Whoever killed your girl, someone tried to bring her back."

Gaines couldn't speak. He just looked at Regis with an expression of utter disbelief.

"As old as God," Regis said. "This shit is as old as God. You take out the heart, you bury the heart elsewhere, a specific place, a specific distance from the body, and then you replace the heart with a wicker basket. Inside the basket is a snake, its tail in its mouth, and you sew them up a special way—thirteen punctures as far as I recall, six on the right, seven on the left, and the stitch crosses itself five times—and then you bury the body near running water. And you never speak a word of what you have done. Not to anyone. Not ever. Even if you do it with someone, even if they were there, you never speak of it between you. If you do, it breaks the spell and the person will not be revived."

Gaines stayed silent. His mouth was dry. His breath felt heavy in his chest.

"That's the revival, Sheriff. That's what was done to your girl back then. You still have her body?"

Gaines nodded.

"Well, you go look, and if there are seven holes on the left side and six on the right, and if she was tied in such a way as to cross those stitches five times, then you have someone trying to revive her."

"Y-you can't be se-serious," Gaines stammered, but already he had begun to understand what had happened. He knew that Webster had done this. It was as if the entire case had turned on its head. All of a sudden, Webster appeared to be the one who'd told the truth. Webster had tried to bring Nancy Denton back. What a sad, desperate, terrible, pointless thing. It was heartbreaking to even consider. He had loved the girl—that was evident from what Gaines had heard, from the almost-visible chemistry between them in their pictures—and he had cut open her chest, removed her heart, and done this dreadful thing in some vain and futile effort to bring her back to life. And that was why he had never spoken of it. Maybe Wade had known this, and such was Webster's belief in what he was doing, such was Wade's certainty that Webster would maintain his silence, that it had not been necessary to kill Webster. Only when Nancy's body had been found, thus demonstrating once and for all that the revival would never work, did Wade need to take care of Michael Webster.

It was utterly unbelievable, but—as Gaines's mother used to say— what we knew of the world was dwarfed by what we did not know.

"I know it sounds like some crazy occult Frankenstein raising-people-from-the-dead thing," Regis said, "but this is hoodoo, and this has an awful lot less to do with what you may or may not believe and a great deal to do with what other folks believe. And what other folks believe has brought about the killing of a young girl and the desecration of her body. If Wade did that, then—"

"I don't think Wade did that," Gaines said, almost to himself. "I think he killed her, and then someone who loved her found her and did what he thought would bring her back."

Gaines tried to picture Nancy's body. He tried to recall the number of punctures in the torso, the way in which it had been laced. He could call Powell, but he knew without even asking that it would be precisely as Regis had explained.

"So it seems you are dealing with something else now," Regis said.

"Y-yes," Gaines replied. "But how do you know this?"

Regis smiled. The scar down his cheek was like the crease in a sheet of paper. "I am a black man from Louisiana, Sheriff Gaines," he said. "You gotta get the spirit of Legba back into them, and Legba is gonna either bring them back to you or carry them over into the afterlife. The serpent represents the power of Legba. It represents healing and the connection between heaven and earth. Whoever does it usually does it for love . . . to make sure that the one they love never gets caught in limbo between this world and the next. And whoever did this to your girl would have suffered terribly, I'm sure, because to do that to someone you love . . ." Regis shook his head. "And you can never say a word . . . never . . ."

"It casts an entirely different light on the whole thing," Gaines said.

"I imagine it would, Sheriff."

"I can't see Matthias Wade doing that to someone, can you?"

"I can see Matthias Wade doing a great many things, Sheriff Gaines, but doing something like that for love is not one of them."

"Thank you for telling me this," Gaines said.

"You are welcome, Sheriff Gaines, but the best way to thank me is to get that note to Della without her brother finding out. That's all I can ask of you."

Gaines and Regis parted company, Regis back into the care of Ted McNamara and a pickup ride to the work party, Gaines out onto the highway once more. It was after eight o'clock by the time he saw the Parchman Farm main entrance in the rearview.

He drove in silence but for the sound of the engine and the wheels on the road. He did not switch on the radio. He just wanted a clear mind with no interruptions as he considered the implications of what Clifton Regis had told him.

That morning, little more than a week before, he, Jim Hughes, Richard Hagen, and the assembled crew had unearthed something from the riverbank. It had not just been the body of a sixteen-year-old; it had been something else entirely. They had brought out the dead, and the unresolved truth of her death was now haunting Whytesburg like a ghost. That ghost would not lie in rest until the facts were known. That ghost was in limbo, and where Michael Webster might have failed to accomplish what he had set out to do, Gaines could not.

Gaines knew that by the time he got back south, it would be too late to go see Maryanne Benedict, and besides, he wanted to find out from Eddie Holland why she'd wanted to see him. Perhaps there was something about the night of Nancy Denton's disappearance that she'd remembered. Perhaps there was something she knew about Matthias Wade but felt safer speaking at first to Eddie Holland rather than Gaines, who, in actuality, was a complete stranger. Gaines could only guess, and guessing served no purpose.

Rather, he spent the hours of solitude between Indianola and Whytesburg turning over all that had happened in his mind. He did not believe Clifton Regis was a liar, just as he did not believe the man was a thief. He believed that Clifton Regis had met Della Wade in New Orleans, just as he'd said, and that chance rendezvous had occurred because of Eugene. Eugene was a musician, as was Regis, and Della appeared to have gravitated toward that lifestyle, the people who lived it. Matthias, staunch segregationist, perhaps racist to the core, had learned of the relationship, had learned also that ten thousand dollars of Wade money had found its way into Clifton Regis's hands. That would have flown in the teeth of everything that Wade intended to preserve about his family's name and reputation. The solution had been simple. A brief visit to Clifton Regis, the recovery of the money, his sister rescued, and Clifton

Regis left behind minus two of his fingers. Whether the subsequent burglary charge that put Regis in Parchman had been Wade's doing or simply another blatant example of racist railroading that was so prevalent in these parts was another matter, and frankly, something that did not overly concern Gaines at that moment. He was content to know where Regis was, encouraged by the fact that Regis was compliant, secure in the knowledge that if he got the letter to Della Wade, then some sort of dialogue might be engendered. How to get the letter to Della without Matthias's knowledge was the next obstacle.

Arriving back in Whytesburg, Gaines did not consider it too late to go visit with Ross and Holland. They were both up, playing cards as it happened, and they welcomed Gaines's arrival. They asked him to join them, to share a few drinks, a few hands, but he said he had no plans to stay.

"I just came to find out why Maryanne Benedict wanted to see you," Gaines asked Holland.

"Because you scared the bejesus out of her, that's why," Holland replied. "A stranger shows up at her door, tells her Nancy Denton is dead, Webster, too, one of them buried in a riverbank for twenty years, the other one burned in a fire without his head. How would you feel?"

"Oh, I think I'd feel pretty much as I do right now, Eddie. Like I'm in someone else's nightmare, and whatever I do, I just can't wake up."

"Well, she's pretty much the same, my friend. She wanted to know if everything you'd said was true. She wanted to know if you could be trusted, as well."

"Trusted?"

"Hell, I don't know why she asked that, John. She just did. Maybe she's gathering up the courage to tell you something."

"I'm plannin' on going over to see her in the morning."

"Because?"

"Because I want her to deliver a message to Della Wade for me."

Both Eddie Holland and Nate Ross looked up from their cards, but neither spoke.

"I got a man called Clifton Regis up at Parchman on a three-to-five that looks like a setup. He was Della's boyfriend. Hell, they were going to elope together. Della gave him ten grand, and then Matthias found out, took her back, cut off a couple of Clifton Regis's fingers, and shipped Della back to the Wade house. As far as I know, she's been there ever since."

"And what did this fella up at Parchman have to say to Della?" Holland asked.

"He says he loves her, hopes that she's waiting for him, hopes that they'll find some way to be together despite Matthias."

"So this Regis has a vested interest in colluding with you any which way to get Matthias out of the picture."

"Yes, seems that way to me."

"And why didn't Matthias take kindly to Della being involved with Mr. Regis?" Holland asked

"That's easy," Ross explained. "Because Clifton Regis is a colored man."

"Right," Holland said. "That'll do it."

"And he told me something else . . . something about why Webster cut Nancy Denton near in half and put a snake in her chest."

"Because he was fucking crazy, right?" Holland said.

"No, Eddie . . . because he loved her more than life itself, and he was trying to bring her back."

"You what?"

"It's called a revival. It's some kind of voodoo ritual, and he did that because he thought there was a chance she could be brought back to life."

"Christ almighty," Ross said. "Now I believe I have heard it all."

"But I cannot deal with that now, not as part of the investigation," Gaines said. "That has been and gone, and whatever Michael Webster thought he might be doing is history now. I have to deal with what I have right in front of me, and that is Webster's death and whether Matthias Wade was directly involved."

"I don't think there's a great deal going on around there that doesn't involve Matthias Wade, one way or the other," Ross said.

"They're Klan, right?" Gaines asked.

"The Wades? Sure as hell they are. A lot of the old Southern families were—and still are. Things have changed, but they changed only a little, and they've changed too damned slow. It's not the way it was in the twenties and thirties, but it's there all right."

"You think old man Wade is Klan, as well?"

Ross smiled. "Earl Wade was all set to be Grand Dragon for this state, possibly Louisiana and Alabama too. He was right in there, politically speaking, but after that church bombing in sixty-three, a good number of senior Klan officers distanced themselves from it, again for political reasons."

"Church bombing?" Gaines asked.

"The 16th Street Baptist Church in Birmingham, Alabama. Four colored girls were killed. That was eleven years ago, and they're still no nearer to finding out who did that. It was Klan, for sure, but no one has been identified as responsible, and no arrests have been made. Then we had those three civil rights kids murdered here in Mississippi in 1964—"

"Chaney, Goodman, and Schwerner," Holland interjected, "and then those two colored kids were murdered here as well, Henry Dee and Charles Moore. There was rumor— still is—that they were killed by someone within the sheriff's department, but—as with all these cases—there is never enough evidence, and no one is ever prepared to make a statement."

"And then Vernon Dahmer was killed in sixty-six. He was Forrest County NAACP president. Got his house firebombed, his wife and eight kids inside. His wife got herself and all the kids out. Dahmer manages to escape, but he's so badly burned he doesn't make it. He dies the next day. That was one time people actually demanded a real honest-to-God investigation, and they ended up indicting fourteen men. Thirteen made it to trial, eight of them on arson and murder charges, the rest on conspiracy to intimidate and such. They even charged Sam Bowers, Imperial Wizard, got him before a judge and jury four times, but each time it ended in a mistrial. All that happened on my doorstep, literally, and it was the kind of thing that really soured a lot of people on Klan membership. They certainly were not in the business of making any new friends down here, and they lost a lot of old ones. Late sixties was when Earl Wade started to get sick, and since then, he's not been physically well enough to be involved in anything like that."

"He's sick?" Gaines asked. "Sick with what?"

"I don't know for sure," Ross said. "Maybe he's just getting old. Heard word he was losing his mind, going senile, you know?"

"But Matthias," Holland said, "well, he's a different animal altogether."

"He's active in the Klan?" Gaines asked.

"Who the hell knows," Ross replied. "It isn't something people openly admit to anymore. Back in the twenties, the Klan had something in the region of four or five million members, some say as high as six million. That was about five percent of the population. One person in every twenty was a self-professed Klan member."

"Well, we know for sure he had a major disagreement with his sister and Clifton Regis getting together."

"And Regis is on a three-to-five, you say?"

"Right."

"And he's been there how long?"

"Seventeen months."

"You want me to check into it?" Ross asked. "I still have a whole network of friends and acquaintances in the legal arena. Hattiesburg, Vicksburg, Jackson, Columbus, Tupelo . . . I can find out who was on it, the judge, jury selection, all kinds of things."

"No," Gaines said. "I have enough going on without worrying about whether or not Clifton Regis was set up by Matthias Wade. Right now, all I am interested in is Michael Webster's death."

"And Nancy Denton's," Holland said.

"No, not as much, Eddie. Webster was killed less than a week ago, Nancy twenty years ago. I think that Matthias Wade killed Nancy. I think he strangled her and dumped the body. I think Michael Webster found her, and then he did what he did. He held on to that secret for twenty years with the deluded belief that she might come back. That's why he never spoke of it, and I think Wade knew he would never speak of it. If he spoke of what had happened, then not only would this revival be compromised, but he would go to jail for what he did to her body, for obstructing justice, and might even have been found guilty of her murder. When she was found, well, everything changed. Then Webster would be free to speak, certain that she wasn't coming back. Wade knew that Webster had to be removed from the equation, and removed he was. If Webster did kill Nancy, well, there isn't anything more the law can do to him now. If Matthias killed Nancy, then even getting him for Michael Webster's murder will serve me well enough."

"And you honestly think that Della is your inside line to that family?" Ross asked.

"I have to try something, Nate. And right now, it's the best thing I can think of."

"And you're off to Gulfport tomorrow morning?" Holland asked.

"Yes."

"You want me to come with you? Maryanne knows me. She trusts me. It might make the difference between her being willing to cooperate or not."

"Yes, that'd be really appreciated."

"Then I'll be ready tomorrow morning," Holland said.

"I'll come fetch you at eight."

"So now there's no reason not to stay and have a drink," Ross said. "Better here with company than home on your own, right?"

Gaines considered the cold and empty house, the closed door of his mother's room, the task that that lay ahead of him, of how he would cope with everything that reminded him of her. He thought of her clothes, her picture albums, her personal possessions.

"Okay," Gaines said. "One drink, a few hands of poker."

"Or a few drinks and one hand of poker," Ross said. "Sounds better that way."

49

Gaines did not leave Ross's house until somewhere close to one a.m. He was asleep before his head hit the pillow, and yet woke suddenly a little more than five hours later.

He paid no mind to that long-familiar sense of bone-deep fatigue. In-country, he had sleepwalked through days, never catching more than an hour or two's rest at a time. He showered, shaved, got dressed, made some coffee, and then drove over to the office. Neither Barbara nor Hagen had arrived, and he appreciated the silence and solitude.

The thought he had woken with, right there at the forefront of his mind, was Michael Webster's photo album, still there in evidence lockup.

He retrieved the album and took it to reception, sat there at the front desk to save having to walk back out every time the phone rang, and he went through it.

Gaines studied each picture carefully, now recognizing both Maryanne Benedict and Matthias Wade without hesitation. And Nancy was there, just as before, always smiling, so full of life. The way in which she seemed to radiate from those simple, faded images was inexplicable. Maryanne was beautiful, too, undeniably, but it was after three or four pages that he recognized yet another girl. She looked a little younger than Maryanne and he suspected this was Della Wade. There was something in the eyes that reminded Gaines of Matthias, but where Matthias possessed a degree of distance, perhaps even coolness, the young Della Wade was afire with vitality and happiness, much the same as Nancy. Possibly Matthias's seeming lack of warmth was due to Webster's presence, the resentment Matthias must have felt as he saw the closeness Webster and Nancy shared. His bitterness would have been directed toward Webster at first, and then perhaps—finally—Nancy herself. Had Matthias killed Nancy to satiate something so petty as spite and jealousy? *If I can't have her, neither can you.* Had that been the motivation? It made sense. Love became soured by rejection, and eventually that sense of rejection, festering among unexpressed thoughts and unrequited hopes, had become bitter and twisted. Finally, Matthias had convinced himself that Nancy was foolish or stupid or ignorant, that someone who would deny him what was rightfully his had no place on this earth. Or perhaps it was simply that he could not bear to be reminded of his loss every day, and the only way to remove that reminder was to remove the person he'd lost.

But Della was there, appearing time and again through some of the later images. She could only have been ten or eleven years old. Had she and Maryanne been close? Would this gamble pay off? Would Della still hold enough feelings of affection toward Maryanne for Maryanne to get to her?

Perhaps nothing more would be served by this venture than the ultimate reunion of Clifton Regis and Della Wade. And all of this was dependent upon the validity of what Clifton Regis had told him. There was always the possibility that Della Wade was as manipulative as Gaines believed Matthias to be, that she had used Regis as a means by which she could escape the clutches of the Wade family. Gaines didn't believe so. He had seen something in Clifton Regis's eyes, and he had believed the man. And good though it would be to help Regis and Della with their personal lives, Gaines was hoping for so much more. He needed a foot in the door. He needed something that would give him leverage on Matthias Wade.

For Gaines, it seemed to no longer be a matter of law, but of justice. They were worlds apart. Gaines was not so naive as to believe they were even related. Justice had long since faded into relative obscurity with the advent of due process and bureaucracy. Hell, it was the law who was responsible for some of the Klan horrors that Ross and Holland had detailed the night before. There was no justice there, and there would be no justice here—not for Nancy or Judith, not for Michael Webster—if Gaines did not pursue this any which way he could.

He thought of his mother. This was what she would have wanted. For him to be doing something worthwhile and purposeful, to be soldiering on, to be in control of what he was feeling and what was going on around him.

In war, horrors were expected. In Whytesburg, Mississippi, such horrors should play no part at all.

Gaines returned the album to the evidence room, and he left the office. He locked up behind himself, drove over to Nate Ross's to collect Eddie Holland, all the while considering the best approach to Maryanne Benedict and the assignment he was going to ask of her. If she said no, well, he was back to square one. For some reason, he believed she was going to help him. For some reason, he believed his visit had reminded her of the life she'd once had, and to now see all aspects of that life broken apart and scattered to the four winds was more upsetting than she could bear. But, in Gaines, perhaps she saw someone who could assist her with the weight of conscience. Perhaps she was now motivated by guilt, the feeling that she could have helped Michael Webster, that she could have been there for him after Nancy's disappearance. Maybe she had loved Michael, too, and yet had never been able to approach him, knowing always that Michael loved only Nancy. To live a life in the shadow of another was to live no life at all. To live a life perpetually compared to someone else would be the most grievous negation of one's own worth. It struck Gaines then that his own choices had perhaps been influenced by his belief that he would never love anyone as much as he had loved Linda Newman. Possibly he and Maryanne Benedict had lived along some strange line of parallel emotions, never committing, never wholly withdrawing, existing somewhere in the middle ground, the places where neither light nor darkness ever really reached. Like ghosts of their former selves, living without really being alive.

He was reminded of something Lieutenant Wilson had once said. "Spend time with the lost and fallen, with the lonely and the forgotten, with the ones who didn't make it . . . That's where you find real humanity." And with that memory came the memory of the last words to leave Ron Wilson's lips, uttered in the handful of seconds between changing his damp socks and the arrival of the bullet that killed him. *The memory of the dead is the greatest burden of all.*

That was the burden Gaines carried, and he vowed to carry it well, to carry it resolutely, never faltering or resting until he could set that burden down at the feet of whosoever was responsible.

And then Gaines was turning off the road and heading toward Nate Ross's house, and he saw Eddie Holland standing on the veranda awaiting him. Less than an hour and they would be in Gulfport, and Gaines would know if Maryanne Benedict was on his side, or had chosen to abandon this game once and for all.

50

En route, they talked. Rather, Holland talked and Gaines listened. Holland spoke of Don Bicklow, of Gaines's mother, of Nate Ross's wife and the circumstances of her death. He told Gaines the details of a murder case that Bicklow and his own predecessor, George Austin, had investigated back in the latter part of 1958. It was the first real-life honest-to-God murder that had happened since his assignment to Breed County.

"Had to stand there for three hours with a dead woman on the floor of her kitchen. Crazy husband bashed her head in with a tire iron and then said she fell and hit her head on the corner of the stove. Made me sick to my stomach, you know, but someone had to stand there while all the crime scene fellas did their thing. However, despite how bad it made me feel, it was also the thing that really convinced me that I had taken the right job. Sounds odd, but before that I reckoned on this line of work being nothing more than a regular salary, a pension at the end, something being better than nothing, you know? But that dead woman, the fact that her husband did her in and then tried to get away with it, well, that started me to thinking that there must be a lot of folks who don't have anyone in their corner, if you know what I mean."

Gaines nodded, kept his eyes on the road. He didn't acknowledge Holland because he didn't want him to stop talking. The sound of Holland's voice took away the incessant barrage of questions in his own mind, and it was good to have a little internal silence for a change.

"So, that sort of resolved it all for me. I came in after the war was over, much like you after Vietnam. I know Webster was in Asia, but I served in Italy." Holland fell quiet.

Gaines prompted him with, "You have kids, right?"

Holland laughed. "However old they get, they're always still your kids, aren't they? Yes, I got kids. Four of them, though the youngest has three daughters and a Chrysler franchise out in Waynesboro . . ."

And off he went with wives' names, husbands' names, kids' names, what happened when they all got together last Thanksgiving. That started him in on his wife and how she died, and how he'd never been able to even consider the possibility of finding someone else. With those last words, Gaines saw the sign for Gulfport, and they took the exit.

Gaines remembered the way to Maryanne Benedict's house, and when they pulled up outside, he was certain he saw the curtain flicker in an upstairs window.

He had been here the day before his mother died—Saturday, the 27th. He had driven away from here, returned home, and it was that night, as Saturday became Sunday, that Alice had gone.

Before Gaines was out of the car, Maryanne Benedict had opened the front door of her house.

Eddie Holland was there first. He hugged her, turned back as Gaines approached, and started to explain their visit.

Maryanne came forward and took Gaines's right hand. "Eddie told me about your mother, Sheriff," she said, "and I want you to know how sorry I am for your loss."

"Thank you, Miss Benedict," Gaines replied. She had told him to call her Maryanne last time he'd been here, but somehow it still did not seem appropriate.

"Please come in," she said.

She released Gaines's hand, went on back, Holland behind her, Gaines following Holland, and she led them through to the kitchen, where she asked them to sit.

Gaines's last visit seemed to belong to some distant other life. Even the room seemed not to be the room he remembered from their last conversation.

Once she had made coffee, Maryanne sat down and looked directly at Gaines.

"Before you ask me," she said, "and despite the fact that I know I should help you, I am not willing to talk to Matthias."

Gaines nodded. "I understand, and that is precisely what I don't want you to do."

Maryanne frowned.

"I wanted to ask you about Della," he said. "Last time I came, you spoke about Matthias, about Michael, you told me about the fire at the plant, about the night that Nancy went missing, but you never mentioned Della, not once. As far as I can work out, she was about ten years old at the time, and I wondered whether you and she had been friends."

"I didn't mention Catherine or Eugene either," Maryanne replied. "Eugene was sixteen, only two years older than me, and Catherine was close to nineteen."

Gaines stayed silent. He just looked at her and waited for her to go on.

"What are you after, Sheriff Gaines?" she asked.

There was something in her expression. She knew there was some intended manipulation, something that Gaines was planning to ask of her, something that he was unable to effect alone.

She did not look at Eddie Holland, despite the fact that she knew Eddie so much better than Gaines. She was smart enough to realize that Eddie's presence was merely a sweetener for the bitter pill.

"Miss Benedict—"

"Maryanne."

"Okay, Maryanne. I have a letter from a man called Clifton Regis. He is a colored man that Della Wade was involved with some time ago. They were together in New Orleans, and Matthias didn't take too kindly to the idea of his younger sister running around with a colored musician. According to Regis, Della planned to run away with him, and she got ten thousand dollars from somewhere and gave it to Regis. Matthias sent someone down there to take back the ten grand, but whoever it was took couple of Regis's fingers, as well. Matthias then had Della brought back to the Wade family home, and as far as I can find out, she's been here ever since."

"And this Clifton Regis is where now?" Maryanne asked.

"Parchman Farm."

"And Matthias put him there for taking this money?"

"No, he's in there for a burglary he's supposed to have done."

"*Supposed* to have done?"

Gaines shrugged. It was obvious from his reaction that Gaines believed Wade complicit, directly or indirectly, in Regis's incarceration, and it did not need to be said.

Maryanne was quiet for a time. She did look at Eddie Holland then, and Eddie reached out and closed his hand over hers.

"Della is a crazy person," she eventually said. "Della Wade has always been a crazy person and probably always will be. When Della was six years old, she poured bleach into a fishpond and killed all the fish. When she was eight, she set light to another girl's hair.

Dealing with Della Wade is like crossing a rope bridge in a storm. You take careful steps, and you move very slowly."

"You knew her as a child?"

"Sure, I did. She was there with the rest of the Wades. Catherine was always around to keep an eye on her and Eugene, but my impression of her then and now are quite different, most of it influenced by the things people have said over the years. At the time, she didn't seem so different from anyone else. She was wild, sure, but so were all of us at that age. After her mother died, I don't really know who took care of her, but from what you say, it seems that Matthias is managing her affairs now."

"I spoke to Regis yesterday," Gaines said, "and he said nothing about her being crazy. He spoke of her with tremendous affection, and I really got the impression that they had been very much in love and intended to move away and have a life together."

"I said crazy, but maybe I didn't mean that kind of crazy. Unpredictable, flighty, a ceaseless energy, but kind of manic and uncontrollable. Then, suddenly, huge bouts of depression, sudden changes in her attitude and personality."

"Schizophrenic?"

"I don't know what you'd call it, and giving it a name doesn't matter. She would just flip wildly from one mood to the next, and you never had any prediction. Sometimes she seemed to be the sweetest little girl you could ever hope to meet, other times a vicious little harpy with the shortest temper and the worst language."

"Did the Wades ever have her seen by a psychiatrist or something?"

Maryanne shook her head. "I wouldn't think so. That's not the way that wealthy families deal with troublesome offspring, is it, Eddie?"

Eddie smiled. "No, they stick them in the basement and keep them secret."

"It sullies the family name to have a lunatic in the ranks," Maryanne said. "Reputation is everything, at least as a facade, if not in reality. It's superficial, but that's the way it is down here. Only other way for the Wades to deal with Della would have been to have her locked up someplace a hundred miles away, and Lillian Wade would never have let such a thing happen. As far as Lillian was concerned, family took priority over everything. You did not betray your own family members, no matter what they might have done."

"You knew Lillian?"

"Sure I did," Maryanne replied. "Lillian was an amazing woman. She loved those children dearly, gave them everything she could."

"But she was an alcoholic, right? She drank herself to death."

"I don't know what to say, Sheriff. I don't know details. For the brief time that I knew the Wades, those few years between the end of the war and Nancy's disappearance, I had a happy childhood. Me, Nancy, Matthias, and Michael, and around the edges of that little universe there was Eugene and Catherine and Della. Sometimes they'd be there, but most times they were off doing whatever they were doing. They were never really part of it, you know? Not that they were excluded, but they just never really figured in our world. We would see Lillian in the house, and she always talked to me like I was a grown-up. She asked my opinion about things. She always wanted to know what I thought about something or other. I remember one time she engaged me in a long discussion about Harry Truman being the new president and how there was now a democratic majority in both Houses of Congress. That was 1948. I was eight years old. She said I should understand such things, and I was always grown-up enough to have an opinion."

"What did your parents think about your friendship with the Wades?"

Maryanne frowned. "Why do you ask that?"

"I'm just curious," Gaines said. "If it bothers you to talk about it, I'm sorry."

"No, it doesn't bother me. It just surprises me a little, as it has no bearing on why you're here. What did my parents think of it? My mother believed that the Wades and the Benedicts were from different worlds, and those worlds should ideally stay separate. However, she never actively stopped me spending time with them. My father was very much the strong, silent type, and if he didn't raise a subject, it was never discussed. My parents didn't exactly maintain an equality in their relationship, if you know what I mean."

"Are they still alive?"

"No," Maryanne said. "My father died in sixty-five, my mother in sixty-eight."

"And you have no brothers or sisters?"

Maryanne frowned. "No, I am an only child." She shook her head, looked askance at Eddie Holland. "What is this, Sheriff? Why all these personal questions?"

"I apologize," Gaines said. "I am just interested. It's in my nature to be curious about people."

"It is also your occupation," Maryanne replied. "I am beginning to feel like I am the one under investigation."

"No, not at all, and that was not my intention," Gaines interjected. "I am sorry for giving you that impression. I am just dealing with so much at the moment, so many different aspects of this thing, and it seems that there are so few answers available—"

"That when you find someone who answers your questions, you have to keep thinking of more, right?"

Gaines smiled. "Maybe," he said. "Maybe something like that."

"Okay, well, let's get back to the issue at hand. You still haven't explained to me what it is that you want."

"Well, to understand what I want, you have to understand what I think has happened here, and then, with all of that in mind, you can make a decision as to whether or not you're willing to help me."

"That's a dangerous word to use, Sheriff Gaines."

"What is?"

"Help. It's loaded, and you know it. You're trying to appeal to the better angel of my nature, supposing, of course that I do actually have a better angel."

"I think you do, Maryanne."

"And what gives you that impression, Sheriff?"

"The fact that you opened the door this morning before we even reached it. I think you want to help, and maybe not just for Nancy's sake but for Michael, as well."

"And then there is also the matter of vengeance, which, to be truthful, is something I had always hoped not to feel the need for, but in this case I might make an exception."

"Vengeance?"

"If Matthias Wade strangled Nancy Denton, if Matthias Wade cut Michael Webster's head off and then burned his body in his own home, then I will start lining up early just to see him sentenced, Sheriff Gaines."

"You'll be in line right after me, Maryanne," Gaines said.

Maryanne Benedict looked at Eddie Holland, nodded in acknowledgment of his silent and reassuring presence, and then looked back at Gaines.

"So tell me what you have in mind," she said, leaning forward.

51

"There is something just so desperately sad about this," Maryanne Benedict said when she looked up from reading Clifton Regis's letter. "How did he meet Della?"

"Through Eugene. Clifton was working as a musician in New Orleans."

"And Matthias cut his fingers off?"

"Not Matthias, but someone who was acting under orders from Matthias."

"And does he know who this person was?"

"No, he doesn't."

Maryanne sighed audibly. "You know, since you were here, just a week ago, I have been thinking more and more about Matthias. I have been trying to remember things that we said to each other, times when I felt that he really cared for me, and I am struggling. It is strange, but it's like my entire perception of what was really going on back there has shifted."

"In what way?" Holland asked, perhaps for no other reason than to feel as though he was a part of the conversation.

"My friendship was with Nancy. I knew Nancy first, and then we met Matthias. It was obvious that Matthias loved Nancy, and then Michael appeared and stole Nancy's heart completely. I mean, Matthias was good to me, and on the face of it, he seemed to treat both me and Nancy the same, but I think he just accepted that I was part of the package deal. If he wanted Nancy around, then he got me. I think if Nancy had not been there, then Matthias Wade wouldn't have had anything to do with me."

"Well, he certainly hasn't made any efforts to contact you since then, has he?"

"No," Maryanne said, "not in any meaningful way. But then he lost his mother in fifty-two, as well, and I can only assume that losing Nancy so soon afterward just compounded the grief he was already carrying—" Maryanne stopped then, slowly shook her head. "Unless he feels no grief for Nancy."

"Because he was the one who killed her," Holland said.

"And Matthias knew that there was no proof of his involvement in Nancy's death," Gaines said. "And there is something else you need to know," he added, "about what Michael did to Nancy and why."

There was silence for a moment, and then Gaines detailed precisely what Regis had told him, and he explained it in such a matter-of-fact way that it now seemed to bear some logic.

Maryanne sighed. "So he did what he did for love," she said. "After all this, he did what he did for love, and he never spoke of it, not even when you found her."

"Seems that way," Gaines replied. "Everything was in limbo until her body was discovered. Up until that point, Matthias didn't need to do anything about Michael. But once she was found, then Matthias had to get rid of Michael, just to ensure that Michael didn't say anything that could implicate him. I have been considering the possibility that whoever visited with Clifton and cut off his fingers was also perhaps responsible for what was done to Michael."

"So I get this letter to Della somehow or other," Maryanne said, "and hope that she doesn't show it to Matthias, and then what?"

"Well, if she really does love Clifton Regis, then there might be sufficient motivation for her to speak to me."

"Because getting Matthias out of the way enables her and Clifton to be reunited."

"Yes," Gaines said.

"Are your murder investigations always this Shakespearian, Sheriff?"

"I have to say that there are very few murder investigations, thankfully."

"I'm sorry. I didn't mean to sound flippant," Maryanne said. "I do understand the importance of what you're asking me to do, but I have to be honest with you. First, I think it's a very fragile plan. Second, and more important, I think you have no idea who you're dealing with when it comes to Della Wade. I can only imagine what her relationship with Matthias is like. If she's been under his control and influence for the last year and a half, I think there's a very strong possibility that I won't even get to her, and if I do, then the first thing she will do with this letter is take it to him. If Matthias did send someone down to New Orleans to cut Clifton Regis's fingers off for getting involved with his sister, then what do you think he might do if he learns that Regis has every intention of getting back with her?"

"I think Clifton Regis would have a fatal accident up in Sunflower County," Gaines said.

"And Regis is aware of this possibility?"

"Clifton Regis is not a fool. If he is not telling the truth, then he is an extraordinary liar."

"You think you can read people that well?" Maryanne asked.

"I think I have a good intuition for people, yes. And right now I'm in a position where I either trust that intuition or reconcile myself to the fact that this will never be solved."

"And you could never do that?"

"No, Maryanne, I could never do that."

"Well, Sheriff, I feel I have a good intuition for people, and that is why I opened the door this morning, and that is why I asked Eddie to come over and see me. Since we spoke, I have felt a greater and greater sense of responsibility, almost a need, to do something about what happened to Nancy."

"And that is really appreciated," Gaines said, "because right now, I feel like I am in this alone."

"And Matthias Wade?" she asked. "What does your intuition tell you about him?"

"That he did something truly terrible twenty years ago, that he has been living with the guilt of what he did for all this time, and it has twisted him into a manipulative and vicious man. If he killed Webster, if he did send someone to cut off Regis's fingers, and if he buried Michael Webster's head in the field behind my house, then he did it to warn me off, to scare me enough to drop this whole thing."

"That is horrific," Maryanne said. "Utterly, utterly horrific. What kind of person are we dealing with here?"

"A very dangerous man," Gaines said, "which is why I need you to look at this in the cold, hard light of day and ask yourself whether or not you are prepared to take the risks that come along with being involved."

"I have no choice, Sheriff Gaines."

"Of course you have a choice, Maryanne," Eddie Holland interjected.

She smiled, almost to herself, and then shook her head. "No, I don't, Eddie. You know me well enough to understand why I don't. I have spent the last twenty years trying to forget what happened to the best friend I ever had, and now I have a chance to—" Maryanne stopped. Her eyes were brimming with tears. She put her hands to her face, and her chest rose and fell as she suppressed her sobs.

Eddie pulled her close and put his arms around her.

John Gaines sat there in silence, feeling as empty as a shell.

52

Leaving the letter with Maryanne Benedict seemed at once the most irresponsible thing to do and yet the only avenue open to Gaines.

He and Eddie Holland said little on the journey back to Whytesburg. It was close to noon by the time they arrived, and Gaines merely dropped Eddie off at Nate Ross's place and drove on to the office.

Victor Powell had been in to see him in his absence. Hagen had spoken with Powell about the bodies of Nancy, Judith, and Michael.

"They can't stay there forever, obviously," Hagen said, "but I told him that until this investigation was over, there wasn't going to be any hope of proper funerals and suchlike."

"And what did he say?"

"He said that he would take them all up to the morgue at Biloxi. He said they had better facilities for long-term storage."

Gaines sighed. "Hell of a thing, eh? Better facilities for long-term storage. This is what it comes down to."

He left Hagen standing there with nothing to say and headed down the back hallway to his office.

Once inside, he closed the door, sat at his desk. and pulled off his boots.

Maryanne Benedict had been circumspect in her strategy for reaching Della Wade. When pressed for any kind of idea, she'd merely said, "I don't know, Sheriff. You're just going to have to leave it with me and let me try to figure something out." Gaines had started to say something else, but Eddie Holland had interjected. "It's okay, John. Leave it be. Let Maryanne work out what to do by herself." So Gaines had dropped it.

And then they had left.

At the front door, just there inside the porch, there had been a strange moment. Holland had gone on to the car, was getting in on the passenger side, and Maryanne had reached out and touched Gaines's arm. He had turned, and she was close to him, oddly so, and she said, "Sometimes it's easier to believe that everything is random, that things just happen, and they happen for no real reason." She was looking directly at Gaines, as if she were trying to read every possible thought in his mind. "But I know that's not true," she went on. "I know there is a rhyme and reason to all things, and even coincidences are not really coincidences at all."

Gaines said nothing, but evidently there was a question in his eyes, an unspoken request for clarification.

"I just find it strange—don't you?—that you are the person now trying to find out who killed my best friend, but you are twenty years too late."

"I don't think I am too late," Gaines said.

"Too late to have the guilty suffer the rightful consequences, Sheriff. If Matthias Wade strangled Nancy, then he should have hanged two decades ago. But no, he has lived the best kind of life, always enough money, never wanting for anything—"

"Except for the very thing he really wanted."

"For Nancy Denton to love him."

"And the knowledge that he was the one who removed any hope of that ever happening."

Maryanne smiled ruefully. "Nancy would have liked you," she said, almost to no one, and then she looked once more at Gaines, and there was a warmth in her expression that Gaines had not seen before. "Yes," she added. "Nancy would have liked you a great deal."

Gaines hesitated. He wanted to hear what she would say next. He wanted to ask her why Nancy would have liked him, or if it was simply a way of Maryanne telling him that she herself liked him.

Perhaps he wanted to see if he had the courage to say something himself, to tell her that talking to her seemed to be the only thing among all this madness that made him feel like a real human being.

But he did not say anything, and neither did Maryanne, and—without another word—Maryanne closed the door after him.

Gaines stood there. He sensed that she was right there on the other side of the door, that she had not yet walked away.

He could hear his own heart. He felt like a teenager. He smiled at his own foolishness and then he walked back to the car.

What Maryanne Benedict thought of him could not now consume his attention. It was not relevant to the situation at hand, and even if she did think of him, then such an issue would serve only to distract and complicate things. Maryanne Benedict was being employed to deliver a message. That was all—nothing more nor less. Maryanne Benedict would succeed, or she would fail, and the resolution of what had happened here in Whytesburg was—at least for now—entirely dependent upon the outcome of that single action, seemingly so simple and yet potentially very profound. Gaines possessed not the slightest doubt regarding the influence that Matthias Wade and his father could bring to bear upon the next sheriff's election. Pursue Wade knowingly and obviously, and Gaines would be without a job. If he was no longer sheriff, there would be no way to remain in Whytesburg. He would have to give up his mother's house and move, not only county, but perhaps state. Back to Louisiana? Or maybe just head west and keep on going until it felt right to stop? Gaines was certain that Wade was directly involved in the death of Michael Webster, and if Wade was capable of that, then perhaps he was capable of killing Gaines. But that would happen only if Wade became aware of what was going on behind the scenes. He could not know about the Regis letter. If he learned of it, then not only Regis, but Maryanne would be in the firing line, too.

Gaines confronted the worst-case scenario—another two dead, Clifton Regis and Maryanne Benedict, and their deaths directly attributable to his actions in this case. And then there would be five dead, one two decades earlier, the other four within a matter of days of one another. From external and objective observation—always the least empathetic view when considering decisions made and actions taken under pressure—it would appear that his failure to obtain a search warrant had prevented any possibility of Webster's further detention. Had Webster been detained, he might be still alive. Had Judith not learned of Webster's release, she might not have taken her own life. Just as Kidd had said, Gaines had allowed his emotions to influence his thoughts. For a man so walled off, so determined to organize his life in such a way as to avoid these complications, he had done a fine job of failing. Granted, there were mitigating circumstances—his mother had died, and he was under a great deal of personal emotional stress, but then, if he had believed himself unable to carry out his duties, why had he not taken some time out, turned the investigation over to his deputy, Richard Hagen? Why, Sheriff Gaines? How did you allow these things to pass so far beyond your zone of control? It was unavoidable—his responsibility for both these deaths—and though he knew he would turn these events over in his mind again and again, though he knew he would ask himself unanswerable questions, he also knew that there was no turning back. It was done. He had gotten caught up in this thing, allowed it to get under his skin, allowed it to disturb him, and out of this he had acted in such a way as to make it far worse. His lack of professionalism was unforgivable, and though he knew others might judge him less severely, he knew he himself would never let it go.

Gaines got up and walked to the window. He was thinking crazy. He was arguing for his own prosecution.

The real issue here was that he could not see any other way to approach this obstacle. Where would he go if he could not reach Della? Eugene? Eugene did not live there and had not lived at the family home for some considerable time. Did Eugene possess some knowledge that would incriminate his brother, or even some burning desire to see his brother incriminated? Or the older of the two sisters, Catherine? Would she help?

Gaines felt boxed in whichever way he turned. Was it possible that Wade would just never be called to account for what he had done? Of course it was. This was the fundamental difference between justice and law. Guilt was no guarantee of punishment. The legal system had created its own Machiavellian intricacies with a view to retaining its exclusivity and self-preservative nature, but in doing so had built in such levels of complexity and loopholes that even the very worst human beings could walk free, every step legal, every step visible, every step taking them closer and closer to the opportunity to perpetrate the same crimes again. A cynical view, but a realistic one.

Ultimately, only those who worked within the courts benefited from the courts. More often than not, those who most needed justice, people whose lives and livelihoods depended upon it, were those who were granted the least. It was a sad state of affairs, but tearing yourself apart about it served no purpose. No one man could change it, and until the very society was ripped apart and built once more on foundations of honesty, then that system would not change. Corruption and deceit had become inherent and implicit in the very fabric of the culture. So, how far would he go? If it came down to it, if all avenues had been exhausted and there was insufficient evidence to secure an arrest, would Gaines take the law into his own hands? Could he just go on up to the Wade house and shoot the man in the head? Could he just run him off the road? Could he pull him over, get him out of his car, engage him in a struggle, shoot him, and then leave a gun at the scene to imply that Wade had threatened him first? Such things had been done, would be done again. Gaines had killed before, at a distance and up close. It had been in war, sure, but wasn't this also some kind of war? Did money and influence always buy you exemption from due process and consequences? Perhaps it did, but that did not make it right.

And if Gaines let it slide, if he decided that a twenty-year-old murder was just another part of this town's forgotten and forgett-able history, and if Michael Webster—crazy son of a bitch that he was—was insufficiently important to warrant any real considera-tion, then what did that say about Gaines? What did it say about him as a police officer, a man, a human being? It said that he was nothing. That he was less than nothing. It said that there was nothing worth fighting for, nothing worth protecting, that the sanctity of human life was not inviolate, that there were people who could just be wiped from the face of the earth and no one would give a good God damn about it. Did Gaines want that to be his legacy, a reflection of the man he was? Is that the kind of man his own father had been? No, his own father had given his life for his country. He had given it for liberty, for the right to be free from oppression and tyranny, the same kind of oppression and tyranny that Gaines had been led to believe he was fighting in Southeast Asia. The moralistic and political issues aside, he had gone to war for the same reason, and was this not the same again, just a smaller field of battle?

Whoever had killed Nancy Denton and Michael Webster—one person, two people, it did not matter—were the enemy. That was the simple truth. The simplest truth of all. It was why he was here. He believed that Maryanne cared, as did Eddie Holland and Nate Ross, but right now Gaines was the only one who possessed any degree of legal authority. And they all cared for different reasons. People were not naturally brave. Bravery seemed more often founded in desperation or lack of choice. You charged forward when there was no way to go backward. Boxed in, you fought to the last man. An avenue of escape, a means by which you could live to fight another day, and the vast majority of people took it without hesitation. It was not cowardice, but the simple and fundamental need and desire to survive, and survive not only for self, but for those who needed you to survive.

Without Gaines, they were—all of them, irrespective of personal motivation or the need for justice—impotent.

Gaines returned to his desk. No, there was no choice now. It was all or nothing. Regardless of whether these people were one and the same or a group working together, the truth was coming to light.

He remembered the photographs of Anna-Louise Mayhew and Dorothy McCormick, ten and twelve years old respectively, their lives snatched away brutally, their bodies worthless now that some desperate and perverse urge had been satisfied. Had Matthias Wade done this too? Was that what he was really dealing with?

If so, then whatever Gaines did, he would be doing it for those children, as well.

53

Gaines had woken immediately when the phone started ringing. He came out of the bed awkwardly, lost his footing, and whacked his knee against the dresser. By the time he actually reached the phone, he believed he would be too late, but it seemed that whoever wanted to reach him was not of a mind to quit.

"I have them both here," Eddie Holland said. "At Nate's place."

"What? Sorry, what did you say?"

"Wake up, John. Get some clothes on. Get yourself over here. I have Maryanne and Della here in the house. Right now."

"You what?"

"I'll see you in five minutes," Eddie said, and hung up the phone.

Gaines looked at the clock. It was twenty to eight. He had slept right through the seven-o'clock alarm, or he had woken, turned it off, and forgotten that he'd done that.

And then his thoughts caught up with the phone call, and he understood what Eddie Holland had just told him.

At first somewhat disbelieving, he then wondered if he wasn't dreaming again, if he would now walk back to his room to find himself deep within undergrowth, once more hiding, tracking someone, being followed.

But he was not dreaming, and the urgency of what had happened suddenly hit him. He was dressed and out of the house within five minutes, covered the distance from his own house to Ross's place within another five, and he arrived to find Nate Ross on the veranda, a concerned expression on his face.

"Jesus, what the hell have you gotten yourself into?" Ross asked him.

"Eddie just called me about Della Wade," Gaines said. "She's still here?"

"I have Maryanne Benedict. I have Della Wade. I have some letter she keeps reading out. And I have a Southern fucking melodrama on my hands that would put Tennessee Williams to shame."

Gaines went on past Ross and through the screen door. Once

inside the house, he could hear voices in the kitchen. He carried on through, found Della Wade, her back to the rear door, in her hand the letter, Maryanne standing by the stove, Eddie Holland seated at the table.

"You are John Gaines," Della said, and as she stepped away from the light of the back-door window, she came into view.

There was a fierce brightness in Della Wade's eyes that intimidated Gaines, a sense of willful petulance, something unsettling, perhaps even unstable. She was petite, perhaps no more than five three or four, but she seemed to occupy the entire room. She was dressed in jeans, a simple cotton blouse, a leather jacket, and her brunette hair, fashioned in something akin to a Gibson Girl upsweep, was tied back with a black ribbon. Gaines knew she was thirty-one, but she looked younger, perhaps twenty-six or seven. Her skin was clear and blemish free, her cheekbones high, almost too pronounced, and yet this merely served to accentuate the size and shape of her eyes. And it was her eyes that got him, made him feel cornered, as if he should back away for a moment, approach her once again more slowly, deferentially perhaps. This was not the crazy woman that Gaines had expected. This was not the cowed and timid girl that Gaines had imagined, controlled by her brother, told what to do, where to be, how to behave. This was a self-assured woman who effortlessly wore the kind of beauty that made husbands wish their wives were six foot deep and forgotten.

"Yes," Gaines eventually said. "I am."

"And you brought this letter and gave it to Maryanne?"

"Yes, I did."

"And you went to see Clifton Regis?"

"Yes, I went to see him."

Della Wade took another step forward. Her expression was fiercely defensive. "Why?"

Gaines looked at Maryanne, at Eddie, turned to look at Nate Ross as he joined them in the kitchen.

"I'm asking you, Sheriff, not them. Why did you go and see Clifton?"

Gaines did not want to lie, but he needed to say something—anything—that would dispel the tremendous tension in the room.

"Because I am a firm believer in true love, Miss Wade, and when I heard what happened, I just had to do something about it."

"Is that supposed to be funny? Is that supposed to make me feel better about what you've done?"

"Maybe you could tell me what you think I've done?" Gaines asked.

"You went to see Clifton Regis, the man I love. You got him to write me a letter. You gave it to Maryanne Benedict. She called the house, and thank God that my brother was not there—"

"I knew he wasn't there before I called, Della," Maryanne interjected.

"Stay out of this, Maryanne, seriously," Della snapped. She took a step toward Gaines, held up the letter. "You know what would have happened to Clifton if Matthias had found this? You know what Matthias did to Clifton?"

"He cut his fingers off," Gaines said.

"Cut his fingers off and got him shipped out to Parchman Farm for five years. That's how much he doesn't want me involved with Clifton Regis, and you, in some kind of blind, stumbling effort to find out what happened to some girl who's been dead for twenty years, you jeopardize everything that I am working toward."

"I am sorry, Miss Wade. That was not the intention."

"Well, I don't even know what to say to that. You think sorry does it for me? You think sorry makes me any less pissed with you? I don't think you even get what I'm talking about here—"

"Like I said, Miss Wade, I apologize for what you think might have happened, but I want you to know that this was a considered action on my part. I went to see Clifton as a means to reach you."

"To reach me? What the hell are you talking about? I live a handful of miles from here. You drove the better part of three hundred miles to see Clifton, got him to write me a letter, used Maryanne as your courier, and never thought of picking up the telephone and calling me?"

"I did not think that you would talk to me."

"Because?"

"Because of your brother, Miss Wade."

"My brother? What the hell has he got to do with whether I talk to the local sheriff or not?"

"Because he'd then know that I was pursuing a line of inquiry that involved him—"

Della Wade opened her mouth to speak, and then she stopped. "I'm sorry?"

"I did not want him to know that I was investigating him."

"Investigating him for what? For what he did to Clifton?"

"No, Miss Wade, for murdering both Nancy Denton and Michael Webster."

Della Wade frowned, her head to one side, and then she seemed to double take. She looked at Maryanne, at Eddie Holland, she started to smile, anticipating that one of those present would suddenly smile with her, that they'd start to laugh, that this would all be exposed as some surreal practical joke.

But no one smiled, and no one laughed, and Della Wade lost all the color from her cheeks and the intensity from her eyes, and she walked two or three steps forward and sort of folded herself loosely into one of the kitchen chairs.

"Oh," she said quietly, and then she looked at Gaines, and Gaines took the seat facing her, and for a while they did nothing but look at each other in silence.

Della Wade broke that silence with, "You think my brother killed Nancy?"

"Yes, Miss Wade, I do."

"And who is this other person?"

"Michael Webster."

Della looked at Maryanne. "Michael?" she asked her. "*The* Michael? Nancy's Michael?"

Maryanne nodded.

"He's dead?" Della asked.

"Yes," Gaines said. "You didn't know?"

Della shook her head. "No, why would I?"

"You don't read the papers?"

"No, I don't read newspapers," she said. "Haven't for years."

"Well, yes, Michael is dead. He was found in the burned-out wreckage of his home, and he had been decapitated."

"I'm sorry . . . what?"

"Decapitated, Miss Wade . . . his head and his left hand had been cut off."

"This is unreal. This is . . ." Her voice faded. She looked at Maryanne, wide-eyed and wordless for some moments, and then she looked back at Gaines and said, "And you think Matthias did this?"

"Let's just say that he is on my list of suspects."

"But Nancy Denton? Nancy Denton ran away, right?" Again Della turned to Maryanne, as if Maryanne were the one she trusted to confirm or deny what she was being told.

Maryanne merely held Della's gaze and said nothing.

"No, Miss Wade," Gaines said. "Nancy did not run away. You weren't aware that we found her?"

Della Wade looked visibly stunned.

Gaines was struck with an intense feeling of déjà vu. He was reprising the conversation he'd had with Maryanne Benedict during his first visit to her home the day before his mother's death.

He glanced at Maryanne. Maryanne shook her head. She had not told Della about Nancy or Michael. She had left that for Gaines to deal with.

Everything went in circles. Life and death and all in between.

"You found her? Where? When?"

"We found her on the morning of Wednesday the twenty-fourth, eleven days ago."

"How? What happened?"

"There was a rainstorm, a very heavy one, and it broke up the riverbank, and we found her buried there. We can only assume that she had been there since the night of her disappearance."

Gaines watched the woman come apart at the seams. Things she believed in no way involved or concerned her now seemed so close to home, and she was struggling desperately not only to absorb what was happening, but also to place it within any frame of reference. Gaines could so easily have told her that there was no context within which such things made sense, but he believed her already fully aware of this.

"And she was killed?" Della asked.

"Strangled," Gaines replied.

"By Matthias?"

"I believe so."

"And Michael was killed? Why was Michael killed? Why would Matthias kill Michael?"

"To stop him from speaking of what happened that night."

Della shook her head. "That makes no sense, no sense at all. Nancy disappeared twenty years ago. Michael Webster had two decades to tell anyone he liked whatever he knew about what happened."

"Michael was bound by his own decision not to say a word."

"But why? What possible reason could he have had for not saying what happened?"

"Because he was involved, too," Gaines said.

"In Nancy's death? No, no way. Michael loved her. Even I could see that. I was just a child and even I could see that." She turned to

Maryanne. "Isn't that right? Michael loved Nancy and she loved him back, and he would never have done anything to hurt her. Tell him, Maryanne."

"He didn't do anything to hurt her," Gaines said. "He did something that he believed would help her, and what he did and why he did it meant that he could never speak about it. Then, when she was found, he knew that what he'd done hadn't worked and now never would. That was why he had to be silenced."

"I do not understand what you're saying. This makes no fucking sense. What the hell are you saying? What did he do to her? What did Michael do to Nancy?"

Gaines paused. He waited until Della Wade's eyes were firmly fixed on his own, and then he said, "He tried to raise her from the dead, Miss Wade. Michael Webster tried to raise Nancy Denton from the dead."

Della Wade did smile then and then she started to laugh, but she stopped suddenly when she again realized that her reaction was singular and without support.

She looked at John Gaines for further explanation.

Gaines said nothing.

54

Maryanne Benedict held Della Wade's shoulders as she cried. She did not cry for more than a few moments, and then she seemed to gather herself together with surprising composure. It was as if she were somehow demonstrating vulnerability, and this facet of herself she did not wish to share with those present in Nate Ross's kitchen.

"Tell me everything," she said. "Tell me everything you know about Nancy and Michael."

Gaines did. He explained the sequence of events from the moment Nancy's body was first discovered right up to the meeting they were now having in Nate Ross's kitchen.

And when he was done, he sat back in his chair and watched as she tried to take it all in.

A couple of times she seemed to have a question on her lips, but then it vanished as she considered some other aspect of what she'd been told. Finally, minutes having passed, she asked the one thing that needed to be asked, the only question that really held any significance or meaning.

"And you have no evidence at all, do you?" she said. "Nothing that directly implicates Matthias in any of this? Not in Nancy's death and not in Michael's."

"No, Miss Wade, I do not," Gaines said.

"So what is this based on? Your intuition?"

"Perhaps," Gaines said.

"Perhaps?"

"My intuition, yes, but also the fact that Matthias was in love with Nancy and yet could not have her, that he was with her the night she disappeared, that Matthias paid Michael's bail, that he was the last person seen with Michael, the fact that he had someone terrorize Clifton, had them cut off his fingers, and just to stop you seeing him, even the fact that—"

"Enough," Della said. "Enough now."

"You're right, Miss Wade. It's all circumstantial or coincidental, and no, I do not have anything that I can prove or substantiate, but sometimes an intuitive feeling possesses more substance than anything else."

"And you thought that because of what happened with Clifton, I might be willing to help you incriminate and expose my brother as a murderer?"

"Miss Wade, I do not know for sure that he *is* a murderer."

"But you believe he is."

"I consider him the most likely contender."

"Jesus Christ," she said, her voice almost a whisper. "This is just a nightmare, a fucking nightmare."

"I understand."

She looked up suddenly. "Do you? Do you even have the faintest idea what it's like to be told that your own brother is a murderer, that he murdered someone twenty years ago, an innocent girl for God's sake, and he's lived with that for two decades?"

Gaines shook his head. "No, I don't. I don't have a clue how this must feel."

Della sighed. "I am upset with you, Sheriff Gaines. I am upset with Maryanne. I am upset that you went to see Clifton. Clifton knows I love him. He doesn't need to ask me. He knows I love him enough to wait for however long it takes. The moment he's out, we are gone, seriously. And we will be gone so far and so fast that Matthias will not even know about it until it's too late to do anything. And it's not only Matthias that makes it difficult for us to have a future together. A white girl and a colored man cannot have a relationship here. It is not possible. That is just the way of things. We should have been smarter. We should have been more careful. I have to accept responsibility for what happened, as I was the one who gave him the money. It was a stupid and impulsive thing to do, and we learned a hard lesson. But I am patient, and I can wait, and then Clifton and I will wish this part of the world goodbye, and we won't be coming back. I want you to know that if Matthias had seen this letter, then Clifton would be dead. You understand?"

"I do, yes," Gaines replied.

"And he asked you to send word back from me?"

"Yes, he did."

"Well, if you go up there again, you tell him that nothing has changed, that everything is the same. But *you* tell him, Sheriff Gaines. No one else. You do not pass on a message. You do not send the message with someone else. And if you cannot go there, then you do nothing. Are we clear on that?"

"Yes, we are. Absolutely."

"Okay then," Della said. She turned to Nate Ross. "What you got that's halfway toward moonshine in this place?"

"Got some good bourbon," Ross replied.

"Well, I need some. I need a good slug in a cup of coffee." She took a packet of cigarettes from her jacket pocket and lit one.

"So how was Clifton?" she said.

"He looked good," Gaines replied. "As good as could be expected under the circumstances."

"You know he's a musician, right? You know I met him through Eugene?"

"Yes, he told me that."

Della smoked her cigarette for a while. Ross brought her the laced coffee. She drank half of it, nodded at Ross, who then added more bourbon.

"Okay, okay, okay," she said, almost to herself. "This is not what you think it is, Sheriff Gaines. This is not just a matter of walking up to the house and accusing my brother of murder and trusting that he will fall apart and confess."

"I appreciate that, Miss Wade."

"So what the hell do you think I'm going to be able to do?"

"Well, the mere fact that you have not leapt to his defense tells me something."

"What, exactly? What does it tell you?"

"It tells me that you believe he might have done this, that such a thing would not have been beyond him."

She smiled sardonically. "My brother is a man of many faces, Sheriff. Those who know him do not really know him, and those who don't know him know more than they think. Who he is, and who he wants the world to believe he is, are two different things entirely."

She hesitated for a moment. Gaines said nothing, his silence the best encouragement.

"He wants everyone to believe that he's the master of his own little world. He runs my father's businesses, or at least he pretends to. He appears every once in a while at the plants, at the refineries. He tells the people there what to do. They listen; they acknowledge him, and once he's gone, they do what they were going to do before he showed up. He knows it, they know it, and it's an arrangement of

309

tacit consent. It works just fine on both sides. They get to make the companies and businesses work, and he gets to take the director's salary."

"And your father?"

"What about my father?"

"He doesn't manage the businesses anymore?"

"My father is seventy-six years old, Sheriff Gaines. He has not been involved in any real capacity in his businesses for at least five years. After the illness—"

"The illness?"

"He was ill, seriously ill. At first they believed it was some kind of heart condition, but it wasn't. Then they said it was a nerve disease, a deterioration of something in his brain, but he didn't have the right symptoms. No one seems to know what was wrong with him, but it got worse and worse, and then it seemed to level out. He reached a state about a year or a year and a half ago, and he doesn't seem to have gotten any worse since then."

"And how is he? What effects has this illness had on him?"

"Everything, Sheriff. Everything about him has changed. He has moments of lucidity, but rarely. The times I have with my father, I mean, really have with him, are so few and far between these days. An hour or two a week, if I am lucky. He is elsewhere. He doesn't remember the simplest things, and yet he can recall precise details of some event that happened fifty years ago as if it was yesterday. He rambles; he talks incessantly about nothing, and then he is completely silent for days at a stretch."

"Is he aware of what happened with you and Clifton?"

"Sheriff, sometimes he doesn't even know who *I* am, and I live with him."

"And if he had known about you and Clifton, what would he have said?"

"You mean, would he have let me get involved with a colored man?"

"Yes."

"No, he would not. Well, I think he would have done everything he could to discourage me, but if I had fought him—and believe me, I would have—he would have finally relented. He would not have let me stay here, but he would not have disowned me, neither in name nor financially."

"And he would not have threatened Clifton or had him sent to Parchman."

Della smiled ruefully. "Whatever has been said about my father, he was never a vindictive man. He was a businessman. He was tough, aggressive, but he was not cruel."

Gaines looked at Ross, at Holland, at Maryanne. It seemed as though he might have been angling for some unspoken moral support, and Della picked this up immediately.

"What?" she asked.

"There's a question I want to ask you, but I don't want to cause offense—"

"Do I seem like the sort of person who is going to take offense at being asked a question, Sheriff?"

Gaines sighed and shook his head. "I don't know what kind of person you are, Miss Wade."

"Well, ask me the question, and if there's gonna be a fistfight, then you've got three friends here to hold me down if it gets dirty."

"Your father . . . his political persuasion, his loyalties, so to speak—"

"Ask the question, Sheriff. Politeness has its place, but directness serves us far better in the long run of things."

"Is he Klan?" Gaines asked. "That direct enough for you?"

Della shrugged. "Well, at least I know what you're asking me now."

"So?"

"Politically, yes, personally, no. But then, such a balance cannot easily be maintained around here, if you know what I mean."

"Explain."

"I don't need to explain, Sheriff. You know precisely what I mean. It's all very well and good saying you're in the club, but saying you are goes only so far. Every once in a while you have to do something that proves you're in the club; otherwise folks start to get fidgety and unsettled. The Klan is on the decline. It might come to life again, but those who are out there with their mouths open, airing their opinions and whatnot, are becoming more and more rare as the years pass. It is not so fashionable nowadays, even down here, and if you are of that inclination, then it is expected that you keep your opinions to yourself, just to keep up appearances, you know? It's a double-edged sword, especially when it comes to business. For some people, you have to say one thing, for others something else."

"But your father has not been involved in business for some time, right?"

"Right, so that is a problem he has not had to deal with."

"And Matthias?"

"I think you know where Matthias's sympathies lie."

"But does that extend further than his concern for his family? Is he just prejudiced when it comes to his sister getting involved with a colored man, or does it apply to everyone?"

"If you're asking whether or not he goes out late at night with a pillowcase on his head, then no, he does not. Where he puts money, what he supports, whom he speaks with, where his allegiances lie, I do not know. You have to appreciate that my brother and I have not maintained the most amicable of relationships for quite some time."

"So why do you stay at the house?"

"Have you seen the house?"

"Yes, I have," Gaines said. "Not inside, but I was there very briefly, speaking to your brother a while back."

"You could lose an entire family in that house. I can go for days without seeing him. It suits me to stay there right now."

"For financial reasons?"

Della looked awkward for a moment, as if caught off guard. "I don't see that—" She hesitated, turned to glance at Maryanne, standing in silence there by the back door. She sighed audibly, seemed perhaps exasperated. "For financial reasons, yes."

"Do you think that if your father were able to maintain some coherence in his mental state, you could then explain your situation to him and he would help you?"

"It would not be a problem I would want to give him, Sheriff. I wouldn't want to put him in the middle of any conflict I might be having with Matthias."

"Are you not able to make financial arrangements to secure your independence from Matthias? Is that not possible?"

Della smiled. "However advanced into the twentieth century things may appear to be, Sheriff, there are some things that stay traditional. I have absolutely no influence or control over any aspect of the Wade fortune. In the event of my father's death, everything comes under Matthias's control. That's the way he wants it, and that's the way it will be. Perhaps that is unusual, but then my father has always been an unusual man. And taking into consideration the fact that my father is not able to manage his own affairs, he might as well already be dead, at least from a business point of view."

Della lifted her coffee cup and drained it. She held it out toward Ross. "Same again, barkeep."

"I think I'll join you," Ross said. "Anyone else?"

Maryanne and Gaines accepted coffee, declined the bourbon. Holland wanted both.

"So how is your life?" Gaines asked.

"Life is a waiting game right now," Della said. "Waiting for my father to die, waiting for Clifton to be released, waiting for a revelation about how to handle this mess better than I am handling it right now."

"You want some help?"

"You think you can help me?"

"I think we can help each other."

"Seriously?"

"You doubt my intentions?" Gaines asked.

"I don't know anything about your intentions, Sheriff Gaines. I appreciate the fact that you are trying to do something here, and I acknowledge that you made the effort to go on up to Parchman and see Clifton, ill-advised though it was, but I don't know what your long-term plan is, no."

"It's very simple, Miss Wade. I want to find out if your brother was responsible for the deaths of Nancy Denton and Michael Webster, and if so, then I want to see him charged, arraigned, tried, convicted, and sentenced appropriately."

"Do we hang folks for murder now, or do we fry them?"

"Not anymore, no. Death penalty has been suspended by the Supreme Court."

"I didn't know. So, it'd be a life sentence then?"

"Yes, it would."

"Up at Parchman. That would be ironic, eh?"

Della was silent. She sipped her coffee. By the time she finished it, she would have gotten through a good three or four shots of bourbon. Maybe that was standard for Della Wade. Maybe that was the way she rounded off the edges of her awkward existence.

Gaines watched her. There was sadness there, no doubt about it, but deep-rooted, buried beneath the brave face she wore for the world. He did not envy the life she was living, and he knew that there was no amount of Wade money, present or promised, that would change the fact that she was desperately alone without Clifton Regis.

"Do you not hate Matthias for what he's done?" Gaines asked.

"Hate him? No, Sheriff, I don't hate him. There is no point hating him. What good would it serve? What problem would be solved by allowing him to upset me that much? No, I don't hate him. I don't trust him, and I don't deal with him on anything but the most superficial terms. I know who he is and how he can be, and there have been times that he has demonstrated tremendous generosity and kindness, but it's as if he's at war with himself. He thinks he needs to be a certain way to survive, and that makes him arrogant and self-absorbed, but I don't believe that's who he truly is. The difficulty is that he's been this way for so long that who he really is has been lost forever."

Gaines nodded. He needed to ask Della Wade about something else, but he did not want to inspire any inherent impulse she might possess to defend her brother. He knew that she sensed this—if not in his expression, his body language, then in the seeming increase of tension in the room. It seemed that everyone was aware of this, for Della Wade pinned Gaines with a hard look and asked him outright.

"This is not all, is it?" she said. "There is something else."

Gaines did not speak immediately. He started to explain, to walk around the edges of what he wanted to ask her, but she cut him short.

"Ask me the question, Sheriff. I cannot promise that I will know the answer, or even that I will answer it, but I am big enough to be asked."

"January, 1968," Gaines said. "Morgan City, Louisiana. Two girls were found murdered—"

"I remember it," Della said.

"At the time—"

"At the time, there were a lot of questions. Some of those questions were asked of Matthias, but nothing was proven. There was no evidence to link Matthias to what happened to those children."

"Just as there is no evidence to link Matthias to either Nancy or Michael."

"You honestly think Matthias could have murdered little girls?"

"I don't know, Miss Wade. I know Matthias even less well than I know you."

Della sat without speaking for a good minute, perhaps two. It seemed so much longer, and the atmosphere in the kitchen was such that no one dared move or breathe. Even more than that, no one dared think.

Finally, she looked away toward Maryanne, not *at* her, just toward her, and then she turned back toward Gaines and shook her head. "I have nothing to say," she said. "I do not want to think that my brother would be capable of such a thing. I know him, and I do not think he has it in him to do something like that. But, then, I did not believe he'd be capable of doing what he did to Clifton. I think what he did to Clifton was done out of jealousy, not prejudice or hatred, but jealousy."

"Jealousy?"

"Jealous of love, Sheriff. Jealous that he does not have it, cannot find it, probably never will. He was jealous of Michael and Nancy, for sure, and he may well have been sufficiently jealous to take Nancy away from Michael. I do not know, and I am not saying that I do not *want* to know, but I am saying that I do not want to believe he did that. It's natural, isn't it? To think the best of people? To believe them good and kind and honest? But they're not, and I'm not naive about these things. I can accept what he did to Clifton. I can accept what he has done to me. I can understand why he believes he should be this way in order to make it through this life, but I am struggling, desperately, when I consider him capable of such horrors. I am supposed to love him. He's my brother. And I do love him, but I don't know why. Maybe I don't actually love him, but I have convinced myself that I do because that is what's meant to happen. You're not meant to hate your own family. Blood is thicker than water and all that. But this? This is someone else's blood, isn't it? Several people's blood. What do you do then? What are you supposed to say? What are you supposed to feel?" She looked up at Gaines. "You don't know, and I know you can't answer that question, so don't bother trying."

She turned to Ross. "Nate, get me another drink, and skip the coffee this time."

Ross brought her more bourbon, poured some into a glass while she lit another cigarette.

Gaines leaned forward. He smiled as best he could, trying perhaps to reassure her that he was here without bias or prejudice, without preconceptions or some unspoken ulterior motive.

"My mother died," he said. "Just a week ago—"

Della opened her mouth, perhaps to express her condolences.

Gaines raised his hand, and she fell silent.

"She had been ill for a long time. I knew she was going to die. I'd known for a long time. But I wasn't prepared for it, and I don't think

315

you can ever be prepared for it. My father died back in the war in Europe, and I never knew him, and so it's easy to feel very little about that at all. If you never had something, then you can't miss it, right? What I'm trying to say, Miss Wade, is that I cannot imagine how you must feel. I am not going to even try to imagine how you feel. All I can say is that every once in a while we drive right into something terrible, something so devastating and overwhelming, something we have no context for, no frame of reference, and we deal with it the way that we deal with it. They say that the things that don't kill you make you stronger, but that's not true. Maybe those things don't kill you physically or emotionally, but they can kill you mentally, even spiritually. I don't know what really happened to Nancy Denton and Michael Webster, just like I don't know what happened to Dorothy McCormick and Anna-Louise Mayhew back in 1968. What I do know is that someone killed those people, and I don't think they deserved it any more than Clifton deserved to get his fingers cut off for loving you—"

"Don't try and blackmail me, Sheriff Gaines. Don't try and make it any more personal than it already is—"

"Della, I don't think it *could* be any more personal. These are people's lives we're talking about. This is not some movie script where everything is going to fall into place at the end and everything's going to get tied up nice and neat. This is a horror story, a real-life honest-to-God horror story, and I am right in the middle of it, and so are you. Maybe you'll get through this, maybe Clifton will, maybe me and Nate and Eddie and Maryanne will all come through this and out the other end, but maybe we won't. Nancy didn't, and even though that was twenty years ago and we don't have to think about it, Michael was killed just a week ago, and that is awful close, as far as I'm concerned. That is just too damned close. And even though I didn't know the man, and despite whatever he might have done however many years ago, I don't think it was right what happened to him. Even if he was complicit in the death of Nancy Denton, then his penalty should still have been legal and equitable. What was done to him was no better than dragging some poor colored man out there and lynching him. Guilt by association, guilt by assumption, guilt because of your color or your religion or your political persuasion . . . These things don't determine guilt. You know that, and I know that. What determines guilt is evidence and confession and proof, and I mean real proof, proof that can be substantiated and validated by reasonable men, men who have no ax to grind, no vested interest." Gaines paused. He felt the passion of what he was saying in his chest, in the way his hands were shaking, in the way his voice wavered. "Now, I don't know about you, Della, but I am of a mind to find out what really happened here and what happened back in Morgan City six years ago. I want to know who killed Nancy Denton, and I want to know who cut Michael Webster's head off and buried it in a field behind my house. My desire to find the truth will not diminish in time, Della, and I won't go away. I am here, and I am here for as long as it takes, and I will keep on digging and looking and asking questions until I find out what I want, or until someone kills me and buries *my* head someplace. That's the simple truth of it, and you can either help me or not. You are not obligated, and I am not going to blackmail you. You can say yes or no. You can stay, or you can walk away. You have no loyalty to me, but you do have loyalty to your family. I know that I am asking a great deal of you, and I know that to be involved in this investigation is a huge risk, but right now I have no place else to go. If you say no, well, I will find another way—"

"Stop talking, Sheriff Gaines. Just for a second, stop talking, okay?"

Gaines nodded, leaned back in his chair, continued to look right at her.

"Okay," she eventually said. "If I said I was willing to help you, what would you need me to do?"

55

It was late morning. The clouded sun gave up a greasy light, and the air seemed thick enough to chew. Sounds were muted, the songs of blue jays and whip-poor-wills fading to silence not six inches from their throats.

Gaines stood on the back porch steps, looked out toward the field where lay buried the memory of Michael Webster's head and hand. Out there in the turnrows, inches beneath the surface, there was blood and wax and hair and whatever else might still remain. And beyond that, toward the horizon—out beyond the barbed-wire fence and loblolly pines, beyond the cypress and goldenrod and blue salvia, through the webs of kudzu, amid the nests of redbirds and brown thrashers, the sound of bullfrogs and squirrels, and the tracks of whitetail deer—was something else. Ghosts, perhaps. Something strange and potent, some aspect of horror that he knew he did not comprehend. Not yet.

What else could he have asked her to do?

What could he have said to her beyond what had already been said?

Piecing together recent events, trying to make sense of them, was akin to reconstructing an already-forgotten dream.

Right there in Nate Ross's kitchen, Della Wade had as much as volunteered to help him.

What would you need me to do?

That's what she asked him.

What would you need me to do?

He looked at her for a while and simply said, "Help me find the truth, Della. Just help me find the truth."

"And how am I supposed to do that?" she asked.

"Find some way of getting him to talk," Gaines replied. "I don't know. I haven't had time to think about this, to make any kind of plan. I didn't expect to be speaking with you so soon, and to tell you the truth, I half-expected never to speak to you at all."

"Because you thought I was some crazy woman out there in that big house who would do something only if her big brother said it was okay."

Gaines smiled. "Maybe so, yes."

He remembered her face then, the way she looked at him.

Revelations aside, her horror at what she was being told, the sheer weight of the mental and emotional burden she must have felt, Della Wade had nevertheless seemed somehow contained, measured, able to absorb what was going on around her and deal with it. And yet now—suddenly presented with the responsibility of assisting Gaines in his investigation—she seemed fragile and afraid. Not for herself. Not that at all. Afraid that she would perhaps fail Gaines, and thus fail Nancy, Michael, the girls from Morgan City. Fail also Clifton Regis.

"I don't know what to tell you," Gaines continued. "I cannot gain access to the house. I cannot look for evidence. I can't ask Matthias questions without running the risk of him finding some way to defend himself even further. But you could look, at least. You could see if there is anything that might tie him to the death of Michael Webster, just something that connects Matthias directly to these recent events."

"Because you simply want him convicted of something, right? Something that will enable you to put him in jail."

"The law is the law, Della. If he killed Michael, then he goes to jail for the rest of his life."

She closed her eyes. She breathed deeply several times as if trying to maintain equilibrium, as if trying not to implode and disappear, and then she shook her head slowly.

When she opened her eyes, there were tears. They welled in her lids, and then they spilled over.

Nate Ross stepped forward and gave Della Wade a handkerchief. She thanked him with a fleeting smile.

"You want me to help you lock up my brother."

She said it so matter-of-factly, so simply, that there was nothing Gaines could do but say, "Yes, Della. *If* he did these things, *if* he killed these people, then he needs to suffer the full penalty of the law."

"Can you even begin to appreciate what you are asking me to do?"

"No, Della, I can't."

"And if I fail—"

"You can't fail," Gaines said. "There is no such thing here. You can do whatever you can do, as much as you are willing, and beyond that there is nothing else. Right now, as it stands, I have nowhere else to go. I am not saying that to make you feel responsible for what happens. I am not saying that to make you feel obligated, Della. I am just saying that because it's the truth. If I had more time, or if I'd had a better way of approaching this, then maybe I would have a better plan. But I don't, and that's all there is to it. I am hoping against all reason that there is something in your house that ties Matthias to one or more of these killings. Something, anything at all. Anything you can find will give me reason for a warrant, and if I have a warrant, perhaps we will find something else. That's all I can hope for."

"And if there's nothing? If I look as best I can and I find nothing?"

"Then I will have to come at this from some other direction."

"And maybe there won't be another direction."

"Maybe there won't be."

"And then what?"

Gaines shook his head. "Then we will never know the truth of what happened to Nancy or Michael or anyone else, and these things will remain unpunished."

"Which is not right," she said. "That can't be right. I understand that. But there's something else to consider . . . the fact that he might not have killed Nancy, that he might not have killed Michael."

"You're right," Gaines said. "Maybe he didn't kill them, but if he is innocent, why is he not willing to even talk to me? Why is he so defensive?"

"I don't know, Sheriff. Maybe because he doesn't want this kind of rumor and hearsay around the family. Maybe because he doesn't want my father to hear about it."

"Do you think that's the case?"

"Oh God, I can't answer that. Jesus Christ, you know I can't answer that. You're asking me to make decisions about things that are impossible to make decisions about. You're asking me to choose Clifton over my brother . . . You're asking—"

"That is life," Gaines said, interrupting her. "If life were always right, then these things would not have happened. Nancy would have married Michael, and there'd be two young women in Morgan City with lives of their own to look forward to. But they don't, and that's because someone kidnapped them and killed them back in 1968."

"Matthias," Della said. Just his name, nothing more, but in the way she said it there was everything she was feeling—despair, loss, fear, horror, refusal, perhaps some desperate sense of hope that what was being suggested here could never be true.

"I am sorry to be the one who—"

"Who what?" she interjected. "You didn't kill anyone, did you? You didn't strangle some poor child and leave her dead somewhere, did you? You didn't make this happen, Sheriff Gaines. What can I say? What can I tell you? Can I say that I wish I'd never known about this, that I'd stayed ignorant, uninformed? Can I say that and believe it, honestly? No, I don't think so. What has happened has happened. We can't go backward, can we? We can't retrace our steps and change it all and make it right. What you say is true. Life doesn't work that way. Life is just going to be however it is, and once a day has gone there is nothing anyone can do to fix it."

"But we can fix tomorrow," Gaines said.

"We can *try* and fix tomorrow," she replied.

"And that's what I'm asking of you."

"I know what you're asking of me, Sheriff."

"And can you help us? Can you do what I'm asking?"

"I can. Of course I can. It's not a question of whether or not I can. It's a question of whether or not I am willing to."

"And are you?"

"Yes," she said. "I am willing to help you, Sheriff Gaines, but I can guarantee nothing."

"I know."

She shook her head. "No, I don't think you do know. I don't think you understand who you are dealing with here. If my brother is anything, he is organized. He is methodical. He is businesslike in everything he does, from the clothes he wears to the things he says, the way he manages my father's companies, the finances, the help, the land we own, everything. Everything is under control; every-thing is precise. If he killed Michael Webster, then he did not kill him. He had someone else do it. That's what he would have done. My brother, believe me, will not have Michael Webster's blood on his hands."

"But maybe there is something," Gaines said. "That's all we have right now . . . the possibility that there is something."

"And there is something I want from you."

Gaines didn't ask her. He waited for her to tell him.

"I need you to do everything you can to help Clifton. If I help you do this, I want Clifton out of there, out of Parchman and back here with me."

"I cannot promise—"

"And neither can I," she said. "We are not asking each other for promises, Sheriff Gaines. We are asking each other to do the best we can. You want me to find evidence that will convict my brother of murder. I want you to dispute and disprove the evidence that put Clifton in prison."

"This is a condition?"

Della frowned, looked at Gaines as if he had insulted her. "You don't get this at all, do you? Maybe you do, and you're just protecting yourself. Of course it's not a condition. What kind of person do you think I am? You think I am going to trade the lives of innocent people for my own advantage?"

"I'm sorry, Della. I didn't mean for it to sound that way."

"Well, I don't know what way you meant for it to sound, Sheriff. It sounded just about right to me. Maybe the Wades have a reputation around here. Maybe people think we're nothing but a bunch of racist, self-interested, hardheaded assholes out to take advantage of any situation that presents itself. Well, maybe some of us have been that way, but I am not one of them, I can assure you."

"Like I said, I'm sorry."

"So no, it is not a condition. You are asking me to do something, to do my best to help you with this, and I am asking you to do your best. That is all."

"I agree. I will do my best to find out what happened with Clifton's conviction and see if it can be appealed."

"And I will look for what you want," Della said. "And I have a suggestion for you as well."

"Which is?"

"Go talk to Leon Devereaux."

"Who's that?"

"He's Matthias's right-hand man. He's not from around here, lives out near the factory in Lucedale. There's not a great deal that goes on as far as Wade business is concerned that he doesn't know about. But you have to understand—anything you say to Leon is going right back to Matthias."

"When you say that this Devereaux is Matthias's right-hand man, do you mean what I think you mean?"

"I am sure . . . I am absolutely sure that Leon Devereaux was the one who visited with Clifton."

"And how do I reach you without alerting Matthias?"

"You don't," Della replied. "I will call Maryanne every day, early morning. If I miss a day, I'll call the following morning. You let her know if you need to talk to me, and we'll figure something out."

"And if I need to get to you in a hurry?"

"Then Maryanne should call the house and say she is my hairstylist and that I need to arrange another appointment."

"Understood."

Della Wade rose to her feet. She looked at Gaines and then turned to look at the other three present.

"I can only hope that you turn out to be utterly wrong," she said. And with that, she left.

Eddie Holland walked out with her, offered to drive her home, but she declined. She had him drive her into town, and from there she took a cab.

By the time Holland reached Ross's house once more, Gaines had left to drive Maryanne back to Gulfport. He returned promptly, said the entire journey had passed with few words exchanged. Seemed that neither he nor Maryanne Benedict had a great deal more to say about what was happening.

Gaines asked Ross and Holland to investigate the Clifton Regis B&E conviction. He was going to follow up on Leon Devereaux as discreetly as he could. Maybe getting something on Devereaux was another route to Matthias Wade.

And then Gaines headed home, and for a while he sat in silence on the back porch steps. He looked out at the field, thought about the ghosts that haunted the turnrows beyond the house, and then he left for the office.

Even though it was Sunday, he found Richard Hagen there. He was typing up speeding tickets and DUIs, stabbing the keyboard as if trying to wake it from sleep.

"So where we at?" Hagen asked Gaines.

"We are in a deep hole and we have to dig ourselves out of it."

"So no change, then?"

Gaines smiled. "Della Wade."

"What about her?"

"I just had a long conversation with her over at Nate Ross's place."

Hagen turned his chair, all ears, suddenly intent. "Is that so?"

"Yes, it is."

"And?"

"She's going to do what she can to find us something on Matthias."

"You're serious? Her own brother?"

"You don't know the half of it, Richard. Right now her boyfriend, one Clifton Regis, is up at Parchman Farm on what could very well be a bullshit rap, and he's got a couple of missing fingers as well."

"Matthias did that?"

"Yes . . . well, Matthias ordered it, and it looks like someone called Leon Devereaux actually did the work."

Hagen frowned. "Who the hell is Leon Devereaux?"

"Lives out near one of the Wade factories in Lucedale. Apparently, he takes care of any extracurricular work that Matthias Wade might need doing when things don't go the way he wants them to go."

"And we're on to him? Is that what we're doing?"

"Yes, that's what we're doing."

"Well, Lucedale is up in George County. I can go out there and chase up anything they have on him, if you like."

"You know anyone up there?" Gaines asked.

"Hell, no. Only thing I know about Lucedale is the Cook Family Singers."

"The who?"

"Cook Family Singers. Gospel singers, you know? Used to tour with the Carter Family. Played the Grand Ole Opry a good few times. Think my wife has a few of their records."

"Didn't know you were a gospel man, Richard."

"I'm not. My wife is into it. Me, I'm more Janis Joplin and the Allman Brothers."

"Well, okay. So I figure you should go home and spend some time with your gospel wife, and I'll go to Lucedale. I don't know what the hell you're doing sitting here typing up DUIs for anyhow."

"Gotta be done sometime, and my wife took the kids on up to see her folks in McComb."

"Well, your call, then. Stay here and finish this, or come with me to Lucedale, see what we can find out about Leon Devereaux."

"I think I'll come with you," Hagen replied.

"Good enough."

Gaines and Hagen took one car, left Whytesburg a little after two for the eighty- or ninety-mile drive. They made good time, and were there before three thirty. Finding the George County Sheriff's Office closed, they made inquiries at the gas station. The sheriff's name was Lowell Gradney, lived out on Seven Hills Road, about a mile down and on the left-hand side. Gaines thanked the attendant, headed the way he showed them, and drove on out there in the hope of finding Gradney at home.

56

Gradney was younger than Gaines had anticipated, early forties perhaps, and looked like he was settled in Lucedale for the duration. This was not a county-assigned property, but a well-kept midsized home with an orderly yard set with flowers and low shrubs, window boxes brimming with color, gingham curtains on the windows, and a couple of young children playing on the veranda.

Gaines went on up there while Hagen hung back by the gate. When the elder of the children—a blond girl no more than five or six—saw him, she went in through the door calling for her daddy. The second child, a boy of three or thereabouts, just sat cross-legged and eyed him without concern or suspicion. Perhaps strangers showing up on a Sunday afternoon was nothing to get agitated about in these parts.

Gradney came out drying his hands. He was dressed in jeans and a T-shirt, no belt, no boots, and when he saw the uniforms, he frowned. Then he smiled and came on through the screen and down the steps to greet his visitors.

"Apologies for the time and the day," Gaines said. "John Gaines, Whytesburg, and back there is my deputy, Richard Hagen."

Hagen came through the gate and extended his hand.

"Must be important enough for you boys to come on over here on a Sunday afternoon, and if it's that important, then the least I can do is accommodate you. Come on up to the house and we'll talk."

The house was cool. That was the first thing Gaines noticed. The second was how well presented each room was, not extravagant, but furnished with pieces that would not have seemed out of place in a much larger and more expensive home. Seemed that Gradney had some money behind him; such a standard of accommodation could not have been maintained on a sheriff's salary.

Gradney walked Gaines and Hagen on through to the parlor, and here they were introduced to Gradney's wife.

"This here is my wife, Sarah. Sarah, this is Sheriff Gaines and Deputy Hagen up from Whytesburg on a little business."

She came away from the sink, and in the light from the window, Gaines saw her clearly. Sarah Gradney was an extraordinarily beautiful woman, but there was something about her that belied the matter-of-fact reality of being a small-town sheriff's wife. This was where the money came from, Gaines felt sure. The way she spoke, the way she moved—these things suggested a background very different from her current whereabouts and social position. Gaines wondered what the backstory was, but he simply shook her hand, apologized for the inconvenience of arriving unannounced and uninvited on a Sunday afternoon, and thanked her for her hospitality.

"Oh, it's no matter at all, gentlemen. Please, be seated. Let me get you something to drink. Perhaps some coffee, some tea, some lemonade."

"Whatever's the least trouble would be fine," Gaines said.

"Well, considering you're here on such a fine day, then I think a little lemonade would best suit."

Gradney indicated a large table to the left of the room, and here they sat while Sarah busied herself with a jug from the refrigerator and glasses for each of them. Once she had served the lemonade, she stood momentarily with her hand on her husband's shoulder.

"I'll be out in the yard with the children," she said. "Anything else you boys need, you just holler."

"Thank you, Sarah," Gradney said.

"Appreciated, ma'am," Gaines added.

Sarah left them to it, closing the parlor door behind her.

"You have a beautiful home," Gaines said, "and a lovely wife."

"Lucky man," Gradney replied. "They sort of came together. Sarah was a Lanafeuille 'fore I married her. They own pretty much everything between here and Pascagoula. Hell of a wealthy family, and they didn't take too kindly to the idea of their daughter up and marrying a policeman. But hell, in the end there wasn't a great deal they could do about it. They're good people, when it comes down to it."

"Well, it seems like you really have made a good life for yourself here . . . and beautiful children you have, too."

"Which is all as well as may be," Gradney said, smiling, "but that sure as hell ain't motivation enough for you to drive over here on a Sunday afternoon. So, what are we talking about here?"

"Leon Devereaux," Gaines said.

"Oh my. Oh my," Gradney said. "So what has the charming and delightful Mr. Devereaux gotten himself into now?"

"You know him?"

"Know him? Hell, I might as well be related to him, the number of times we visit with each other. He's a thief and a liar and a cheat and pretty much anything else you can think of. A drunk as well. Far as he's concerned, life is just something that gets in the way of him and his liquor. I keep tellin' him, he ain't gonna find nothin' worth much of anythin' in this life if he just keeps lyin' about everythin', but he doesn't seem able to restrain himself. If he isn't somewhere maneuvering to sleep with some poor son of a bitch's wife, then he's someplace else sleeping off a drunk or hiding from a husband with a gun."

"Sounds like a fine, upstanding citizen."

"Well, like many a folk, somewhere along the line he got the idea that rotgut whiskey was the curative for all that might ail him now or in the future. But Leon goes a little way further than that. Took me a while to appreciate where he was at, but there ain't much good goin' on in there, and that's the truth. I always try to give folk the benefit of the doubt, you know? Seems when it comes to most bad people, there's always someone good trying to clamber on out and show their face. With others, well, they're just bad right through to the core. Leon Devereaux falls into the second category."

"You know he works for the Wades, right?"

"Works? Is that what they call it? Leon doesn't do a great deal of that, I can tell you right now. Maybe he has some sort of agreement with the Wades, but that factory he's supposed to manage, well, I don't know that they see him there more than once a month."

"Do you know what his relationship with the Wades is? Matthias Wade, specifically?"

"Don't know, and don't know that I *want* to know. Somehow or other, he always manages to wind his way out of trouble. I've had him for DUIs, B&Es, harassment, statutory rape, criminal damage, aiding and abetting an escaped felon, grand theft auto, pandering. The list is endless. I've had him locked up more times than anyone in my career, but never for long. Somehow or other, the witness always retracts their statement, the judge gives him a fine, a warning, anything but a custodial sentence, and Leon Devereaux goes back to doing whatever Leon Devereaux does, thankfully much of it outside my jurisdiction, as far as I can see."

"We have a report that he cut a man's fingers off and did so under orders from Matthias Wade," Gaines said.

"Wouldn't surprise me," Gradney replied. "You came on in here and told me that he'd raped both your wives, drowned your kids, drank all your liquor, and then robbed the Whytesburg Savings and Loan, I'd ask you what he did after lunch."

"When did you last have him in your office?"

"Oh, must be a month or so ago."

"For?"

"Lord, I can't remember. Got drunk and walloped a few people, more than likely. He ain't such a big guy, but he won't go down. Hit him as many times as you like, he won't go down, stubborn son of a bitch that he is."

"Where does he live?"

"Well, when he's here, he lives down off Collins Road. Has a couple of trailers down there."

"And he's been here a long time?"

"Longer than me, and I been here six years."

"Is he from here, originally?"

"No, he's from Louisiana. Born and raised in Lafayette, went into the army down there, served in the war—"

"He's a Vietnam veteran?"

"Sure is," Gradney said. "Says it was the best vacation he ever took."

"Crazy before he went out, or just when he came back?"

"Oh, I reckon he was as crazy as a shithouse rat from the moment he was born, Sheriff Gaines. I think the first thought when he came out of his ma was how many folks he could fuck with in his three score and ten."

"Married?"

"No."

"Kids?"

"Oh, I should think so. Probably a coupla dozen from a host of different women between here and Memphis, though I don't figure him for the settlin' down type, you know?"

"And when he's not here, he's just on the road?"

"I guess so. He drives a black Ford pickup, more rust than anything else. God knows how it stays together. When the car's here, he's around. When it's not, he's gone. He can be gone for weeks at a time, and then I get a call to say he's busted some poor fella's nose in a bar someplace and he's getting ready to bust a great deal more. I go down, pull him in, keep him in a cell until he's slept off the drunk, and then I kick him out again. Whoever he bashed never presses charges, or there's someone ready to stand up and say it was self-defense. This has been going on for all the years I've been here, and I am sure it will continue this way until someone wallops him so hard, he don't get up again. Shame is that whoever winds up doing that will probably get life for it, and in all honesty, he should get a medal pinned on his chest and a county pension for life."

"Do you know if he's here in town now?"

"I don't believe he is," Gradney replied. "Friday and Saturday night went by without a single word on Leon, so I guess he's elsewhere."

"And do you know if Matthias Wade has ever been down here to visit with him?"

"Couldn't say. Leon is not someone I go looking for, and I don't keep tabs on him unless I know he's causing trouble somewhere. There have been times when I've known he was in town, but there's been no trouble to speak of. How his deal works out with the Wades is his business, and I'm happy to leave it that way. Simple truth is that you go looking for Leon, you're going to find trouble of one variety or another."

Gaines looked at Hagen. "Anything else you can think of?"

"No, I think we've got what we need," Hagen said. "Think the next thing is to go down and make a visit."

"Like I said, down on the Collins Road. Head back toward town. Second intersection on the right is signposted for the state line. You head on down there a half mile or so and then take the road signposted *Pascagoula*. Follow that road for a good mile and a half, and you'll see Devereaux's trailers set back on the left-hand side. If his truck is there, he's home. If it ain't, he ain't."

Gaines finished his lemonade and got up from the table.

"Much appreciated, Sheriff."

"You're welcome," Gradney replied. "You let me know how this goes, but if you need any help, I ain't home." He smiled.

They shook hands, and Gradney showed them out of the house. Sarah Gradney and the kids were in the yard. Gaines and Hagen thanked her for her hospitality, apologizing again for disturbing their Sunday afternoon.

The kids waved as Gaines and Hagen drove away.

"Good people," Hagen said.

"Unlike our Mr. Devereaux," Gaines replied.

330

57

Devereaux's trailers had seen many better days. One was single wide, the other a double, and where once they might have looked as fine as anything tethered behind a pickup, all fresh chrome and streamlined design, they had now settled in for some slow, inevitable process of deterioration. Those trailers would never move again, for to hitch them to anything and pull away would be to see them come apart at the seams.

There was no sign of Leon Devereaux's black Ford, and when Gaines pulled to a halt and got out, there was nothing but silence to greet him in that small clearing.

The trailers were obscured from the road by a tall bank of cypresses, and on the ground between them, amidst the scatterings of goldenrod and cattails, were broken bottles, empty gas canisters, busted furniture, a rusted-to-hell barbecue, a bicycle frame, a dilapidated sofa, the stuffing escaping through rends and tears. Gaines imagined the interior of the trailers would be just as bad, if not worse.

"I want to check inside," Gaines said.

"I know you do," Hagen replied.

"You got a problem with that?"

"See no evil, hear no evil, speak no evil."

"You okay to stay here and keep an eye out?"

"Sure am."

Gaines headed for the larger of the two trailers. The door was locked, but he fetched a knife from the car and pried the lock without any difficulty. He would be able to close it again and leave no sign that the door had been forced.

Once inside, he was assaulted by the smell. It was like Webster's place—worse in fact—and he knew before he even reached the small bathroom in the back of the trailer that something more than rotten food and dirty clothes had made a stench like that.

If you'd been to war, well, you never forgot that smell.

Gaines reached out and gripped the door handle. He turned it

331

until he felt the latch click back from the striker plate. He held his breath for a second, and then he pushed the door open.

The blood, and there was much of it, was concentrated within the tub itself. It had dried in swirls on the porcelain, and Gaines could clearly see clearly where someone—presumably Devereaux—had gripped the edge of the tub as he worked.

Gaines thought that word—*worked*—and he shuddered. The bile rose in his throat. He gritted his teeth, clenched his fists, swallowed the foul taste.

Back to the tub. There must have been two pints of blood, maybe three, and in places it was thick and congealed, raised in relief against the surface.

He believed he knew exactly what had taken place here. He was certain that this was Webster's blood, that this tub was where the removal of Webster's head and hand had occurred. Perhaps that had been the sequence of events. Wade had bailed Webster out, best of friends, just helping a guy in trouble, and he'd suggested they drive over to see another friend in Lucedale, get a drink, have a good old time after Webster's ordeal. The friend in Lucedale? Hell, he was a vet, too. He and Webster would get along just fine. And Webster went, unaware that he was being delivered to his own death. Devereaux killed him, or maybe Wade did that himself. Into the tub he went, head and hand were removed, and then the body was shipped back to Webster's cabin and the place was torched.

Gaines pictured Devereaux kneeling right there beside the tub, one hand holding Webster by the shoulder, perhaps in the tub himself and kneeling on the body. Christ almighty, it didn't bear thinking about. But Gaines could not help thinking about it. More than that, he could picture the horror playing out before his very eyes. His next question—what had Devereaux used to do this thing?—was answered when he saw the blood-streaked, foot-long hunting knife beneath the tub, a razor-sharp blade on one side, a serrated edge on the other. Gaines had seen such knives many times in Vietnam. This was not so much a knife as both a machete and a saw combined. A weapon such as that would have decapitated a man effortlessly.

Gaines kneeled down, covered his hand with the sleeve of his jacket, and lifted the knife out carefully. He set it near the door.

Devereaux, it seemed, had made no effort to cover his tracks, no effort to clean up the place, no effort to hide the evidence of his actions. There were no indications of a struggle, no jagged splashes of blood on the walls or the tub, barely any blood on the floor. Michael Webster had most definitely been dead before this was done. That, if nothing else, was some small saving grace.

Of course, Gaines could have been wrong. This could have been someone else's blood, someone else's nightmare enacted in this narrow, confined space. Taking that knife back to Victor Powell and typing the blood would support his belief that someone had been butchered here, but it would do nothing to prove it was Webster. And again, just as was the case with the things he'd taken from Webster's room, taking the knife would also be the illegal removal of evidence from a crime scene. His failure to do things by the book last time had seen Webster released and then murdered. Simply stated, his failure had seen a man killed. But what choice did Gaines have? Had there been any probable cause for his entry to the trailer? No, there had been no reason for him to access the trailer. Was there any outstanding warrant for Leon Devereaux? Not that he was aware of, and Gradney had made no reference to such a thing. And to track Devereaux down and hound him for something that would justify a search warrant would give Devereaux time to contact anyone he wished, more than likely Wade, who could have half a dozen people down here within an hour, and they could remove every single scrap of evidence from these trailers and vanish it all into nowhere.

There was the line. As state's AG, Jack Kidd, had so clearly pointed out when he spoke to Gaines about the illegal search and seizure at Webster's cabin, it was a sad state of affairs when the law prevented you from seeing justice done. But this was the nature of things. This was the system within which he had to work—until he decided to work outside of it.

John Gaines looked at the swirls of blood in the tub and then back to the knife. He did not hesitate long before he reached down and—once again covering his hand with the sleeve of his jacket—retrieved the knife and headed out to the car.

"Got there?" Hagen asked.

"Well, as far as I can guess, this is the knife that was used to cut Michael Webster's head and hand off."

"Taking it back to Whytesburg?"

"Want Vic Powell to type the blood."

"He works fast. We could have it back here safe and sound before anyone's the wiser."

"I have no intention of bringing it back," Gaines replied.

"But—"

"But nothing, Richard. Word gets out that we're looking at Devereaux for this, and I guarantee these trailers will go the way of Webster's cabin before the ink is even dry on the search warrant. I'm not prepared to take that risk. I need something that ties these people to Webster. If he returns and notices it gone, then so be it. At least he will not be able to get rid of it."

Hagen didn't say a word in response.

Gaines put the knife in the trunk of the car. He went back with a cloth and wiped down any door handles or surfaces he might have touched. He secured the door of the trailer and returned to the car, where Hagen already had the engine running.

"I called in to the office," Hagen said, "told Barbara to get Victor out to his office, that we need him pronto."

"Well, let's get the hell out of here, then," Gaines said.

Hagen gunned the engine to life, and they drove away from Leon Devereaux's trailers.

58

While Gaines waited for the test results, he sat in his car, windows open, and considered what he had done. Matching blood types to Webster didn't prove a damned thing, but it would at least be something circumstantial.

He'd had Hagen call Sheriff Gradney and ask that Gradney alert them if there was any sign of Leon Devereaux. After that, he'd told Hagen he could go on home. Gaines figured that waiting was something that didn't require both of them.

Powell was an hour, no more, and then he came out.

"Same type," he said. "But that ain't the only type on that knife. I got an A, an AB and an O. Webster was an A."

"Right," Gaines said. "Seems our boy has been busier than we thought." He opened the door and got out of the car. His first thought was whether one of those other blood types was that of Clifton Regis.

"I'm not going to ask you where this came from," Powell said.

"And if you asked me, I wouldn't tell you."

"I can tell you that a knife like that would have been more than sufficient to decapitate Webster."

"Good. That helps."

"And I can also tell you that the O is the oldest, and the other two are far more recent. I'd say both of them are no earlier than a week or ten days ago, the A first, the AB later, but not by much."

"So if the A is Webster, then that knife was used on someone else even more recently?"

"Certainly looks that way. What do you want me to do with it?"

"I'll take it off your hands," Gaines said. "I'll put it in the office lockup."

Powell went back inside to fetch the knife, wrapped in a mortuary bag ordinarily reserved for removed organs. Gaines put it in the trunk of his car.

"So you getting somewhere with this?" Powell asked.

"Have some ideas."

"Any evidence . . . legally obtained evidence?"

Gaines shook his head. "Lot of hopefuls, but nothing solid."

"Well, I can do nothing but wish you all the luck in the world, John. If they come asking for me, I didn't see that knife and we didn't have this conversation. I'm not going to give them a hand when they try and bury you."

"Appreciated, Victor."

Powell stood in front of the building and watched Gaines drive away. Gaines headed home, was there by nine, took the knife from the trunk and hid it behind the steps leading down to the basement. Maybe he would leave it there as opposed to taking it back to lockup. That way he would better prevent any possibility of implicating Hagen in this matter.

Gaines sat in the kitchen for a while. He was hungry. He opened a can of tuna, ate all of it, but it served merely to remind him of how little he had eaten that day.

There was a steak in the fridge, but it didn't smell so good. He went out back and hurled it into the field. Some dog would find it, and better that than have it go to waste.

He paused there on the steps. There was nothing out there but darkness and deeper darkness—and the memory of Michael Webster's head and how it'd been buried in the dirt. Buried in such a way as to be found. Maybe Leon Devereaux had been the man to do this thing. Maybe Matthias Wade had delivered Webster on up to Devereaux for the last drink of his life. Or maybe Gaines had misread everything, and he was dealing with a series of events that possessed no connection to Wade, to Devereaux, to anyone that he was aware of. What he'd said to Powell was right—a lot of hopefuls, nothing solid. Nothing probative, nothing conclusive, nothing damning. Not a shred of substantive evidence.

So where did he go now? Just wait and see if Della Wade came back with anything? Wait to see if Leon Devereaux noticed that his knife had been taken and thus prompt him to take some action that would be self-incriminatory? No, these things were no good. If Gaines was going to resolve this, he would have to be the one to act. Offense was the best form of defense.

These people—whoever these people were—had brought a war to Whytesburg. A small war, but a war all the same. Perhaps it really was time to take the war to them, to deliver it right to their doorsteps, to present it in such a way that it could be nothing other than fought.

And it was with this consideration that Gaines returned to the kitchen, taking care to ensure the back door was locked behind him.

He fetched down some bourbon. If he was not going to eat, he would drink. If he drank sufficient, he would sleep, and in sleeping he would at least evade the relentless churning of thoughts in his mind.

He could not shake that image. The scene in Devereaux's narrow, stinking bathroom. The image of what had taken place there. And then the added revelation that there was not only one blood type on that knife, but three. Whose blood was this? Who was this man? A solider, a Vietnam veteran, a casualty of war himself, and yet still capable of things that should have stayed back there in the jungles of Southeast Asia? Perhaps this was the reality that Gaines had to face—that the means and methods being employed were the same means and methods he would need to counter this offensive. He poured a second drink. He closed his eyes. He breathed deeply, exhaled slowly.

Maybe he would have to fight fire with fire.

Maybe it was that simple.

59

Four went out. Three came back.

That's what they said.

Four went out. Three came back.

No one knew why. No one had an explanation.

It didn't make sense to me that Nancy would run away. I mean, I knew she loved Michael. Everyone knew she loved him, and everyone knew that he loved her. If she had run away, well, she would have run away *with* him. That was the point. It was just one of those things that everyone knew but no one spoke about. He was older than her, of course, but he was so handsome, and people respected him so much for who he was and what he represented. I mean, he was like every father's favorite son, the son that every mother wished for. He was the boyfriend for every girl, the husband for every wife. And it was a different time, a different age. And it was the South, of course. The difference in years between people wasn't such a big deal.

I lay there in the closing evening light, and the warmth just seemed to seep up through the earth and fill every part of me. I had my eyes closed, and Matthias sat beside me but we did not speak. We did not need to speak. The silence between us was just perfect. The music played on, and Michael and Nancy danced on, and it seemed that every minute of that last hour stretched into another hour and yet another, and time became something languid and fluid and we were all just swallowed up inside it. I let my mind drift, and maybe I even slept for a while. I do not remember, and at the time it did not matter, for even had I slept for an hour, for two, I would have woken and merely a minute would have passed in the real world. I did not question it because I did not need to understand.

And then the record ended. I remember now the very last song that was played. It was "Pretend" by Nat King Cole, and I listened to those words and thought that I was the only one who needed to pretend something—pretend that it was Eugene who was right there beside me, not Matthias—and that Michael and Nancy needed only to pretend that two or three years had already passed, and they could marry and find a home and start a family.

That's what I was thinking as I listened to that beautiful record.

And then it was finished, and Michael walked toward us, Nancy holding his hand, and he said, "We're going to take a little walk . . . just for a few minutes. Wait here, okay? We'll be back soon."

And I smiled, and Matthias said, "Sure. We're not going anywhere, right, Maryanne?"

"Nope, goin' nowhere," I replied, because I didn't want to move a muscle, didn't even want to waste as much energy as it took to *think* about moving.

And they went—Michael and Nancy—hand in hand, ever so slowly, out toward the edge of the field.

"You ever been in love, Maryanne?" Matthias asked me.

I didn't want to talk, not even about love, but I said, "Maybe. I don't know. I am wondering if you really know whether you're actually in love the first time . . . because it'd be the first time, right, and you'd have never done it before."

"I guess so," he said, and then he sighed. He closed his eyes and he didn't say another word.

We were there just a little while, it seemed, though time was playing its own game, so maybe it was half an hour, an hour perhaps, and then Michael came back alone.

Michael Webster took Nancy Denton out into the trees at the end of Five Mile Road, and then he came back alone.

He seemed confused, disorientated. He said he didn't know what happened. He said they were together and then they were not. She was there, there right beside him, and then she was gone. Just gone. Where did she go? That was the question that was never answered. Where did Nancy go?

Now I know I should have gone with her. Maybe I would have disappeared as well, but at least I would have known. At least I wouldn't have had that question hanging over me for the rest of my life.

The present becomes the past, unstoppable and inevitable, and then we look back and hindsight shows us our cruelest lessons.

I should have gone with her.

I should have kept them from going.

I should have said something.

If I had, she would still be here, still be alive, and we would still be the very best of friends.

I know this. I know it with everything I possess, because that was how we were. We had always been, and always would be, the very best of friends.

My sister from another mother. That's what she used to say. You are my sister from another mother.

Because things have not been the same since, not for any of us.

We used to be inseparable. If you saw one, you saw all. Maybe Nancy was the glue that held us all together, and when she vanished there was just nothing to make us stick anymore.

They say that Michael went crazy. I can imagine he did. I can imagine that losing Nancy was like having his heart torn right out of his chest. Life would have had no meaning anymore.

Maybe he believed he was paying the price for surviving the war, that now some kind of universal balance had been restored. Maybe he believed that some kind of debt was owed for his own life. How would that have made me feel? It would've made me feel like I was directly responsible for what had happened. It would've made me feel like Nancy's disappearance was my fault, even though I'd had nothing to do with it. Even though I wasn't there, I would still have felt guilty.

That's what it would have done to me.

I had been right about remembering that day, that evening.

We went out into the field along Five Mile Road, and—like so many times before—we played old records on a gramophone, the wind-up Victrola that Matthias had fetched from the house, and Nancy danced with Michael on the grass, and he had on his shoes, and she—as always—was without them, and for a while she stood on his shoes, and she did not, and then he danced so well that he never stepped on her toes. Didn't even come close. They were like that. *Symbiotic.* That's the word. I didn't know it then, but I have learned it since. It described who they were and how they seemed together. Matthias was jealous because he also loved Nancy. And when he asked me that question—*You ever been in love, Maryanne?*—I knew that he was talking about what he felt for Nancy. And whether that really was *love* didn't matter, because Matthias believed it was, as all of us do, and that was all that mattered.

Matthias did not carry his heart on his sleeve. He carried it in his hands, and it was right out there in front of him for the whole world to see. But Nancy was with Michael, and that was the way it would always and forever be.

So we played the records—Peggy Lee and Buddy Clark and Nat

King Cole, and we laughed, and Matthias acted the clown because that's the way he hid the fact that his heart had been broken. Me and Matthias and Michael and Nancy. The Famous Four. The Fabulous Four. The Unforgettable Four.

It was the 12th of August, 1954, a day and date that would be forever burned in our minds.

Perhaps it was true that Michael could never survive without her. I think of the times I've seen him since, and each time I haven't wanted to see him. And Matthias? Matthias just frightens me. I don't know how to describe it. He just frightens me. Frightens me like his father used to frighten me when I was a little girl. Maybe Matthias, too, believes himself responsible. Maybe he, too, believes that had he loved her more, had he told her how he felt right from the start, then she would have been with him, and this thing would never have happened. For all that Michael was—the war hero, the decorated soldier, the luckiest man alive—he could not protect her against whatever shadow swallowed her. And swallow her it did, like Jonah into the whale.

Every day I opened the door of my house, and every day I expected to see her standing there—smiling, laughing, just as I always remembered her—and saying how there had been a misunderstanding, a prank perhaps, but she was back now, and it was all fine, and there didn't need to be any questions because it was just one of those things that happened. Life was like that, you know? Odd and funny and surprising. But it was all back to how it once was, and we were all going to be together again, and things were going to be just how they were before that night.

But she was never there. Not through any door.

After a while I stopped expecting her.

After a while I stopped looking.

After a while I stopped remembering her smile, her laugh, the way her eyes shone when Michael danced with her.

That night, I think we ceased to be children. Perhaps, more accurately, we lost that small fragment within us of the children we once were, the children we still remembered. Some people hold on to that fragment all of their lives. They grow old disgracefully, and they never forget to laugh at themselves. We were children together, at least the three of us. Then Michael came, and it was as if everything that had gone before then made sense. We were an odd number, and then we were even, and it all made so much sense. So perhaps Michael was the one who held us together. And then when Nancy disappeared, Michael lost his mind, and when he lost his mind, we lost whatever magic had existed for all that time.

And now here I am. Here we all are. We exist. We survive. We deal with each new day just as we did the day before.

We do not speak to one another. We do not see one another. We do not care to speak of that night in August of 1954.

What could any of us say?

Have you seen Nancy?

Have you heard word of Nancy?

The answer will always be no.

No, I have not seen her.

No, I have heard no word.

You can see it in our eyes. You can read it in the language of our bodies. It is the ghost we all share, the ghost that haunts us. And now—in some strange way—we have one thing in common that we never possessed before, and yet that is the very thing that keeps us apart.

The mystery did not hold us together against adversity and fear. It drove us away from one another in a way that could never be repaired.

We danced in the field, we laughed as we always had, and then Nancy walked into the trees at the end of Five Mile Road and was never seen again.

60

Considering all that he had on his mind, Gaines slept a great deal longer than he'd anticipated. It was seven thirty when he woke. He showered and shaved, made some coffee, remembered that this was the morning that the bodies of the Dentons and Michael Webster were being shipped out to Biloxi. There they would stay until the case was finally closed. And if it was never closed? Well, at some point someone would have to make a decision to bury those people and be done with it.

Gaines did not plan for such an eventuality. Gaines wanted to see the thing finished, of course, but in such a way as people were named and sentences were passed down on them.

Shortly after arriving at the office, Hagen still yet to appear, Gaines took a call. It was Nate Ross.

"This Clifton Regis thing," he said. "It looks like a bag of bullshit from the get-go. Apparently, he was witnessed leaving the scene of a robbery, but the facts are so vague, the testimony of the witness so doubtful, that I am amazed it even went to arraignment."

"Who was he supposed to have robbed?"

"Some woman called Dolores Henderson, and from what I can gather, she has somewhat of a record herself. Did two years for aiding and abetting a felon back in sixty-five, some guy called—"

"Devereaux, by any chance?" Gaines interjected.

"Devereaux? No, no Devereaux is mentioned here. Who the hell is Devereaux?"

"No, forget it. Just someone else I'm following up on. Who was the felon she aided and abetted?"

"Escaped con called Daniel James Levitt. Bank robber, was doing a dime at the county farm and got out. She hid him for a few days, and then he was off again. He was gone for a week. He took her car, and she never reported it stolen. That's how they got her. She had a string of things before that, though, misdemeanors and whatever, and I think they decided it was best to teach her a lesson."

"And where is Levitt now?"

"Dead," Ross replied matter-of-factly. "He got out in sixty-nine, kept himself out of trouble until seventy-one, and then tried pulling a job in Lucedale and got himself shot."

"Lucedale?"

"Yes, Lucedale . . . up northeast a hundred miles or so, right near the state line."

"I know where Lucedale is, Nate. I was there just yesterday following up on this Devereaux character I mentioned."

"You get anything?"

"Nothing that you wanna know about right now."

"So, back to Dolores Henderson."

"She dead too?" Gaines asked.

"No, seems she's alive and well and living in Purvis. She moved up there right after the Regis conviction."

"And I bet she moved on up there with a little financial assistance, eh?"

"I figured I might go on up there with Eddie and see what she has to say for herself."

"No, not yet, Nate. But what I would ask of you is to find out whatever you can about her and this Daniel Levitt character. But as discreetly as you can. See if there is any connection to Wade, also to this Leon Devereaux—that's D-E-V-E-R-E-A-U-X—out of Lucedale. Any which way that these people tie together would be very useful."

"Can do. I'll call you if I find anything."

" 'Preciated."

Ross hung up. Gaines sat there for a while turning over this additional information. So Regis gets himself involved with Della. Matthias takes a dislike to the promise of a colored man in the family and gives him as clear a warning as he can. Then, just to really make sure he's got the message, railroads him up to Parchman on a bogus B&E. The victim of the B&E—upstanding citizen of the year, Dolores Henderson—moves to Purvis, and all's well that ends well. Della is back in the fold, Regis is out of the picture, and life goes back to normal. Meanwhile, the ghost of an earlier crime, the body of Nancy Denton, surfaces from the mud. Michael Webster comes out of retirement and looks like he might start talking, and Matthias Wade, doing nothing more than protecting his own interests and guaranteeing his rightful inheritance, calls up an old friend, Leon Devereaux. They take Michael out for the evening and then out of the picture for good.

If it went down that way, then it was a pretty straightforward sequence of events. But knowing what happened and proving what happened were very different matters. Regardless of what Nate Ross and Eddie Holland might learn about Dolores Henderson and the evidence she gave against Clifton Regis, it was doubtful that she would change her tune. People like Dolores were more than aware of people like Leon, and to retract her statement and contribute to Regis's case being reviewed, even appealed, meant she would put herself in the firing line for the same kind of visit that Leon had made with Michael Webster. That was something Gaines felt sure she would not even consider. Gaines's thoughts turned back to Devereaux. By all indications, he was neither the most careful nor the most concerned about what he had done. Not only was there a bathtub half-full of blood in his trailer, but there was every possibility that the knife he had used to decapitate Michael Webster had been left behind, too. Well, that knife was now in Gaines's own basement, and there it was going to stay . . .

Gaines stopped mid-thought. He lifted the phone, called Nate Ross, and Nate picked up immediately.

"Nate, it's John again."

"Hey."

"The Regis case. Where was it tried?"

"Circuit."

"Who was presiding?"

"Hang on," Ross said. Gaines heard him call out to Eddie Holland, asking the question that Gaines had asked.

Ross came back. "Marvin Wallace."

"Who is based in Purvis, right?"

"Yes, he is."

"And who arraigned Michael Webster and posted his bail?"

"Marvin Wallace."

Neither spoke for a few seconds.

"I've known Wallace for twenty years," Ross said.

"Meaning?"

"Hell, I don't know, John. Meaning nothing. Meaning that if he's involved in this, it doesn't matter how long I've known him."

"It could be nothing. He's the circuit court judge. He pretty much hears everything, right?"

"Well, what he must have heard the day that Clifton Regis was up before him was a yard and a half of make-believe, and yet he still sent him upstate. That doesn't give him the benefit of the doubt, as far as I can see."

"You think that Wade might be paying off Wallace?" Gaines asked.

"Well, if Marvin Wallace went that way, then he was paid, for sure, or Wade has something on him. But you know as well as I that this is all supposition. I'm sticking with what you told me before . . . gonna find out as much as I can about Henderson, Levitt, and this Leon Devereaux character."

"Well, while you're checking into Devereaux's arraignments and appearances, just see if Wallace was presiding, would you?"

"For sure," Ross replied, and then added, "And if this is some big hole you're digging yourself into, John—"

"Nate, someone else dug the hole. I'm just following them into it."

"Well, son, make sure you take a flashlight and a shotgun, eh?"

Ross hung up. Gaines got up from his desk and walked to the window.

He looked out as the day got going, as cars and trucks headed out along the freeway to whatever business concerned them. It was Monday the fifth, his mother had been dead for eight days, and yet it still felt like she'd be home if he went there right now.

Gaines believed that he wouldn't even appreciate her absence, wouldn't even begin to come to terms with it until this case was done, until his mind finally settled, until he was able to lay the ghosts of Nancy Denton and Michael Webster to rest once and for all.

61

Hagen appeared just after nine thirty, apologizing for his lateness. "The little 'un has croup," he explained.

"You need to be home?" Gaines asked.

"It's okay now. He's sleeping. Mary'll call me if she needs anything."

Gaines got Hagen up to speed on recent developments, the information that Nate had given him on the Regis case, the fact that Dolores Henderson and Daniel Levitt has been added to the cast of characters in this particular drama.

"Tell me what you know about Marvin Wallace," Gaines said. "You've been here your whole life. You know much about him?"

"Seems like a decent man," Hagen said. "Tough, doesn't take any crap, but still has a heart for a sad story, you know?"

"What do you mean?"

"Has a tendency to let himself be persuaded that folks are better than they actually are. Tends to give people the benefit of the doubt."

"He married?"

"Yes, has been for as long as I recall. Wife's name is Edith. He has two kids . . . I say kids, but they're adults now, out and about in the big, bad world. A son and a daughter. Daughter lives with her husband and kids somewhere like Magee or Mendenhall, far as I remember, and the son is a lawyer in Vicksburg. He's married, too; don't know if he has any kids yet. She's a few years older than him. He's about my age, late twenties, and she's half a dozen years older than that."

"Names?"

"Marion and Stanley. And Stanley, by the way, is married to Jack Kidd's daughter, Ruth."

"State's AG, Jack Kidd?"

"Only one Jack Kidd I know of."

"And is the daughter married to anyone we know?"

Hagen smiled. "Probably. This is the South, you know? Everyone knows everyone else, and if you don't know 'em, then you're probably related anyways."

"That's what it's starting to look like."

Gaines thought back to his conversation with Hagen, the fact that Ken Howard had spoken with Kidd and Kidd had come back and told Howard that Webster could not be held for more than a couple of hours. Kidd could have overridden that point; he could have decided that Michael Webster was in no fit state to recall anything he might or might not have said about taking things from the cabin; he could have concluded that Webster's failure to make any calls upon his arrest was Webster's choice, not a failure on Gaines's part to provide Webster his basic legal rights. Kidd could have done whatever he felt was appropriate, but he said that the murder charge should be dropped, that Webster should be charged solely with destruction of evidence, and he also advised that the arraignment be held in front of Marvin Wallace. In that way the bail was held down as low as possible, and Wade could just walk in and pay it. From there it was a simple drive over to see Mr. Devereaux, and the matter was closed. Everything stayed in-house, neat as paint.

Wade, Wallace, Kidd. Was that what was going on here? Were these guys in league with one another? And if so, why? Was it a simple matter of Wade money putting people in the state attorney general's office and on the bench, and when a favor was needed, it was all too easily extended? Or was there more to this? Were Wallace and Kidd somehow connected to what had happened to Nancy Denton? Was that why Wade never concerned himself with silencing Michael Webster? Not simply because of Michael's own belief that to break his silence would preclude any possibility of Nancy's return from the dead, but because Wade knew that Webster could never touch him. Never even get close. The law would always be on Wade's side. Webster could have an accident or meet an unfortunate end just anytime Wade chose, and Wade would never be held to account. Even if Webster had come forward, Wade had everyone from the local circuit judge to the state's AG on his payroll. That was the way it worked, the way it had always worked, the way it would always work in the future. This was just the way things were done down here.

"Sheriff?"

Gaines looked at Hagen.

"Where d'you go to?"

"A dark place, Richard . . . a dark fucking place."

"So what's next?"

"Well, I got Ross and Holland finding out everything they can about Leon Devereaux and the others, and we are also waiting for any word from Della Wade."

"She can be trusted?"

"Hell, I don't know, Richard. She seemed like she wanted to help us. If not for her own sense of moral rectitude, but because of Clifton Regis and what her brother did to him."

"But that doesn't change the fact that she's a Wade."

"I am well aware of that," Gaines said. "So to answer your question, no, I don't trust her."

"These people got it in them to kill Webster, to do what they did to Regis, then we are sure as hell in the firing line."

"We are, but that's why we wanted a uniform in the first place, right?"

"Hell no. I did it for the job security and the health benefits."

Gaines smiled, a moment of levity. Hagen was good people, no doubt about it.

"Well, I'm not one for hanging around," Hagen said. "I can go over and help out Nate and Eddie, if you like."

"Sure, you do that, but you go out of town, let me know."

"Will do, Sheriff."

Gaines sat in silence once again. Seemed the hole these people had dug was growing ever deeper. Either that, or the hole was simply a manifestation of Gaines's own imagination, and there was nothing here at all.

He hoped it was the former. He had to believe it was the former. He was not prepared to accept that the death of Nancy Denton had begun and ended with Michael Webster. He just couldn't believe it of the man. Not now. Not after learning the reason for what he'd done to her body. Crazy he might be, but a murderer? Gaines didn't think so. He had looked in that man's eyes; he had sat with him in the basement cell; he had listened to his ramblings and monologues, and yet never once had he said anything that convinced Gaines he was evil.

He lifted the phone once more, called Nate Ross a third time.

"Nate, it's John. I've sent Richard Hagen over to help you out. I'm thinking of taking a trip up to Purvis to see this Henderson woman myself."

"That'll put your flag in the yard, John. You go speak to her and it'll get back to Wade."

"If she's involved, Nate, only if she's involved."

"Seems pretty clear that she is, wouldn't you say?"

"Well, I don't know what to tell you. I'm beginning to think that if we don't take some direct steps to get to the truth of this, then we may never find it. I don't see anyone walking on in here to explain all of this to me."

"You want company?"

"No, I'm gonna go alone. Did you get an address for her?"

"No, not yet, but if she's still in Purvis, she shouldn't be too hard to find."

"She'll be in the system somewhere, I imagine," Gaines replied. "And if you run out of things for Hagen to do, send him back here to hold the fort."

"Sure thing."

Gaines hung up, searched out the number for the Lamar County Sheriff's Office, called them and spoke with a deputy up there who knew precisely who Dolores Henderson was and where she lived.

"She a handful of trouble for you folks?" Gaines asked.

"Always has been, always will be," the deputy replied. "Had her in here just a couple of days ago on a drunk and disorderly, resisting arrest, a bunch of other stuff. Public lewdness, as well, I think. Woman's a nightmare on a good day. What you interested in her for, Sheriff?"

"Not her, but someone she knows," Gaines replied.

"Oh, I should think she knows pretty much the worst of the worst from here and half a dozen other counties."

"Well, I'm hopin' that's the case, and I'm gonna drive on up and see for myself, if that's okay with you."

"You make yourself at home, Sheriff Gaines, and if you can find a good reason to get her out of Purvis, we'll all be in your debt."

Gaines thanked the deputy for his assistance.

He collected his hat, his jacket, went on out to the car, and headed north.

62

If Dolores Henderson wasn't strung out on something, then she had been very recently.

Gaines wondered, even as he stood inside the porch of her house, whether it would have been smarter to visit out of uniform.

The momentary sense of curiosity on her face as she opened the screen and looked at him was immediately replaced with an expression of distaste and derision. "Who the fuck are you, and what the fuck do you want?" she said. She spat her words out, as if each was something rank and bitter.

Dolores Henderson couldn't have been more than thirty-five. She had the sallow, dry skin of a junkie, the facial laxity of a drunk, and the personal hygiene of a three-dollar hooker. She was not in good shape, not at all, and Gaines imagined it would have been the easiest thing in the world to convince her to testify against Clifton Regis.

But one time she must have been good-looking. Gaines could see that as well. Though her dishwater-blond hair was lank and unwashed, there was a memory there of how it might have looked when she was in her teens. Here was a life gone sour, a life that slid off the tracks someplace. From appearances, she was slow-motion killing herself to save anyone else from doing it for her.

"You won the lottery," Gaines said.

She sneered. "You a fucking comedian, or what?"

"I sure am," Gaines replied. "That's what we do now. We send comedians dressed as cops to let you know when you've won the lottery."

"You got any smokes?"

"Yes, thanks."

She took a step back, seemed as if she were going to lose her balance, and then grabbed the edge of the door for support. "Well, ain't you even fuckin' funnier than I thought," she said. "Jesus Christ, what gives with you people, eh? Why do you always have to be such assholes?"

"I think it's a condition for the job," Gaines said. "They have an asshole test at the academy, and if you're not a big enough asshole, you're out."

Dolores was elsewhere before Gaines had even finished. She was looking back inside the house, as if someone or something was in there demanding her attention.

"So can I come in, Dolores?" Gaines asked.

"You got a piece of paper that says I have to let you in?"

"No, just a polite request."

"Well, you can go fuck yourself, then," she replied. "You don't got no warrant, you stay on the fuckin' porch . . . in fact, I don't even have to let you into the yard. This is private property."

"It is, and you're right," Gaines said. "But I need to ask you about a couple of things, and then I'll let you get back to your busy social schedule."

"Ask whatever you like, asshole. Just 'cause you ask doesn't mean you get an answer."

"Clifton Regis."

She hesitated, frowned at Gaines. "What about him? He out already?"

"Nope, he's still up there in Parchman."

"Best fuckin' place for him. That son of a bitch broke in here and tried to rob me. Hell, if I hadn't a screamed the fuckin' place down, he'd have more 'an likely tried to rape me as well."

Oh, dream on, sister, Gaines thought. "So it was Clifton Regis who broke into your house and tried to rob you?"

"Yes, he did."

"And you testified to that effect?"

Dolores stood silent for a moment, perhaps wondering what this was all about, and then she dropped her hip, put her hand on her waist, and assumed her most defensive tone.

"What gives?" she asked.

"I'm just asking about Clifton Regis."

"What the hell for? That was a long time ago. I done said what needed to be said, and that's all there was to it."

Gaines took a punt. "And did you say what Leon told you to say, or did you make it all up yourself?"

Suddenly she was alert. "What the hell you talkin' 'bout Leon for? What's he done now? What's he said? He tryin' to get hisself out of some fix by settin' me up?"

"Maybe," Gaines said.

"That son of a bitch!" Dolores replied. "What's he done said about me?"

"Said that maybe the evidence you gave wasn't all good, you know? Maybe that there were some inconsistencies."

"That fuckin' son of a bitch. Jesus Christ, goddammit, I knew I should never have taken him back. Fuck! Fuck! What you got him for?"

"Oh, a whole mess of stuff, Dolores. Stuff you wouldn't even wanna know."

"And he's tryin' to make a deal with you? Tryin' to get hisself off the hook by diggin' a hole for me?"

"I didn't say that."

"So what's happened? What's the deal here?"

"I can't tell you that, Dolores."

"What the fuck d'you mean, you can't tell me that?"

"Whatever he's done is a matter for us and him, and whatever might be going on between you two, well, that's something that you're going to have to talk to him about."

"Motherfucker!" she said, and thumped the frame of the door. "Goddammit, that son of a bitch, I know I should never have gotten involved in that bullshit."

"The Clifton Regis bullshit?"

She stopped suddenly. She looked askance at Gaines. "What did you say your name was?"

"I didn't," Gaines replied.

"I figured so. And which county you from?"

"I didn't say that neither."

"Hey, what the hell is this, mister? What the hell is going on here? I ain't sayin' anythin' else. You hear me? I ain't sayin' a single goddamned word more. You don't get nothin' outta me."

"I got what I needed, Dolores," Gaines said, and took a step back down from the porch.

"What the hell is that supposed to mean? You got what you needed? What the fuck is that? I didn't say a goddamned thing." She came down the steps after Gaines, followed him as he back-tracked to the gate, the street beyond, his car parked against the curb.

"You even spoken to Leon?" she asked. "You even *have* Leon?"

"Oh, I have Leon all right," Gaines said, "and I've got a few more questions to ask him now, thanks to you."

"That's horseshit, mister. I didn't say a goddamned thing, and if you tell Leon that I've been talkin' to you, I'll—"

"You'll what, Dolores? You'll have someone come over and cut off my fingers?"

"Hey, I had nothin' to do with that, goddammit! I wasn't even there when they did that to him."

"So it wasn't only Leon, then?"

"Fuck you!" she snapped. She reached down suddenly, picked up a stone from the yard, held it in her hand, her expression like a loaded gun.

Gaines reached the car, felt behind him for the door lever.

"I'll pass on your regards to Leon," he said, and opened the door.

"Asshole!" Dolores shouted, and even as he got into the driver's seat, the stone thumped noisily against the fender.

Gaines started the car, pulled away, and watched Dolores Henderson diminish to nothing in the rearview.

A mile away, he felt the tension of the situation unravel inside him. He felt that knot in his stomach, the way his hands shook, and he knew it wasn't out of fear. It was a sense of vindication and all that it involved. Nothing probative, of course, nothing in writing, nothing that he could share with anyone but Hagen, Ross, and Holland, and certainly nothing that would stand up before Wallace or Kidd or anyone else. But he had something. He had a connection between Dolores Henderson and Leon Devereaux. Gaines would have bet his house on Regis's blood being one of those that remained unidentified on the knife he'd taken from Devereaux's trailer.

And if Leon Devereaux had been influential in Regis's incarceration, then he was most definitely in the employ of Matthias Wade. Wade had used Devereaux for that job, so perhaps he had also used him for Webster. Same knife for two different tasks. And who was the third?

Gaines drove the seventy miles to Whytesburg with his foot to the floor. He was back at Nate Ross's a little after one.

63

Ross, Holland, and Hagen were all at the house. They had been making calls, trying to piece connections together between Henderson, Devereaux, and Levitt. Gaines recounted his conversation with Dolores Henderson, to which Hagen said, "Devereaux finds out she spoke with you, implicated him like that, I'm thinking we might be finding another body soon."

"Sounds like she's gonna get the justice she deserves," Holland said. "Things have a way of working out like that."

"If we were good people, we'd have her in protective custody until this Devereaux character was locked up," Ross said.

"Seems we ain't good people," Gaines replied. "Far as I'm concerned, I have about as much concern for her welfare as she had for Clifton Regis."

"So we need to find Devereaux," Hagen said.

"And we need to tie Devereaux to Wade. We need something on Devereaux that'll make him give up Wade, and then we can look at closing this thing once and for all. I want Wade for one of them, and if it can't be Nancy, then it'll have to be Webster."

"Well, maybe Dolores Henderson will testify against Devereaux. She's certainly showed her willingness to testify before, right?" Ross said.

Hagen shook his head. "She's about as credible a witness as . . . well, as the worst kind of witness you could imagine. She's a felon and a junkie. A greenhorn with no courtroom experience at all could pull her credibility to pieces in five minutes."

"Which makes it all the more unbelievable that she was capable of putting Regis in Parchman," Holland said.

"Exactly," Gaines said. "She's no use to us, believe me, beyond substantiating our suspicions about Devereaux, and she pretty much confirmed that he was the one who cut Regis's fingers off."

"Which leaves us Wallace," Ross said.

"Which leaves us Wallace," Gaines echoed.

"Damned shame, man like that, all those years behind him, and he winds up a yes man for the Wades."

"We don't know that for sure," Gaines said.

Ross shook his head. "I think we do, John."

The four of them sat there in silence for a good thirty seconds.

"You want to take a visit with me?" Gaines asked Ross.

"We're going as friends, I'll come with you. We're going official, you better take Hagen."

"As friends," Gaines said. "We don't know what we have here as far as Wallace is concerned. We don't even know that we have anything at all. Not really. We can go see him, tell him what we're looking at, see if he gives us anything. We just have to let him know the direction we're headed, and then if he wants to run interference or do something that absolves himself, so be it. We give him the benefit of the doubt and see what happens."

"Good enough," Ross said. "I'll make some calls, see where he is."

Gaines turned to Hagen. "You go on back to the office. Say nothing on this. Soon as I know where we're at, I'll get word to you."

"And me?" Eddie Holland asked.

"Looks like you're the fifth wheel, Ed," Gaines said. "Don't think it'll suit to have all three of us arrive unannounced at Marvin Wallace's house."

"Suits me," Holland said. "Got some things I need to do anyway. I'll be here if you need me."

"Appreciated."

Ross came back to the kitchen from the hallway. "He's in his office up in Purvis," he said. "He's not in court today, according to his secretary. We have an appointment with him at three."

"We're outta here, then," Gaines said.

"Get him on a hook and make him wriggle," was Holland's parting comment.

Gaines didn't reply. He didn't think that the conversation with Judge Marvin Wallace would be anything like the conversation with Dolores Henderson. Wallace was a state-appointed legal authority, a man of considerable standing and reputation, and he had a great deal of friends. This was not going to be a turkey shoot, not at all. This was where any possibility of keeping their investigation under wraps was going to be blown into shreds.

Now there would be nowhere to hide from the influence and

connections of Matthias Wade. Maybe Gaines would wake to find Leon Devereaux standing over his bed, asking if he please couldn't have his knife back as there was urgent work needing to be done.

64

For a child of eleven, Kenny Sawyer was pretty damned smart. Already he understood that when it came to life, what you deserved and what you got were never the same thing.

Kenny's mother, Janette, was only thirty-seven, yet already exhausted with disappointments. She'd become the sort of person who figured that hope was merely there to remind you of all those things you'd yet failed to do.

At twenty-five, she'd married a man of forty, name of Ray Sawyer, and they'd rented a place in Lucedale. Ray had already been married, already had two sons—Dale and Stephen, fourteen and seventeen respectively. Ray had been widowed by a wife who committed suicide. Why she'd committed suicide, well, Kenny didn't know, and it never seemed right to raise the subject.

A year into the marriage, Janette Sawyer was pregnant, and the result was Kenny, born in 1963.

Six years later, having contracted an aggressive cancer, Ray went from fit and well to dead in less than three months. There were pictures of him toward the end, a shadow of his former self, his clothes hanging off of him like there was room enough inside for two or three more folk of about the same stature. Kenny could barely remember his father, and his ma spoke of him rarely. Only thing that remained of Ray Sawyer's memory was the house that he and Janette had taken. Janette had taken up with a string of men in the subsequent five years, some of them good, most of them not.

Both Dale and Stephen had shipped out pretty much as soon as their father was buried. How and why they felt no burden of responsibility for their stepmother was a mystery to Kenny. Kenny had felt that burden, and so he'd stuck around. That he'd been six years old at the time did play a part in his decision, for sure, but he liked to believe that if he'd wanted to, well, he could have up and left just like Dale and Stephen.

Kenny did not appreciate all the angles, but he was sure of one thing: What you deserved and what you got were not the same thing. Not ever.

The absence of a father was never that prevalent in Kenny's mind. Folks asked him about it, and he said that what you never had you couldn't miss. The kids didn't really understand that sentiment; the adults were impressed with his philosophical attitude, and they favored him for his seeming honesty and sensitivity. He was an artistic boy, loved to draw and paint and make clay models, and there were those who believed he might be one of those who made it out.

"He could be an architect, a painter, a designer, or something," the art teacher once told Janette Sawyer at a parent–teacher conference. "He certainly has a talent, Mrs. Sawyer, and I am sure he will do well."

If Janette had possessed the energy to be proud, she might well have been. But she did not. She did not possess the energy for a great many things these days. She was not yet forty, and yet she felt as old as her own mother. *Drained* was the word she used. "I feel utterly drained, Kenny," she would say. "Make yourself some soup and crackers. I'll do some proper dinner later." But mostly there was no *later*, and Kenny would take a couple of quarters from her purse and go get fried chicken.

It was on one of the fried chicken expeditions that he first met Leon Devereaux. Not a great deal more than a year earlier, he'd walked on up to the diner on Gorman Road, started back with the greasy paper bag, in it two wings, two legs, a tub of slaw, in his other hand a cup of root beer, and a black pickup had slowed alongside him and come to a stop.

Kenny Sawyer was not a suspicious child. He was young enough to take people at face value, to trust them until they gave him a reason not to, and yet old enough to consider he could take care of himself. Perhaps life had dealt him a mediocre hand, but it was with a mediocre hand that the best bluffs were undertaken.

"Got there?" a voice said.

Kenny stopped and turned left. "Chicken."

"Where d'you get that?"

"Diner."

A face then appeared at the window, the arm on the edge of the door, said arm scattered with jailhouse tats, the man's hair closely shorn, a tooth missing on the left side of his crooked smile. But to

Kenny it seemed like a good smile, an honest smile, and there was something about the man that seemed of decent humor.

"Back there?"

"Sure, back there. Half a mile, no more."

"And it's good chicken, you say?"

"Good enough," Kenny said.

"You don't get no supper at home?"

"Some."

"But not today."

"No, sir, not today."

"Sir? What you done call me sir for?"

Kenny frowned. "Politeness, sir."

"Well, shee-it, kid. I don't recall that there's ever been a time someone called me sir."

"Well, maybe you ain't knowed a great deal of polite folks."

"I'm thinkin' that may be the case. I think maybe you just hit the nail damn square on the head right there, son."

"Maybe so," Kenny said, and thought about his chicken getting cold.

"So that chicken is good, then, you say."

"You wanna try some?" Kenny asked, and he took a step toward the pickup and held up the greasy paper bag.

"You'd let me have some of that there chicken you got in the bag?"

"Sure. Not all of it, mind, but you could maybe have a wing and see if it was good, and if you wanted more, you could drive right on down there and get yourself some."

The man paused, tilted his head to one side, and looked at Kenny Sawyer like this was something altogether different.

"You're a good kid, you know that?"

Kenny looked back at Leon like this was something altogether different for him, too.

"So, you want some?"

"Sure, kid. Let me have a wing there and we'll see how it is."

They agreed the chicken was good, not the best either of them had ever had, but fit for purpose.

"Where do you live, son?" Leon asked.

"Back a ways there, over beyond the clear-cut."

"With your ma and pa?"

"Just my ma."

"Your pa done run off?"

"Nope, he died."

"Sorry to hear that."

"Yup."

"You got brothers and sisters?"

"Two stepbrothers, Dale and Stephen, but they lit out when our pa died."

"So they wasn't your ma's boys?"

"No, sir. They come with the package."

Leon laughed. "Yes, indeed, you're a good kid, and you're smart, too. Bet you there ain't a great deal of people who can get past you."

"I'd like to think not."

"So, I'm gonna go down to that diner there and get myself some of that chicken. You wanna come?"

"Why for?"

"No reason. Just for company."

"Ain't s'posed to go no place with strangers."

"What's your name, son?"

"Kenny."

"Well, Kenny, my name is Leon, and I'm pleased to meet you."

"Pleased to meet you, sir."

"Well, seein' as how we's on first-name terms, and seein' as how we already shared some dinner there, looks like we ain't strangers no more, wouldn't you say?"

"I guess."

"Well, hop on up here and show me where this diner is, and then once we've eaten, I can give you a ride back home."

Kenny hesitated for no more than a second, and then he went on up in the passenger seat and gave directions. Not that there were a great many directions to give, but he gave them anyway.

Seemed that there may have been some odious and disreputable reason for Leon Devereaux's initial exchange with Kenny Sawyer, but then again, maybe there wasn't. Maybe he was just looking for company, and Kenny Sawyer was there to provide it. Whatever the deal had been, the deal was now something different. Leon Devereaux went on into the diner and bought more chicken. He got French fries and a cup of ketchup and cookies that were still warm from the oven. The cookies were for Kenny. They ate together, right there in the cab of that pickup, and they didn't talk a great deal. When they were done, Leon was good to his word and he drove Kenny home.

"You know the trailers parked up over yonder?"

361

"The ones where that crazy dog is at?" Kenny asked.

"That's the ones."

"Yes, I do, sir."

"Well, that's where I live. You ever want some company, you come on by there. And don't mind the dog. That's General Patton. He's always chained up secure, and he ain't half as mad as he sounds. He just does it to show off."

"You want me to bring chicken?"

"Sure, son. You bring some chicken if you like."

"Okay," Kenny said.

"Well, okay," Leon replied.

And so it had become a friendship of sorts, Kenny Sawyer taking the long way back from school to see if Leon's pickup was out at the trailers, and—if so—heading for the diner, getting chicken for them both, and then walking back.

Most often Leon was not there, and so their meetings were few and far between. But when they did meet, they picked up the conversations where they'd left off—baseball, comic books, church, what was best to eat, girlfriends, the benefits of cats versus dogs or vice versa, other such things. Leon showed Kenny lumberjack fighting, taught him a few slick moves— how to throw a punch and make it matter—and Kenny never asked where Leon had been for the past week or so, and Leon never ventured an explanation for his absences.

And so it was, late afternoon of Monday, August 5th, that Kenny Sawyer came back from school and checked to see if Leon's pickup was home. It was not, hadn't been for near on two weeks, but this time there was something strange. General Patton was there, unchained, running back and forth between the trailers and barking like a crazy son of a bitch. Kenny called him, and General Patton came running, near bowled him over with enthusiasm to see a familiar face.

"What's up, boy?" Kenny asked him. "Where's your pa, eh? Where's Leon at? What you doin' here by yourself?"

Each day Kenny had been down this way, he had seen the trailers but no pickup and no dog. This didn't make sense. No sense at all. Couldn't understand how Leon was absent but the General was here, untethered, running loose.

Kenny went on up to the big trailer, the one where he and Leon would sit and talk and eat chicken. He knocked, waited, figured that maybe Leon was in there with a girl again like he'd been a couple of times before. But Leon was not here. Of course he wasn't. How the hell had he got here without the truck? Maybe he'd broken down someplace and had taken to walking back, had let the General run on ahead. A handful of minutes and he'd be turning the corner and asking where the chicken was at.

Kenny headed for the smaller trailer, the one where Leon slept.

He knocked again, knew he wouldn't get an answer, and reached up to open the door.

Five minutes later, stopping once again to heave violently at the side of the road, Kenny Sawyer could still smell Leon Devereaux's decaying corpse, still see just the one eye staring back at him. The other eye had been shot right through, left a hole the size of a quarter and then some, and whatever meatballs and tomato sauce had been inside that skull of his was decorating the wall above his head.

He'd been shot right there in his bed, had perhaps leaned up to see who was coming through the door, and taken a bullet right through the eye.

By the time he reached home, Kenny could hardly breathe, let alone speak. It was a while before Janette Sawyer appreciated the full import of what had happened, a while after that before she reached the Sheriff's Office. Gradney himself went out to those trailers and saw what Kenny Sawyer had seen, and once he had the scene under control, once photographs had been taken, once the coroner had been called, Gradney took it upon himself to try to understand why an eleven-year-old kid would have a friend like Leon Devereaux. Gradney also knew that what you deserved and what you got were not the same thing, and that applied to friends as well. Kenny explained what he could, and then Gradney sat with Janette Sawyer and tried to get her to see that keeping an eye on who her son was spending time with might be a wise investment of her attention. After the Sawyers had left, Gradney called the dog pound, told them he had a mutt that needed collecting. Once the dog was gone, only then did he think to check the other trailer. He saw what Gaines had seen in the bathtub, and he was disturbed beyond measure. He did not know what Leon Devereaux had been doing, but he wondered whether Kenny Sawyer might have been the next intended recipient of whatever it was. Lastly, Gradney made a call to the Breed County Sheriff's Office. He didn't reach Gaines, but Hagen. He explained what had happened, that Leon Devereaux had been found dead in his trailer by a child.

"A child?" Hagen asked, incredulous.

"That's what I said," Gradney replied. "Seems Leon Devereaux kept some unlikely company. Little kid of eleven or twelve, said he'd been coming out here and visiting with Devereaux and General Patton—that's Devereaux's dog, by the way—for some time. Brought chicken after school, talked about girls and whatnot."

Hagen lied convincingly. He said that he and Gaines had been out there, but had not ventured into the trailers. Gradney said that aside from Leon Devereaux's corpse in the smaller of the trailers, there was evidence of some other foul play in the larger of the two vehicles. A great deal of blood had been found in the bathtub, blood that looked to have been there a good deal longer than Leon's dead body.

"Of course, he could have decided to gut a pig in there," Gradney suggested, "but I doubt it. I am concerned we might find that some poor son of a bitch has gone missing, and when we find him, he ain't gonna have a great deal of blood left inside of him."

And then he added, "Ironic, eh? Fact of the matter was that your boy was home all along, 'cept he wasn't in the mood for taking visitors. Someone shot him in the eye, decorated the wall with most of his head, and then just left him there in bed. Coroner says he'd been there about a week. The man neither looked so good nor smelled so good at the best of times, so you can imagine what he's like right now."

Hagen thanked Gradney, told him there might be a chance he and Gaines would come out and take a look at the trailers, but today was unlikely. Gradney said they were welcome anytime, but to give him fair warning so he could be present. Hagen thanked him for calling, and the conversation was over.

Hagen knew he wouldn't reach Gaines on the radio, and so he called Judge Marvin Wallace's office and left a message for Gaines to call him back as soon as possible.

Set to leave his office, another call came through. It was Maryanne Benedict.

"Is Sheriff Gaines there?" she asked.

"No, Miss Benedict. He's out of town right now. Can I help?"

"It's Della Wade," she said. "She called me, said she was coming over to see me, said she had some information about what happened to Clifton."

"I'm leaving now," Hagen said. "You tell her I'm on the way, and that she's not to leave until I see her."

"I'll do my best," Maryanne said, and hung up.

Hagen left the office, told Barbara to get him on the radio if there was any word from the sheriff. She said she would, and as she watched Hagen's car pull away, she tried to remember the last time there had been such aggravation and commotion in Whytesburg. She could not recall such a time, and did not believe there ever had been.

65

Judge Marvin Wallace of Purvis was a man used to dealing with liars. He believed he could spot a liar at a hundred paces, that those selfsame liars recognized in him a man who'd waste not a second in listening to whatever mendacity was planned.

Such a faculty served him well as a judge and arbiter of law, for alibis became transparent, evasiveness in the face of direct questions received no quarter, and folks intent on deception were rapidly undone in the precise application of his pronouncements and edicts. Ken Howard knew him well, as did all the state defenders and prosecutors through every relevant county and a few beyond.

Branford was the county seat, and Frederick Otis ran a tight ship as far as that function was concerned, but Wallace was circuit and thus managed a far wider jurisdiction.

The appointment that he'd agreed to for three o'clock on the afternoon of Monday, August 5th, was—he imagined—related to some outstanding warrant, an ongoing case, a matter of *t*'s to be crossed and *i*'s to be dotted. Wallace had scheduled a meeting for thirty minutes later, certain that whatever Sheriff John Gaines had to discuss would take no more than that.

Wallace greeted Gaines politely, Nate Ross also, and when Gaines opened the conversation with, "Judge Wallace, thank you for seeing us. We wanted to talk to you about Matthias Wade," there was a definite sense that the temperature in the room had dropped a degree or two.

"Matthias Wade?" Wallace asked. He shifted in his seat. He glanced at Ross, then looked back at Gaines. "What about Matthias Wade?"

"In the absence of any probative evidence, even anything significant of a circumstantial nature, we are nevertheless of the viewpoint that he may have been involved in the recent death of Michael Webster, and before that, all of twenty years ago, the death of Nancy Denton."

Wallace showed no surprise. He was implacable, and after looking back at Gaines in silence for a good ten seconds, he smiled and then shook his head ever so slowly.

"So?" he asked.

"Well, I wanted to know your reaction to that suggestion. That he might have been involved."

"I have no reaction, Sheriff Gaines. What kind of reaction did you think I might have?"

"I wondered whether or not your relationship with Matthias Wade—"

"I'm sorry, my *relationship* with Matthias Wade?"

"Okay, your friendship. I wondered whether your friendship with Matthias Wa—"

Wallace raised his hand and Gaines fell silent. He leaned back in his chair and steepled his fingers together.

For a little while the only sound was the fan in the ceiling.

"I think you have caught me on the back step," Wallace said. "I feel as if I am coming late to the game and the score has already been decided. I have absolutely no idea what you are talking about. You use the word *relationship* and then *friendship* when referring to Matthias Wade, and you use them as if they actually mean something of significance. I do not know what you are talking about."

"Are you saying that you're not friends with Matthias Wade?"

Wallace's mouth smiled, but his eyes did not. "Friends? With Matthias Wade?" He was silent for a moment and then said, "Okay, Sheriff Gaines, let's get one thing straight right here and now. If you have a question for me, then you ask it. You do not come into my office with this attitude. You do not present questions to me as if I am withholding something from you. You do not employ interrogative techniques when you ask me something, you understand?"

"Interrogative techniques?"

"The way you ask your questions. Am I saying that I am *not* friends with Matthias Wade? As if I am trying to deny some earlier statement. You know exactly what I am talking about, Sheriff, and don't try and tell me you don't. If you have a question for me, then ask me that question and not something else. I have no time for games."

Gaines paused before speaking. "I apologize," he said. "This has been a high-strung business for us, you know? Not often there's a murder, and now we have more than one and a suicide as well. We just need your help, Judge, and there are some things that make sense and some that don't, and we thought you could help clarify a few points."

"Fire away, son. We're all on the same side here, and if there's a question I have an answer for, then you'll get the answer."

"Do you remember a man called Clifton Regis?"

Wallace was pensive, and then he slowly shook his head. "Can't say I do, no."

"You committed him to a term at Parchman Farm."

Wallace smiled. "Hell, I commit someone to a term at Parchman half a dozen times a month. When was this?"

"Eighteen months ago—"

"Eighteen months ago? You have any idea of the number of cases I hear in a week, let alone eighteen months?"

"I just thought you might remember this one."

"And why would that be, Sheriff Gaines? Please enlighten me."

"Missing some fingers on his right hand. Charged with breaking and entering, eyewitness statement from a single individual, nothing to corroborate her statement, and you found him guilty."

"Well, Sheriff, if I found him guilty, there is a very strong likelihood that he was guilty. Circumstantial evidence can be damning if there's enough of it."

"I understand this, but it seems that there was no other evidence aside from the witness statement."

"Well, then she must have been very convincing and the defendant must have been very unconvincing. I do not commit someone to a term of detention lightly, Sheriff, and I think you know that."

"Do you remember the case?"

"Not specifically, no."

"So there's nothing you can recall that we might have missed about this case? We have looked and looked, and we just can't understand why he was sentenced to a jail term."

"Like I said, son, if I sent him to the Farm, then I must have had very good reason to do so."

"Do you remember if Matthias Wade had anything to do with that case?"

"What is it with you and Matthias Wade? He upset you somehow? What on earth would interest Matthias Wade about this Regis person?"

"The fact that Clifton Regis and Della Wade were in a relationship together."

Wallace hesitated and then said, "And this Clifton Regis is a colored man, I presume."

"Yes, sir, he is a colored man."

Wallace nodded slowly. "Oh. Well, now I understand why Matthias Wade might want this man in Parchman Farm, but my decision to incarcerate was not influenced or coerced in any way by Matthias Wade. Of that I can assure you."

Gaines sat back in his chair, seemed to relax. "Well, Judge, I am greatly relieved to hear that."

"I am curious as to why you might have thought me involved with Matthias Wade. His father I know, of course. Anyone of my generation was well-known to Earl, and vice versa, but Matthias no, not so readily. I understand him to be a little headstrong, a little impetuous, and I can appreciate why he might have possessed some concern about his sister becoming involved with a colored man."

"Why would he be concerned, Judge?"

Wallace smiled; the question was so meaningless as to not warrant a reply.

"So that's all there is to this?" Wallace asked.

"Yes, sir, that's all."

Wallace got up, indicated the door. "Well, if there's anything else I can assist you with, let me know."

Gaines reached the door, Ross right there beside him, and then he turned and looked back at Wallace. "Do you remember the woman, Judge? The one who gave the statement in court?"

"The Henderson woman? No, I don't remember her, sorry."

"Okay. Thank you for your time, sir," Gaines said, and left the room.

Ross closed the door gently behind him. There was a moment's hesitation, and then he smiled and said, "The lying son of a bitch."

66

There was a message from Hagen at Wallace's office. Gaines was given it as he and Ross left. Gaines asked if he could use one of their telephones.

Barbara took the call back at Breed County, told Gaines that Hagen had received word from a Sheriff Gradney in Lucedale and also a call from Maryanne Benedict, that Hagen had driven out there to see her. Gaines asked if Hagen had given the reason for Gradney's call.

"He didn't say, Sheriff," she replied. "The calls came back-to-back, the other sheriff first, then Miss Benedict, and Richard just hurried on out of here."

Gaines called Maryanne's house, spoke with her briefly, learned that she had received word from Della Wade, and that Della Wade was en route to see her.

Gaines—just as Hagen had done—told her to do whatever she could to keep Della Wade there until he arrived.

Gulfport was a good sixty or seventy miles, and Gaines floored the accelerator.

Ross was the first to reference Wallace's misstep, that he had inadvertently used Dolores Henderson's name without Gaines ever referring to her directly.

"You ever wish you didn't know, Nate? You ever wish that you'd taken some other job where this kind of shit didn't take over your life?"

"Nope," he said. "This kind of shit is the thing that keeps me interested in staying alive."

Gaines smiled sardonically.

"It does make me wonder how far it goes," Ross said. "I want to know if Kidd is involved and if it's about money or if it's about something else."

"Ninety-nine times in a hundred, it's money. That's my experience," Gaines replied.

"Well, Wallace is not in the poorhouse, and Kidd sure as hell is a wealthy man, so I don't know what the Sam Hill they're after."

"You go down that road, no matter how much you have, it's never enough."

"Crazy sons of bitches," Ross said.

"Wallace'll be on the phone to Wade now. I'd bet my house on it," Ross said.

"I reckon he is," Gaines replied. "Tell you the truth, I am just sick and tired of beating around the edges of this and getting no straight answers. Figured it was time to bring it to their doorsteps rather than wait for them to kill someone else."

"You think Matthias started all of this by murdering that poor girl?"

"I do, Nate. I do. I reckon he was as jealous as hell, couldn't believe that she wanted Michael Webster and not him, got it into his head that he had to have her. Maybe he tried to tell her that in the woods that night. Maybe she laughed at him, made him mad, and then he choked her. Maybe he didn't mean to kill her, but she wound up dead. Michael found her, tried to bring her back the only way he could think how."

"Scary shit, that is," Ross interjected. "I read about that stuff and it scares the living Jesus out of me."

"Well, I think Webster was already fragile from his experiences in the war, and then the grief . . . well, I think he just lost his mind. I don't think he even understood what he was doing or why. I think he just did something, anything, rather than accept the fact that the girl he loved was dead."

"But putting a snake inside of her . . . What the hell?"

"Oh, believe me, there's far worse than that. I mean, look at what happened to Webster. Someone cut his head off and buried it out behind my house. Made his hand into a fucking candle, for Christ's sake."

"Wade did that, you think?"

"I think Wade got Leon Devereaux to do it, and it was done in Devereaux's trailer. That's why we need to find him. I honestly believe that we can get him to turn state's evidence against Wade if we present him with the choices. People like that will always work for whoever offers the most money or the most threat to their survival."

"Well, maybe Della has something," Ross said. "Maybe she can help us with this Leon Devereaux."

371

Little else was said for the remainder of the journey. Gaines seemed in a world of his own, Ross similarly distracted by his own thoughts. They made good time, and it wasn't yet five when they pulled up in front of the Benedict house and got out of the car. Hagen's car was already there, but there was no sign of any other vehicle that might have ferried Della to Gulfport.

Maryanne had seen them from the window and came out to greet both Gaines and Ross.

"She's not here yet," she said before Gaines had a chance to ask.

They went on through to the kitchen, and it was here that Hagen informed Gaines and Ross of the discovery of Leon Devereaux's body.

"Shot through the eye," he said. "Gradney called me, told me someone had found his body in the other trailer, the one we didn't check."

Gaines was left without words. Ross couldn't believe what he was hearing.

"Said he'd been there the better part of a week," Hagen went on. "Some kid found him, apparently."

"A kid?" Gaines asked.

"That's what Gradney said. Said that some kid was a friend of Devereaux's, went out there with fried chicken and visited him, and he was the one who found the body."

"Jesus Christ almighty," Gaines said. "I don't think this could get much worse."

Maryanne came in from the front hall. "She's here," she said. "Della. Outside."

Gaines got up, Hagen also.

"Stay here," Gaines said. "I don't want her to feel overwhelmed by the number of people."

Gaines stood by the kitchen doorway, waited for Maryanne to get Della Wade into the front hallway before he presented himself.

"Sheriff Gaines," she said.

"Miss Wade," he replied.

"I think it was Leon Devereaux who hurt Clifton."

67

Gaines had to tell Della Wade that Leon Devereaux was dead.

"Dead?" She looked at the faces around her—Maryanne, Nate Ross, Richard Hagen, and then back to Gaines.

"Someone shot him," Gaines said.

"Shot him? Who? Who shot him?"

"We don't know, Miss Wade. Someone found him today in his trailer. Apparently, he'd been dead for about a week."

"Matthias?" she asked. "Did Matthias kill him?"

"We don't know, Miss Wade. Do you think it might have been Matthias?"

"Of course," she said, not a moment's hesitation in her response. "I think Devereaux did what he did to Clifton, and I think he might have killed Michael Webster, too. I think Leon Devereaux has been doing a lot of things for Matthias, and with all of this going on, I would think that Matthias would be scared that Devereaux would be caught. And then he might talk, and that would be the end of Matthias."

"I understand that," Gaines said, "but where did you get this name from? How do you know about Leon Devereaux?"

"Well, he's been around for years. But as far as being directly involved in this business now, Eugene told me."

"Eugene? Your brother?"

"Yes," Della replied. "I called him. I told him that I was afraid of Matthias, that I thought Matthias might have done something bad, and he said that I didn't need to be worried about what Matthias might do, but about someone called Leon Devereaux."

"And did Eugene say how he knew about Devereaux?"

"He said that Matthias told him that Leon Devereaux would come visit him if he caused any trouble."

"And why would Matthias threaten his own brother like that?"

"When Eugene left, he went without anything. He didn't want anything from our father, and he wanted nothing from Matthias. Apparently, Matthias told him that he was going to disown him, that he would no longer be a Wade, that there would be nothing in the estate for him when our father died. Eugene told him that he couldn't do that, that Matthias might have control of the family estate, but Eugene was still legally entitled to some recompense from the will. Matthias said there wouldn't be any will, that it would all come to him as the eldest son. He said that's what their father wanted, and that's the way it was going to be. He said that papers had already been signed, and there was nothing anyone could do about it. They argued, of course. Matthias said he could have Eugene killed, that he knew people who would do that. He said that if he tried to take any legal action against the estate or Matthias himself, he would send Devereaux to shoot him in the head."

"He said that? Those precise words, that he would send Devereaux to shoot him in the head?"

"That's what Eugene told me."

"And do you think Eugene would confirm any of this?" Gaines asked.

"Legally? No, I don't think he would. I think he is out of the family and has absolutely no desire to become involved in any way. I think he has gotten used to whatever life he lives now, and no amount of money would ever bring him back here."

"So you don't believe he'd make a statement to this effect, that Matthias had threatened him, said he would get Devereaux to shoot him in the head?"

"No, I don't think he would."

Gaines leaned back in the chair. He looked at Hagen, at Ross, at Maryanne.

"Christ almighty," he said. "This just gets crazier and crazier."

"So what can you do, Sheriff? Can you arrest Matthias? Can you put him somewhere where he won't hurt me or Eugene or anyone else?"

"Right now I have nothing, Della. I have your suspicion that Matthias killed Leon Devereaux. I have our suspicions that Devereaux attacked Clifton, maybe that he killed Michael Webster, but there is no evidence."

"I don't know exactly what happened to Clifton," Della said. "As far as I can tell, he was literally picked up off the street, and they took him someplace and did whatever they did to him."

"And then he was framed for the Dolores Henderson robbery, and well out of the picture."

"Right," Della said.

"Okay," Gaines said. "We have work to do. We have things to follow up on. The question I have for you is whether or not there's any way you can stay away from the house."

"Not a hope, Sheriff. I am there for my father. I have to be."

"He doesn't have nurses?"

"Sure he does, but a nurse is not a daughter. Besides, I am under house arrest, pretty much. I am there because Matthias says I have to be there. Matthias wants to know I am not off somewhere with people he disapproves of."

Gaines didn't speak for a time. He tried to maintain Della's gaze, to make her feel as if he were the only person in the room.

"I need to ask you, Della, and I need you to answer me as honestly as you can. From what you know of your brother, do you believe that he is capable of what happened to Nancy Denton? Do you think that he could have strangled her, and that twenty years later he had Michael Webster killed to prevent him from talking about what happened that night? And do you think he was the one who shot Leon Devereaux because Devereaux could implicate him in Webster's death and what was done to Clifton?"

Della Wade did not look away. She neither glanced at anyone else, nor averted her eyes, nor showed the slightest flicker of emotion. She simply nodded once and said, "I do not want to believe these things, Sheriff Gaines, but I think he is more than capable of all of them."

"And does Matthias know that you spoke to Eugene about this?"

"No, I don't see how he could. He was away this afternoon, and I called Eugene from outside the house."

"And you honestly feel that you have no choice but to go back to the house?"

"I have no choice, Sheriff. None at all."

"Where does Matthias think you are now?"

"He doesn't know that I'm out. He hasn't returned yet, or he hadn't when I left."

Gaines glanced at his watch. It was close to six o'clock.

"You have any idea of when he will return?"

She shook her head. "He could be back now; he could be away until tomorrow."

"Okay," Gaines replied. Considering all options, he did not see any way to avoid sending her back to the house.

"How did you get here?"

"Took a cab."

"And you'll take a cab back?"

"No other way. Anyone gives me a ride and he sees me being dropped off, there will be the third degree. Matthias knows when I am lying," she added, and smiled ruefully. "I have tried it, and I can't get away with it. I am not one of life's natural liars."

"Okay, so go back now," Gaines said. He turned to Maryanne. "Can you call Della a cab?"

"Of course," Maryanne said.

"Do not talk to him about anything but regular things," Gaines went on. "Only if you feel he is aware that you are speaking to us, only if you feel your life is in danger, do you do something. You get ahold of me, of Maryanne, of Hagen, Ross, anyone, and let us know you are in trouble, and we will be there. I am hoping that such a situation won't arise."

"And you? What are you going to do?"

"We are going to do whatever it takes to get Matthias in a room where we can ask him enough questions to trip him up. If we can wear him down, if we can find anything incriminating at all, then we have a prayer."

"The gun," Della asked. "The gun that was used to kill Leon Devereaux. Was it there at the scene? Did whoever killed him leave it behind?"

Gaines looked at Hagen.

"Gradney never mentioned it," he said. "He didn't give me any details."

"Why d'you want to know?" Gaines asked.

"I know a little about guns," Della replied. "Enough to know what's a revolver, what's not. If there was no gun there and Matthias did kill him, then maybe the gun he used is in the house. I know where he keeps his guns."

"Call Gradney," Gaines told Hagen.

Maryanne got up to show Hagen where the phone was. Hagen was no more than a minute or two. He returned to the kitchen and said, "They don't have ballistics confirmation, but Gradney says that from the look of it, it wasn't a big caliber. He says maybe a .22 or a .25. Not a .38. Said there wasn't enough frontal damage for a .38."

"I'll look," Della said. "I know the difference between a .38 and a smaller-caliber gun. If I find something, I'll contact Maryanne."

"You have to take care, Della. Seriously, we've had three deaths here in the last week and a half—granted one of them was a suicide—but this is all tied together. I do not need another killing in Whytesburg."

Della Wade got up from her chair and straightened her coat. "I have no intention of dying just yet, Sheriff Gaines. I have a man up at Parchman expecting to come back and find me very much alive."

Gaines rose also, took Della's hand, held it for just a moment. "What you are doing is very much appreciated," he said. "I want you to know that."

"I am not doing it for you, Sheriff," she said. "I am doing it for myself and maybe for Nancy Denton and Michael Webster. Seems that maybe Leon Devereaux might have got what he deserved, but I can find no justification for what was done to Nancy and Michael. They loved each other. Was that their crime?"

She turned and looked at Maryanne. "You knew them," she said. "They didn't deserve that, did they?"

"No," Maryanne said. "They did not."

"Take care," Gaines said, and he released her hand.

Maryanne showed her to the door, waited with her for the minutes before the cab arrived.

She returned to the kitchen, found the three men in silence.

It seemed to be some small eternity before anyone uttered a word.

68

She came to him in his dreams.

Della Wade.

Of course it was not her, not in appearance, but in her words, it could have been no one else.

And in listening to her, he knew that she had lied to him.

The war raged about them, and they stood in some clearing. Through the overhanging trees, he could still see the ghosts of tracers, the way the phosphorous hung above the ground, and there was the smell of cordite and blood and the stagnant water that seemed to find its way into everything—your fatigues, your boots, your skin.

For a while she looked like a little Vietnamese girl. She stood silent, and there was blood on her *ai do*, and there was blood on her hands.

It was the blood on her hands that told Gaines that she had lied.

The blood on her hands made him think about what she had said.

And then the little girl opened her mouth, and though she did not make a sound, Gaines could understand what she was saying.

War cleanses men of all that is best in them.

It cleanses with fire, with bullets and blades and bombs and blood.

It cleanses with loss and pain.

But the only things that can kill you out here are faithlessness and shortness of breath.

Later, when Gaines woke from the dream, the memory of it fading from his thoughts too rapidly, he recalled Della's words.

He would send Devereaux to shoot him in the head.

It was that statement, those few words, that did not ring true.

Gaines, sitting there on the edge of his bed, looking out the window and awaiting the ghost of dawn that slept just a few inches beneath the horizon, did not believe that Matthias Wade had said any such thing to his younger brother.

Matthias Wade, if nothing else, was a smart man.

Matthias Wade may very well have threatened Eugene, but he would not have used Leon Devereaux's name.

That did not make sense.

Gaines could have been wrong, of course. He knew that. He knew he could be wrong about Michael Webster. He may have been the one who stole Nancy Denton away that night and strangled her. He knew he could be wrong about Marvin Wallace. He could be wrong about Matthias Wade. Matthias could be no more responsible for the death of Nancy Denton than he was himself.

This was not detective work. This was a blunt and brutal fist of a thing, constantly hammering away at nothing in the hope that some small truth might be revealed. He was surrounded by liars, people who knew things that they would not share, people who themselves had been misled, deceived, betrayed. He had no leads. He had nothing of significance or consequence, and it had been this way right from the start. He had made guesses and assumptions. He had chased shadows and specters. He had asked questions of those who did not wish to be asked and read a second meaning into their answers.

And this was what he had, in and of itself the merest shadow of the truth, and it served in the absence of anything else.

However, Gaines knew he had to believe in something, so he chose to believe that Della Wade had lied to him about Eugene and Leon Devereaux.

Gaines showered and dressed. He made coffee. He stood on the back porch and looked out toward the trees.

He closed his eyes and spoke to his mother. He hoped she was well, that she had found peace, that there was something beyond this life that made this life make sense.

He dared to believe that there might be something, for what was here made no sense at all. The world made no sense, people made no sense; what they did to one another, what they said. How man treated his fellow man, not just in war, but also in peace, for peace seemed to be nothing but a charade to pass the time between each outbreak of violence. He had read this one time, that there had been eleven days of peace in the last two thousand years. Why would people want to live this way? Why would such a thing be considered a worthwhile existence?

He drank his coffee. He smoked his cigarette. He knew he had to go up to the Wade house and confront the truth.

Once inside, Gaines pressed a clean shirt, shined his shoes, cleaned, and reloaded his gun, even gave a sheen to the worn leather holster he had used since he'd first joined the Breed County Sheriff's Department.

Today was the day.

Today something would happen.

Enough of the lies, the deceptions, the mysteries, the unknowns.

Today the truth would out, and if the truth would not be coaxed out with words, then perhaps something else was needed.

Perhaps a war.

Perhaps that's what he would deliver into the hands of Matthias and Della Wade: a war.

Someone should go with him. But not Hagen. Hagen was a married man, a man with children. Nate Ross or Eddie Holland. Perhaps both of them.

And then Gaines decided against it. This was a matter of law, and he represented the law. Eddie was retired and no longer possessed any official authority. Nate was a lawyer, not a policeman. If Gaines could not deal with this alone, then he could not deal with it at all.

And so he waited, waited until the sun had broken the horizon and started its slow ascent. He stood inside the front doorway of his mother's house, and he watched as the colors of the fields and trees were revealed, as the shadows lengthened, as the redbirds and thrashers finished their chorus, and then he walked down to his car, started the engine, and drove away from Whytesburg toward that beautiful old house on the banks of the Pearl River.

This was the end of it.

It had to be.

69

Sheriff John Gaines, standing there between the high pillars of the Wade house entranceway, was permitted by one of the staff to step inside.

Gaines told them he had come to visit with Mr. Wade, and yet they did not ask which one. Gaines was shown into a small library to the right of the reception hall, and here he waited for Matthias Wade to appear.

He waited a good fifteen minutes, and then the door opened, and through that door—pushed in a bamboo and wicker wheelchair—came Earl Wade, smartly dressed, a cream-colored three-piece suit, an open-necked shirt with a neatly tied cravat, the expression on his face one of curiosity, interest, a slight degree of concern, perhaps.

Gaines rose from where he had been seated.

Earl Wade, all of seventy-six years old, smiled at Gaines and said, "Excuse me, sir, for not rising to greet you, but my legs refuse to cooperate this morning."

Gaines walked toward him, extended his hand. "A pleasure to meet you, Mr. Wade."

They shook. Wade's grip was firm and resolute.

"They came and told me a sheriff was here, someone asking for Mr. Wade. I imagine you came to visit with Matthias, but Matthias is not here."

"I did come to see Matthias, sir, but I do appreciate your courtesy."

"Well, I understand that he will not be long, that he is attending to some small matter at one of the factories. Meanwhile, you and I shall keep company, and he will be here momentarily."

Wade turned to the elderly woman who had pushed him into the room. "I will have tea, Martha," he said. He turned back to Gaines. "Coffee, Sheriff, or will you join me in some tea?"

"Tea would be fine," Gaines said.

"Tea, Martha, for two, and I will have lemon."

Martha acknowledged the request and left the room.

Gaines watched the old man. He was smiling, but not at Gaines. His attention was directed toward something in the middle of the room, though Gaines could not determine what he might have been looking at.

For a short while, it was as if Gaines were not there at all.

"There are moments, are there not?" Earl Wade said, and yet he did not turn his attention to Gaines until he had asked the question.

"Moments, sir?"

Wade smiled. "I remember when we had dinner with Ron Richardson. You remember that?"

Gaines opened his mouth to speak, to suggest that Wade might have mistaken Gaines for someone else, but Wade went on as if Gaines were not present.

"He was a drinker, no question about it. Never known a man who could drink so much and still stand up." Wade laughed. "Remember what he said about his wife? Said she set a mattress down on the garage floor for when he stumbled home drunk. She didn't want to be woken by his noise or his stink or his crude advances. 'Need my beauty sleep.' That's what she said. 'Hell,' Ron said, 'she could sleep straight through till Judgment Day; ain't gonna make a mite of difference.' You remember when he said that?"

Gaines said nothing.

"One time he shot that dog. Shot it clean through the head. Thought it was deer, he said. I asked him how the hell he could mistake a dog for a deer. I mean the damn thing was some sort of spaniel, some sort of little thing, you know? 'I was drunk,' he said. 'I was just drunk.' 'And that's your get-out clause?' I asked him. 'You were drunk?'"

Wade's laughter at this recollection was interrupted only by Martha returning with tea. She served them both without a word, and then she left the room and silently closed the door behind her.

"Matthias isn't here?" Wade said.

"So I understand," Gaines said.

"I don't know where he is and I don't know what he's doing. That boy is a law unto himself. All of them are. Useless, the lot of them. Useless children."

"I think he is attending to some business matters at one of the factories," Gaines said.

"Yes, I think you're right, sir," Wade replied. "And what has he done now? Is he in trouble with the law again?"

"Again?"

"Oh, you know Matthias. He's always in some sort of difficulty, always having to explain his way out of some hole he's dug for himself. Only two weeks ago he decided it would be a good idea to urinate in the fish pond. I mean, seriously, what possible purpose could be served by urinating on the fish? Unfortunately, his mother has banned me from beating him."

Earl Wade sipped his tea. His attention drifted again.

Gaines's attention was distracted by the sound of footsteps above their heads.

"Do you have cigarettes?" Wade suddenly asked.

"Yes, sir, I do."

"Oh, let me have one. They don't let me have cigarettes anymore. Treat me like a goddamned child."

Gaines fetched the packet out from his shirt pocket. Wade took the cigarette excitedly, his hands trembling as Gaines lit it for him, and then he greedily inhaled, leaning his head back and closing his eyes.

Wade turned back to Gaines, but his eyes were closed. "It is a sad state of affairs when you start to despise your own children," he said. His voice was measured and precise, as if he were giving a sworn statement. "Matthias is a son of a bitch; Della is a whore, Eugene is a churchgoing Bible-quoting queer who thinks he can sing, and Catherine thinks she's too damned good to have anything to do with us anymore. I hate them all."

Wade took another draw on the cigarette and smiled. "A bastard, a whore, a queer, and a bitch. Those are the fruits of my loins. They say that friends are the family you choose. If I had the choice, I'd see all of them off with nothing, and I'd give all my money to my friends."

"Marvin Wallace," Gaines said. "He is one of your friends, isn't he?"

"Marvin. Marvin Wallace. Yes, Marvin Wallace is a good man. Marvin sorted out that terrible business, you know?"

"Terrible business?"

Wade reached for his tea. It seemed for a moment that the cup would slip from his fingers, but he regained control of it.

"What terrible business, Mr. Wade?"

"My wife was beautiful, you know?" Wade said. "Did you ever meet my wife?"

"No, sir, I didn't." Gaines edged forward on his chair. He wanted to rewind the conversation before it drifted even further. "I was wondering what you meant when you said that Marvin Wallace helped you sort out some terrible business."

"Yes, he did, God bless him. Lillian never really liked Marvin, you know, but then a man's friends and a man's family are better kept apart, wouldn't you say?"

"Lillian was your wife—"

"Lillian is my wife, yes. She's been gone for quite a while now, and I don't know what she thinks she's doing. She was supposed to be back hours ago." Wade dropped the smoked cigarette into his teacup and asked for another.

Gaines gave it to him, helped him light it.

"You, sir, will be in the deepest trouble imaginable when they find out that you have been giving me cigarettes."

"I think they might have more serious things to concern themselves with, sir."

"Serious, yes. Why do they always have to be so serious? When did everyone become so damned serious?"

Gaines hesitated. He let Wade's words hang in the air for moment, and then he said, "Marvin Wallace said that there was some trouble that needed sorting out."

"Marvin Wallace needs to learn how to keep his mouth damned well shut. Man needs to get some backbone."

"He's been saying things, you understand."

Wade frowned, leaned forward out of the chair. "There are things that you talk about and things that you don't. Marvin Wallace needs to learn the difference, or we're all going to pay the price."

Gaines didn't understand what was happening. It was like listening to Webster again. What was Wade talking about? Pay the price for what?

Gaines knew there was no way to force Wade to speak, but questions—gently directed questions—could perhaps prompt him to say more.

"Wallace said that Matthias—"

"You spoke to Wallace?" Wade asked suddenly.

"Yes, I did."

"When?"

"Yesterday."

"Did you go and see him, or did he come to you?"

"He came to see me."

Wade sneered derisively. "I knew it. I knew he was weak. I knew he would be the first one to speak. Goddamn him!"

"He told me some of what happened."

"Did he, now?"

"Yes."

"And what did he tell you? What did he tell you exactly?"

"He told you nothing, Sheriff Gaines."

Gaines turned suddenly.

Della Wade stood there in the doorway. She took three steps forward, snatched the half-smoked cigarette from her father's hand, and dropped it in the teacup.

"Martha!" she shouted. "Martha, get in here right now!"

Martha hurried into the room.

"I don't know who the hell you thought this was, or why you let him in, but he has been in here with Father, upsetting him and giving him cigarettes. Take Father upstairs now."

"Sorry, ma'am," Martha said. "I thought it was some sort of official business."

"See?" Wade said to Gaines. "See the kind of crap I have to put up with from these inconsiderate, selfish . . . Jesus Christ, this is intolerable." He looked up at Della as he was wheeled from the room. "Whore!" he snapped.

Della closed her eyes for a moment and said nothing until her father was gone. She closed the door behind him and then stood there looking at Gaines as if Gaines had himself been the one to curse at her.

"What are you doing here?" she asked.

"It has to end, Miss Wade. This has to end. I can't let this go on anymore."

"Let what go on, exactly? What is it that you think has to end?"

"All the lies. Whatever happened to Nancy, whatever happened to Michael Webster and Leon Devereaux. Your brother knows the truth, and if he is involved, then he needs to be held accountable for what he's done."

"You came to me for help. I helped you. I am doing this my way, and that is the way it is going to be done."

"I can't let that happen. This is police business. People have been killed. Not only killed, but their bodies—"

"I know what has happened, Sheriff, and I told you that I would help you. What I did not expect was to find you in my house, talking to my father."

"Your father said—"

"What my father said or did not say is neither here nor there,

Sheriff. My father does not understand what he is saying, and even if he does, it bears no relevance to what is happening here."

"He said that Marvin Wallace needed to keep his mouth shut or they were all going to pay the price. What did he mean, Miss Wade? What did your father mean by that?"

For a split second, the air of self-possession became transparent. Had Gaines not been looking directly at her, he would not have seen it.

"I do not know, Sheriff Gaines. I have absolutely no idea what he might have meant."

"I think you do, Miss Wade. I think you know precisely what he meant."

Gaines got to his feet. He looked back at her unerringly.

"So what? You're now going to start accusing me of being involved in what has happened here? What my brother is involved in is not something I know about, or want to know about."

"I don't believe you, Miss Wade," Gaines said. "I don't think Matthias spoke to Eugene, or maybe he spoke to him but he did not tell him about Leon Devereaux. I think Matthias is far smarter than that. He would not name names, would he, Miss Wade? He did not threaten you with Leon Devereaux, did he? That's not what you said. You said that he threatened Eugene. And Clifton never mentioned Leon. Clifton did not know who cut his fingers off. That name came from you, and only you."

Della Wade waved Gaines's comments aside. "You are imagining connections where no connection exists, Sheriff," she said.

"No, Miss Wade, I don't believe I am. I think this is a family matter. I think this has always been a family matter, and you each are doing whatever you can to protect the precious Wade name. I think something happened here in 1954, and something else happened in January of 1968 out near Morgan City, and your older brother, the black sheep of the family, was responsible. I think your father knew, and I think you knew, and I think you have been hiding the truth for all these years."

"You really are reaching, Sheriff."

"And Leon Devereaux? I think he killed Michael Webster, and he was told to do this by Matthias, and then maybe Matthias got scared that Devereaux would talk, or maybe you finally found out that Devereaux was the one who hurt Clifton, and you went out there and you shot Devereaux. Devereaux was dead two days after I found Michael Webster's head buried in the field behind my house. Leon

Devereaux was dead five days before you even showed up at Nate Ross's place, and you performed so well, Miss Wade. You acted your part so very well, and you made us all believe that you knew nothing of what was going on."

Della Wade smiled quietly. "You don't know anything about me, Sheriff, and you know nothing about my family. Matthias is the very last person in the world I would protect. Matthias is a vicious son of a bitch, intent on nothing more than controlling everything and everyone around him. He keeps me here, he keeps our father here, and anyone who does not agree with him—Catherine and Eugene most of all—he disowns them, doesn't speak to them, threatens them to stay away from here or he will ruin them. If Leon Devereaux killed Michael Webster, then it was Matthias who told him to do it. And if Leon Devereaux is dead, then either Matthias killed him or he sent someone to do it. I spoke to Eugene, and Eugene told me that Matthias had threatened him. I have no wish to see my father suffer for what Matthias may or may not have done, but I have even less of a desire to protect Matthias from the consequences of his actions. If Matthias killed Nancy Denton, then so be it. If that is the truth, then he should be charged and tried and sentenced like anyone else. If he killed Michael Webster, or he was involved in his death, then he should suffer the penalty for that as well."

"Did Matthias kill Nancy Denton, Miss Wade? Or did someone else kill her?"

Della Wade stood silently. She did not blink.

"Was it Matthias, or was it someone else? Someone you could never have challenged as a child, someone who would have been believed so much more than you? Is that why your mother drank herself to death, Miss Wade? Is that why your father is so afraid the truth will come out? Did your father kill her, Miss Wade? Did he strangle Nancy Denton? Did he kill those girls in Morgan City in 1968? Is that the truth, Miss Wade?"

"Enough!" she snapped. "I will not have you stand here and accuse my father of being a murderer—"

"But you are not defending him, Miss Wade. You are not denying it, are you?"

"You need to leave now, Sheriff. You need to leave this house right now."

"And what about Michael Webster, crazy son of a bitch that he was, believing that he could bring her back to life? You didn't know

387

he did that, did you? You didn't know that that was what had happened to her body, did you? You just thought that your father had buried her somewhere, or maybe thrown her down a dry well or something. You never thought she would be found, did you? How much of a surprise was that? It came back, after all these years, and now your father is sick; now he's lost half his mind, and there is no way he could ever be brought to trial for this. So what do you do? You want Matthias to pay for your father's crimes. You want Matthias to pay because he's caused you so much upset. You want him to pay for what he did to you and Clifton. You want Matthias to spend the rest of his life looking out through the bars of a prison cell—"

Della Wade did not say a word. She smiled, and she slowly shook her head.

"You are more like Michael than you think," she said. "You went to war. War makes men crazy. There is no way a man can return from war and be a whole man ever again. You left some piece of yourself there, just like Michael did. Nancy was ours. She belonged to us. To me and Matthias. Then he came back and he took her from us. And I was glad when she disappeared. I was pleased she was gone, because life could get back to how it was before. But that didn't happen, because she wasn't there. Michael came home, and because of Michael she was gone, and then everything was ruined—"

"Did Matthias kill her, Della? Or did your father kill her?"

Della Wade glared at Gaines. Her expression was cold and hateful.

"Was it Matthias, or was it your father, Della? Which one of them killed Nancy Denton and left her in that shack for Michael Webster to find?"

Della Wade closed her eyes and lowered her head. She inhaled slowly, exhaled again.

"Was it neither of them?" Gaines asked. "Someone else?"

Della just stood there—motionless, silent—and yet something about her said that she was bearing a burden that was almost impossible to carry.

"Someone else?" Gaines repeated. "Was it someone else? Have you all been protecting someone else?"

There was a thought there, right at the front of his mind. Something that Webster had said, or was it something he had dreamed? It was there, right there, and he couldn't grasp it.

Della Wade raised her head and looked at Gaines. There were tears in her eyes.

"Is that what your father meant when he said that if Wallace spoke, you would all pay the price? You and Matthias and your father? All of you? Why, Della? Because you all withheld the truth that it was someone else entirely? And who could that have been, eh? Who would you all want to protect?"

"You need to leave, Sheriff Gaines. There is nothing for you here. You will find no resolution, no answers, no peace. It is all history now. It is all too old for anyone to care about anymore. Nancy is dead, as is her mother, Michael, too. And Leon Devereaux, whoever he was and whatever he might have done, he is gone as well. There is no one left now. There's no one who cares but you, and you don't need to care, Sheriff. You really *don't* need to go on caring about people no one else even remembers."

"But I do, Miss Wade. I do need to go on caring, and the fact that no one else remembers these people is precisely why I need to go on caring."

"The truth is relative, Sheriff, and the truth is rarely found even when people want you to know the truth. More often than not, the truth people tell you is just the truth they want you to believe."

"The truth can be found, Miss Wade, and it will be. That I can assure you."

"And if you find the truth, Sheriff, what will you do then? It won't bring them back. It won't bring any of them back. Not Nancy, not Michael, not your mother. The truth does not set you free, Sheriff, especially if you have decided to be a prisoner of that truth."

Gaines knew he should have felt such anger inside, but he felt very little at all.

He knew that Della Wade had been dying from within, maintaining such lies, such deceptions, such secrets.

The return of Nancy Denton had brought it all home again, had carried the terrible reminders of the truth to the door of the Wade house, had started to undermine the very foundations of everything they had created and maintained for twenty years.

Perhaps she'd had enough. Perhaps her mention of Leon Devereaux to Gaines had been intentional. Perhaps she had wanted someone, anyone, to finally learn the truth of what had happened.

Perhaps they were not guilty of these crimes themselves, but they were guilty of withholding what they knew, of perverting the course of justice, of aiding and abetting a killer, of building a wall around themselves that had withstood all attempts to breach it.

Ironic, but a dead girl had brought everything crashing down around their ears, and now they were scrabbling desperately through the rubble trying to rebuild a castle that would never stand again.

"I am going," Gaines said. "I have an investigation to pursue."

Gaines took his hat from the table.

He glanced once more at Della, and she opened her mouth as if to say one final thing.

Gaines looked at her expectantly.

She shook her head. A tear escaped her lid and rolled down her cheek. "Nothing," she said, her voice cracking. "It is nothing."

70

As he drove, Gaines considered every aspect of this, and believed without doubt that Della Wade knew the truth.

This started and ended with the Wade family—perhaps Earl, perhaps Matthias, perhaps someone else—but it was all about the Wades.

Once at his office, he went back to the evidence locker. He took the Morgan City file, the photo album, and Webster's Bible to his office.

He opened the photo album, and he looked at those faces. They looked back at him from some long-ago history.

Those four people—Michael, Matthias, Nancy, and Maryanne—and then there were the other Wade children . . .

And then there was the Bible.

Gaines picked up the Bible, opened it, and studied it properly for the first time. Battered, weatherworn, the leather dry and cracked, it had nevertheless been a very expensive thing at one time. The kind of Bible given as a gift, perhaps at a first Communion, perhaps for a birthday.

Her name was there—inscribed beautifully—three or four pages in.

Lillian Tresselt.

And Gaines had been right, because directly beneath it were the words, *Given on the occasion of your first Communion, with love from your mother and father.*

Lillian Wade, née Tresselt. Her Bible. Her *own* Bible, given to Webster by *E.*

This helped me. E.

Gaines opened the Bible. He saw something underlined.

I know your works. Behold, I have set before you an open door, which no one is able to shut.

He flicked through the pages, and it seemed that within a few further pages of wherever he looked, there was something else underlined. So many passages to which he had paid so little attention, all of them possessive of one common theme.

I am the door. If anyone enters by me, he will be saved and will go in and out and find pasture.

Strive to enter through the narrow door. For many, I tell you, will seek to enter and will not be able.

Behold, I stand at the door and knock. If anyone hears my voice and opens the door, I will come in to him and eat with him, and he with me.

For a wide door for effective work has opened to me, and there are many adversaries.

And then Gaines took up the Morgan City files, and as he looked closely at the pictures of the two dead girls, it became so clear. He recalled something that Michael Webster had said, and he had not understood its significance at all. Not until now. Not until this very moment.

She was just there, just right there in a shack at the side of the road. Just lying there in the doorway.

Had Gaines not looked at the Bible, it would have gone unknown forever.

Those girls had been laid out intentionally, right there in the doorway of a shack, much the same as how Michael had described the position in which he had found Nancy Denton.

The doorway. Place a body in a doorway in such a way as to prevent the door from being closed.

It was beyond belief. It stretched Gaines's mind. The implications, the emotional and mental implications; what must have been going through his mind as he gave this to Michael Webster; what Webster must have felt as he received it, believing that someone was trying to help him, to give him respite, succor, a safety net, and yet all the while unaware that this someone was responsible for taking away the very person for whom Michael Webster lived.

It was staggering.

And what must have gone through his mind when he had done these things? What had he been trying to do?

Gaines sat down in his chair. It felt as if a great weight had been lifted and then lowered once again upon his shoulders with even greater force.

He knew where he had to go, but he could not go alone. He needed someone with him who would recognize who he was looking for.

Gaines called Hagen in, explained the situation rapidly, sent him east to bring Maryanne Benedict from Gulfport. Once Hagen had left, Gaines set to work.

Finding someone who did not wish to be found was difficult, but Clifton Regis had given Gaines enough of a direction to pursue. At least Gaines knew where to look, the kind of people he needed to talk to.

By the time Hagen arrived back with Maryanne Benedict, Gaines had determined that the only hope he had was to drive there and look for himself.

"I need you to come with us," he told Maryanne. "I think we are going to be too late, but I need you to come with us."

"You have to tell me where we're going and why," she said. "You have to tell me what's happened."

Gaines sat with her in his office. He explained as best he could. She said she could not believe it, but she did not challenge Gaines.

"I knew him," she said after a while. "I even loved him, in my own childish way."

"So did Nancy," Gaines said. "She knew him, trusted him more than likely, and never would have suspected that he was going to do what he did."

"And they knew? The family? They all knew and they hid it?"

Gaines shook his head. "I don't know the details, Maryanne. I don't know exactly what happened, or why, or how."

"And the girls . . . the other girls, the ones from Morgan City?"

"I think so, yes. I think he killed them, too."

Maryanne sat in silence for a while, and then she got up from the chair and walked to the window. "But why? What was he trying to do? What was the meaning of strangling little girls and leaving them in a doorway somewhere?"

"I don't know," Gaines replied. "Maybe he thought the door through which they left was also a door through which someone could come back. Maybe he believed that he was trading lives. That is something only he can explain to us."

She turned and looked at Gaines. "Lillian," she said, and it was not a question.

Gaines nodded. "That's what I think, too."

"If they knew what he'd done . . . if they actually knew what he'd done and they said nothing, then they—" She shook her head, disbelieving, confused. "And what happened with Clifton Regis? What happened with him and Della?"

"I think Della loved him, still does, and they wanted to get away. I think it happened exactly as she said, exactly as Clifton told me. Matthias found out, and Clifton got a visit from Leon Devereaux. Then, just to make sure that he couldn't get to his sister, Matthias used whatever influence he had with Wallace to get Clifton sent up to Parchman. I don't think that Matthias is capable of killing anyone, but I think he's more than capable of warning them in the very strongest terms. Clifton Regis ends up in jail for his trouble, and Della's under house arrest. I think Matthias has them both good and scared."

"And Earl Wade?"

"I think he knew. I think it comes back to him every once in a while, but I don't think he even understands what he knows anymore."

"And why not tell the truth? Why not just tell the truth of what happened and be done with it?"

"I don't know, Maryanne. The family name, the reputation, the shame, the fact that this is something that started, as far as we know, all of twenty years ago, and even after the first week of hiding it, any one of them could have been charged with aiding and abetting a felon, of obstructing justice, any number of things."

She was pensive then, an air of defeatism hanging over her, as if her fundamental belief in the rightness of life, her certainty regarding the natural balance and order of things had been tilted wildly from its axis. Such a change in perspective could not be reverted. Such a conviction could never again be restored.

"I am sorry," she said

"For what?"

"I don't know. I really don't know what I should be sorry for, but I feel I should be. Sorry that I didn't ask more questions. Sorry that I didn't remember her more often. Sorry I forgot that she was dead."

"You can't be sorry for such things," Gaines said.

"Maybe not, but I am," she replied. "So what do we do?"

"We go and find him."

"Do you think we will?"

"Yes, I do. I don't know where, but I think we will find him."

71

It was easier than Gaines had expected to find Eugene Wade. Gaines had not known what obstacles he would encounter. New Orleans was a big city, and if a man wished to be lost, then he could be lost so very easily. But it seemed that Eugene did not want to be lost; he did not want to be invisible, and within an hour they had an address from the phone directory, an old address granted, an address where Eugene no longer lived, but the current tenant was a friend of Eugene's and gave them the address to which he'd moved only weeks before.

Gaines, Hagen, and Maryanne Benedict drove over there. Gaines asked Maryanne if she would be willing to stay in the car while they went up and checked out the place.

"Are you serious?" she asked. "Really? After fetching me all the way from home, you want me to stay in the car? Not a hope, Sheriff. If what you think is true, if Eugene Wade killed Nancy Denton and that family hid this thing for all these years, then I want to see the son of a bitch's face when you confront him."

They crossed the street and knocked on the door. An elderly woman answered, asked after their business. Gaines produced ID, said they were hoping to see Eugene Wade.

"More than likely he ain't here," she said. "Music playing so loud all the time when he is, but you go on up and check. You go see for yourself. All the way to the top in the attic. His room's up there."

Gaines went first, Maryanne behind him, Hagen last.

They had spoken little on the drive over, and though they had been in the car for more than an hour, it seemed as though that hour had vanished within a moment.

"It makes sense," Maryanne said at one point. "I don't want it to make sense, but it does. That night, the night he left with Catherine and Della. He must have gone back to the house and then left again to find us. Maybe he came down through the woods and saw her with Michael. She wouldn't have been alarmed, not to see Eugene.

Maybe she went to speak to him, left Michael behind for a moment, and . . . and he must have just . . ." Her voice trailed into silence.

Gaines did not speak. She was putting these things together just as he had and seeing a truth that she did not want to see.

"Eugene was sixteen when Nancy went missing," Maryanne said. "He strangled her. Michael found the body, did what he did, and then Matthias found out. I think Matthias has known all this time. Earl, too. Maybe even Della. And they hid this from everyone."

"What else were they going to do?" Gaines asked. "This is the Wade family. This is the Wade name. This is a dynasty that's supposed to go on, generation after generation. They can't possibly tell the world that they have a killer in their midst."

"And they just let him get away with it?"

"They let him get away with a great deal more than the death of Nancy Denton. There was Morgan City as well. I think Eugene killed those two little girls, and that's when Matthias knew he had to get Eugene away somewhere. I think we'll find that Eugene's rent, his bills, everything is paid for. And it's paid for by Matthias. He's the one directing this, dictating how it goes. He has his own situations to deal with, his own secrets, believe me. I think he has done everything he can to keep the Wade name free of scandal. I think he used Leon Devereaux to do a great many things that we will never know about, least of which was separating Della and Clifton."

"And Matthias killed Devereaux?"

"Again, I am not sure. Maybe he did, or maybe Della killed him. We are going to find out." Gaines shook his head resignedly. "Or maybe we'll never know."

Maryanne fell silent again, looking from the window as they crossed the bridge, trying perhaps to come to terms with what was now unfolding around her, trying perhaps not to think of it at all.

They went quietly, Gaines at the head of the trio, stepping lightly on the edges of the risers so as to make as little sound as possible. Why he felt it necessary to do this, he could not have explained. He was delivering an unwanted message, a statement of the truth to someone who wished for such a truth to never be known. He felt as if he were invading someone's life, someone's reality, and though it was necessary, though it was vital that such an invasion occur, it nevertheless felt strangely cruel. It was not something that Gaines considered greatly, for there had been so many strange and disparate emotions throughout these past days that something further was of no great concern.

Gaines stopped on the uppermost landing and waited for Maryanne Benedict and Richard Hagen to reach him. They stood together, they looked at one another, and for a moment Gaines held his breath.

His heart did not race, nor his pulse, nor the blood in his temples. He felt no rush of adrenaline, no agitation of nerves in his gut. He felt calm, unhurried, as if he had all the time in the world.

He raised his hand and knocked on the door.

"Mr. Wade?" he asked. "Eugene Wade?"

There was no immediate answer.

"Mr. Wade . . . this is the Breed County Sheriff's Department."

Not a sound came from inside the room.

Gaines unclipped his holster.

"You going in?" Hagen asked.

Gaines nodded.

"Warrant?"

"Not gonna get one, and right now I don't care," Gaines replied.

He reached out and turned the handle. The door was locked.

"Back up," he said. Maryanne and Hagen did so, and Gaines, stepping away two or three feet, then raised his right foot and kicked the door just at the side of the lock. The frame was not substantial, and the door opened suddenly, slamming back against the inside wall.

The smell was immediate and unquestioningly familiar.

Gaines told Hagen to stay with Maryanne for a moment, and he went on inside.

He held his hand to his face. This was two days', three days' dead, and he knew that at least some small part of this mystery was now resolved.

Later, the autopsy complete, the coroner would estimate time of death somewhere between six a.m. and noon on Saturday the 3rd.

Eugene Wade had not known how to hang himself. He did not understand the basic mechanics of weight versus speed of descent, factoring in such things as the length of the drop and how this determined the force brought to bear upon the cervical vertebrae.

Hanging people was a science. A simple science perhaps, but a science all the same.

Eugene had been dead for three days, and it seemed at first that no one had known.

But later—once the facts of his injury was made known to Gaines—it became obvious that Eugene had been visited by someone. It did not take a great leap of imagination to determine who that might have been.

Eugene Wade's left hand was bandaged tightly, and once those bandages were removed, it was evident that one of his fingers was missing. The wound had become infected, and had he not received treatment, the blood poisoning alone might have killed him. It was also noted, confirming Gaines's suspicion regarding the identity of his assailant, that Eugene Wade's blood type was AB.

Later, Gaines tried to imagine the conversation that had taken place between Eugene and Leon Devereaux. What had Matthias sent Devereaux to tell him? That he should disappear out of the state? That he should disappear for good? Had Eugene responded by saying that he would tell everything, that he would confess to the killing of Nancy Denton, that he would ruin the Wade name for all time?

Leon's visit must have changed everything. Leon sang a different song. Perhaps he told Eugene that he was now on his own, that the game was over. The girl's body had been found, and the soldier who loved her was dead. Eugene had no way out. If he confessed, well, Matthias had a judge in his pocket. Eugene's accusations—unfounded, a lone voice of protest—would be ruled inadmissible by Marvin Wallace. Eugene would be charged also with the murder of Michael Webster, and he would go up to Parchman Farm for life. And perhaps that life wouldn't be so long: there would be a disagreement, an exercise yard altercation, and Eugene Wade would be found bleeding out from a stomach wound in the dirt. Maybe Matthias Wade would get Clifton Regis to do it, the perfect irony, and Clifton would be promised exoneration and release, a reunion with Della. Of course, Della and Clifton would never be able to stay at the house; they would have to move away, to disappear and make their own life with whatever Wade money they could get, but a sister married to a colored was far and away a better burden to bear than a serial killer for a brother.

Had Matthias told Leon to hurt Eugene, to physically harm him, or had Leon taken the law into his own hands and exceeded his brief?

So Eugene had no more money, and time was at his heels. He was caught between Leon Devereaux and an altogether unknown future.

Perhaps Eugene had long since decided that he would never

run, that he would make his escape more final, more complete, an escape that could never be undone.

The guilt he carried for the deaths of Nancy Denton, Anna-Louise Mayhew, and Dorothy McCormick had finally brought sufficient pressure to bear on him that he knew he could hide no further.

Or maybe he had considered some thought like Judith Denton. Maybe if I go now, I will find that my mother is still waiting for me.

So it came back to the other option, the easiest one of all.

And it was that option he decided to take in the early hours of Saturday, the 3rd of August, 1974.

He hung himself right there in his own attic apartment from a rafter in the ceiling. The rope he had selected was too fine for such a job, and—in the few hours after he had choked out his last breath—the weight of his body had brought such constriction to bear upon his throat that his face was almost black. His tongue protruded, distended and swollen, and his eyes were a deep red.

He had hung there for three days. No one knew, save perhaps Leon Devereaux and Matthias Wade. No one else had cared enough to find out where he was.

Gaines looked at that black and distended face for a long time, and then he walked back out to the hallway.

"Go down and call it in," he told Hagen.

Maryanne accompanied Hagen. Hagen asked the landlady for the use of her phone.

Gaines returned to Eugene's room and made a cursory search. He did not expect to find anything that would directly implicate Eugene Wade in the murder of Nancy Denton, nor the murders of Dorothy McCormick and Anna-Louise Mayhew. But just as had been the case so many times in the preceding weeks, what he expected and what he got were not the same thing.

Gaines found the small leather suitcase open at the foot of the bed, left there—it seemed—to be found.

Within it were newspaper clippings, photographs, odd and unrelated articles—a faded yellow ribbon, a small gold locket, a dried flower—now little more than dust—pressed inside a folded sheet of paper, a silver bangle with a turquoise stone. Other such tokens and mementos.

It was the newspaper clippings that told a story that John Gaines could barely believe.

He sat there on the edge of Eugene Wade's bed, and it seemed that where he was—that stinking attic apartment with a corpse hanging from the rafter—seemed to vanish from his awareness. He leafed through the clippings, scanned the headlines, grasped the import of what he was reading, and he began to understand what Matthias Wade had unleashed when he had chosen to hide the truth of his brother from the world.

He realized he was holding his breath. He inhaled forcibly and perceived the edges of his vision blurring. He felt as if he would lose his balance, and he held on to the edge of the bedframe.

Eventually, he rose, gathered up the small case, and walked back to where Eugene Wade hung from the rafter.

Gaines looked at the man's face, almost unrecognizable though it was, and he knew he was looking at the face of the devil.

72

Gaines left Hagen behind to deal with the local authorities. He did not speak of the leather case. He did not speak of the newspaper clippings he had found. Hagen was instructed to explain to the attending officers that the dead man was responsible for a twenty-year-old murder. Details were of no great concern now. There were no living relatives to inform of the ultimate justice that had befallen the perpetrator of Nancy Denton's murder. There would be no charges to file, no arraignment to schedule, no jury to select. Gaines would go back and bring closure to the families who had lost their children, of course, but right now that was not his foremost concern.

Maryanne accompanied Gaines to the car.

"We're going back to Whytesburg," he said, "and I'll have one of my deputies drive you home."

She was there on the passenger seat beside him for some minutes before she spoke.

She had seen him set the small case on the rear seat. She had watched as he closed his eyes for a moment before starting the car, the way he had clenched and unclenched his fists, the way his hand shook ever so slightly as he tried to get the key into the ignition.

And then she reached out, and she placed her hand over his, and he looked at her.

"Tell me," she said.

Gaines shook his head. He looked away through the window, and she could see his knuckles whitening as he gripped the steering wheel.

"John?"

And then he nodded, as if reconciling something within himself. He reached behind himself, retrieved the case, and handed it to her.

She held it in her hands and then placed it on her lap.

She placed her fingers on the latches, but she did not open it.

"Look," Gaines said. "You want to know . . . then look."

Maryanne hesitated, and then she flipped the latches. The sound was sharp and loud in the confines of the car.

The smell of musty paper filed her nostrils, and she started to look through the newspaper clippings within.

On the morning of March 19, 1957, a bright and cool Tuesday morning, Jeanette Ferguson, a fourteen year-old girl from Lyman went missing on the way home from school. She was reported missing that same evening. She was found four days later in a derelict house.

On Saturday, November 10, 1960, just a day after John Fitzgerald Kennedy became the youngest man ever to win the presidency, Mary Elizabeth Duggan was found strangled in the back of a Greyhound bus. Mary Elizabeth had boarded the bus in Hattiesburg, Mississippi, bound for Monroe, Louisiana. She was eighteen years old. The bus had made stops in Collins, Magee, Mendenhall, Jackson, Vicksburg, Tallulah, and Rayville. Mary Elizabeth's cousins—Stan and Willa Blakely—had waited in the depot for Mary Elizabeth to disembark. She did not. Puzzled, they asked if they could perhaps search the bus to see if she had somehow remained asleep. The driver said there was no one back there, but he gave them permission to look anyway. At the very back of the vehicle, there beneath the seat, they found Mary Elizabeth on the floor, wrapped from head to toe in a blanket. She was not sleeping. She was dead.

A lengthy and extensive investigation was undertaken. Police departments from both Mississippi and Louisiana were involved. An attempt was made to locate every single passenger who had used that service between Hattiesburg and Monroe, but anyone could buy tickets and no identification was required; nor was any record maintained beyond the number of tickets sold and their respective costs. The investigation, it appeared, had come to nothing.

On Saturday, October 7, 1961, Frances Zimmerman, a nineteen-year-old from Monticello, ironically the girl chosen to present Vice President Richard Nixon with flowers upon his arrival at the Mississippi State Fair in 1958, was found strangled in the men's restroom at Brookhaven train station. She had been left in an open doorway.

August 19, 1962, just two weeks after the death of Marilyn Monroe, Kathleen Snow, a fifteen-year-old, was reported missing from her afternoon classes at St. Mary Magdalene Catholic School for Girls in Jackson. Her friends said she had left the school at lunchtime to *meet someone*. The identity of the person was unknown to her friends, and Kathleen had assured them she would be gone for no more than half an hour. They had promised they would cover for her. Kathleen did not return. Her body was found the following day by a volunteer crossing guard. Kathleen had been strangled, but strangled with such force that the hand prints of her killer were visible on her throat as dark welts.

And so it went on—through '63, '64, a year or two skipped here and there, but those reports seemed endless. And then Maryanne found them. Morgan City, January of 1968, the faces of Dorothy McCormick and Anna-Louise Mayhew.

She held up the clipping. Gaines looked at those faces, and they looked back at him, just as they had from the files he had read in Dennis Young's office.

Fourteen victims spanning seventeen years.

"I can't believe—"

She shook her head, and there were tears in her eyes, and they welled over the lids and rolled down her cheeks.

Gaines started the car.

"You're going to see him . . . Matthias?" she asked.

"Yes."

"I don't want to see him, John."

"You won't, Maryanne. Go home, or even stay in my office, but don't see him."

There was silence between them for the rest of the journey, and once they arrived, Gaines had Forrest Dalton fetch a squad car to take Maryanne home.

It was then, as she left Gaines's office, that she hesitated. She touched his arm, looked at him directly, unerringly, and said, "Enough people have come to grief. Enough people have died. And this man—"

"This man is not going to kill anyone," Gaines replied. "I do not think he has ever killed anyone. I think he got Devereaux to kill Webster, and he hid his brother from the law. I don't even know that he was aware of what Eugene had really done. His crime was his silence, the same as Della, the same as Earl."

"And Devereaux? Didn't he kill Devereaux?"

Gaines shook his head. "I don't believe he did, no. I think Devereaux was killed in revenge for something else entirely."

Her expression was questioning, but it was obvious Gaines was not going to explain further.

"Be careful," she said, and there was something in that entreaty that touched Gaines, as if she really meant it, as if she really wanted to ensure that he came back safely.

"I will," Gaines replied, and then she left.

Half an hour later, Gaines was again at the Wade house. He pounded on the door with the side of his fist, and the door was hurriedly opened. He did not wait to be invited across the threshold. He walked in, the leather suitcase in his hand, said that he needed to see both Matthias and Della, and then he crossed the hallway and entered the same library where he had spoken with Earl Wade only that morning.

Della appeared within a minute.

"What is it?" she said. "What is going on?"

"Where is Matthias?" Gaines asked.

"He's upstairs with Father. Why? Why have you come back here?"

"Eugene is dead," Gaines said matter-of-factly.

Once again, real or perfectly portrayed, Della Wade expressed utter disbelief and shock in her expression, in her absence of words, in the way in which the color drained from her face and her eyes widened.

"Dead?"

"He hung himself, Della. He committed suicide. He has been dead for a few days, and I think it would interest you to know that Leon Devereaux might very well have been the last person to see him. That is an assumption on my part, but I think it will prove to be fact."

Della walked to the window, back to the door, looking sideways at Gaines as if reminding herself that he was in the room, that this wasn't some hideous nightmare from which she could force herself to wake.

"I have a question for you, Della."

She paused, looked directly at him.

"Did you kill Leon Devereaux?"

"Say nothing, Della."

She turned, her mouth open as if to speak, silenced by the sudden appearance of Matthias, entering the room and interrupting proceedings just as she herself had done with her father.

"Do not say a word to this man," Matthias went on. "He has no right to be here. He has no warrant. He has no evidence, no nothing."

Gaines did not speak. He set the leather case down on the table, opened it, and withdrew the sheaf of clippings. He took three or four steps toward Della and held out his hand.

She took them from him.

"What is this?" Matthias asked, and he reached out to take them from Della.

Della snatched her hand back, walked away toward the window and Gaines felt the tension in the room increase in proportion to the slow-dawning realization that was taking place. Perhaps, once again, it was his imagination; perhaps no one but he could sense it, but it was there. He felt sure of it.

When she turned, tears in her eyes, there were many things written in her expression.

For the first time since he'd met her, Gaines believed that now she was going to tell the truth.

"This?" she asked. "This is what?"

"This is what you have done by saying nothing," Gaines said.

"Saying nothing about what? About—"

"About nothing," Matthias interjected. "About some wild flight of imagination that Sheriff Gaines has convinced himself is the truth."

"About the fact that your brother Eugene was the one who killed Nancy Denton. Matthias knew, your father as well, and Judge Wallace, and maybe even Leon Devereaux. I don't know how many more people knew what really happened back then, twenty years ago, but I think Matthias was the only one who knew what happened afterward, right, Matthias?"

Matthias Wade didn't respond. He looked back at Gaines implacably, as if Gaines had commented on nothing more consequential than the weather.

"And this?" Della said, holding out the clippings. "This is Eugene's doing? These are people Eugene has murdered?"

"Seems that when you release a monster from the cage, he doesn't stop being a monster," Gaines said.

"Matthias?" Della said. "Matthias, is this true? Is Eugene responsible for all of this? Did Eugene kill Nancy? Is that what happened?"

She looked back at Gaines. "All this time, I wanted to believe it had nothing to do with us."

"Della," Matthias Wade said, his tone authoritative, almost threatening.

"She just ran away from home. That was all. She was scared,

something happened, something we knew nothing about, and she ran away from home. I wanted to believe she would come back, just like Michael did, and I never even imagined that she had been murdered by someone in my own family—"

"Della, seriously, enough is enough." Matthias took a step forward.

Della turned and looked at him, her expression one of dismay and horror. "And then I talked to Sheriff Gaines, and he told me some things, Matthias. He told me some painful things, and it got me to thinking that it might have been you. You could have done this terrible thing. You sent that terrible man to frighten Clifton, and that man cut off his fingers. Did you tell him to do that, or did he just get inventive?"

Matthias advanced again and was now within arm's length of his sister.

"Yes, I started to think that you could have killed Nancy. And then I thought no, you could never have done that. You weren't capable of murder, surely. And then I started thinking that if it wasn't you, then who could it be? Who would you be so eager to protect? There was only one person. There could only have been one possible person, right? Our father. That's who you were protecting. All this while doing nothing but hiding the truth from everyone, trying to protect our father, trying to protect the family name, trying to protect your inheritance and not see it wasted on defending—"

Matthias lashed out and caught her across the side of the face. She fell awkwardly, the newspaper clippings spilling from her hand.

Matthias Wade stood silently, staring at Gaines, ignoring his sister as she struggled to her feet.

"My brother is dead," Matthias Wade said, "and so are Nancy Denton and Michael Webster and Leon Devereaux. They are all dead. No one's coming back, Sheriff. No one's going to substantiate what you are saying. No one is going to make any statements or testify in court, and even if there were someone to help you, I think you would find that the courts were not going to give you whatever justice you were hoping for."

Della was on her feet. "This is true," she said. "What he is saying is true, Matthias? Eugene killed Nancy, and he's been doing this . . . these things, and all this time you knew about it? Is this true?"

Matthias looked back at his sister. "Don't even talk to me, Della. Don't you act judgmental with me. How fucking dare you? Drugs, abortions, sleeping with colored men. You are a fucking whore just like Father says you are. You are a worthless fucking whore, a worthless human being, and if you weren't my sister, maybe Leon would have come and visited with you as well."

Della snatched a handful of clippings from the floor and thrust them at Matthias.

"You did this," she said. "You are as guilty as Eugene. You knew what he did to Nancy. You knew what he's been doing since, and you did nothing? You did absolutely nothing?"

"What would you have had me do, Della? Kill him? Is that what you would have had me do? Kill my own brother? He was sick. He was mentally ill. Like our mother, alcoholic that she was. Drowning her depression in whiskey. You have no idea how much time and effort and energy it takes to control what happens around this family. You have not the faintest clue how much trouble you have caused for me. Eugene was your brother, too, Della, and just because he lost his mind when our mother died, you think that gave me license to neglect him, to abandon him, to pretend he was no longer part of us. You can't explain what he did. He believed he was doing the right thing. He believed that maybe he could bring her back. He honestly believed that. And our father? Lost his mind, too, eh? What would you have me do? Kill all of them, anyone that doesn't meet your standards of sanity? Oh, and what a standard that would be, Della. What a fucking standard that would be!"

Della slapped her brother. The sound was ferocious. He looked at her as if she had barely touched him.

He smiled strangely, and then he lowered his head as if dismissing her from the room.

Della, her eyes ablaze, tears rolling down her cheeks, caught somewhere in the midst of a whirlwind of emotions, stormed out.

Gaines heard her as she ran across the hall and started up the stairs.

Matthias Wade turned back to Gaines. "It's over," Wade said. "The game is finished. The people who really did these things are dead. Perhaps it is time for you to just accept the fact that sometimes things happen, and there is nothing you can do to influence or change any of it."

"I don't believe that, Mr. Wade."

Wade nodded slowly. He looked down at the clippings on the floor, and then back up at Gaines. "Who's to say that one life is worth more than another? Not for us to say, right? I don't know about you, Sheriff, but I tend to be fatalistic about these things. If I were a religious man, if I held to the view that God created all men in His own image, then He created Eugene just the same as He created me or you or Della or these children. Maybe there is a balance in all things. Maybe He gives and at the same time He takes away, and there is nothing we can do to change that. Perhaps these people were all meant to die, and if it had not been Eugene to take care of that, then it would have been someone else—"

"Is that how you have justified your decision all these years?"

"My decision, Sheriff?"

"Your decision to say nothing when you found out that Eugene killed Nancy Denton."

Wade smiled. "Are we still playing that game, Sheriff? What I say here has no bearing on anything. Whatever you think I might be admitting to will be so strenuously denied. It is your word against mine, Sheriff Gaines, and I believe I know enough people of enough significance to make anything you say sound like the ramblings of a war veteran with some inexplicable personal grudge."

Gaines looked at the man, and he saw it in his eyes. There never was a decision. Nancy Denton did not matter, not compared to the shame and discredit that could have been directed toward the family.

"You are no different," Gaines said. "You may as well have killed her yourself. You may as well have killed all of them. You knew what had happened, and you let it go. You just stepped away and did nothing."

"I think you are delusional, Sheriff. I think that maybe you are shell-shocked, a little mentally unbalanced. After all, war can have such a destructive and deteriorative effect on a man's mental stability, can it not?"

"You killed your own brother, Matthias. You sent Leon Devereaux up there to tell him that Nancy Denton's body had been found, that the truth was going to come out. You knew what he would do, didn't you? You knew he would kill himself. There was no other way out for him, was there? Did you think he would just be forgotten? Another lonely suicide somewhere, hushed up by the Wade family, everything forgotten? Is that what you anticipated?"

Matthias Wade waved the questions aside as if they were irrelevant.

"Life might be a matter of doing the things you want to do, Sheriff, but surviving is a matter of doing the things that need to be done. Sometimes people agree with those things, and sometimes they do not. Sometimes others feel that the things you choose to do are not acceptable, and that is their right. People should have a right to disagree, Sheriff, but that doesn't necessarily give them the right to try to prevent you from doing those things. For me, it is very simple."

"And for me, too."

Matthias Wade turned as Della came into the room. She had a gun in her hand, a small revolver, and she aimed it unerringly at her brother.

"What is this?" Wade asked. "What the fuck is this, Della?"

"Justice, Matthias. Plain and simple."

"Put the fucking gun down, Della. You are not going to use it."

"You don't think I'm capable?"

"Capable? Capable? What I think you're capable of is getting drunk and fucking some colored man, you ignorant bitch. That's what I think you're capable of."

"You think I don't possess some sense of pride, Matthias? You think I don't want to do everything to save our father from the shame and disgrace you are going to bring on this family?"

"Oh, enough, Della. Put the gun down and go away for Christ's sake."

Della took another step forward. She steadied her shaking hand. "Say goodbye, you asshole," she hissed, and she pulled the trigger.

The bullet, a .25 caliber, entered Matthias Wade's throat at the base. It did not possess sufficient force to exit through the rear of his neck, but it punctured his trachea and lodged in the vertebrae.

Matthias Wade did not fall or stagger backward, as if he could not believe that his sister had shot him, and such was his certainty that he was able to defy the physical reality of its occurrence.

Nevertheless, the physical reality could not be denied, and blood started to choke out of the puncture in his throat. It soaked the front of his shirt, and when he saw that blood, he started trying to gather it up, as if returning it would somehow reverse what had happened.

Matthias dropped to his knees. He just stared back at his little sister and opened his mouth to say something.

Whatever he had planned to say never made the distance from his mind to his lips. He keeled over sideways and lay on the floor. He was motionless aside from his right leg, which kicked back and forth a half-dozen times and then stopped.

Della Wade looked at Gaines. Gaines looked back at Della.

"Is there another gun in the house?" Gaines asked, his voice direct, not to be questioned. It was as if every ounce of adrenaline available to him was coursing through his body. He felt certain, focused, not even shocked. He felt utterly calm.

Della just stared back at him as if she had not heard him.

"Della. Look at me. Is there another gun in the house? A gun that belongs to Matthias?"

She nodded once, twice, and then seem to snap to. "Y-yes," she said. "He has—"

"Go get it," he said. "Hurry!"

Della moved suddenly, crossing the room, heading down the corridor and away.

She was back within a minute, in her hand a .38.

Gaines took the revolver from her, wiped off her prints with his shirt-tail, and then put the gun in Matthias's lifeless hand. He held the gun level, and then fired a single shot somewhere into the wall behind where Della had been standing.

Della jumped, startled, and dropped the .25.

He looked back at Della. "Self-defense," he said. "You shot him in self-defense. Do you understand?"

Della was speechless.

Gaines was up on his feet, had her by the shoulders, started shaking her, getting her to focus, to look at him, to get her attention.

"You understand what I'm saying?" he said.

"Ye-yes," she said. "Yes, self-defense."

"Now, go to your room. Stay there. Don't say anything. Don't call anyone. Don't do anything until I tell you, okay?"

She looked at him blankly.

"Okay?"

"Yes, yes okay," she said, and with that she hurried from the room.

Gaines turned back and looked at Matthias Wade.

He saw the dead teenager, the one who carried a single grenade, the one who got in the way of the bullet.

The gods of war were fickle. They didn't care who they took, or why.

Most often they were just dispassionate and indifferent, but every once in a while they got it right.

410

73

Della Wade sits quietly in the basement cell. It is not the cell that housed Michael Webster, but the one that faces it.

She is there partly for her own protection, to keep her away from the horde of journalists that seem to have descended on Whytesburg, but there also while Gaines deals with the issues surrounding the deaths of Matthias Wade and Leon Devereaux. There are things that have to be made right, things to be settled, and while they remain unresolved, she is best served by being in his care rather than anyone else's.

Eddie Holland sits on a chair six feet from the cell. He doesn't speak to her. She doesn't speak to him.

Gaines is upstairs dealing with the reporters, the photographers, the official necessities surrounding such a situation. The reception area of the Sheriff's Office reminds him of the Danang Press Center.

It is the following morning when Gaines comes to speak with her. Wednesday, August 7th. It is somewhere after nine in the morning, and Gaines has received word that Della Wade has still not eaten a thing since he brought her in.

Lyle Chantry is keeping watch on her, and Gaines sends Chantry away. He lets himself into the cell, pulls the door closed behind him, and sits beside her.

He clears his throat, and then he starts talking. "When I was in the army," he says, "I went to war. It was a war that other people had decided was a good idea. It wasn't my decision, nothing to do with me, but the law said I had to go, and so I did." Gaines turns and leans against the back wall. He lifts one foot and places it on the edge of the bunk. He takes cigarettes from his shirt pocket, lights two, passes one to Della, and goes on. "War is a lottery. War is like some kind of doorway into hell, and you run through that doorway into oncoming fire, and you see people die all around you, people whose names you don't even know, and yet you are all supposed to be fighting for the same thing. I asked a lot of people, and no one seemed to know what we were fighting for. I had this lieutenant. His name was Ron Wilson—"

"Sheriff?"

"Yes, Della."

"Are you going to charge me with the murder of Leon Devereaux?"

"No, Della, I am not."

"Why?"

"Because I believe it was the right thing to do, and if I had been in your situation, I would have done the same thing."

"I was afraid that he would get away."

"Devereaux?"

"No, Matthias. I believed he had killed Nancy. I *really* did believe he had killed Nancy, but I thought he would get away with it, and I couldn't bear it. After what he did to Clifton, and then when you came and started asking questions, and you were convinced he had done this, then I thought that Leon Devereaux should die—"

"And that Matthias would be blamed?"

She doesn't speak for a moment, and then she nods her head. "Yes," she replies. "I wanted him to be punished for killing someone, even if it wasn't the right person."

"He was complicit in the deaths of many people," Gaines tells her. "Perhaps there were more, but we have evidence that implicates Eugene in the deaths of at least five girls. Those are ones we have something substantive to corroborate, some physical evidence that we found in his apartment."

"Physical evidence?"

"Items of clothing, jewelry, things like that."

"And Matthias knew he was killing these girls . . . these children?"

"He knew about Nancy. I am sure of that. And he knew about the two girls in Morgan City. They were both daughters of Wade employees, and Matthias got so involved in that case that he himself was suspected for a long time. There are still people who think Matthias was the one who murdered them."

"And now he is dead. And Eugene, too."

"Yes."

"And Michael?" she asks. "He did that terrible thing . . ."

"He did something to try to bring her back," Gaines replies. "Michael Webster loved that girl more than life itself. Without her . . . well, he was devastated, and he did the only thing he could think of doing."

"He did it for love," she says. "But to do that to someone you love? I can't even begin to imagine what that did to him."

"I know what it did to him," Gaines says. "He lost his mind, Della. He truly lost his mind."

"Such a waste of life," she says.

"Yes, it is," Gaines replies, and wants to add, *Just like in war*, but he does not.

He reaches out and takes her hand, and he holds it reassuringly, and he looks at her for a very long time and neither of them speak.

74

On an unseasonably cool day, August 8, 1974—as America and the world watched events unfold around the resignation of Richard M. Nixon—a funeral was held in the small Mississippi town of Whytesburg.

It was a strange funeral, perhaps more a memorial service, and though there were no family members there to represent any of the deceased, that same small church that had seen Alice Gaines's funeral just one week earlier was filled to capacity. Nate Ross, Eddie Holland, John Gaines, Richard Hagen, Officers Chantry and Dalton were front right. Front left were the Rousseaus, Bob Thurston, Victor Powell, Maryanne Benedict, and Della Wade. In the seats behind were many of the eldest Whytesburg citizens—those who remembered Nancy Denton, those who had perhaps been involved in those initial searches for her whereabouts on the day after her disappearance.

Gaines spoke this time. He did not say a great deal, but his words were meaningful and heartfelt, and he felt sure that they would be heard.

Later, the gathered attendees walked out to the cemetery, and there—in plots paid for by the county purse—Judith and Nancy were buried side by side, and next to Nancy they laid the body of Michael Webster, the man who loved her enough to do what he did and try to live with the consequences.

In some days' time there would be a funeral for Eugene Wade, another for Matthias, but there would be few attendees, and those funerals would be held far from Whytesburg. Della would not attend, and neither would Earl Wade, his health and mental well-being having deteriorated to the point where he was bed-bound much of the time.

Della Wade told Gaines that she had tried to explain things to her father, but her father did not, or could not, understand.

Catherine Wade had been apprised of all that needed to be known, and Catherine—now the eldest—was making plans to have her father deemed legally incapable of managing his own affairs. She would act as proxy, and she—with Della's agreement—had decided to sell the house. There was a great deal of money. They were taking equal shares. The Wade dynasty would end right there with the death of Earl, and Della did not believe it would be long before he passed away.

"I think he knows what happened here," she told Gaines. "I think he is drowning in his own lies and secrets."

Gaines did not say anything directly, but it was evident in his expression that he agreed.

The events of that day, primarily the self-defense shooting of Matthias Wade by his sister, were corroborated by John Gaines. Gaines also wrote a report that identified Matthias Wade as the killer of Leon Devereaux. There were those—Richard Hagen and Victor Powell among them—who were required to say certain things, to sign certain things, and they did so without question.

Gaines also visited with Marvin Wallace. He took Nate Ross with him. Wallace was informed that there would be no further financial or political support from the Wades. Gaines told him that it was possibly a good time to retire, that he should sell up and move on, perhaps head south in search of warmer climes and better golf courses. Wallace listened carefully, and he had no questions. Gaines asked him to sign a declaration of proxy assigning Catherine Wade as the manager of all Wade affairs. He did so without hesitation. He was then told to authorize a complete review of the Clifton Regis case, to suggest in his letter that if the review did not exonerate Regis of the Henderson B&E, an appeal should be lodged at state level. Again Wallace complied without hesitation or question. Within two weeks, Judge Marvin Wallace had tendered his resignation, and his resignation had been accepted.

Gaines made a careful and thorough investigation into any possibility that Jack Kidd might have been involved in the numerous dismissed cases and exonerations afforded Leon Devereaux in Wallace's courtroom. Gaines found nothing incriminating, and he dropped it.

And so it was that on August 12th, exactly twenty years to the day since Nancy Denton had walked into the woods at the end of Five Mile Road, John Gaines—who had lately, and by providence or default, come to the position of sheriff of Whytesburg, Breed County, Mississippi, and before that had come alive from the nine circles of hell that was the war in Vietnam, who was himself born in Lafayette, a Louisianan from the start—stood on the back porch of his mother's house and looked out into the darkness.

The darkness was constant, as were the shapes and sounds within it, and within those shapes and sounds would forever be the memory of what had happened here, of the people who had died, the voices that would no longer be heard.

Nancy, Michael, Judith, Leon, Matthias, Eugene.

And there was Alice, of course.

There would always be those who killed for greed, for revenge, for hate, for something they believed was love. And there would always be those who died.

Here was to be found the precise and torturous gravity of conscience.

Here was to be found the true and onerous weight of the dead.

The dreams of these events would come—fractured, surreal, some of them understandable, some of them without any meaning or significance he could fathom. Gaines knew that. He anticipated those dreams, even longed for them, for in dreaming, he would then find wakefulness, and in waking he would know that some part of the dream had thus been left behind, and in such small increments he would recover his own self and one day become something of the person he had been before he went to war.

Not the same person, but better, wiser, more sensitive and empathetic.

Someone who could, perhaps, share his life with another.

There is something silent within him now, and he finds this reassuring, as if a small place has been established into which he can withdraw when the world becomes too crowded. And yet, strangely, he feels this place is too spacious for himself alone.

It is with this thought that, one evening, he calls Maryanne Benedict, and when she answers the phone and he tells her who it is, she does not seem surprised.

He has not seen her, nor spoken to her, since the funeral.

"I have something," he says, "and I am not sure if you want it, but I thought to ask you."

"Something?"

"It's Michael's picture album."

"Oh," she says.

416

"You are in it, Nancy, Matthias, Michael . . . all of you, and I wondered—"

"No," she says. "I don't want it, John."

"What shall I do with it?"

"I don't know," she replies.

"Okay," he says. "I will figure something out."

Neither of them speak for a moment, and then they speak together.

"I was—" he says.

"Are you—" she starts.

"You first," Gaines says.

"I was just going to ask if you were okay."

"Okay?" he echoes. "Yes, I'm getting there."

"Good," she says.

"And you?" he asks.

"As can be. Considering all that has happened, you know?"

There is silence once more. Just for a moment.

"What were you going to ask me?" she says.

"Nothing," he says.

"John," she prompts, as if she understands how hard this is and is trying to make it easier.

"I was going to ask if you wouldn't like to . . . maybe, I don't know, maybe—"

"Ask me, John," she says.

"I was wondering if you would like to perhaps go out sometime. We could have dinner or something. We could just talk, you know? Just talk for a while and see—"

"It's okay, John. You've asked me. You don't need to say anything else."

"Okay," he says. "Sorry, I was just—"

"I know," she says, and he can hear a smile in her voice.

"So?" he says.

"I'll have to see," she says. "I'll have to check my calendar."

He hesitates. "Oh," he says. "Okay. Yes. Check your calendar."

He hears her laughing before he has finished talking.

"I am teasing you, John," she says. "Of course we can go out. We can go out, and we can have some dinner, and we can talk. We can do whatever we want."

He smiles. "Okay," he says. "Good. Thank you."

"Friday evening," she says. "Come and get me at seven."

"I will," he says. "Friday at seven."

"Until then," she says.

"Yes, Maryanne, until then."

She hangs up.

Gaines stands there for a little while, and then he hangs up, too.

In the kitchen, he pours himself a drink, and then he returns to the back porch and watches as the last ghosts of color fade behind the distant trees.

He knows that he will never forget the war.

He knows that he will never forget his mother.

But maybe one day he will forget Nancy Denton and all that happened here.

There is silence in his thoughts, perhaps for the first time in his life.

He does not hear the distant chatter of CH-47s, the crack and whip and drumroll of the 105s and the Vulcans, nor Charlie's 51 cals and 82mm mortars.

He does not hear the relentless rain as it hammers down to earth. He does not feel the ground swelling beneath his feet. He does not feel as if he is being watched from the shadows.

He hears the sound of his own heart, feels the pressure of blood in his veins, and he knows he can make it.

After all that has happened, he can make it.

One day his life will perhaps turn full circle, and he will remember what it was to be a child, and he will know how it is to love and to be loved, and there will be things that make sense and things that do not make sense but they will not matter.

One day, perhaps, he will see it all for what it is . . . a circle, a wheel, something with neither beginning nor end . . . like the snake that devoured its own tail, and finally, irrevocably, disappeared.

Bright lights
hide dark truths

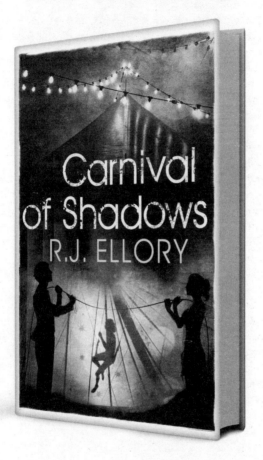

The powerful new thriller from R.J. Ellory

Available in Orion Hardback and eBook

May 2014